ALEXANDRE DUMAS

THE
MOHICANS OF PARIS

Elibron Classics
www.elibron.com

Elibron Classics series.

© 2005 Adamant Media Corporation.

ISBN 1-4021-7510-8 (paperback)
ISBN 1-4021-0752-8 (hardcover)

This Elibron Classics Replica Edition is an unabridged facsimile of the edition published by George Routledge and Sons, London and New York.

Elibron and Elibron Classics are trademarks of Adamant Media Corporation. All rights reserved.

This book is an accurate reproduction of the original. Any marks, names, colophons, imprints, logos or other symbols or identifiers that appear on or in this book, except for those of Adamant Media Corporation and BookSurge, LLC, are used only for historical reference and accuracy and are not meant to designate origin or imply any sponsorship by or license from any third party.

THE
MOHICANS OF PARIS

BY

ALEXANDRE DUMAS

TRANSLATED AND ADAPTED BY JOHN LATEY, JUN.

LONDON:
GEORGE ROUTLEDGE AND SONS
THE BROADWAY, LUDGATE
NEW YORK: 416, BROOME STREET

THE MOHICANS OF PARIS.

Chapter I.—A Carnival Meeting.

Paris in the year 1827! That day of supreme folly, the *mardi gras*, was fast drawing to a close. It was, indeed, on the stroke of midnight when three young men, arm-in-arm, descended the Rue Saint-Denis: two of them singing the most catching airs of the quadrilles they had heard at the Colosseum *bal*, where they had spent the evening; the third contenting himself with biting the gold knob of his cane.

The two singers wore the favourite carnival livery of the day—the costumes of market-porters.

Their companion—the one who was as silent as the others were lively, who seemed the eldest and was certainly the most serious of the trio, who was a head taller than his friends, between whom he walked as if in a reverie—wore one of those large cloaks with velvet collars, only seen now on the frontispieces of Chateaubriand's or Byron's works.

He had just left a soirée of artists in the Rue Sainte-Appoline.

If anyone had ventured to lift his brown cloak he would have seen at a glance that the black evening suit which the stranger wore beneath had evidently come from the studio of one of those renowned tailors on the Boulevard de Gand, and had been made for one of those young men of fashion who were then styled dandies, and who later earned the name of lions. Yet the wearer seemed to have not the slightest pretension to pass for a dandy. There was far too much freedom and independence in his bearing for him to be mistaken for one of those marionettes of fashion who dared not move their necks lest there should be a wrinkle in their cravats or a fold in their collars. Besides, as a final protest, as it were, against the fetters of fashion, he had released his hands from his gloves, revealing on the index finger of his right hand a large gold signet-ring.

The garb of the two other young men formed a singular contrast to the Byronic costume of their companion. Clad, as already mentioned, in the carnival dress of market porters; white plush vests with cerise collars, satin pantaloons with blue and white stripes, a red cashmere scarf swathed round the waist of one, and a yellow cashmere scarf round the other; wearing silk stockings and shoes with diamond buckles; gaudy from top to toe in ribbons of all colours; their white hats encircled with garlands of red and white camellias, the smallest of which would, at that time of the year, have cost a crown at Madame Bayou's or Madame Prévost's, the two florists most in renown; their faces flushed with the healthy red of youth, fire in their eyes, joy on their lips, gaiety in their hearts—these two young men were the very incarnation of French vivacity, as their friend seemed its very antipodes.

What brought these young men together, when the total dissimilarity of their costumes was apparently of a piece with the variance of their natures and temperaments? And why were they wandering at so late an hour in one of the fifty muddy streets which furrowed Paris from the Boulevard Saint-Denis to the Quai de Gèvres?

The answer is very simple. The two personifications of French gaiety found no carriage on leaving the Colosseum *bal*; whilst the young man in the brown cloak in vain sought one in the Rue Sainte-Appoline. The latter was clear-headed enough, having taken nothing more intoxicating than a glass or so of gooseberry syrup. He was making steadily for his apartments in the Rue de l'Université, when he encountered his two friends by chance at the corner of the Rue Sainte-Appoline and the Rue Saint-Denis.

"Hallo! Jean Robert!" exclaimed the two latter, who had evidently drunk more punch than was good for them.

"Ludovic! Pétrus!" exclaimed at the same moment the young man in the brown cloak. (In 1827, be it explained, Pierre was called Pétrus, and Louis, Ludovic.)

All three shook hands heartily. Jean Robert was induced to join his friends in quest of supper at Bordier's near the Halle; and it was thither they were bound when they were first introduced to the reader: Pétrus (an artist) and Ludovic (a doctor), humming lively snatches of dance-music; Jean Robert (poet), buried in his own thoughts, seemingly.

When they arrived within twenty paces of the Cour Batave, Jean Robert suddenly stopped.

"Where is it we are going to sup?" he asked.

"At Bordier's!" answered Pétrus and Ludovic with one voice.

"Bordier's! Hadn't you better reconsider the matter? Instead of supping tranquilly at Very's, at Philippe's, or at the Frères-Provvençaux, will you pass the night in some hole in which we shall have to drink an infusion of logwood for Bordeaux, and eat cats in place of rabbits?"

"Ah! ah!" answered Pétrus, laughingly; "Jean Robert has made a great hit at the Théâtre Français, you see, Ludovic! He gets five hundred francs every other day, and his pockets are full of gold. He has become an aristocrat!".

"You can't say it's for the sake of economy, my dear fellows, that you're going to Bordier's!" retorted Jean Robert.

"No;" said Ludovic. "It's to see a little life. And, now we're so near the Halle, I shall either sup there or not at all."

"Let us sup there, then. It will have one good result; it will so disgust you that you will never sup there again while you live!"

Humming a bacchanalian song to counteract the effect of Jean Robert's sober counsel, Pétrus walked on again; and the three friends were soon quickening their pace to make up for the few moments lost.

As the clock of Saint-Eustache struck half-past twelve they gained the market place; and, at the last moment, Ludovic hesitated as to which cabaret they should patronise.

"Shall it be Paul Niquet's, Baratte's, or Bordier's?" he asked.

"Bordier was recommended to me," said Pétrus, decisively. "Let's try Bordier's."

"Bordier's let it be!" echoed Jean Robert.

"Here we are, then!" answered Pétrus. And, placing his hat rakishly on one side of his head, Pétrus stepped into the cabaret with the ease and effrontery of an habitual frequenter of Bordier's.

His two friends followed him.

* * * * *

What was Bordier's?

Bordier's was one of the cabarets used by the criminal population of Paris.

There were seven:

The Chat Noir, Rue de la Vielle-Draperie, in the Isle of the City —rendezvous for pickpockets and for thieves who followed their vocation by means of false keys.

The Lapin-Blanc, opposite the Gymnase—rendezvous for garrotters and burglars.

The Sept Billards, Rue de Bondy.

Hotel d'Angleterre, Rue Saint-Honoré.

Paul Niquet's, Rue aux Fers.

And, finally, Bordier's, at the corner of the Rue Aubry-le-Boucher and the Rue Saint-Denis.

To watch over this population of bandits and thieves, burglars and ticket-of-leave men, there were only six inspectors and an "officer of peace" in each parish; the sergeants-de-ville had not then been established, and were not organised till 1828 by Monsieur de Belleyme.

At the present day not one of these low cabarets remains; some disappeared with the demolitions necessary for the embellishment of Paris; the rest are either closed or extinct.

Bordier's alone survives; but the cabaret of 1827 has become a smart grocer's shop, wherein dried fruit preserves and liqueurs are sold, but which contains not a jot of the evil surroundings amid which we are unwillingly obliged to conduct our readers.

CHAPTER II.—AN ADVENTURE AT BORDIER'S.

THE cabaret was full to overflowing. The low saloon on the ground-floor—damp, clouded with smoke and nauseous—was thronged with a horde of men and women, intermingled, pell-mell, in what seemed to be an inextricable confusion of the most diverse costumes.

This seething crowd in masquerade finery laughed, talked, sang with such inexpressible incoherence as to be beyond all description.

An ominous murmur greeted the three friends on their entrance.

Punchinello stopped himself in the act of spinning round again.

A grand Turk rose to give his welcome in person—only to fall back across a table, which gave beneath the weight of the intoxicated Turk.

A nimble lad in the guise of a monkey leapt on the shoulders of Pétrus, and, amid the laughter of the company, commenced picking the flowers from the wreath round his hat.

"If you take my advice," whispered Jean Robert to Pétrus, "you'll leave this place at once!"

"Go before we have entered!" protested Pétrus. "What are you thinking of? They would think we were afraid, and would chase us through the streets of Paris, like his Majesty Charles X. chases the deer in the forest of Compiègne!"

"What's your opinion?" asked Jean Robert of Ludovic.

"I think now we are here we had better see all the fun that is to be seen."

"On we go, then!"

"Attention!" added Pétrus. "We are observed. Jean Robert, dramatist as you are, you know all depends upon a successful début!"

And, walking boldly up to the spot where the grand Turk had come to grief, and had fallen like the letter V amid the ruins of the table, leaving only his boots and his turban in sight, Pétrus said,

"Seigneur Mussulman, you remember the famous saying of your master, Mohammed, nephew of the great Abou Thaleb, Prince of Mecca?"

"No!" roared a deep heavy voice, in reply.

"Since the mountain will not come to Mohammed, Mohammed must go to the mountain!" answered Pétrus.

Then, seizing the monkey by the neck, and lifting him with a graceful sweep, as though he were doffing his hat, Pétrus gravely saluted the Turk with the words,

"My respects, Seigneur Mussulman!" The salute finished, he replaced the monkey on his shoulders, but the gamin slid down his back and made off for one of the obscurest corners of the saloon.

This example of courtesy and ready wit gained for Pétrus general applause.

The wavering hand of the Turk grasped the hand held out to him, and, with a good, strong pull, Pétrus lifted him to his feet—a very insecure base for so shaky a column.

"Phew! We are three too many here, decidedly," muttered Pétrus to his friends. "Let's go up stairs!"

"Just as you like," said Ludovic; "though this spectacle is not without interest."

A waiter, who had followed them assiduously from the moment they entered, now joined incontinently in the conversation.

"Would you like to sup on the first floor, gentlemen?"

"We shan't be sorry to quit this room, anyhow," answered Pétrus.

"There's the staircase," said the waiter, pointing out what was little better than a spiral ladder to them.

This was speedily ascended by our three friends, amid the continued shouting and laughter of the roysterers in the saloon.

On the first floor, as on the basement, the cabaret was thronged, and there was not a seat to spare, and the company seemed more repulsive than ever.

"Oh!" said Jean Robert, who was the first to gain the door and the first to leave it with a look of ineffable disgust. "It seems that the hell of Bordier is quite the opposite of Dante's hell; the higher one gets the lower one descends."

"Up we go again, then!" said Pétrus.

And they continued to mount by the staircase, which became narrower and grimier at each flight. The same spectacle was repeated on the second floor, only the air seemed fouler and the smoke denser. On the third floor the scene was more degrading. On the tables and under the tables, on the benches and under the benches, were some fifty human beings—if men descended to the level of brutes deserve to rank in the scale of humanity. One faint, flickering light revealed these fifty human beings—lying in all directions, sleeping off the fumes of drink, their faces and clothes stained with wine, their pillows broken bottles.

Jean Robert's heart sank within him at this sight; but he was master of his will; and seeing that there was yet another floor above, still ascended, though the staircase had now degenerated into what was no better than a miller's ladder. Assuming a fearlessness and ease he was very far from feeling inly, Jean Robert called back to his comrades encouragingly,

"Higher! Higher!"

At length they opened the door of the fourth-floor room.

They saw five men seated round a square deal table, on which stood eight or ten bottles, ranged like so many skittle-pins. The five men were clad simply in the working-garb of Paris ouvriers.

The three friends entered, the waiter following them. They cast a hasty glance round the dingy room, and Jean Robert gave a shrug, which said, "This must do."

"Parbleu! we can sup like princes here," said Pétrus gaily.

"Yes; we only want a little air fit to breathe now," added Ludovic.

"We can soon have that by opening the window," replied Pétrus.

"Where would you like the cloth laid, Messieurs?" demanded the waiter.

"There," answered Jean Robert, pointing to the end of the table not occupied by the five men.

The ceiling was so low that Jean Robert was obliged to take off his hat upon entering the room; and, as it was, his head almost grazed the plaster.

"What would you like, Messieurs?" added the waiter.

"Six dozen oysters, six mutton cutlets, and an omelette!" replied Pétrus.

"How many bottles?"

"Three bottles of chablis, to begin with, and some seltzer-water, if you have any."

At this order, one of the five men whom the new-comers had interrupted turned towards Pétrus, and said,

"Oh, oh! Chablis first, and seltzer-water, eh? We are honoured by the company of dandies, it appears, then?"

"Sons of a noble house, mayhap!" echoed another.

"Or citizens with a noble pedigree!" exclaimed a third.

Thereupon they saluted our three adventurers with a volley of insulting laughter. As the "Memoirs of Vidocq" had not then familiarised society with slang, Jean Robert, Pétrus, and Ludovic could not see that they were being covertly laughed at as swell thieves.

Heedless of their presence, Jean Robert deposited his cloak on the back of a chair, and his cane in a corner near the window.

The waiter was about to hasten away to fulfil his orders when he was detained. The bully of the five, the one who had spoken first at Pétrus, held the waiter by his apron.

"Well?" he demanded.

"Well?" echoed the waiter.

"Didn't I ask you for a pack of cards?"

"Yes."

"Why haven't you brought them, then?"

"Because, as you know very well, cards are not allowed at this late hour."

"Why?"

"Ask Monsieur Delavau."

"Who is Monsieur Delavau?"

"The Préfet of Police."

"What has the Préfet of Police to do with me?"

"He may be nothing to you, but he is something to us."

"What?"

"He could close the cabaret, in which case he would deprive us of the pleasure of serving you again."

"But if we are not allowed to play, what on earth *can* we do here?"

"You are not forced to remain here."

"You are not over civil, young man. Take care, or I shall warn your master!"

"Oh! warn the Pope, if you like!"

"Thousand thunders! Bring us the cards, you rascal!" snouted the bully, rising to his feet and striking the table with his mighty fist.

But the waiter was already half-way down the stairs; and the bully had to resume his seat sulkily with his demand unsatisfied.

"The rascal forgets," he muttered, "that I am Jean Taureau, and that I can kill an ox with one blow of my fist. I must make him remember!"

And lifting a half-empty bottle from the table he drained it at a draught.

"Jean Taureau is put out," murmured one of his comrades to another; "and his rage will soon find vent upon someone, you see."

"Let the dandies look out, then," was the reply.

The window had by this time been opened by Pétrus.

This simple act roused the wrath of Jean Taureau.

"Shut the window!" he shouted to Pétrus.

"Monsieur Jean Taureau," answered Pétrus, in a tone of ironical politeness, "my friend Ludovic here is a distinguished physician, and he will explain to you in two seconds the elements of which air ought to be composed to be respirable."

"What does he mean with his elements?"

"He means, Monsieur Jean Taureau," replied Ludovic, in a tone of courtesy equalling Pétrus in suavity as well as in quiet raillery, "he means that the atmosphere, in order that it may not be injurious to the lungs of an honest man, ought to be composed of from seventy-five to seventy-six parts of nitrogen, from twenty-two to twenty-three parts of oxygen, and two parts of water, a little more, or a little less."

"I say, Jean," interrupted one of the five men in blouses and jackets, "I fancy he is speaking Latin to you."

"I'll answer in French, at any rate," growled Jean Taureau. "Shut that window!" he roared out again.

Pétrus simply planted himself firmly before the open window, and crossing his arms over his chest, gazed fearlessly at Jean Taureau.

"Thousand thunders! Shut that window!" repeated the bully, springing to his feet menacingly.

"Pooh! There's no thunder nor lightning either here," calmly answered Pétrus; "so the window shall remain open!"

Jean Robert saw that blows would soon follow these violent words, but did his best to delay the impending collision. It was fortunate that he maintained his sangfroid.

He moved towards Jean Taureau with the intention of calming his fury.

"Monsieur," he said, "we have just come from the open air; and, on entering this room, we were almost suffocated."

"I should think we were," added Ludovic; "for one breathed nothing but carbonic acid!"

"Permit us to keep the window open a little longer, just to let in a little fresh air; and then it shall be closed directly."

"But you opened it without my permission," snarled Jean Taureau.

"What then?" said Pétrus.

"Had you asked me, I might have given you permission."

"Enough!" exclaimed Pétrus, impatiently. "I opened the window to please myself, and it shall remain open as long as I please."

"Gently, Pétrus!" remonstrated Jean Robert.

"What? Be gentle with fellows like these?"

At this sneer, uttered by Pétrus with scornful emphasis, the four comrades of Jean Taureau rose from the table and advanced with him to settle the dispute by brute force.

Judging by their fierce bearing and threatening gestures, they welcomed this interruption of their monotonous drinking bout as holding forth a promise of a noisy finish to their night of carnival debauch.

It was easy to guess the occupation of each of these five burly carousers. The one whom Jean Taureau addressed now and then as Croc-en-Jambe was evidently a rag-picker. Another not unnaturally went by the sobriquet of Sac-à-Plâtre, seeing that his lime speckled and dust-covered face unmistakably betrayed him to be a mason. Sac-à-Plâtre was bound to Jean Taureau by the most indissoluble ties of gratitude. He owed him not only his own life, but the lives of his wife and child.

It was an act of true heroism, this rescue of Jean Taureau's. It was also a remarkable display of herculean strength. As Jean Taureau is destined to play an important rôle in this romance, the valiant action may as well be described here as elsewhere.

One night a house on the Isle of the City was on fire. The staircase, the first to be attacked by the flames, had fallen in. A man, a woman, and a child were crying "Help!" from a window on the second floor.

The man was a mason. He cried—and his whole heart was in the cry—for a ladder or a rope. With either the ladder or the rope he hoped to save his wife and child.

But the busybodies in the crowd lost their heads. Ladders were brought not half long enough—cord too weak to support the weight of one person was alone forthcoming.

The flames gained in strength. The smoke rolled out in dense volumes from the windows, preceding the glowing body of fire which seemed already scorching the unfortunate creatures appealing for help.

Jean Taureau was passing.

He stopped.

"What, have you neither ladder nor rope yet?" he shouted, with indignation. "Would you let the poor devils burn?"

Jean Taureau gave one quick glance round, and saw there were no signs of their being rescued by anyone else.

"Come, Sac-à-Plâtre!" he called up, cheerily, at the same time holding out his arms as he took his stand beneath the window; "trust the child to me!"

The mason, recognising the voice, quickly lifted his child in his arms, kissed him on both cheeks, and dropped the precious burden into the arms of Jean Taureau.

A cry of suspense escaped the crowd as the child shot through the air. Jean Taureau received him safely in his arms, and at once handed the child to someone behind him.

"Now, your wife!"

The mason took his wife in his arms with the same confidence, and, despite her entreaties to be allowed to remain with him, dropped her as he dropped the child.

Jean Taureau received the woman in his arms with equal safety; but her weight made him stagger back one step.

"There she is!" he said, depositing her on her feet in a half-fainting state, whilst loud shouts greeted the stout-hearted, strong-limbed Jean Taureau.

"Now, it's your turn!" he sang out to the man at the window, rooting his legs to the ground as firmly as oaks, and screwing up his thews and sinews for the final shock.

Two thousand persons were gazing breathlessly at the herculean form of Jean Taureau below, and at the figure of the mason aloft—a silhouette against a background of fire.

The mason mounted to the window-sill, made the sign of the cross, and, murmuring an appeal to Heaven, dropped to what seemed to the throngs of spectators a certain death for both himself and his valiant friend.

The shock was terrible: Jean Taureau bent beneath the mason's weight, and staggered back three paces, but by a violent effort kept himself from falling.

A loud cheer rose from the multitude. There was a dash towards him to carry him in triumph. But before anyone could reach him, Jean Taureau fell down, beaten at last, a crimson tide flowing from his mouth.

Neither the child nor the woman nor the man received a scratch.

Jean Taureau had burst a blood-vessel in his lungs. He was conveyed to the Hôtel-Dieu, whence he came out well again in two days.

Jean Taureau had a certain natural mother-wit; and he had given to another of his comrades on this night of the *mardi gras* the cognomen of Toussaint-Louverture, after the revolutionary negro hero of St. Domingo, whom he thought Toussaint—coalheaver by profession—might probably resemble, from the blackness of his coaly face.

His fourth and last comrade was a man of about fifty years of age, with quick eyes and rapid gestures, answering to the name of Father Gibélotte. He was clad in a velvet jacket, and a vest and cap of catskin; and he exhaled a strong and pungent odour of valerian.

Jean Taureau himself alone remains to be described. He was a man of about five feet six inches in height, strong and firm as the oak-trees, which, as a carpenter, he planed so deftly: a kind of

Farnese Hercules, seemingly cut from a block of granite, and, at first sight, apparently quite equal to the task of mastering Jean Robert, Ludovic, and Pétrus by himself, without the aid of his fellow-roysterers. Jean Taureau's face was enframed by a crisp beard and a head of short, curly hair; and he boasted a neck so thick as to justify the name he had bestowed upon himself, with the sanction of all who knew his bull-like strength and obstinacy. His age was between thirty and forty. He was clad in the jacket and dress proper to a carpenter; and, that there might be no mistake whatever as to his profession, a T square stuck from one of his pockets, whilst a compass hung from another.

Such were the five antagonists with whom the three new comers bade fair to be engaged in hostilities should the diplomatic pleading of Jean Robert be of no avail.

CHAPTER III.—THE FIGHT.

Now a conflict seemed inevitable, it was characteristic of each of our heroes that they bore themselves with a calmness which was the greatest possible contrast to the excited demeanour of their five opponents.

Pétrus, leaning with his back against the open window, stood with a nonchalant air, regarding the gesticulating ouvriers with a look of indifference and defiance.

Ludovic scanned the herculean proportions of Jean Taureau with a curiosity that greatly diminished the gravity of the situation in his eyes: for, man of science as he was, he said to himself that he would willingly give a hundred francs to have so excellent a subject to dissect. Perhaps, in his heart of hearts, he felt that he would even have given two hundred francs, for it would be a palpable gain to science if he could have Jean Taureau extended before him stark and dead as a door nail instead of being in front of him, full of life, and in the threatening attitude of a probable assailant.

As for Jean Robert, the maxim of Marshal Saxe recurred opportunely to his mind, and he resolved to act on the maxim that when hostilities must take place 'tis a palpable advantage and a moral gain to strike the first blow.

A good hand at boxing, and a good foot at the *savate*, thanks to the lessons of a master in the manly art of self-defence, Jean Robert, endowed, moreover, with great physical strength, did not shrink from the coming contest. With such native power was he blessed, indeed, that had his antagonist been only a little less of a Hercules, a wrestle between them would have been anything but a sure victory for Jean Taureau.

"For the last time, I ask, will you shut the window?" exclaimed Jean Taureau.

"No!"

The colossal carpenter flushed afresh at this negative answer, which same simultaneously from the lips of the three friends.

He was about to rush upon Jean Robert, when the muscular poet stepped forward and said boldly,

"We may well open the ball, for we are both Jeans: you are Jean Taureau, I am Jean Robert."

"It's true I am Jean Taureau," answered the carpenter defiantly; "but you lie when you call yourself Jean Robert: you are Jean F. . . . ."

The young man in evening dress did not let him finish. He sent his left fist full on to the temple of Jean Taureau, felling him to the ground.

Pétrus achieved a similar victory. He was unusually dexterous at singlestick, and very nimble at the *savate*. In the absence of a good staff, he availed himself of his knowledge of the latter art, and dealt the mason a blow in the chest with his foot that sent him rolling by the side of Jean Taureau.

Ludovic, meantime, in his quality of anatomist, shot out his right with such damaging effect on the coalheaver that he could be seen to turn pale under the coaly mask which blackened his face.

Whilst Jean Taureau and the mason rose to their feet in a few seconds, Toussaint, almost bending double with pain, sank into a chair.

But this was merely the skirmish before the battle.

So the three friends prepared or a renewal of the attack with more fury and with additional strength, inasmuch as the two who had not hitherto taken part in the fray, but had been almost stupefied for a moment at the downfall of their champion, were now ready to join in the combat.

"Thousand thunders!" cried Jean Taureau, as he staggered to his feet. "See what comes of being taken by surprise: a child could vanquish one!"

"Very well! Be on your guard now, Jean Taureau," answered Jean Robert; "for I intend to send you sprawling on the floor again soon."

Jean Taureau's reply was a rush and a terrific lunge with his right arm. The blow must have broken Jean Robert's ribs had it reached home. With the agility of a practised boxer, however, Jean Robert leapt on one side, and gave his adversary such a sidelong kick in the chest that his words came true, and Jean Taureau once more fell like a log on the floor.

As for Pétrus, he had been equally successful with two of his assailants. The ragpicker he had settled with a smart tap on the head from a stool, and he sent the mason rolling over by butting at him suddenly with his head, in true Breton style.

Ludovic, in his ignorance of the art pugilistic, could only grapple with Gibélotte, whom he threw, after a long wrestling bout. But, instead of profiting by his advantage, Ludovic got his antagonist upon his knee, and endeavoured to find out how it came that he smelt so strongly of valerian. He was indefatigably pursuing his search when the mason and the ragpicker, seeing their leader again overthrown, began to fear the fight was going against them, and cried out,

"Let us knife them!"

The waiter appeared on the threshold at this moment with the oysters. He saw the situation at a glance, and hurried down stairs more quickly than he had ascended.

Meanwhile the noise above had roused the curiosity of the drunken company on the third floor. The appeal to the knife reached their ears. There was the noise of many feet and the roar of husky voices. It was the scum of the cabaret mounting to the top.

The doorway was presently filled with brutal faces and grimy forms, at sight of which Jean Robert, the most impressionable of the three friends, felt a shiver of disgust involuntarily run through him, and could not repress the exclamation,

"Ah Pétrus! Where have you led us to?"

But Pétrus was equal to the difficulty. He improvised a new system of defence.

To the appeal to knives, Pétrus replied by the cry of

"Barricades!" which had not been raised in Paris since the famous day which gave birth to them. With this cry of "Barricades!" on his lips, Pétrus, drawing Jean Robert after him, and forcing Ludovic to follow, sought refuge in an angle, which he at once separated from the rest of the room by forming an impromptu rampart with the table and forms.

Pétrus had already profited by the pause in the hostilities to wrench the gilt curtain-rod from the window; and this pole formed his lance.

Jean Robert was armed with his cane.

Ludovic had to depend on the arms nature had furnished him with.

"Look!" said Pétrus to his two comrades, pointing to a pile of bottles, broken plates, aud oyster-shells in the corner of their improvised fortress. "You see munitions of war will not fail us!"

"No," replied Jean Robert; "but are either of you hurt? I fancy I gave a few blows; but I haven't received one!"

"Safe and sound," said Pétrus.

"And you, Ludovic?"

"I? Oh! I fancy I received a blow between the jaw and the collar-bone; but that doesn't bother me."

"What does bother you, then?" asked Jean Robert.

"I should very much like to know why my particular opponent smells so strongly of valerian."

Chapter IV.—Monsieur Salvator.

The sight of the crowd of people from below who now blocked up the doorway gave Jean Taureau and his comrades renewed courage. There was a dash at the barricade. It was gallantly repulsed, the ragpicker retreating beneath a steady fusillade of bottles skilfully aimed by Ludovic, Toussaint falling stunned from a vigorous crack on the skull dealt by a stool which Jean Robert wielded as deftly as a cudgel, while the mason and Gibélotte were driven back by the scientific lance thrusts of Pétrus.

Exasperated by the blood-stained faces of his companions, and their inglorious defeat by the little garrison, Jean Taureau drew his formidable compass from his pocket, and, holding it dagger-wise, prepared for a deadly attack on Jean Robert. Brandishing it over his head he was about to make another mad rush, but hesitated when Jean Robert gave a jerk to his cane, which fell like a sheath to the floor, leaving a flashing poniard in its owner's hand. They were now equally matched. Excited by the shouts of the spectators, Jean Taureau no longer delayed his attack. He sprang forward with murderous intent, when he was suddenly arrested by a powerful hand, which gave so vigorous a twist to his wrist that his compass dropped from his grasp.

The carpenter turned back with a terrible imprecation on his lips. But, directly he saw who it was face to face with him, his voice dropped involuntarily from an accent of menace to a tone of respect.

"Monsieur Salvator! Pardon!"

"Monsieur Salvator!" exclaimed Jean Robert, Pétrus, and Ludovic. "Who can he be?"

The personage who had appeared so suddenly and so opportunely on the scene, resembling, as it were, one of the gods of old, who intervened just in time to give a peaceful turn to affairs when they were at their worst, looked a young man of about thirty years of age. An eagle glance around the scene of the late tumult made him master of the situation; and, as his brows were knit and a flush of anger rose to his pale face, Jean Taureau and his comrades fairly cowered before him, as though he were their Judge.

Monsieur Salvator is the principal hero of our history. He was at that age when manly beauty is seen in all its strength, and manly strength in all its beauty. His hair was curly black. His moustache and beard grew as nature meant them to grow, and were as soft as silk. His oval face was pale; his well-cut features were of a determined cast, his eyes were of a limpid blue, clear in their lustrous depths as the blue waters of a lake. As for his dress, he wore a black velvet paletôt and a cap of the same stuff, and the general picturesqueness of his costume struck Jean Robert and Ludovic, but particularly Pétrus, who said to himself,

"Sacrebleu! The very model for my Raphaël! I would willingly give him six francs a sitting!"

The sudden silence occasioned by the appearance of the mysterious stranger, who went by the name of Monsieur Salvator, was broken by Jean Taureau. The humbled carpenter abjectly excused himself, and tried to shift the blame for the riot upon the shoulders of Jean Robert and his friends. But he was sternly rebuked all the same.

"It is the old story over again, Jean Taureau! You are drunk, and must pick a quarrel with some one, so you hit upon these gentlemen. Just because you have had high words at home again, you would make the innocent suffer for the infidelities of Mademoiselle——'

"Stop, Monsieur Salvator. Don't pronounce her name," interrupted the sobered carpenter. "She will be my death!"

* * * * * *

A few minutes later the same room was the scene of a merry supper. The magic influence of Monsieur Salvator had dispersed the riotous spirits who had turned the place into a hell. With graceful ease he had received the hearty thanks of Jean Robert, Ludovic, and Pétrus, and had consented to join them at supper. The wine had not been spared by Pétrus and Ludovic, who, after repeating their favourite stories and jokes for the twentieth time, rolled off their chairs, and soon sank into a heavy sleep underneath the table.

As if inviting him to the fullest confidence, Monsieur Salvator now turned to Jean Robert, and asked,

"Whatever induced you to pass a night at the Halle?"

"Only to please my two friends."

"Only?"

"Only."

"Ah! you reckon without yourself, Monsieur Jean Robert. Those friends of yours, who are sleeping so soundly down there, are but the pretext—not the cause. Shall I tell you why you have come? You have come as philosopher, observer, painter of manners, poet, romancer—you have come to study the human heart, haven't you?"

"I must confess there's truth in what you say," answered Jean Robert, laughingly. "Hitherto, I have only written for the theatre; but it is my ambition to write a romance; and my idea is to write it after the style adopted by Shakspeare in his dramas, including every grade of society, from the gravedigger to Hamlet, Prince of Denmark."

"Your idea is a good one. Excuse my frankness, Monsieur Jean Robert. Chance has thrown us together. When we part we may never meet again. Let me give you a little advice. But you think me presumptuous?"

"Oh! not at all, I assure you."

"Have you chosen the subject of your romance?"

"No; not yet."

"Pardon! It is already begun?"

"Since when?"

"Since the hour in which your friends said, 'Let us sup at the Halle.'"

"You are joking."

"No; 'pon my honour, I'm not. The characters are before you, which to choose. Jean Taureau will be a personage in your romance, and Gibélotte, and Toussaint-Louverture, and Sac-à-Plâtre, and Croc-en-Jambe, and myself, if you deem me worthy to be included, and your two friends, who sleep in happy ignorance of the fact that we are distributing their rôles, shall also be personages of your romance. One thing you must ever bear in mind is that you are yourself an actor in the great drama of humanity of which the world is the theatre, having cities and forests, rivers and oceans, for its scenes ; and in which everyone is seemingly moved by his own personal interest, caprice, or pleasure, but is in reality controlled by the invisible and all-powerful hand of destiny. The tears that flow in your romance must be veritable tears, the blood spilt must be veritable blood ; and you yourself must mingle your tears with the tears of your characters. Come ! it is a beautiful moonlight night. Let us set out, and search for the continuation of the romance, in the opening chapters of which you have figured !"

"But my friends ?"

"They will be quite safe. I'll leave word with the waiter; and, when it is known that they are under my safeguard, the hardest Bohemian in the cabaret will not dare to touch a hair of their heads."

Monsieur Salvator forthwith gave the promised caution to the waiter, and beckoning Jean Robert to follow, descended the ladder.

Jean Robert paid for the supper. Slipping five francs into the waiter's hand for himself, he whispered,

"Who is that gentleman ?"

"Monsieur Salvator, Commissionaire of the Rue aux Fers."

"Monsieur Salvator said the truth," murmured Jean Robert to himself; "we have commenced such a romance as has never been written before."

Chapter V.—Fragola.

It struck two as Jean Robert and Monsieur Salvator left Bordier's arm-in-arm. It was, indeed, a magnificent moonlight night, as the Commissionaire of the Rue aux Fers had announced.

Arrived at the Place du Châtelet, they both instinctively stopped. The river ran at their feet. Notre Dame towered above them in all its majesty. The Sainte-Chapelle raised its crest above the neighbouring houses. They might almost have fancied themselves in the Paris of the fifteenth century.

The two young men traversed the Pont-au-Change, and soon gained the narrow and sombre Rue Saint-André-des-Arcs.

Between the Rue Maçon and the Place Saint-André-des-Arcs, Monsieur Salvator stopped at a small white house. He opened the door with a key, and, turning courteously to Jean Robert, said,

"It is, of course, understood that you pass the rest of the night under my care ?"

"I accept your gracious offer," said Jean Robert.

A light suddenly appeared at the top of the staircase, and a sweet voice was heard inquiring,

"Is it you, Salvator ?"

"Yes ; 'tis I," was the cheery answer.

At the sound of his master's voice a noble dog bounded down the stairs, placed his fore paws on Monsieur Salvator's shoulders, and greeted him with cries of inexpressible tenderness.

"Down, Roland! That will do. Your mistress has something to say to me."

The dog gave a growl as he caught sight of Jean Robert, but was quiet directly Salvator said,

"Silence, Roland! That's a friend."

Roland—a magnificent dog, with the coat of a lion, a cross between a St. Bernard and a Newfoundland—fell behind, and licked Jean Robert's hand as the poet ascended the stairs behind his master.

The fair girl who held the light on the landing above was a pretty, graceful blonde of about twenty. Her blue eyes were filled with pleasure. The sweetest of mouths was parted with a smile, revealing two rows of pearls within the ripe lips red as cherries. A slight birth-mark, a true beauty spot, above her right eye, resembled at times the tint of a strawberry, and had won for her a poetical name, the justice of which Jean Robert would soon be the first to acknowledge

A shade of anxiety passed over Fragola's charming face as she saw Salvator was not alone; but the bewitching smile soon returned when she received the assurance,

"A friend, Fragola!"

Having received a tender, almost respectful, kiss from Salvator, Fragola turned to Jean Robert and said, with winning frankness,

"Welcome, friend of my friend!"

CHAPTER VI.—ROLAND'S CONFIDENCES.

THE witching smile of frankness rendered Fragola's welcome irresistible to Jean Robert, who at once followed Salvator and his fair hostess, with Roland, into the room which seemed to serve them as a dining-room.

"It was not anxiety for me that kept you from your bed, dear?" asked Salvator of Fragola, with a touch of tender concern in his voice. "I should never forgive myself if it were."

"Oh, no!" was the reply, in a sweet, low accent; "I have received a letter from that friend I have often spoken to you about."

"Which? There are three friends of yours, Fragola, familiar to me by name."

"You might even say there are four."

"True; but which do you refer to now?"

"Carmelite."

"Has anything happened to her?"

"I have a presentiment that she has met with some misfortune. To-morrow she, Lydia, Regina, and I were to meet, as usual, at Notre-Dame, to attend mass together; and now we have a rendezvous with her at seven o'clock in the morning instead."

"Where?"

Fragola smiled as she answered,

"She wishes that to be kept secret."

"Oh, keep it, then, my angel!" said Salvator, earnestly. "A secret! You know my opinion on that point : a secret should be sacredly kept."

Then, turning towards Jean Robert, he added,

"I'll be with you in a minute. Meanwhile, amuse yourself by glancing round the room—'tis an exact copy of the poet's at Pompeii ; and, when you are tired with that, you can have a chat with Roland."

Salvator then entered the next room with Fragola ; and the dog, with a sigh of satisfaction, planted himself at full length on the mat before the door, which had just been closed upon his master and mistress.

Left alone, Jean Robert lifted the light mechanically, and looked around him as Salvator suggested, but it was the fair face which had just dazzled him that occupied his thoughts. There arose before him, as in a vision, the lovely figure of the young girl whom he had first seen on the landing, the light she was holding suffusing her beauteous face, and irradiating her azure eyes, with a lustrous warmth, and making her wealth of blonde hair shine like wavelets of gold, whilst the undulating beauty of her graceful, albeit slender, form seemed to gain in charm by the artistic play of light and shadow. He saw in his mind's eye Fragola, whose appearance was not less astonishing to him than was Salvator's, the one being the complement of the other, as if to make the living and waking dream of the poet complete. Then the name she mentioned—Regina—had recalled an aristocratic souvenir, which could scarcely have any connection with his new acquaintances in their humbler sphere of life, but which, nevertheless, made his heart beat with a delightful pit-a-pat long strange to him.

By degrees, however, the veil of fancy before his eyes became more and more transparent. The visionary world no longer held sway over his imagination ; the reality succeeded the dream : and Jean Robert found himself face to face with a faithful representation of the decorative painting of antiquity. He was charmed with a series of mural landscapes, each of which he seemed to see through the cunningly painted columns of a peristyle, or the no less skilfully limned casement of a window, whilst the imitation of the Pompeian original was rendered perfect by the fanciful embellishments which archæological science has since rendered popular, such as the hours of the day, dancers, the grasshopper drawn in its car by a pair of slugs, and doves drinking from one cup, &c:

These chaste designs, painted in good taste, and with a fidelity of tone which showed them to be the work of a true artist, would have been a fresh surprise to Jean Robert if anything connected with his strange host could surprise him now.

Still admiring the beauty of the paintings on the wall, he sank into a chair. His eyes wandered round the room till they rested on the dog.

He suddenly recollected the words of Salvator—"When you are tired chat with Roland!"

Jean Robert smiled at the remembrance. Nevertheless, the recommendation, which might have been regarded by others simply as a bit of pleasantry, seemed natural enough to him. It touched another chord of sympathy between him and Salvator.

Poet as he was, Jean Robert cherished the idea in his heart of hearts that it was not upon man alone that God had bestowed a soul. Often he had pictured to himself man in the infancy of the world, preceded by the animals now deemed our inferiors, and it had appeared to him not irrational during this reverie on the past to think it was then the brute creation, and even those tender sisters of the animal world, the flowers and plants of the earth, that served as the first guides and preceptors to humanity. According to this favourite fancy of his, the creatures who obey us now swayed over us then, guiding our wavering reason with their certain instinct—acting, in short, as our counsellors and friends, and then uncomplainingly subsiding, their great work achieved, into the slaves of man. Jean Robert went so far as to believe that in his boyhood he had had a personal exemplification of this universal brotherhood, and could understand the language of dogs, the songs of birds, and even the tender, sweet exhalations of the rose. What had broken that simple tie which bound him fraternally to flowers and animals alike? Alas! it was pride.

Jean Robert humbled himself before Roland, then, and called him towards him.

The dog came to him readily, leant his head upon Jean Robert's knees, and regarded him with confidence.

"Poor dog!" said the poet, caressingly.

Roland answered with a tender, plaintive whine.

"Ah! ah!" said Jean Robert, "Monsieur Salvator was right; we shall understand each other perfectly."

At the name of Salvator the dog looked intelligently towards the door, and gave a low, friendly bark.

"Yes," replied Jean Robert, "he is in the next room with your mistress, isn't he, Roland? Come, let us see what our father and mother were. Give me your paw, if you please."

The dog lifted his large paw and placed it daintily and lightly in the small white hand of Jean Robert.

"Ah! I thought so," exclaimed Jean Robert, after examining the paw with care. "Now for your age!"

And he opened Roland's heavy lips, discovering a double row of formidable teeth, white as ivory for the most part, but rather yellow at the back of the jaw.

"We're no longer young, I see," was the next comment. "If we were a woman, Roland, we should have concealed our age for ten years or more; if we were a man we should begin to be a little uncertain about it."

Roland remained motionless. It appeared a matter of indifference to him whether Jean Robert knew his age or not. Seeing this, the poet continued his examination, hoping to discover something presently that would arouse the dog's sensibilities.

It was not long before Jean Robert found what he looked for.

Roland had, as already mentioned, the yellow coat of a lion; but his hair was longer, save on one spot, between the fourth and fifth rib of the right side. There Jean Robert saw a large white mark.

"Why, what is this, poor Roland?" he said, at the same time placing his finger on the white spot.

Roland winced, and gave a pitiful moan.

"Halloo!" cried Jean Robert, "It's a scar."

He looked on the opposite side, and soon discovered a similar scar, only rather lower down.

On his pressing his finger on this second scar, Roland shivered and a deeper moan escaped him. Jean Robert knew that a burn or a wound destroys the colouring oil which circulates in the capillary tissues; and the size of the scar, and the dog's evident pain when it was touched, confirmed his suspicions that it was a severe wound Roland had received.

"Poor Roland!" he said, caressing the dog. "It appears you have been in the wars like your namesake."

Roland raised his head, and gave a loud wailing bark, which made Jean Robert shudder again.

The bark was so lugubrious that Salvator quickly re-entered the room, and inquired anxiously of Jean Robert,

"What is the matter with Roland?"

"Nothing," replied Jean Robert, laughingly. "You told me to have a chat with him. I asked him for his history, and he was in the act of relating it to me."

"And what did he tell you? Come, I should like to know," said Salvator, evidently curious, and at the same time filled with inquietude.

"It's soon told. I asked him whose son he was. He told me he was a cross between a Saint Bernard and a Newfoundland. I asked him his age. He told me he was between nine and ten years old. I asked him the cause of the two white marks he has, one on each flank. He told me that it was the trace of a bullet which had entered his right side and had broken a rib in piercing through to his left side."

"Marvellously exact! But did he tell you nothing more?"

"No. You came in just as he had told me that he had not forgotten his wound; and that, should he have an opportunity, he would, in all probability, remember the man who had fired the shot. I expect you to tell me the rest of the story, Monsieur Salvator."

"I am sorry to say I know no more than you do."

"But how did you come across him?"

"That's easily explained. One day, about five years ago, I was enjoying a day's shooting in the suburbs of Paris. . . ."

"You indulge in sport, then?"

"*Ma foi!* no. A Commissionaire cannot afford to be a sportsman. I should have said I was out on a little poaching expedition, when I found that poor dog in a ditch. He was covered with blood, wounded to death, on the point of giving up the ghost. He excited my compassion. I drew him to a spring, washed his wounds with some of the cold water, dashed with a little brandy, and saved his life. It then occurred to me that I should like to be the master of so fine a dog. I sent him home in a gardener's cart, nursed him carefully until his wounds were healed, and that's all I know of Roland. . . . Ah! pardon me, Roland; I forgot that you have shown me a gratitude which puts the gratitude of man to shame. I forgot that you would gladly face death on my behalf, or on behalf of the friends I love—wouldn't you, Roland?"

At this appeal, Roland gave a joyful cry, stood on his hind legs, and, placing his fore paws fondly on his master's shoulders, kissed Salvator's face.

"Good Roland! Good dog!" whispered Salvator. "But lie down now and take care of your mistress, Roland."

Roland at once obeyed his master, and resumed his station on the mat whence Jean Robert had called him.

"And now shall we take a stroll for fresh adventures?" asked Salvator.

"Willingly; but I fear I am trespassing on your time."

"Why?"

"Because your fair companion has a visit to make in the morning, and perhaps counts upon your accompanying her."

"Oh, no! Didn't you hear her say she couldn't tell me where she was going?"

"And do you venture to allow her to go unaccompanied to a place of the whereabouts of which you are ignorant?" demanded Jean Robert, laughingly.

"My dear poet, don't you know that there can be no love where there's no confidence? I love Fragola with all my heart; and I would sooner doubt my mother than doubt her."

"Quite so; but even then isn't it imprudent to allow a young girl to go out alone at six o'clock in the morning, and trust herself with a cabman in Paris?"

"It would be if she were not to take Roland with her; but with Roland for guardian I would let her travel round the world without the slightest fear."

"That settles the matter," answered Jean Robert, wrapping his cloak around him. "By-the-way, didn't I hear the name of Regina mentioned as one of her friends?"

"Yes."

"It is a rather uncommon name. I once knew a marshal's daughter with the same name."

"The daughter of Marshal de Lamothe-Houdan?" questioned Salvator.

"The very same!"

"That is Fragola's friend. . . . But let us be off now."

Jean Robert followed without another word, wondering what could be the next surprise that might happen on this night of surprise on surprise.

CHAPTER VII.—JEAN TAUREAU'S SAVIOUR.

DURING his stay of ten minutes in his bed-chamber Salvator had completely changed his dress.

He entered in a velvet costume. He came out in a light overcoat, a high waistcoat buttoned up to his neck, and dark trousers. Thus clad, it was impossible to tell precisely what class he belonged to; but from his bearing and conversation he would have been assigned a good standing in society.

"Where shall we go?" asked Salvator of Jean Robert, as he shut the front door behind him.

"Wherever you please. Am I not in your charge for the night?"

"Let us do as the ancients did," suggested Salvator. "Let us throw up a feather and follow wherever the wind may blow it."

They were now in the centre of the Place Saint-André-des-Arcs. Salvator tore a piece of paper from his pocket-book, threw it up, and the wind blew it in the direction of the Rue Poupée. The two friends followed the paper, which was borne before them like a butterfly. They were led by their will-o'-the-wisp to the Rue de la Harpe; and a second piece of paper, committed by them to the wind likewise, drew them to the Rue Saint-Jacques.

Without knowing in the least whither they might be led, they wandered at the will of the wind, ready for any adventure that might chance to befall them. Two or three times Jean Robert attempted to learn the secret of his mysterious companion's life; but each time Salvator avoided his questions like the fox by some adroit feint sometimes gives the slip to the hound pursuing him. At last, driven to reply more directly, Salvator said,

"What we are seeking is a new romance; what you wish me to relate to you is a romance concluded. Were I to yield to your wish we should be making a retrograde step. Let 'forward!' be our motto."

Jean Robert perceived that his companion wished to remain unknown, so did not press him further. Besides, the current of his thoughts was changed by an incident.

A crowd of men and women was gathered round a man lying on the pavement.

"He is drunk," said some.

"He is dying," said others.

There was an ominous rattle in the man's throat.

Salvator pushed his way through the throng, knelt down and raised the man's face, then suddenly looked up at Jean Robert and said,

"'Tis Jean Taureau! He will die of congestion of the brain if I don't bleed him this instant. Look! There ought to be a chemist's near. Find one, and knock him up."

Jean Robert looked quickly round him. He found they had strolled, without knowing it, into the Faubourg Saint-Jacques, near the hospital. Facing the hospital Jean Robert read above one shop this sign:—

| PHARMACIE DE LOUIS RENAUD. |

The name of the chemist was nothing to Jean Robert, provided he opened his door. He knocked a matter-of-life-or-death knock. After a delay of five minutes the door was opened, and M. Louis Renaud appeared on the threshold in his cotton nightcap and fustian trousers, demanding what was wanted of him at that late hour of the night.

"Get a basin and some bandages ready at once," quickly answered Jean Robert. "Here's a man who must be bled directly, to save his life."

The limp body of the unconscious carpenter was tenderly borne into the shop.

"Is there a doctor present to bleed the poor man?" demanded M. Renaud, with some anxiety. "I am totally ignorant of the art of bleeding. I am a herbalist—not a surgeon."

"Don't be alarmed," replied Salvator. "I have been a medical student, and so will undertake the operation."

"But I haven't even a lancet."

"Luckily, I have my case of instruments with me," was the reassuring response of Salvator.

The crowd filled the shop.

"Will any of you gentlemen like to be of use to this poor man?" next inquired Salvator.

"Certainly, Monsieur Salvator," promptly said one young man, holding forth his hand at the same time.

Salvator grasped the hand, and Jean Robert thought he saw the Commissionaire exchange a masonic sign with the new comer.

"Monsieur Salvator!" was repeated by some of the bystanders, in a low voice, from one to the other.

"Very well," said Salvator. "While I bleed him, you run round to the hospital and tell them to get ready for another patient."

Forthwith, three or four men, headed by the one who had spoken first to Salvator, set off on their errand; whilst the herbalist undid Jean Taureau's necktie, opened his waistcoat, and withdrew his shirt-sleeve from one inert arm.

The veins in his neck were swollen almost to bursting.

"Shall we bandage the arm?" asked Jean Robert.

"There's no bandage ready," replied Salvator. "Squeeze the arm tight below the vein, Monsieur Robert; I think that will do."

Jean Robert obeyed. Another ready hand held the basin; a third the lamp.

Monsieur Salvator applied the lancet with a skilful touch, and the angry, black blood gushed out into the basin.

"*Ma foi!*" exclaimed the deft operator; "it was high time!"

Jean Taureau drew a deep breath. When he had lost half-a-pint of bad blood he opened his eyes. The first glance was dull and heavy. Little by little his eyes grew less and less stony, until a divine ray of intelligence shone from them once again, and he regarded with astonishment the amateur surgeon, who yet stood over him, lancet in hand.

"Monsieur Salvator!" he cried, feebly. "Thank Heaven for sending you! It was you who bled me, wasn't it?"

"Yes—in more senses than one, I'm afraid, Barthelemy Lelong," answered Salvator, addressing Jean Taureau by his proper name, and wiping the blood from his lancet.

"Well, certainly," came the low response, "I had a terrible fall when you sent me spinning down stairs at Bordier's. It was too bad of you to take the part of that dandy. But I must not complain now you have brought me round again, Monsieur Salvator."

"Why, that dandy, as you call him, Barthelemy, has helped to bring you back to life. So you see he bears you no more malice than I do."

Jean Robert thereupon offered his hand to his late opponent.

"Let bygones be bygones, my friend," he said, in a propitiating tone.

"Thousand thunders!" answered Barthelemy Lelong, making use of his favourite exclamation, but in such a faint voice that it sounded ludicrous coming from his lips. "You will kill me with kindness now! Ah, Monsieur Salvator! what a stupid a man must be to make a fool of himself simply because a woman . . . But you will, perhaps, excuse me, Monsieur Salvator, when I tell you she came back from Bobino's again with that little wretch!"

"Come, come; be calm, Barthelemy!"

"It's easy enough for you to say that, Monsieur Salvator, when you have an angel to keep your home for you; but you deserve her, seeing you only live to do good to your neighbours and all who need your aid. Yet I am a good father, and I have done nothing that should make them take away my little daughter! For three days have I been searching for the little one. She has hidden her somewhere—at her wretched mother's, mayhap. She cries out 'Assassin!' directly she sees me, and with such good effect that I have had to pass the last two nights in a cell at the Salle Saint-Martin. But I am determined to find my little darling. Poor petite. She will be two years old next summer."

And the prostrate Hercules turned his head to hide his tears.

"You see his heart is in the right place," murmured Salvator in Jean Robert's ear.

"True," answered Jean Robert, watching the strange spectacle with great interest.

"Cheer up, Barthelemy," said Salvator, aloud. "Your daughter shall be returned to you."

"Will *you* see that she is, Monsieur Salvator?"

"Yes; I give you my promise."

"Oh! Thank you! Thank you! Now I have your promise I'm sure to see her soon—sure to clasp my little one soon in my arms again. Grant me this boon, Monsieur Salvator, and my life will be at your service, and you may do with it what you will. But when will you be able to find my little Fifine?"

"In three days' time you shall have news of her, Barthelemy."

"Sooner, if possible?"

"Yes; as soon as I can trace her out."

Salvator then waved his hand. Two of the messengers who had by this time returned from the hospital lifted Barthelemy Lelong—no longer a Jean Taureau in strength or ferocity—to his feet, and supported him out of the shop.

"Remember," cried Barthelemy, as he was being borne to the hospital, "you promised to bring me news of Fifine in three days at the latest, Monsieur Salvator. I shall live on the hope you have given me."

Chapter VIII.—A Strain of Music.

THE operation over and the patient gone, Salvator and Jean Robert were shown by the herbalist into the courtyard, there to wash the blood-stains from their hands at the pump.

A strain of sweetest music attracted their attention.

In the midst of the silence and calm of that serene night there suddenly vibrated through the air, as if by enchantment, the most melodious notes.

Whence came these soft, sweet strains of harmony? From what celestial choir?—from what divine instrument? Yonder rose the high wall of a convent. Had the east wind stolen into its dulcet organ in order to waft rarest æolian-harp melody to the passers-by in the Rue Saint-Jacques? The soul of some gentle novice—was it mounting to heaven on the wings of divinest music?

In sober earnest the air the two young men overheard was neither a snatch from some opera nor the solo of some gay musician returning from a carnival *bal masque*. It seemed, rather, a psalm or a hymn from some biblical library, for, on listening to it intently, there were recalled to the two entranced listeners, like plaintive shadows of the past, all the sacred tunes, all the hallowed hymns of their boyhood—the simple, soul-touching compositions of Sebastian Bach and Palestrina.

The one appropriate name for this fascinating fantaisie would have been "Resignation."

Who was the musician?

The music rose into rich volumes of harmony, and then dropped into cadences the most soft and melancholy. It held Salvator and Jean Robert spellbound.

Five francs slipped by Jean Robert into the herbalist's hand amply satisfied him for his trouble, and they were free to remain in the courtyard as long as it pleased them.

Salvator stepped gently towards a window, through the shutters of which light was streaming. He drew the shutters open. Then, through an opening in the curtains, they could see a young man about thirty years of age, seated on a stool, playing a violoncello.

Though a piece of music was before him on a music-stand, he never looked at the notes: he appeared lost in a melancholy reverie, and seemed utterly unconscious of what he was playing. His eloquent fantasia was plainly an improvisation—a soliloquy in which the inner life of the young player with all its sorrows was laid bare. As he played, there was evidently some contest going on within his heart. At last there escaped from the violoncello a heartrending strain, as from a man in agony; the bow fell from the player's nervous fingers; and a hand was placed before his eyes to keep back the welling tears.

The two young men watched this solitary drama with the keenest interest.

"There's the romance you seek," at length said Salvator, pointing to the violoncellist. "It is within this poor house, it is in that young man suffering before our eyes, it is in that violoncello which wept and rejoiced with him !"

Chapter IX.—Justin's Battle of Life.

"Do you know him?" asked Jean Robert.

"No," answered Salvator; "I don't know his name; I have never seen him before; but it is not necessary to know him to tell you that his is one of the most sombre pages in the book of life. See ! he has dried his eyes, and has begun to play again. The man who does that with such simplicity is a man with a great heart, I could swear. Let us go in and find out his history."

"Do you mean it? Do you really imagine he will relate the story of his life to any idle questioner?"

"But we are philosophers, not idle questioners. Besides, we bear the stamp of honest men in our faces. Moreover, all men are brothers, and should assist one another; all troubles are sisters, and deserve succour."

These last words were uttered by Salvator with a melancholy accent quite foreign to him.

He knocked at the door. It was presently opened by the young violoncellist without the least sign of astonishment.

"Whom have I the honour to speak to?" he asked of Jean Robert and Salvator.

"Friends, although we're unknown to you," said Salvator.

"Come in, then," was the answer, without a word of protest against so untimely a call at that late hour of the night, or, rather, of the morning.

Our two adventurers followed him into the room in which they had first caught sight of him through the curtains.

"Monsieur," said Salvator, "permit me to ask you whether it is in the power of man to relieve you from the grief which is seemingly weighing you down?"

"No, Monsieur," replied the violoncellist, in the same tranquil tone..

"Then we will retire. Let me only say a few words to excuse ourselves for this interruption. Monsieur (said Salvator, pointing to Jean Robert) is about to write a romance, in which he wishes to include the sorrows as well as the joys of man. He studies when and where he can. He and I accidentally overheard you playing, and then saw you repressing some heartfelt sorrow. Allow us to offer you our purses if you are poor, our arms if you are weak, our hearts if you are afflicted."

The sad pale face of the violoncellist was lit up momentarily with a smile of gratitude.

"I pity those," he answered, "who hide their wounds from their fellowmen. To show one's wounds to one's brothers may, at least, teach them how to avoid these heart sores. Sit down, my friends, and listen."

The story he told won the sympathy of his hearers.

The room, which served both as sitting-room and bed room to Justin —for that was the name of the violoncellist—was the neatest of chambers, with its white muslin curtains round the bed of snowy linen, with its neat and simple furniture, and that nameless charm which told of a woman's beautifying touch. But many long years ago the room was the dingy abode of a poor schoolmaster—poor in the goods of this world, but rich indeed in the learning and wisdom which are far above the dross that is accumulated to rust the hearts and cloud the souls of money-grubbers. It was at once the dwelling-place and the school of good M. Muller at that period.

Justin, the son of a poor country farmer who had sent his boy to Paris to be educated, was M. Muller's favourite pupil. Into his young mind the old schoolmaster poured his stores of learning, stimulating his fancy by the grand verse of Virgil and Homer, those two high priests of Nature, whose works served as texts when master and pupil took long Sunday walks together through the woods of Versailles, Meudon, or Montmorency.

Purest pleasure of all was it to Justin when M. Muller one day revealed to him the great passion of his life—his love for music—and opened a new world of thoughts to Justin when he made his violoncello speak to him with all the pathos and skill of a German musician. To learn to play this wonderful instrument which had such power to move the heart strings was the next source of delight to Justin. Daily practice, and the able lessons of M. Muller, soon made him familiar with the choicest pieces of Weber and Bach, Mozart and Haydn; and thenceforth he had in his violoncello a friend ever ready to sympathise with him, to rejoice in his joys, to grieve over his sorrows, to respond to every varying phase of his sensitive nature.

One Sunday in the February of 1814 the weekly letter arrived, as usual, for Justin; but it was sealed in black, and it was addressed neither in the hand of his father nor his mother. Justin opened the letter with trembling hands. He read with a sinking heart that the

Cossacks had devastated his father's farm, emptied the granaries, and burnt the house; that his mother, in rescuing her daughter from the flames, was so severely burnt that she was blind; that his father, a veteran soldier of the Republic, wild at the outrage committed by the enemy, took down his gun, shot nine Cossacks, and then fell dead with a dozen balls lodged in his body!

Tears of sympathy were shed by M. Muller; but Justin was inconsolable. The old schoolmaster, however, was his one friend left in the world; so Justin ultimately acted upon his advice. He brought his mother and sister to Paris. Then began his battle of life. For a long time he sought work in vain. Then he gave lessons in music at a ladies' school for a miserable pittance. Then he kept a tradesman's books for twenty-five francs a year. Then he succeeded to the arduous post of a printer's reader. Then came a severe attack of fever, and he lost all his engagements, one after the other; and, to cap his misfortunes, M. Muller left Paris to spend a long holiday in Dresden, to be near the idol of his heart—Weber—once more.

"Work is prayer!" This holy motto became Justin's. One by one he got a few pupils together, till by the time M. Muller returned the number was increased to eighteen. Their few pence just enabled Justin, his mother, and sister to live—that is, kept them from dying of hunger.

Laugh, if you can—you who have never had occasion to want food or fuel for those who are dearest to you! But laughter seems a sacrilege to me, who have also had to keep a mother and a son on a hundred francs a month.

Justin's life had become, in short, a life of complete self-abnegation, when the hand of God lifted him from the abyss of misery into which fate had plunged him, and gave into his care a bright young creature to be the sunshine of his home.

One beautiful June evening Justin was returning with his old master from a little holiday on the plain of Montrouge, when they perceived a little girl of about nine or ten years of age sleeping amid the poppies and the corn.

This little fairy, slumbering so peacefully, was surely sent to reward Justin for his heroic virtue and self-sacrifice.

Chapter X.—The Foundling.

The fair little maiden whom Justin and M. Muller had discovered cradled amid the golden corn lay peaceful as a dove in her nest: she formed a picture of rare beauty, and one that the two friends might have gazed at in silent admiration had they not been filled with inquietude at the thought of the dangers the innocent sleeper ran in being left there unprotected on the plain of Montrouge.

Was it possible so young a child had been left alone! Or, might not her mother be resting close by? Far and near Justin and M. Muller searched for her natural protector; but not a soul could they see save the gentle slumberer, whom they at length resolved to awaken.

"Have you lost your way, my child?" asked M. Muller, as the little one's eyes opened and looked up at them with surprise.

"No, Monsieur," was the reply, accompanied by a trustful glance, as if the little speaker were satisfied with her questioner's kind intentions. "I was very tired, and could walk no farther. So I sat down here and fell asleep."

"But where are your parents?"

"My parents?" answered the young girl, sitting up, and regarding the old professor with an air of perplexity implying an utter ignorance of what parents might be.

"Yes; your parents?" gently repeated Justin.

"I have no parents," replied the little one in the same tone in which she might have said, "I don't know what you mean."

"Have you no father?" pursued M. Muller, after exchanging a glance of astonishment with Justin.

"No, Monsieur."

"Where is your mother?"

"I have none, Monsieur."

"Who has brought you up, then?"

"My nurse."

"Where is she?"

"She is in the ground, Monsieur."

The young girl burst into tears as the last words escaped her lips. The hearts of her new friends were filled with warmest sympathy for her; and, when her sobs grew fainter, M. Muller gently asked,

"How came you to be all alone here, my dear?"

"I came from the country," was the trembling reply.

"From what part?"

"From Bouille."

"Near Rouen?" asked Justin, in a tone of glad surprise, being himself from the neighbourhood of Rouen.

"Yes, Monsieur," was the simple answer of this rosy-cheeked little Normandy pippin.

"But who brought you here?"

"I came alone."

"On foot?"

"Oh! no, Monsieur: by diligence to Paris."

"To Paris?"

"Yes; and I walked from Paris as far as this pretty field."

"What part of Paris were you going to?"

"To the Faubourg Saint-Jacques."

"What number?"

"To my nurses's brother. I have a letter for him from the curé of Bouille."

"Asking your nurse's brother to take care of you, my dear, I suppose?"

"Yes, Monsieur."

"How is it, then, that we find you here?"

"Because the diligence was late; and everybody in Paris seemed asleep. So I walked and walked till I came to these fields——"

"With the intention of waiting here till morning?"

"Yes, Monsieur; and then to set out to find the Faubourg Saint-Jacques. But I had not been in bed for two nights, and was so tired that I fell fast asleep where you found me."

More than ever did it seem that Providence had placed this little orphan in Justin's path to show him that there were even creatures more to be pitied then he was under the blue, starry dome of the heavens.

To Justin and to the old professor simultaneously it occurred that common humanity called upon them to see the poor girl safe for the night, and the little one accepted their friendly help as frankly as it was offered. When they were fairly on their road the child, leaning on the arms of her two new friends, and regarding them with the trustful confidence of youth which knows no evil of anyone, the conversation was renewed.

"What is the occupation of your nurse's brother, dear?" inquired M. Muller.

"He is a cartwright."

"At No. 111, Faubourg Saint-Jacques?"

"Yes, Monsieur; I know his name and number by heart. He is Monsieur Durier."

Justin and M. Muller looked at each other uneasily. Their silence did not stay the child's busy tongue. She chatted on, and they were soon familiar with her little history, which was not without romance and interest.

One night, in the year 1812, a carriage stopped at the village of Bouille. A gentleman descended from it. He carried in his arms a bundle which he held with care. Arrived at the door of a cottage near the end of the village, he took a key from his pocket, opened the door, walked boldly in, placed his burden on the bed, left a letter with a purse on the table, and then departed as secretly and silently as he had come.

When the good woman who lived in the cottage returned home an hour after from a marketing visit to Rouen, it was with no little surprise she heard a baby's cry coming from the bed she had left vacant. She quickly lit a lamp, and found it was an infant about a year old. Looking round with astonishment, she then perceived the purse and the letter on the table, and hastened to see what explanation the note might give of the little stranger's arrival. The following words met her eyes:

"Madame Boivin,

"You are well known as a good and honest woman; this is

what has made a father who is compelled to quit France resolve to confide his daughter to your care.

"You will find the purse on the table contains twelve hundred francs; this is the first year's payment for board and lodging in advance.

"On and after the anniversary of this date, the 28th of October, next year, you will receive, through the curé of Bouille, one hundred francs a month.

"This sum will be remitted to a bank in Rouen, and the curé will have no knowledge as to whom it comes from.

"Give the child the best education in your power, and see, particularly, that she makes a good house-keeper. God knows what her destiny may be!

"Her christian name is Mina; she need not bear any other, since I have not thought fit to reveal the name that belongs to her.

"28 *October*, 1812."

When Madame Boivin had mastered the contents of the letter, she seized the baby in her arms and ran to the curé's to get her pastor's counsel on the weighty matter.

The curé advised the good woman to accept the charge thrust upon her, and to bring up the child as well as she could.

Madame Boivin acted upon this advice. The child took the place of her son, who had died two years previously. The letter she carefully treasured with the papers of her husband, a sergeant in the Old Guard, then engaged in the disastrous retreat from Moscow.

Nothing more was heard of Sergeant Boivin by his wife. It never came to the poor woman's ears whether he was taken prisoner or whether he was dead.

For seven years the foster-mother was paid regularly for Mina's board. Then the payments ceased for two years and a half. But not a whit less kind and attentive was Madame Boivin to the charge she had come to regard as sacred.

It was death that deprived Mina of her trusty protectress. She left the orphan in the charge of the curé, who was to intrust her to the care of Madame Boivin's brother in Paris.

This brother was the Monsieur Durier who lived at 111, Faubourg Saint-Jacques.

Such was the brief and touching story that Mina had confided to Justin and M. Muller by the time they arrived at their destination.

Late though it was, Céleste flew to the door to welcome her brother. At first sight of Mina, Céleste was charmed with her fresh young beauty, caught her in her arms, and embraced her with a wealth of affection. Then, without stopping to learn who the little stranger might be, Céleste bore her off to her mother, who in her turn, at once yielded her heart to Mina, seeming to know insensibly, blind as she was, that it was one of God's fairest and sweetest creations that had just been brought into her presence. Madame Corby let her hands linger caressingly on the child's head, and appeared to be conscious of Mina's beauty from the simple touch of her sensitive fingers—the eyes of the blind.

While Céleste led Mina to her bed to sleep off her fatigue, Justin and the old professor recounted to Madame Corby all that they knew of the little foundling of Bouille.

CHAPTER XI.—DURIER'S CONSPIRACY.

BEFORE school-hour in the morning Justin called on one of the neighbours of the cartwright to whom Mina was intrusted. Toussaint was the name of the neighbour—the same that Jean Robert encountered in the broil at Bordier's.

Justin learnt that Toussaint and Durier were friends, and that Durier had taken part in the famous conspiracy of Nantes and Bérard to gain possession of the fort of Vincennes, and so give éclat to the outbreak of a plot that had been spread throughout France.

Durier had been led into the affair by a Corsican named Sarranti who attached great importance to his joining the conspiracy by reason of the number of ouvriers he might be able to influence. On the eve of the outbreak, about midnight, Toussaint heard a violent knocking at Durier's door, and on looking out of the window, recognised in the noisy stranger a man whom he had frequently seen with Durier. Toussaint then saw them both make off in the direction of the barrier, and had not beheld Durier or Sarranti since. He heard from the police, however, that Sarranti was "wanted" not only for his concern in the conspiracy, but also for having stolen from one of his friends something like fifty or sixty thousand francs, with which sum he had, no doubt, been enabled to reach Havre, in company with Durier, and to take passage thence together to India.

No news of either had since reached Toussaint. He added, however, for Justin's benefit, that possibly Monsieur Sarranti's son—a pupil at the school of Saint-Sulpice—might know something of their whereabouts. If the son did know aught of his father and his companion in flight, he would be discreet enough, Justin thought, not to impart ny of his knowledge to a stranger. Wherefore Justin returned home without calling upon Monsieur Sarranti's son.

Secretly pleased at the non-success of his search for Mina's new guardian, Justin acted the hypocrite for the first time, and informed Céleste and Madame Corby of the bad news.

"Bad news!" exclaimed his mother, not concealing her delight. "on the contrary, it is good news—the best of news; since God has thereby given an angel into *our* charge."

CHAPTER XII.—SUNSHINE IN THE HOUSE.

THE resolution to adopt Mina having thus been taken, Justin wrote to that effect to the Curé of Bouille, who quickly sent back his blessing and grateful thanks, with his sanction to Justin, and promised,

3

moreover, to let them know directly if he should hear from the little orphan's unknown protector.

Heaven would reward them, the good Curé added, for their humanity; and Heaven did reward them, in the person of Mina herself, whose sunshiny presence soon lit up the house with joy.

At first the dulness of the gloomy Paris house, compared to the rustic freshness of the cottage at Bouille, naturally damped the high spirits of Mina. What a difference did she not find between Céleste's sober bed-room and the little nest she occupied at Bouille! True, the walls of her little nest could boast no paper; but they were of snowy whiteness. Nor did her window have a red and yellow curtain, such as adorned Céleste's; but it opened on a fragrant garden, full of flowers in spring and summer, and full of fruit in the autumn; and as Mina was wont to strew a few crumbs on her window-sill every night, she was ever awakened by the sweetest carollings of her host of feathered friends.

That sweet country life—the pure, exhilarating air, the inspiriting sunshine, the beauty of the ever-changing foliage, the singing of the birds—had instilled into Mina's heart the essence of joy, had made her little cheeks the colour of peaches, and had filled her with a gaiety that soon rose triumphant over the depressing surroundings of her new life in Paris, buoyed up as she was by the loving tenderness of Madame Corby, Justin, and Céleste.

"Well, Mina," said Céleste to her one morning; "you are quite one of us now, you see! Our mother is your mother, and Justin and I are brother and sister to you; and though we're not rich we will do all we can to make you happy, dear."

And thus Mina glided into their lives, returning their goodness a hundredfold by her infectious gaiety, making each day seem a holiday, and life one long Sunday.

She became supreme. The house was her empire; and as spring clothes the earth with beauty, leading winter captive with vernal garlands, so Mina transformed the former wintry life of Justin's household into a springtide of gladness, a season of laughter and brightness unceasing.

Youth has the enchanting property of rejuvenising all it approaches; and Mina had scarcely been a member of the household two years when she had made Justin younger by ten years, and had imparted to the dull rooms something of country light and cheerfulness.

Now it would be an apronful of daisies and wild violets that she had gathered from the very field in which Justin and the old professor had first found her; and these simple flowers arranged round the rooms gave them an indescribable air of charming freshness. Later it would be a rose or two that a neighbouring gardener gave her; and a little bouquet of the queen of flowers would be placed by a little hand for the adornment of Justin's bed-chamber, beautified by that time into a marvel of the blanchisseuse's art, creamy white with damask curtains, and pretty and neat as Justin could desire.

Mina soon came to be called the "angel of gaiety."

One enjoyment she deprived Justin of—his violoncello, against which she felt a strong aversion, and tyrannically interrupted him whenever he went to seek solace from his favourite instrument. But what was the use of the violoncello now, when he never felt ennui? Was not Mina a living song? Was not her sweet voice the softest music to him?

Chapter XIII.—The Spring-tide of Love.

ONE charming summer evening, when the birds made amends for their silence all day long by trills and bursts of sweetest warblings, transforming their leafy orchestra into Heaven's own choir, and when flowers and birds and bees and butterflies were celebrating one of Nature's holidays, a young man had thrown himself down in the cornfield on the very spot where, five years before, he had discovered a little fairy who had become the one joy of his life.

It was Justin.

More than the enjoyment of Nature's delightful holiday filled his heart. Had he suddenly come into a fortune? Had some long-looked for ship come home laden with gold and happiness? Or had Work, that veritable mine of wealth, at length brought him the sweet leisure that always rewards those who know how to labour and to wait?

Fortune had, indeed, shone upon him at last; but he attributed it all to his good angel—Mina. Since she had come to brighten his existence, pupil after pupil had sought tuition from the favourite young schoolmaster of the quarter. He had as much as he could do, and was well paid for what he did, and so had been enabled to put a good round sum by in the shape of savings.

So Justin had gone to the corn-field of Montrouge to send up his thanks on high for the treasure that had been granted him.

It was then the month of June, in the year 1826, and Mina was about fifteen, tall, bewitchingly lovely, and full of the graceful lissomeness and winsome ingenuousness of girlhood. She might very well have sat for an Undine. Her blonde hair fell naturally in luxurious curls, the colour of golden wheat; her eyes were a sweet azure; her cheeks were rosy with the red of health.

When Justin and Mina walked out together through the corn-fields of Montrouge in the balmy Sunday mornings during which they unconsciously enjoyed the spring-tide of their love. What a happy couple! was the cry that would often have saluted their ears had they not been deaf to everything save the sweet confidences they exchanged.

Justin loved Mina with all the strength of his quiet nature.

It was on the Thursday of the Fête-Dieu that he first found out his love for her.

Mina formed one of the charming procession of young girls in pure white who at that time marched in procession through the chief streets of Paris, which were gay with garlands, and wreaths, and flags in their honour.

Justin stood to see the cortége of maidens go past, keeping his eyes on the alert for Mina. He thought he simply had a brotherly desire to note how his foster-sister looked in the procession; but, just as he caught sight of Mina's fair face, he chanced to look up at a window opposite, and there saw a young man who seemed to be devouring Mina with his eyes. A flame shot up into Justin's face. His heart gave a strange leap. He knew all at once that he was jealous and in love at the same time!

From that day of the Fête-Dieu Justin grew more and more in love, but did not venture to betray the secret of his heart to Mina.

Madame Corby, on her advice being sought, made the rational suggestion that, as Mina was so young, she should go to boarding-school for a year, at the end of which period it would be time enough for the marriage to take place, supposing Mina should then know her own heart well enough to be certain whether she could accept Justin for her husband. M. Müller chimed in, and mentioned the name of a schoolmistress at Versailles ("The only woman whom I could have loved, if I had only had time to love," said the old professor) to whom Mina could be safely intrusted.

So it came about that, on the first Thursday in the July of 1826, Mina (suffering a terrible heart-wrench through the temporary separation) was escorted by Justin and M. Muller to the Versailles pensionnat for young ladies, there to remain seven months in ignorance of the fact that, at the expiration of that time, she would return home as the bride of Justin—if no unforeseen occurrence should interfere with the arrangements of the Corby family.

Chapter XIV.—The Wedding Eve.

The summer months flew by less unhappily for Mina than she anticipated at the pensionnat, for she soon found a bosom friend, in whom, in all her artless innocence, she placed the most implicit confidence. The time flew by also with great rapidity for Justin, for he was engaged every day in preparations for the wedding, as were all the inmates of his little household, from his mother, whose bridal gift was the rich lace which had adorned her own wedding-dress in the happy long ago, to M. Müller, whose surprise was a handsome pianoforte.

Mina was to leave the boarding-school on the 5th of February, 1827, and the marriage was to take place the next day, according to the programme settled, perhaps with too much certainty, by Madame Corby, and agreed to willingly enough by Justin, and sanctioned, moreover, by the good curé of Bouille, who had promised to bestow his benediction on the fair bride in person.

The momentous evening arrived; Justin, with his mother and sister and the old professor, drove to Versailles to fetch Mina; and, as his carriage rattled up to the door, a dashing fiacre was just leaving.

Let it be remarked emphatically that it was high time they came.

Mina's new bosom friend, Mademoiselle Suzanne de Valgeneuse, had so won the affections of Mina that it was evidently a painful surprise to her to learn that she was suddenly to be separated from her gay young companion. Though still in the dark as to how her heart had been disposed of without her consent, Mina, however, soon recovered her natural lightheartedness before her benefactors, and welcomed them with all her old warmth and witchery of manner. Yet when she reached her own little room, to which she had insensibly become attached, Mina flung herself down on the simple prie Dieu adorned with our Saviour on the cross, and prayed for the happiness of all the gay-hearted young school-girls who had become as sisters to her. Then dressing herself rapidly, and bidding farewell to each treasured object in her little sanctuary, Mina hastened down stairs; and her face beamed with smiles as bright as of yore upon learning that Madame Corby had invited Madame Desmarets (the schoolmistress) and Mademoiselle Suzanne to spend the morrow with her at the Faubourg Saint-Jacques.

Whilst Mina and Justin, with their party, regained their carriage in the best of spirits, Mina's new bosom friend hastened to her room, and wrote the following note to her brother, Monsieur Lorédan de Valgeneuse:—

"Just as you left, the family arrived. They have taken Mina away with them. Something extraordinary is clearly going to happen in the Rue Saint-Jacques. Madame Desmarets and I are invited to spend the day there! If you wish to learn what is going on, take Madame and me there in your carriage to-morrow morning.

"Your loving Sister,
"S. DE V."

Chapter XV.—The Wedding Morn.

JUSTIN awoke with a rare feeling of buoyancy in the morning. He was down at six. He breathed a joyous prayer for Mina as he passed her door. He seemed to walk on air, for the moment of his supreme happiness was near at hand.

At eight o'clock his heart gave a great leap, and a thrill of love ran through his veins. He heard Mina and Céleste moving overhead. Would Céleste reveal the secret of secrets to the fair maiden to whom he was betrothed without her knowledge? He was soon to know.

When Mina was fairly awake, the surprise upon surprise prepared began to dawn upon her.

The apartments destined for the young bride and bridegroom were on the same floor. When Céleste stepped thither to give a last glance round, Mina first discovered the lace-decked robe of white muslin, the jupon of white taffeta, and the white silk stockings arranged on the bed.

Mina regarded these articles of bridal beauty with the greatest astonishment.

"For whom can these be?" she laughingly inquired of Céleste, on her return.

"Why, for you dear."

"A wedding-dress for *me?* Who is going to be married, then?"

"That's a secret."

"A secret! Oh, tell me, dearest Céleste," beseeched Mina.

"You must ask Justin," was the smiling reply.

"Oh, Justin will be sure to tell me if I ask him. Where is he?"

"He is waiting till you are dressed."

"Then he shall not have long to wait."

And Mina, aided by the willing hands of Céleste, was dressed in the twinkling of an eye.

Justin was awaiting the fair young bride in the nuptial chamber, holding in his hand a wreath of orange-blossoms, the one ornament wanting to complete Mina's bridal costume.

Presently, the dainty maiden in white, looking dazzlingly lovely, appeared on the threshold.

One glance at Justin revealed the secret to her.

A little cry of joy escaped her. Her arms were held out towards him. In another instant they were heart to heart, lip to lip; and, as Justin sipped the sweet nectar of her lips, he placed the wreath on her fair brow, crowning her at last his happy, loving, and beloved bride.

Then entered Madame Corby to give her blessing, Céleste to add her warm salute, and M. Müller to congratulate the loving pair.

"She loves me," whispered Justin to the old professor; "I am the happiest of men."

Justin was right. That was the culminating point of his happiness.

They were now joined by the schoolmistress and Mademoiselle de Valgeneuse. No sooner had they offered their felicitations than a smart English "tiger" made his appearance, and handed to Mademoiselle Suzanne a pencil and a note, adding,

"From M. Lorédan. I am to wait for an answer."

The note was laconic enough. It was simply as follows:

```
?
```

Suzanne understood the question. She hastily wrote the following reply:—

> ? A marriage! She weds her gawky school-master!
> Say adieu to your fancy! Keep your love for another object!
>
> S. DE V.

"Here, Dick, take the answer to your master!" she said, refolding the paper, and handing it to the "tiger."

Justin could not repress a presentiment of coming misfortune as he noticed the delivery of the note and the departure of the "tiger" with the reply.

He went to the window to see for whom the note was intended.

He saw an elegantly-dressed young man in an open carriage. When he tunred his face as he took the note from his servant, Justin recognised the very same young man who had first excited his jealousy by his open admiration of Mina on the occasion of the Fête-Dieu.

In Monsieur Lorédan de Valgeneuse, then, Justin thought, with burning cheeks, he had a rival.

*   *   *   *   *

A little later, the Abbé Ducornet, curé of Bouille, arrived; but the news of which he was the innocent bearer did not increase the joy of the bridal party.

First, he announced that he had brought a dowry for Mina in the shape of a cheque for ten thousand eight hundred francs, which Mina's unknown protector had sent to make up for years of remissness. Then he read the following letter, which he had received with the cheque.

"My dear Abbé,

"A long stay I have made in India is the reason you have not had news of me for nine years. But I know you and Madame Boivin well, and am certain you have not allowed Mina to want.

"I have just returned to Vienna, and haste to send you the ten thousand eight hundred francs I am indebted to you for the maintenance of Mina.

"Henceforth you will regularly receive the twelve hundred francs for my daughter till the date of my return.

"Vienna, January 24, 1827."   "MINA'S FATHER.

Mina turned to Justin with a glad smile when she learnt that her father still lived. Not a thought had either for the moment that the news would have the effect of separating them.

It was Madame Corby that awakened Justin to a sense of his duty. With a trembling voice she called Justin to her side, and whispered to her son,

"You will understand, Justin, of course, that you ought not to go on with this marriage now. Whilst Mina was a poor orphan it was right enough; but now—you know she is rich—now you know her father lives, surely——"

A silent pressure of his mother's hand told her that, despite the struggle that was going on in his heart, he had bravely resolved to take her advice.

"What is the matter?" cried Mina.

Justin mastered his emotion as he answered as firmly as he could that now they could only wed with the consent of her father.

Mina fell senseless in her lover's arms as she learnt this terrible truth.

* * * * *

An hour after this interruption of what was to have been a wedding, Mina, overpowered with grief, returned to Versailles with Madame Desmarets and Suzanne. But before their departure Mina's bosom friend had time to send a fresh note to her brother:—

"The marriage has not come off! It appears that Mina is rich, and the daughter of a Somebody. We return to Versailles with the inconsolable bride. "S. DE V."

CHAPTER XVI.—THE ABDUCTION.

JUSTIN was like one lost for the next two days. He wandered about Paris purposelessly. He at length found solace in his forsaken violoncello; and it was his heart-touching symphony that attracted the attention of Jean Robert and Salvator.

The story that has just been told was the story Justin related to Salvator and Jean Robert. It aroused their warmest sympathy. It did more. When Salvator heard the names of Suzanne and Lorédan de Valgeneuse he started, and evidently regarded them with secret repulsion.

"Monsieur," said Jean Robert, "we will not bore you with the expression of the sympathy we feel for you. Here are our addresses. If at any time we can be of service to you regard us as your friends."

They parted with hearty shakes of the hands.

But before the two friends could gain the street, there was a loud knock at the door.

It was quickly opened.

A veritable gamin de Paris stood before them.

"What! Is it you, Monsieur Salvator!" exclaimed the urchin.

"What do *you* want here at this hour, Master Babolin?" was the answer.

"Oh! I have brought a letter here for M. Justin. Mother found it going her rounds to-night."

Looking at the address outside the letter, the gamin read:—

"Monsieur Justin,
20, Faubourg Saint-Jacques.
A reward of a louis to the person who
may bear this letter to him.
MINA."

"Run!" cried Salvator. "Take it to Monsieur Justin this instant!"

The gamin rushed with the letter to Justin, who presently came in great haste after the two friends, holding the open letter in his hand.

"Ah! Thank God you are still here!" he exclaimed. "Read this."

Salvator took the open letter from him and read,—

"I am being taken away by force. I am a prisoner. They are taking me I know not whither. Save me, Justin! Save me, brother! or avenge me, husband! "MINA."

"Ah! friends," appealed Justin; "Providence has sent you to aid me!"

"Well," said Salvator aside to Jean Robert; "you were in want of a romance. We are now fairly engaged in one, my dear fellow!"

CHAPTER XVII.—PURSUIT.

THE news of Mina's abduction astonished Salvator and Jean Robert as much as it did poor Justin. Not a minute did they lose, however, in vain expressions of sympathy. The tearful lover asked his two new friends for their help, and their help was at once freely given.

Salvator soon recovered his sang-froid.

"Pray be calm, Monsieur Justin," he pleaded. "It is a difficult task we are about to engage in; all our faculties must be on the alert if we would rescue Mademoiselle Mina."

"Be calm when my darling is being spirited away, who knows whither?" exclaimed Justin, in despair, "when she appeals to me for succour or for vengeance?"

"Exactly! That is the very reason why we must first find out who is the abductor, and where he has fled to with her. . . . Can you depend upon Mina?"

"As I can on myself!"

"Then rest assured she will know how to defend herself. As for us, we have no alternative but to trace her step by step."

Cold comfort (though wisest counsel) for Justin! He was for starting in pursuit that instant; and his impatience became hard to restrain when his heart sank within him at the thought that Mina might that very moment be growing weaker and weaker in her vain resistance to some terrible outrage.

"Babolin must first be questioned," added Salvator. "Give him a louis for his mother and something for himself to begin with."

Justin having handed the gamin a gold and silver piece, Salvator turned to the lad and asked him,

"Where did your mother find this letter?"

"How should I know?" answered Babolin, frankly enough. "You had better ask her that question herself."

"He is right," said Salvator. "Monsieur Justin, you follow Babolin, and get what you want to know from *la Brocante* yourself."

"Monsieur Jean Robert," continued Salvator, "I must next give you a rôle in this drama."

"Be it so! And as active a part as you like. I've had some experience as an author; and I shall not be sorry to be an actor for the nonce."

"Very well. Hasten you, and find out one of the fleetest horses in Paris, and gallop with it to 11, Rue Triperet, where you will meet Monsieur Justin and me."

"Meanwhile," added Salvator, "I will hurry round and inform the police of the abduction."

CHAPTER XVIII.—WHAT THE CARDS SAID.

WHILST Jean Robert was hastening to the Rue de l'Université, and Salvator was speeding to the Rue de Jérusalem, Justin, whom we will follow, was striding fast at the heels of Babolin, who, true gamin of Paris as he was, quickly conducted him by the shortest cuts to the Rue Triperet.

It was before one of the gloomiest tenements in one of the dirtiest and narrowest of Paris streets that Babolin stopped.

"Here we are," he said.

"You go first; I'll follow," answered Justin, upon whom the dirt and misery had no effect, for the most anxious fears for Mina's safety filled him, heart and soul and mind.

Following his young guide, Justin climbed a steep and narrow flight of stairs, more like a ladder than anything else, and found himself at the door of *la Brocante's* kennel, as it might well have been called, for the first sound that greeted Justin's ears was the discordant barking of several dogs.

"It's me, mother," Babolin shouted through the keyhole. "Open the door, for I have some one with me!"

"Quiet, dogs!" was the exclamation that came, in a harsh voice, from the interior. "I can't hear anything for your noise. Down, Cæsar! Quiet, Pluto!"

"You can come in now," continued the same harsh voice, when silence was restored. "Push the door open; it's not locked."

When Babolin had obeyed this command, what a den of dismal poverty it was that Justin beheld!

There, in a kind of fœtid loft, with damp walls, and a ceiling of laths and plaster supported by a dingy upright and a dingier crossbeam, the gaps in the roof letting in cold blasts of air;—there, amidst all this misery, sat a woman in rags, with a fair girl of remarkable beauty leaning against the beam immediately behind her, with a pack of dogs of different species growling in the corner, and with a rook perched on the beam overhead, to add to the weirdness of the scene.

Justin could at first but faintly discern these objects by the feeble light shed from a small lamp. When his eyes became accustomed to the comparative darkness of the room, he could see that *la Brocante* was a middle-aged repulsive-looking woman, clad in the dismallest of brown rags, and that she regarded him with a half-suspicious, half-cunning look that gave him little encouragement to hope for tidings of Mina from her.

"Monsieur Justin has come, mother," said Babolin, "to learn from you what I can't tell him."

"And the louis?" demanded *la Brocante*, with a cunning smile which suggested that she had confidently looked for this visit.

"Here it is," replied Babolin, slipping the piece of gold into her hand; "and you ought to buy Rose a nice warm gown with it."

"Thank you, Babolin," said the little girl, warmly, and accompanying her words by a grateful glance from the sweetest of azure eyes; "but I am not cold."

Even as she timidly said these words, there came from her a hacking cough which told plainly enough how sadly she did in reality need warmer clothing.

"Madame," said Justin, in trembling, hurried accents, "you sent this letter to me, didn't you? Where did you find it?"

"In the quartier Saint-Jacques, of course."

"Yes; but in what street?"

"I didn't notice the name of the street. It must have been somewhere near the Rue Dauphine or the Rue Mouffetard."

To anyone familiar with the Bohemian tribe, upon one of whom Justin had lucklessly hit, it would have been clear enough that *la Brocante* was beating about the bush, with the idea, mayhap, of making the highest possible figure of her secret.

"Try and remember, I beg of you," pleaded Justin. "Here's something to quicken your thoughts."

And Justin gave her another louis.

This fresh bribe did but excite her cupidity the more.

"I fancy it was. . . . Yes; it must have been there," stammered *la Brocante*. "But the cards will tell us for certain."

"Where must it have been?"

"In the Place Maubert that I found the letter."

"If you can tell me no more I must make that information do," answered Justin, moving towards the door. "Thank you. I had better join Monsieur Salvator now."

"Stay, Monsieur Justin!"

The young man turned back; and, looking in the direction in which *la Brocante* was pointing, observed that the rook was wildly flapping its wings overhead.

"Do you know what that signifies?" she demanded, still pointing her lean finger towards the fluttering rook.

"No."

"It signifies—it signifies that you will not find the person you are in search of as quickly as you anticipated, for you are in search of some one, aren't you?"

"Yes; and I would willingly give all I possess in the world to find her, Madame."

"Well; the bird's flapping of its wings is but typical of your probably fruitless movements hither and thither, unless you commence your search with the necessary information—that is to say, unless you listen intently to the revelation of the cards!"

"Let them begin their revelations, whatever they may be, at once, then!"

La Brocante pocketed the fresh louis that Justin gave her, and indulged in a little cabalistic demonstration before displaying the cards.

An unearthly cry escaped her lips. Thereupon, the twelve dogs set up the most lugubrious howls, then bounded forward, and surrounded her as a body-guard; the rook at the same time circling round her, and finally perching on *la Brocante's* grey head.

The pseudo fortune-teller meanwhile placed a flat piece of wood, in the shape of a gigantic horseshoe, on her lap to form a table; and, after uttering some unintelligible words, began to shuffle a pack of cards, which Justin had to cut with his left hand.

"It is one you have a great love for that you have come to inquire after, isn't it?" asked *la Brocante*, with a slightly wheedling inflection of her harsh voice.

"One whom I adore," was the prompt response of Justin.

"Good! It is evident this Knave of Clubs is meant for you—it stands for an enterprising and adroit young man."

Justin could not repress a bitter smile, for these were the very qualities he lacked.

"*She* is the Queen of Hearts—in other words, a sweet and loving girl."

The cards were shuffled and cut again and again. Each time they were cut three cards were dealt by *la Brocante*, until there were eighteen before her—the Knave of Clubs still representing Justin, and the Queen of Hearts still representing Mina.

Touching the seventh card to the left from the Knave, she said,

"She whom you love is a fair young girl, from sixteen to seventeen years of age."

"True," cried Justin.

"An unaccomplished design!" she next exclaimed, placing her finger on the seven of spades. "There was some arrangement between you that could not be carried out?"

"There was, alas!"

"What interfered with your arrangement," she continued, holding up a nine of clubs, "was the sudden news of some dowry or legacy."

The ten of spades was the next card pitched on by *la Brocante*.

"And, strange to say," she resumed, "that money, ordinarily the cause of so much joy, only brought tears to you both!"

Continuing her calculation, she fixed on the ace of spades, and said,

"The letter I sent you comes from the young girl, who is in danger of being imprisoned."

"Imprisoned!" exclaimed Justin. "Impossible!"

"But the cards say so, and they never err. Prison, seclusion, sequestration!"

"Go on, woman; you've been right, hitherto!"

"The letter arrived, then, when you were engaged with some friends."

"Yes, yes; good friends and true!"

La Brocante's hand then alighted on the Queen of Spades, face downwards.

"'Tis a dark lady who has caused her disappearance," was the next revelation of the cards.

"Yes; Mademoiselle de Valgeneuse."

"The cards only say a dark lady; they don't tell her name."

She resumed her study of the game—easy enough, though seemingly magical—she was playing, and came to the eight of spades.

"The arrangement that came to nothing was a marriage."

Justin stood confounded by the exactness of her reply.

Encouraged by his surprise and wonderment, she quickly touched one of the three aces she had placed side by side.

"Oh! oh!" she murmured. "A conspiracy! A plot!"

The King of Clubs now appeared.

"You are aided at this very moment," continued the witch, "by a trusty and loyal friend, longing to render you a service."

"Salvator!" cried Justin, recognising the portrait.

"But hindered in his good work," added *la Brocante*, "by some unforeseen occurrence."

"What of the young girl?" exclaimed Justin, impatiently, then murmuring softly to himself, "What of my darling? What of Mina?"

La Brocante held up the Knave of Spades, and answered.

"Her abductor is a dark young man, of rough manners."

"Woman!" gasped Justin, in a frenzy of excitement. "Where is she? Only tell me where she is and all I have shall be yours."

Plunging his hand thereupon into his pocket, he drew forth a handful of silver, and was about to dash the money on the little card-table, when his arm was grasped from behind.

Justin turned round to remonstrate with the stranger who had ventured to take this liberty, and recognised Salvator.

He had entered unnoticed just in time to save Justin from this foolish expenditure of money.

"Put the silver back in your pocket," he gently said to Justin. "You will find Monsieur Jean Robert's horse waiting for you in the street. Mount it, and gallop at the top of your speed to Versailles. See that no one enters Mina's room, and watch that no one leaves the pensionnat by the play-ground. It is now half-past seven: at half-past eight you ought to be at Madame Desmaret's."

"But . . ."

"There's not a moment to lose."

"But . . ."

" Start at once, or I can answer for nothing."

" I'll fly then !" replied Justin, adding, to *la Brocante*, as he gained the door,

" We shall meet again."

He then flew down stairs, took the reins from Jean Robert's hands, sprang into the saddle, and dashed off at full gallop by the Rue Copeau for the shortest route to Versailles.

CHAPTER XIX.—HOW THE CARDS CAME TO TELL THE TRUTH.

LA BROCANTE dropped her cards at sight of Monsieur Salvator, and a thick deep sigh escaped her; while the rook flew up to its coign of safety and the dogs rushed helter-skelter to their corner.

When Jean Robert entered, in his turn, the squalid den was not without a certain picturesqueness. It was a scene that would have rejoiced the artistic eye of his friend Pétrus.

The fortune-teller still seated on her stool, Babolin crouching at her feet, and the lissom figure of Rose leaning against the beam which served as a pillar to the roof, were all of interest to the poetic mind of Jean Robert, who stored up these pictures of the dark side of Paris life for use on a fitting occasion.

La Brocante plainly awaited with no little inquietude whatever Salvator might say. To her great surprise, however, he appeared to take no further notice of the game she had been playing.

" Well, Brocante," he said, " how is Rose getting on ?"

" Very well, thank you, Monsieur Salvator," replied the young girl, in a sweet, tender voice.

" It is not you, I'm asking, Rose. It is this woman."

" She still coughs a little," answered *la Brocante*, apologetically.

" Has the doctor been ?"

" Oh, yes, Monsieur Salvator."

" What did he say ?"

" That this lodging must be left at once."

" And well he may have said so," replied Salvator. " I have frequently told you the same thing. How is it you've not given the poor girl any stockings yet ?"

" Because they cost so much : and I am so poor, Monsieur Salvator."

" 'Tis false ! You're *not* poor ; and they're not dear. If in a week's time you have not found a good room for yourself and Babolin, a little room for Rose, and a proper kennel for your dogs, I shall take Rose under my guardianship. So I warn you."

" You would deprive me of my child !" cried the old woman, flinging her arms with many affectionate demonstrations round the fair girl.

" In the first place she is not your child," said Salvator, "for you stole her."

" Saved her ! saved her ! on my oath, Monsieur Salvator !"

HOW THE CARDS CAME TO TELL THE TRUTH.

"Saved or stolen, you will have to discuss the matter with Monsieur Jackal, if you don't do what I have told you."

La Brocante was silent at this threat, but she clasped the girl more closely to her, as if she were a treasure she would guard with her life.

"But what I came for just now was on the business of that poor fellow you were gulling and robbing when I arrived," continued Salvator.

"I was not robbing him; I simply took what he gave me of his own accord," was the sulky response.

"But you were gulling him."

"It was only the truth I was telling him."

"How did you know it was the truth?"

"By the cards."

"You lie!"

"Monsieur Salvator, on my oath, what I said was the simple truth."

"What did you tell him?"

"That he loved a fair young girl of sixteen or seventeen years of age."

"Who told you that?"

"The cards."

"Who told it you?" repeated Salvator, imperatively.

"Babolin, who learnt it from Monsieur Justin's neighbours."

"Proceed, Brocante. What else did you tell him?"

"That the girl loved him, that a marriage had been arranged, but that it was prevented from taking place by the unexpected news of some dowry."

"And who told you all those things?"

"Why, the ten of clubs signified the money, and the eight of spades the interrupted marriage."

"Who *told* you?" demanded Salvator, growing more and more impatient.

"A good old curé, Monsieur Salvator—a good old curé, whom I overheard saying, as he left Monsieur Justin's house, 'Only to think that it was the sum of ten or twelve (I forget which) thousand francs I brought that caused all this trouble!'"

"Very good, Brocante. Continue."

"I then told him that Mademoiselle Mina had been carried off by a dark young man."

"How did you know that?"

"Monsieur Salvator, the Knave of Spades was before me, and the Knave of Spades——"

"How did you know the young girl was being carried off?" insisted Salvator.

"I saw her."

"Where?"

"In the Place Maubert."

"You saw Mina in the Place Maubert?"

"Yes; last night. I was walking along the Place Maubert. Suddenly a carriage almost flashed past me. The window was opened. I heard someone cry, 'Help! Help!' and the fair head of a pretty young girl was just seen by me. At the same moment the face of a young man appeared at the window—the face of a dark young man with moustaches. He drew the girl back and closed the window, but not before she had thrown out a letter."

"And that letter?"

"Was the one addressed to Monsieur Justin, and sent by me to him at once."

"What was the hour?"

"About half-past five."

"Good! Is that all?"

"Yes, Monsieur Salvator, I assure you."

"And why didn't you tell M. Justin all this without producing those stupid cards, Brocante? You'll play this game once too often, if you don't take care. . . . However, here's a louis for speaking the truth; but mind you buy some warm clothing for Rose, or you'll know what you may expect!"

Then, after giving the poor girl an affectionate farewell greeting, Salvator beckoned Jean Robert to follow him, and left *la Brocante's* den.

"Who's your fair little protegée?" asked Jean Robert, when they had gained the street.

"Heaven knows!" was Salvator's reply. "I only know that, seven years ago, Brocante found her by the roadside in the suburbs of Paris; and that, when chance threw her in my way, I kept my eyes on her, and did all I could for the poor child's welfare. There's evidently a great mystery surrounding the girl. Time alone will reveal it."

Salvator had just finished when they reached the Pont Neuf.

"Here's our rendezvous!" he exclaimed, leaning against the railings round the Henri IV. statue.

"What are we to wait for?"

"A carriage."

Before ten minutes had elapsed a carriage, drawn by a pair of spirited horses, stopped opposite the statue.

A man of about forty years of age opened the door from the inside, and said, in a commanding tone of voice,

"Come, quick!"

The two friends promptly responded to the invitation.

The horses resumed their gallop, and the carriage was whirled off in the direction of the Quai de l'Ecole.

CHAPTER XX.—"WHERE'S THE WOMAN?"

WHO and what was the personage in whose carriage Salvator and Jean Robert drove off, viâ the Quai de l'Ecole?

Let the question be answered by a simple statement of Salvator's visit to him that same morning in the Rue de Jérusalem—the Scotland-yard of Paris.

Salvator entered the Préfecture with the air of one who was quite at home in the sanctuary of the police. Of the doorkeeper he asked, "Has Monsieur Jackal arrived yet?"

"Yes, Monsieur Salvator."

Crossing the courtyard and mounting to the second floor, Salvator gained M. Jackal's office in a few minutes, and bade the usher announce him to his master:—

"Tell him that Salvator, the Commissionaire of the Rue aux Fers, wishes to see him particularly."

The usher had no sooner delivered his message than M. Jackal rose from his chair to answer it in person. The door opened, and, before Salvator could catch sight of M. Jackal, he could hear him giving a parting instruction to some one:—

"Pardieu! Where's the woman? Seek her."

The head of a fox, and the body of a polecat! There you have in one sentence an idea of the combined astuteness, cunning, and finesse which were M. Jackal's mental characteristics, as well as of the suppleness and agility which were his physical qualifications for the high post he held.

Half closing his eyes, the better to pierce the darkness of the corridor, M. Jackal recognized his early visitor, and said, cordially, "Ah! it's you, my dear Monsieur Salvator. What brings *you* so early to the Rue de Jérusalem?"

"I have a very grave affair to bring before you," answered Salvator, who appeared to repress with difficulty the repugnance he entertained for the crafty Chief of the Police. "Had I not better give you the particulars in your room?"

"My dear Monsieur Salvator, you know very well there's no private business I would not leave off immediately to be of service to you; but, just at this moment, unfortunately, there are twenty persons waiting to speak to me, and it is important that I should attend to them at once."

"How long will you be engaged with them?"

"About twenty minutes: a minute each person. I must be at Bas-Meudon at nine o'clock."

"May I ask what calls you there?"

"A case of asphyxia—two young people tired of this world."

"Suicide! Poor wretches!" exclaimed Salvator, adding, as he thought of the urgency of Justin's case, "I am sorry I cannot have your valuable assistance, Monsieur Jackal."

"An idea!"

"What is it?"

"I am going to Bas-Meudon in my carriage. Come with me. You can tell me your story en route. What is the upshot of it, by-the-way?"

"An abduction."

"Where's the woman?"

"Parbleu! That's the very thing we want to find out."

"Oh, no! not the woman who's been carried off."

"Who, then?"

"The woman who assisted in the abduction of the other."

"You think there was a woman at the bottom of it, then?"

"There's a woman in everything, Monsieur Salvator. That's what makes our work so difficult. Yesterday word was brought me that a mason was killed in falling from a roof."

"And you asked, 'Where's the woman?'"

"That *was* the very first question I asked."

"Well?"

"They laughed at me. Nevertheless, they looked for the woman and found her."

"Where?"

"The poor fellow had just turned his head to watch a girl at her toilet in the opposite attic; and he found so much pleasure in the sight, *ma foi!* that he quite forgot where he was. His foot slipped and down he fell. So, you see, no matter how trifling the affair may be, a woman's sure to be mixed up in it. . . . Is it settled that you come with me to Bas-Meudon?"

"Yes; but I have a friend."

"There are four places in the carriage. Where shall I pick you up in half-an-hour's time?"

"Let the rendezvous be the statue of Henri IV.

There they accordingly met at the appointed hour; and thus did Jean Robert first make the acquaintance of M. Jackal, who had risen by his marvellous cleverness and aptitude to the high office of Chief of the Police.

M. Jackal knew all the thieves, pickpockets, and Bohemians of Paris: all the ticket-of-leave men and thieves of every grade roamed seemingly at large in that Lutetian pandemonium, but never out of sight of the sleepless eyes of M. Jackal. When told of such and such a crime, he would at once say, "Oh! I know the man; it's So-and-So's style of workmanship."

Rarely was he mistaken.

M. Jackal, moreover, had the power of disguising himself and of assuming the most various characters with wondrous skill. By his impersonations of a General of the Empire, a grand or humble concierge, a grocer, a Peer, he would have eclipsed the most able comedian on the stage.

It was the custom of this Protean Chief of the Police to wear a pair of large green spectacles when he wished to observe anything closely without calling attention to his scrutiny. These were at once put on when Jean Robert entered the carriage after Salvator. A piercing glance or two satisfied M. Jackal as to who Jean Robert was, for he immediately recognised him as the popular dramatist.

"Ah!" exclaimed M. Jackal, allowing the spectacles to fall on his nose, nestling in one of the snug corners of the carriage, and indulging in the luxury of a huge pinch of snuff. "Now tell me all about this abduction."

The leading features of Justin's history and of Mina's abduction were then succinctly related; but the details did not alter M. Jackal's opinion one jot.

"And haven't you sought out the woman yet?" he asked.

"No time has been lost," replied Salvator. "We only knew of the abduction at seven this morning; and directly we knew we dispatched Justin on horseback to the school at Versailles."

"Good! And now, if the woman is only found, all will be well."

"But I don't know any friend of Mademoiselle Mina that the slightest suspicion can be attached to," hazarded Salvator.

"You should suspect every woman."

"Isn't that a somewhat sweeping assertion, Monsieur Jackal?"

"You say it is a young man who has carried off your Mina?"

"My Mina?" said Salvator, smiling.

"The Mina of the young Professor, then—the Mina in question?"

"Yes; *la Brocante* heard her crying for help from a carriage, and saw a young man pull her back from the window."

"Then, find out the woman, I repeat. Evidently a woman has had a hand in the matter—to what extent I can't tell yet. You see no woman to suspect near Mademoiselle Mina. I see numbers. There are mistresses, sub-mistresses, and their friends, chamber-maids, and even her very schoolfellows. Regard any one of these as a magazine of combustibles, ready to be set alight and go off at the first touch of the torch of love, as they might poetically style the cause of all mischief. Clearly, some woman is concerned in this mysterious drama. You may say that a most watchful mistress keeps a good guard over her flock; but suppose it was one of the lambs that let in the wolf?"

"Impossible! Mina adored Justin."

"Be sure, then, a friend of hers has been the prime cause of the mischief. That's why I say once more, find the woman!"

"I begin to be of your opinion," answered Salvator, as a suspicion he had not previously thought of entered his mind.

"Make your minds easy; we shall find Mademoiselle Mina and her false friend both all in good time. . . . Now, let me tell you a little of my business. As I stated to you before, Monsieur Salvator, it's a double case of death from asphyxia which calls me to Bas-Meudon. These suicides of lovers are becoming quite common now. The fashion set by some enamoured couples more idiotic than the run of these young fools, self-murder is, of course, the thing with shallow-pated, cowardly lovers, who deem themselves wronged by Fate, forsooth! and so put an end to their worthless lives. At this moment I am en route to make an official inquiry concerning the suicides of a Mademoiselle Carmélite and a Monsieur Colomban—"

M. Jackal paused, for he observed that his two companions were visibly startled at the mention of these names.

"Pardon me," interrupted Salvator, in an agitated voice; "but was the Mademoiselle Carmélite you refer to a pupil at Saint-Denis?"

"She was."

"And was Monsieur Colomban a young nobleman from Brittany?" inquired Jean Robert, with equal agitation.

"Right again."

"I understand now," murmured Salvator to himself, "the purport of Fragola's letter."

"Do you know what caused them to take this terrible step?" pursued Jean Robert. "Is it a secret, or are you at liberty to tell the story?"

"Ma foi! It's no secret. Would you like to hear the story in detail? Ah! Monsieur Jean Robert, you need only change the names to make it a romance of the greatest interest."

And, as the carriage rolled along the Quai de la Conférence towards the bridge at Sèvres, Monsieur Jackal recounted the following sad history, which will be found to have the closest connection with the personages already introduced to the readers in this romance.

CHAPTER XXI.—A PARIS TRAGEDY.—THE DEATH-BED FRIENDSHIP.

THE hero of M. Jackal's story lived in a modest dwelling in the Rue Saint-Jacques, one of those Parisian streets possessing the rare charm of delightful gardens, the fragrance of whose roses and jasmines stole into humble rooms and filled them with the sweetest incense.

He was a Breton—that could be plainly seen in the energy and firmness stamped upon his face. Colomban de Penhoël, on leaving college, had been sent by his father to Paris to study for the law. With the noble self-abnegation common to many poor gentlemen in France, the father shared with his son all that remained of his income. The Comte de Penhoël almost lived the secluded life of a hermit in a Breton tower that was the sole débris of a feudal castle built during the Vendéan wars, and his thrift enabled him to spare Colomban twelve hundred francs a year.

Colomban had just begun his third year of hard study in Paris. It was one cold night in the January of 1823. He was sitting by the fireside in his little sitting-room on the second floor, studying the Justinian code, when he suddenly heard the sobs and tearful cries of some one evidently in great grief. In a moment he had opened the door. He saw before him a young girl in the deepest sorrow. She was in tears, and was crying for help. Colomban recognised his young neighbour, who lived with her mother on the same floor.

"Monsieur! Monsieur!" she said, wringing her hands. "My mother is so ill—so ill that she cannot speak. Oh! what can I do? What can I do?"

"She has probably fainted," answered the young man, with the warmest sympathy, following the young girl into the room wherein her mother lay white and motionless on a bed.

A shiver ran through Colomban at the sight of the poor woman. Her pallid, rigid features recalled the death of his own mother, the one terrible grief of his childhood, and as the ineffaceable image of the Comtesse de Penhoël's noble face, white and cold as marble, rose in his mind's eye, he felt unutterable pity for the pale and trembling girl by his side, for he knew only too well that she, too, would never see a mother's smile or hear a mother's voice again.

"Well, Monsieur? . . . Well?" asked the young girl between her sobs.

In order to prepare her for the shock that must soon follow, Colomban still endeavoured to persuade her that the poor woman had fainted from extreme weakness.

"But why does she look at me so fixedly? She wants something, and cannot speak. Mother! Mother, dear, what can I do—what can I do to relieve you?"

"Alas! all that you can do, Mademoiselle," Colomban felt himself, at length, compelled to say, though scarcely able to restrain his own tears, "is to close her eyes and pray for the repose of her soul!"

"But she cannot be dead!" exclaimed the young girl, in her agony.

Bending over the inanimate form until her lips touched the cold white brow, she at last realised the truth.

"Dead! Dead!" was the cry wrung from her young heart. She tottered, and would have fallen to the floor in a swoon, had not Colomban received her in his strong arms and gently placed her on her bed.

The poor girl's cries had by this time brought up some of the women living on the floors below, and, seeing that they had able and willing hands as well as sympathetic hearts, Colomban, from motives of delicacy, left the orphan and the dead to their care. Ten minutes later one of the women knocked at Colomban's door, and informed him that the young girl had regained her senses.

"Has she any relatives?" he asked.

"Not that we know of," was the answer.

"Any friends in the neighbourhood?"

"Not one, Monsieur. Madame Gervais was the widow of a captain killed during the campaign of 1814 at Champ-Aubert. She lived on a pension of twelve hundred francs and on a little she earned by needlework; but her pension dies with her, I fear."

"What is the daughter's name?"

"Carmélite."

"What's to be done?" continued Colomban. "The poor girl cannot remain in the chamber of the dead."

"I would willingly offer a room, but we have no bed," replied the good woman. "Stay! My husband can sleep in the attic, and I can put up with a chair."

Self-sacrificing devotion like this is common with some unselfish women among the humblest classes. They would offer a table, a room, a bed, more readily and with greater disinterestedness than a well-to-do shopkeeper would offer a glass of water. Whether it is grief to assuage or misfortune to relieve, a fellow-creature in pain or in want, they proffer their consolation or their services with a willingness and utter forgetfulness of self that are worthy of the highest admiration.

AN IDYLL OF SPRING.

Pity grew akin to love, indeed, in the breast of Colomban when Carmélite, seized with brain fever through the loss of her mother, rose from the shadow of death, and, with her senses fully restored, recognised in the anxious watcher by her bedside the same young man who had hastened to her assistance when she was stricken with the deepest sorrow of her life. A sad, sweet smile of gratitude lit up her wan face, which the fever could not rob of its beauty. Her thin, white hand was raised to press his; but Colomban bent down and kissed it with the lowly reverence due to a Queen, sealing the loving compact which both hearts insensibly made at one and the same moment.

As the youth of Carmélite triumphed, and she gradually regained her health, a rare delicacy kept Colomban from intruding on the company of his fair neighbour. But he knew she was fond of music; so, from the seclusion of his little room, he sent forth the most dulcet notes that the pianoforte could give expression to, certain that the melodious airs would reach her ears through the open window at which she loved to sit.

Well might Carmélite love to sit there! Her senses were at once rejoiced with sweetest harmonies, with the scent of many flowers, and with the view of charming gardens and wide expanses of green. It was a veritable Garden of Eden that greeted her eyes. To the right was a large inclosure thickly planted with poplars and larger trees; to the left a succession of gardens, full of acacias, lilies, and jasmines; the luxurious trees of the Luxembourg in the distance; whilst in the centre grew a perfect field of roses, about twenty acres in extent, offering up their sweet incense, as it were, to the tomb that rose in their midst. Every country under the sun seemed to have surrendered its most cherished flowers to do homage to the saint enshrined in the tomb—a monument erected in the seventeenth century, resembling some of the ambitious structures in the cemetery of Père la Chaise. There bloomed the rose of Caucasus, the rose of Kamschatka, the speckled rose of China, the rose of Carolina, the rose of the States, the May rose, the rose of Sweden, the rose of the Alps, the rose of Siberia, the yellow rose of the Levant, the rose of Damascus, the rose of Bengal, the rose of Provence, the rose of Champagne—in short, a unique collection of the two or three thousand varieties of roses known at that period.

Gloriously beautiful though this fragrant field of roses was, the young girl at her window was lovelier still. Carmélite had all the charming freshness of the queen of flowers, with the added witchery of budding womanhood. Her supple and undulating figure was inexpressibly captivating. Her rich profusion of hair, though seemingly wild and unsmoothable, was as soft to the touch as silk. Eyes of sapphire blue, lips of coral red, but sweet as rose leaves, and teeth like strings of whitest pearls, settled the fate of any man who once beheld this graceful young creature.

It was one evening towards the end of May that Carmélite first saw this field of roses in all its beauty. The day had been sultry; but a few showers cooled the mild spring air. Looking from her window, Carmélite was astonished to see that what had been but rosebuds in the morning had burst into flower. The glowing sight tempted her to stroll in her own little garden; and she soon found herself separated only by a little boundary of lilies from Colomban, drawn thither, mayhap, by the same subtle influence of the flowers. What an insight was it for Carmélite into the admirable order of Nature when Colomban made clear to her the formation of plants! From the flowers of earth they rose to the brilliant flowers of the heavens; and, as he explained to her the secrets of the planetary world, gazing up at the stars that studded the blue vault above, the night sped pleasurably on, they forgot the everyday world around them, and glided imperceptibly into the ethereal regions of platonic love.

What wonder, then, that their sweet converse made them oblivious to time? Reminded by the stroke of midnight that it was high time to retire, they hastened in-doors with some little confusion, but paused once again before wishing each other good-night. The moonlight shone so brightly through the open window that they were both induced to have one last look at the gardens.

"Whose tomb is that?" asked Carmélite, pointing to the monument in the centre of the field of roses.

"It is the tomb of Mademoiselle de la Vallière" said Colomban, who felt a delightful thrill run through him as Carmélite unavoidably leant against him, so narrow was the casement. "More than a century ago she lived for thirty-six years in the Carmélite convent to which these gardens belonged; and on her death she was buried there, and that monument was erected over her grave."

"Oh, how dearly I should prize a few roses from that sacred ground!" exclaimed Carmélite.

"May I offer you mine?" was Colomban's prompt reply. "Those rose-trees you see on my window-sill were brought from that very garden. Do accept them as a souvenir of this happy night!"

As Carmélite turned to look at the roses, her curls brushed Colomban's cheek; and again he felt a delicious thrill pulse through his veins.

The young girl, feeling Colomban's warm breath upon her face at the same moment, involuntarily blushed scarlet, and murmuring "Good-night" at last, hurried to her room with a timid excuse for keeping Colomban so late and a glad acceptance of his proffered gift.

A SUMMER STORM.

A letter from Louisiana arrived for Colomban in the morning. It announced that Camille Rozan, his most intimate college chum, would very soon follow the letter, and greet his "dearest friend" in person. Joyful news for Colomban! The young Breton felt an affection passing friendship for the gay young creole. His deep and earnest nature seemed to have found its complement in the light-hearted and buoyant spirit of Camille. He welcomed the news of his coming, then, with heartiest pleasure. He even bethought himself that they might contrive to live together. He did not conceal his delight from Carmélite, who could not help smiling at the exstravagance of his praise. He described the young creole to her a, the incarnation of manly beauty and youthful vivacity and gaiety and pictured to her what pleasant evenings they would enjoy when her rich contralto voice mingled with the sweet tenor of Camille in the most dulcet of duets.

"Colomban! Colomban!" was called out in a cheery, ringing voice that very same evening, and a lithe young man, bounding up the stairs, greeted the young Breton with a warmth and an effusion that made his heart leap for joy.

Better would it have been for Colomban if he had hugged a serpent to his breast!

It was a sybarite, a roué, an idle pleasure-seeker, with whom he now shared his little home.

Camille Rozan was not long in ingratiating himself with Carmélite. There was a fascination about his gay, sensuous nature which proved as irresistible to the innocent maiden as it did to Colomban.

Apparently, with all the ingenuousness in the world, the creole entered into the spirit of the musical evenings. He sang his best. He outdid himself in cheerfulness and brilliancy. In one word, he cast a spell on all who came within reach of his fascination.

Carmélite's evident pleasure in Camille's society, and the love which Colomban thought he saw growing up between them, made the Breton's heart sink within him. He did but wince; a struggle with his soul, and he subdued the passion that he had secretly cherished as the dearest treasure of his life. The brave young student said to himself,

"It is clear they love each other, and it is but natural, for they seem made for one another. Yet I had dreamed—ah, how fondly! —of one day claiming Carmélite as my own dear wife! But Camille will make her the happiest wife. Let them be one, then!"

This decision come to, however, he felt he could not remain to witness the lover's happiness. In spite of Carmélite's tears—tears of simple friendship, as he thought—in spite of Camille's futile attempts to conceal the passion he felt for the young girl, Colomban bade them farewell ; and his last words to the creole were that he should respect and honour the person of Carmélite as he would his sister until she became his wife.

"I swear before Heaven I will !" was the oath Camille Rozan took. Mark how he kept his word !

He laid siege to her heart with the most insidious skill. He put aside his vices, his follies, his luxury for the time being.

Carmélite innocently believed that this transformation was partly occasioned by regret at the loss of his friend Colomban, and partly from love of her. She was insensibly flattered at the thought that Camille had resigned all his Bohemianism for her sake. Little by little she yielded to the pleasure of having a lover so devoted constantly by her side ; and, by-and by, even Colomban suffered by comparison with the fidelity of the creole. Thus the time slipped past till there came one memorable night in August, when the sultry air was almost stifling, and a storm was brewing, but no rain fell to refresh parched Nature. Once again Carmélite had descended into the garden to breathe more freely, her companion being this time Camille.

What an abyss between that blissful evening in May with Colomban and the burning evening of that summer night !

Between those two nights, as between the Breton and the creole, there was the difference of spring and summer.

Gone was the spring, young, fresh, timid, scarcely daring to unfold its buds.

Present was the summer, vigorous, luxuriant, and scorching, wantonly scattering its flowers.

On the one side, infancy with its hesitation, troubles, and fears. On the other, youth with its brilliancy, transports, and pains.

On that spring day of sweet memories the thunder had crashed loudly, too, and life seemed suspended for awhile ; but down poured the rain, and the vegetation was saved from death.

During this summer night, however, the plants in vain sent up their prayers for revivifying showers ; the flowers drooped, shed their etals one by one, and died.

And so the guardian angel of a maiden's innocence flew up to heaven, blushing at the wrong that had been done.

Regaining her room, Carmélite saw that the rose-tree given her by Colomban was also stricken by the storm. With burning cheeks she approached and plucked the drooping flowers one by one, wrapped them in a white veil, and softly placed them in a drawer, murmuring to herself, mournfully, "Colomban's roses are dead, dead as his love !"

FALSE LOVE AND TRUE LOVE.

"Love in a cottage"—a life of lazy pleasure in a suburban villa, smothered with roses and fragrant climbing plants, and sheltered by noble trees—that was what Camille Rozan enjoyed with Carmélite whilst his passion lasted.

His ardour soon burnt out. Bas-Meudon became too dull, and there was ever the temptation of Paris close by to gratify his every wish. So he soon came to spend every day in Paris, only returning to Bas-Meudon very late at night or early in the morning. This neglect first grieved Carmélite (whose affection had been won by Camille's enthusiastic devotion to her), and at length aroused her contempt and indifference as she came to learn the utter selfishness of the man to whom she had given her heart.

One morning, when Camille was absent, as usual, on some mission of pleasure, there was a ring at the bell. As no one answered, Carmélite pushed open the Persian blinds and looked out of the window, to see who it might be.

A little cry of surprise and fright escaped her, involuntarily.

It was Colomban!

Carmélite hastened down stairs to intercept the servant, and found her in the passage.

"Nanette," she whispered, "conduct the gentleman at the door to the pavilion in the garden and don't tell him I am here!"

A strange tremor ran through Carmélite as she gazed from her window at Colomban—a feeling as though she were no longer alone in the world—a wistful longing to impart a sweet secret to him who should have been her husband; and with this tremor her heart of hearts throbbed with the emotion that Colomban first awakened within her on that delightful May evening when her dreams were all of roses and love.

* * * * *

Colomban, with his natural generosity, at first attributed Camille's change of abode to a considerate delicacy on his part. He imagined the creole had come to Bas-Meudon, and had left Carmélite in Paris, to avoid the scandal that might have been caused by their living in the same house in the Rue Saint-Jacques before their marriage.

Camille himself soon undeceived Colomban. Unabashed, the creole welcomed his friend to Bas-Meudon and introduced him to Carmélite. Colomban's sternness alone brought him to realise the necessity of at least hastening his marriage with Carmélite. He made but one stipulation. It was imperative to obtain the consent of his father; and to do this he must be his own ambassador, and must make a special trip to Louisiana. He was so earnest in assuring Colomban of his speedy return that the trustful Breton once more confided in his honour, and promised his friend that he would protect Carmélite during his absence. So Camille departed on his mission with a light heart; but Carmélite was singularly apathetic when farewell came to be said. It seemed that nothing could restore the confidence she once placed in Camille.

* * * * *

With Colomban near her every day, Carmélite could not fail to contrast the simplicity of his noble, unselfish nature, with the restless egotism and vanity of Camille. For three months she had endured the society of the ignoble, heartless, soulless creature whose seductiveness she now felt ashamed that she had not had the power to resist. If it was thus that Carmélite thought of Camille when he had only been gone a few days, how immeasurably great her contempt for him became when time passed on and did but magnify the virtues of Colomban!

She gradually felt a great and irresistible love obtaining possession of her heart and soul. She grew to adore Colomban. His passion for her returned, meanwhile, with tenfold force. Unknown to each other, they loved one another with a fervour all the stronger for the apparent hopelessness of their love. The spark that ignited their love was applied by Camille himself. A letter from him announced that he had at length gained the consent of his father, and that he was already en route to claim Carmélite as his bride. The letter dropped from the hands of Carmélite. A heartbroken sigh escaped her lips, and the loving look of appeal she gave Colomban made him cast off all the restraint he had hitherto imposed upon himself. He threw himself passionately on his knees before Carmélite. There was a warm embrace that betrayed their mutual love, and Colomban addressed the idol of his heart in impassioned terms,

"Too late I see my cowardice, Carmélite, in leaving you alone in Paris with Camille. Too late I know we love one another heart and soul. But adieu to love in this world! Carmélite, have you the courage to face death with me?"

Chapter XXII.—"To Die! to Sleep!"

"Dear Carmelite,
"I have at last obtained the consent of my father to our marriage, and I will be with you on the 7th of next month.
"Camille."

Carmélite read this laconic letter with sorrowful eyes for the last time on the morrow of Colomban's avowal of his love. The man to whom she had intrusted her happiness was hastening to make amends for the wrong he had done her—was, perhaps, entering port that very moment—but never was her loathing for him or her love for Colomban greater.

"He will arrive to-morrow!" she exclaimed, casting a despairing look at Colomban. "Is there no escape for me but one, Colomban? Ah! you cannot know the depth of my love for you. Life had become a burden to me. The day of Camille's departure I had resolved to seek the living death of a nun in a convent. Your dear presence turned me from it. Day by day my love grew until you became a part of my life——"

"As my heart, my soul, my life are yours, Carmélite," broke in Colomban.

"Let us leave France, then! Let us fly to the other end of the world, and live together in some isle of the southern seas, forgetting all, forgotten by all!"

"Carmélite," answered the young Breton with an air of supreme resignation, "love each other fondly, dearly, madly as we may, is our love free? Not in this world! Camille, base as he has been, would be equalled in baseness by me were I to fly with you. . . . . Death alone——"

"Welcome death, then, since that will unite us, Colomban!"

"Will you die without regret, Carmélite?"

"With joy! And it must be at once, Colomban, for he will be here to-morrow."

"I have only two farewells to write, Carmélite; and then we will meet never more to be parted."

"And I have my adieux to make to three dear schoolfellows, before we are united for ever, Colomban!"

A warm embrace, and they separated for one last communion with the friends they loved best in this world, Colomban watching her loved form as she hastened from the pavilion across the garden to the home where "love in a cottage" had been so short lived.

Colomban had soon written his first letter. Tear-stained, and full of the love whose martyrdom he could not survive, it begged a father's forgiveness for the crime he was about to commit. It was addressed to Comte Edmond de Penhoël. The second letter was written to Colomban's one friend in Paris, Dominique Sarranti, a devoted Dominican monk, whom he prayed to pay the last funereal rites to his body, and to hasten to assuage his father's grief.

To the friends of her heart, to the three dearest companions of her happy school days in Saint-Denis, did Carmélite send her adieux in a touching letter, recalling to Régina, Lydie, and Fragola the simple joys of their youth.

"I love," she wrote in one eloquent sentence, "the man of my choice, the man of my taste, the man of my dreams—one in whom every manly virtue is predominant; and, as Fate is against us, our betrothal takes place here on earth to-night, and our marriage will be celebrated in heaven to-morrow."

Carmélite then wrote three brief letters bidding her friends hasten to Bas-Meudon at seven o'clock the next morning. Calling Nanette, she asked,

"Is there another post to day?"

"Yes, Mademoiselle," replied the girl. "You can just catch the four o'clock post, and your letters will be delivered in Paris at nine.'

"Put these three letters in the post, then, Nanette."

"Yes, Mademoiselle," said Nanette, the more willingly as she had a favour to ask. "And as the fête of the *mardi gras* is to-day, will Mademoiselle spare me for a little holiday in Paris? The blanchissenses of Vanvres are going to have a carnival masquerade, and I want very much to take part in it with five or six friends, if Mademoiselle will have the kindness to let me go."

"You can go, Nanette," answered Carmélite, glad to be rid of her servant for the night. "Enjoy yourself, and return at whatever hour may be convenient. We shall not want you."

A smile lit up Carmélite's face as the girl tripped gladly away, for she knew that Colomban and she could now spend their last hours together in strictest privacy. Night came. When Carmélite and Colomban met, and bade farewell to the sombre, leafless trees beneath which they sauntered, it almost seemed to them that they had already lost sight of the world, and were but shadows of themselves. The dead leaves that rustled under their feet, the gaunt branches that stretched above them like the arms of some weird giant, the cold, grey sky overhead, all appeared to invite them to the death they sought. They were silent; but what need of words when soul spoke to soul? Silently they gained the pavilion, silently they entered the room that had been prepared as a mortuary chapel.

Colomban locked and bolted the door, and gave a final look round the gloomy chamber to see that the windows were fastened, and that there remained not a single loop-hole whence the fatal fumes which were to steal their senses away could escape. Obeying an appealing glance from Colomban, Carmélite sat before the pianoforte, and while her fingers glided over the ivory and ebony keys, raised her rich voice in a song which might well have been the hymn of death, so mournfully sweet, so plaintively touching, was the air. It touched a chord in Colomban's heart that had vibrated long ago at the sound of the same dulcet voice. He paused in his work of lighting the charcoal, and gazed at the singer with all his soul in his eyes. Minute after minute sped by, and yet he regarded Carmélite with the same fixed look, heedless that the deadly vapour was meanwhile filling the room.

"Carmélite!"

The young Breton tottered as he called his love, and fell on a couch, giddy from the subtle fumes. Carmélite, whose voice had insensibly grown fainter and fainter, staggered towards her lover, threw herself down beside him, and gasped out an entreaty for one last adieu. Colomban clasped her to his heart, imprinted a kiss upon her pale, damp brow, and then his arms fell nerveless on the couch, and he could only look his love as life ebbed from him. The flickering light of the burning charcoal and the deadly veil of vapour which hung around the pallid lovers made the scene one of gloomy ghastliness. They were so near death that its shadow was already upon them. Yet at that very moment Chance was racing hard against Death to snatch them both from the river of darkness into which they were sinking.

Chapter XXIII.—Ludovic to the Rescue.

It will not have been forgotten that Salvator and Jean Robert, on leaving the cabaret in the Rue Aubrey-le-Boucher, had first seen Pétrus and Ludovic safely asleep under the table, and had intrusted them to the watchful care of the waiter.

Ludovic was the first to wake. The noise that roused him came from a lively masquerading party mounting to the fourth floor in search of a room for themselves. The first words the young doctor heard were words of dispute between the hilarious crew of pleasure-seekers and the waiter, who would fain have barred their entrance to the cabinet which Salvator had instructed him to keep sacred for his two new friends. Ludovic imagined directly that the foes with whom they had gallantly fought were returning to the attack. Peals of crisp, joyous laughter soon disabused his mind, however, of these fears, and even made his too-susceptible heart long for the fair companionship evidently so near at hand.

He opened the door, then, with a smile of welcome on his face. A throng of pierettes and pierrots burst into the room, sweeping Ludovic back by their impulsive attack. A pair of soft arms entwined round his neck, and a musical voice with the most vivacious of accents, completed his conquest. The voice was that of the Princesse de Vanvres, most bewitching of blanchisseuses, and——but let her wash her dirty linen at home.

"Do you mean to say—you luxurious darling, you!—that you have had the selfishness to retain this room for yourself alone? You're going in for celibacy with a vengeance, then!" laughed this gay coquette of a blanchisseuse.

In the same light, laughing tone Ludovic replied, pointing to the half-awakened Pétrus.

"If your Highness had only given yourself the trouble to look around you would have seen that I'm not alone."

"What! Is it Raphaël himself I see under the table?" cried the lively blanchisseuse, running to assist Pétrus to his feet. "Shall I pose myself for one of Monsieur Raphaël's fallen angels?"

"Surely I know that plump figure!" ruminated the artist, slowly regaining his senses.

"'Tis Chante-Lilas!" exclaimed Ludovic.

"As I'm known I'll doff my mask," answered the frisky pierrette. "Besides, one can drink better without a mask. So, a glass! a glass! I am dying with thirst!"

This chorus was joined in zestfully by all her party; half-a-dozen blanchisseusses, not to say washerwomen, of Vanvres, three or four housemaids, and their followers.

"Silence!" called out Ludovic. "This is our room, and we must do the honours as hosts. Waiter! Six bottles of champagne."

"And six for me, waiter!" added Pétrus.

A veil may be drawn over the gay carnival scene that followed—

a scene of folly, but withal of unrestrained merriment not uncongenial to the slightly Bohemian tastes of the young doctor and the young painter.

"Now," broke in the Princesse de Vanvres, with characteristic frankness, when the last glass had been drained, "it's high time to return to Vanvres. There's Nanette, there, who promised her mistress to be home at eleven, and who has a letter to give her. It's three o'clock."

"Four o'clock," said Pétrus.

"And Missis rises at five!" cried Chante-Lilas. "*En route! En route!* all of you."

"And I go with you to fetch home my linen myself; that is, if you will permit me," said Ludovic.

"Bravo! Bravo!" answered the Princess of Washerwomen, with animation. "We'll have a good draught of milk at the dear old mill at Vanvres where I met that dainty friend of mine, Monsieur Camille, in the summer. Will you come with us, too, Monsieur Raphaël?"

"Sacrebleu!" replied Pétrus, looking glum. "I should be most happy to join your jolly party; but I have an engagement this morning—a sitting, unfortunately."

"Then Fornarina grants Raphaël leave of absence," said Chante-Lilas, bending with mock dignity to Pétrus.

The bill having been paid, Ludovic, determined to drain his night of carnival pleasure to the dregs, followed the Princesse de Vanvres down stairs, and soon found a seat beside her in the huge waggon that had brought the blanchisseuses from Vanvres to Paris. Pétrus, who lived in the Rue de l'Ouest, bade farewell to his friend, and responded with interest to the noisy adieux of the roysterers.

"But where the deuce are we going to?" Ludovic presently asked. "It seems to me we are going to Versailles, not to Vanvres, Princess."

"If Raphaël had not gone," aptly answered Chante-Lilas, "he would have told your Majesty that all roads lead to Rome."

"I don't see the point."

"You see Nanette?"

"Yes."

"What do you think of her?"

"She's rather pretty."

"Very well. Pretty Nanette only came with us on the condition that we should set her down at the door."

"But why?"

"Why, because she has a letter marked 'Immediate' for her master."

It was five o'clock in the morning when they arrived at Bellevue— tame, spiritless, sleepy, vapid as stale champagne. The cold morning air made them shiver again. Reaction was following their spasmodic gaiety. At last the waggon stopped before the house of Carmélite at Bas-Meudon. Nanette leapt to the ground, sang out a cheerful parting greeting, and had soon let herself in with the key.

But the waggon had proceeded but a short distance on the road to Vanvres when its sleepy occupants were alarmed by the shrill cries of Nanette:

"Help! help! Monsieur Ludovic!"

"What can she want me for?" asked the young doctor of Chante-Lilas, as he jumped out of the waggon and helped Chante-Lilas out also.

"Something terrible must have happened from her cries," replied he quick-witted blanchisseuse, hastening towards the house.

Nanette, pale with fright and greatly agitated, met them, and appealed to Ludovic afresh, "Quick, quick, Monsieur! I fear they are both dead."

"Who?"

"Mademoiselle Carmélite and Monsieur Colomban."

"Colomban! Colomban de Penhoël?"

"Yes; Monsieur Colomban de Penhoël and Mademoiselle Carmélite Gervais. What a terrible misfortune! So young and so good as they were!"

Ludovic was in the garden in an instant. He gained the pavilion, and at once perceived what had filled Nanette with alarm.

She had pushed Colomban's outer door open, and had been nearly suffocated by the fumes of charcoal which rushed out into the air. The carbonic acid repulsed Ludovic likewise, but did not deprive him of his wits.

"Break open all the windows! Burst open the door!" he cried, to the sobered maskers. "Let in the life-giving air!"

A few good kicks opened the door; but the deadly vapour was so thick that entrance was impossible for the moment.

"Nanette," continued Ludovic, in order not to lose an instant, "hurry back to the house and warm some serviettes. Quick! And send to the chemist's for some ammoniac and salts. Meantime, bring me some vinegar."

Ludovic then rushed into the mortuary chamber. The man of pleasure had become transformed into the man of science. This young and ardent student in the noblest of professions was about to bring all the resources of his grand art into play to save a dear friend and his mistress if possible. All was dark. The lamp had gone out. The last embers of the charcoal had even died out. No light could pierce the gloom from the windows, the curtains being drawn in front of them. Ludovic felt his way to the windows. Wrapping his handkerchief round his right hand, he smashed pane after pane, and soon established a current of air. It was high time, for Ludovic felt he was himself yielding to the subtle influence of the fumes which yet hung about the room. With a great effort, however, he tugged at the curtains and pulled them down, then opened the windows and breathed freely again.

"You can come in now; there's no danger," exclaimed Ludovic. "The first thing to be done is to light up the room."

Lights were brought, and every object became visible; the pan containing the ashes of the charcoal, and the couple locked in each other's arms, stifled, mayhap, by the fatal fumes. Ludovic, wasting not a moment in fruitless wondering at the causes of the tragedy which had been enacted, bent over them, and scanned their ashy faces with the closest scrutiny.

"Too late! too late! I fear," he murmured to himself.

The lips of Colomban and Carmélite were black. Ludovic raised their eyelids. The eyes of Colomban were swollen and glassy; whilst Carmélite's were duller. Not a shadow of a breath came from either.

"Too late! too late!" Ludovic repeated. "Never mind; let us try every remedy. Mesdames, you take care of the young lady. I will take charge of the young man."

"What shall we do first?" demanded Chante-Lilas.

"Carry her to the window; and bathe her temples with vinegar."

While these instructions were zealously carried out, Ludovic did the like for Colomban. Continuing his directions to Chante-Lilas, he said,

"Now cut a quill pen, like I cut this one. Open her teeth. Place the quill tube in her mouth; and blow some of your superfluous life into her lungs, Chante-Lilas."

With an ivory knife, the young blanchisseuse forced open Carmélite's clenched teeth. With a quick intelligence and dexterity peculiarly her own, she then obeyed Ludovic's orders to the letter; and before long her heart gave a leap of joy, for she felt sure a spark of life yet burned in the bosom of the fair young girl whom she was striving to resuscitate. Do all he could—bleed him, chafe his cold breast and limbs, send his own warm breath into the lungs of the senseless Breton—Ludovic was rewarded with no sign of returning life in Colomban. Meantime, Chante-Lilas grew more and more successful.

"Monsieur Ludovic! She breathes!" the blanchisseuse at length exclaimed. "The colour is coming back to her lips. She is raising her hand to her head. Heaven be praised!"

"Then one will be saved, thank God!" exclaimed Ludovic. "Remove her now from this room instantly. Take her into the house, and carry her up to her own room without losing a moment, so that she may not see her poor lover when she awakens. And, mind, open every window in the room; and light a good bright fire."

So, as Carmélite was gradually being restored to consciousness, she was removed from the pavilion.

"Continue to treat your patient just as you have been treating her," said Ludovic to Chante-Lilas, "and you will have the happiness of knowing that you have restored a fellow-creature to life!"

"And if she should ask what's become of her lover?"

"Oh! she will not be able to speak for another hour or two."

"And then?"

"And then either Colomban or I will be there to answer her."

Chapter XXIV.—M. Jackal on the Scene.

At nine o'clock in the morning the carriage in which M. Jackal had travelled post haste from Paris with Salvator and Jean Robert stopped at the house of the poor girl whose history the Chief of the Police had recounted en route to his two interested listeners.

They found three other vehicles already stationed outside the same house—a cab, a carriage of humble pretensions, and a brilliant carriage with armorial bearings.

"All three are here!" murmured Salvator.

Monsieur Jackal exchanged a few words in secret with a man in black at the door. A moment after the man in black mounted a horse waiting for him close by, and started off at full gallop.

"I've sent him off on Monsieur Justin's business," explained M. Jackal to Jean Robert and Salvator.

The two friends expressed their thanks and entered the house. Almost on the threshold they were met with a welcome cry by a large dog, which came bounding towards them, and ended by springing up and placing his forepaws familiarly on Salvator's shoulders.

"Roland! Roland!" said Salvator. "Quiet! I know all about it. Your mistress is within. Be our guide, Roland."

The dog dashed up stairs, the two young men and M. Jackal following, and paused outside Carmélite's door. M. Jackal, as one who had a right to lead in all affairs of mystery, opened the door, and would have walked in had not the scene that met his eyes stopped him. What the Chief of the Police, Jean Robert, and Salvator saw might have served for a picture of profound devotion. Kneeling at Carmélite's bedside, praying for the recovery of the pale girl lying still as death, were three lovely maidens of the same age as Carmélite; each attired in the neat, dark costume of the Saint-Denis *pension*, whereat all four became bosom friends.

Jean Robert at once recognised Fragola, and so, of course, did Salvator, who raised his finger to his lips, however, as a signal for silence. To their surprise, they observed a faint movement on the part of Carmélite, whose resuscitation, under the directions of Ludovic, they were entirely ignorant of.

"Ah!" exclaimed M. Jackal, with the indifferent air of one accustomed to such scenes; "she is not dead, then?"

"No, Monsieur," said one of the three friends—the one who seemed to have an innate right to speak for her companions.

Jean Robert looked earnestly at the speaker, whose musical voice he fancied he knew; and he recognised her as Mademoiselle Régina de Lamothe-Houdan.

"And the young man?" inquired M. Jackal.

"There's still a lingering hope for him," replied the young girl. "He is in good hands. The clever young doctor who has him in charge has not yet given him up."

At that very moment, however, the group at the door was joined by a new comer; and, to Salvator and Jean Robert's growing astonishment, they saw it was Ludovic, clad now in his everyday costume, not in the carnival finery in which they left him at Bordier's.

"Well!" was the one exclamation that greeted Ludovic.

"The priest is with him," was Ludovic's ominous answer. "There's absolutely nothing more for me to do. He is beyond recovery, poor fellow!"

"Messieurs," broke in M. Jackal, with business-like brusqueness, "it is clear we are not wanted here. Let us leave the poor young lady with the doctor and her friends; and, directly I have made the *procès-verbal*, we can all set out for Versailles."

Salvator and Jean Robert signified their readiness. Both followed M. Jackal, after Salvator had whispered a word or two to Fragola. They left the Chief of the Police to complete his formal duty, and proceeded to the pavilion. Colomban lay rigid as death on the same couch whereon he had inhaled the fatal vapour of the charcoal. By his side was a young Dominican monk, the one friend Colomban had beseeched to come to him, in earnest prayer. The monk rose and saluted Jean Robert and Salvator upon their entrance; but he knew neither. He was known, however, to Salvator, from whom an exclamation of joy escaped when he first caught sight of the Dominican.

"Father," said Salvator, addressing him by the name Religion entitled him to, "without knowing it you saved the life of him who now stands before you. I have never seen you since; but I owe you a debt of deepest gratitude. My life is at your disposal. I will offer it to you freely at any moment."

"I may accept your offer one day, Monsieur," replied the monk, gravely; "although I am ignorant of how I can have rendered any service to you. But men are brothers, and are sent into this world to help one another. So when I have need of you I will seek your aid."

Salvator then gave the monk his name and address, which he folded and placed between the leaves of his prayer-book. All three were joining in prayer for the repose of the young Breton's soul, when a servant in livery, and almost breathless, begged the monk to hasten with him to receive the last confession of his dying master. The duty he was engaged in—Colomban's wish that he should see to his funeral, and then comfort the Comte de Penhoël—Dominique firmly insisted would prevent him from complying with this sudden demand.

Expostulate as he might, the servant could get no other answer till Salvator quietly suggested, "Are not your consolations likely to be of more importance to the living than the dead, father?"

"Besides," added Jean Robert, "we could undertake to prepare everything, so that you would not be delayed in your departure to-night with poor Colomban for Brittany."

"What shall I say to my master?" repeated the servant, anxiously.

"Tell him I will follow you directly, my friend."

"Thank you! Thank you!"

"Whom shall I ask for?"

"Monsieur Gérard, of Vanvres."

"What street? What number?"

"Oh! Monsieur, every one knows Monsieur Gérard round here. Any one will show you the house."

"I can depend upon finding the hearse ready here by four o'clock, then," said the monk, turning with a searching glance to Jean Robert and Salvator.

"Rely upon us," answered Salvator.

The monk imprinted one last kiss on the cold brow of his friend, and then departed on the mission which was to concern him so closely that a dark shadow which had rested on his young life was to be dispelled for ever.

M. Jackal entered the chamber of the dead five minutes later. He took a good pinch of snuff, and then, placing a letter in Jean Robert's hand, said, emphatically, "That letter proves the utter fatuity of this poor fellow in committing suicide. Read it, and you will see that at the very moment the charcoal was being prepared there was something close at hand which would have made them as happy as they could desire to be in this world. The letter is from the fickle Camille. The dog is married to another woman. Plenty of women in the case, of course! And the inconstant creole makes a virtue of necessity, and coolly hands his discarded mistress over to his friend. Had not Nanette gone for her carnival holiday last night she would have delivered this letter to Colomban in time to prevent this wretched bit of business. See what comes of being your own Providence. Pshaw! I have no patience with these morbid suicides.

"Now," added M. Jackal, "I must be off to look after the fiancée of Master Justin, at Versailles."

Chapter XXV.—M. Gerard's Confession.

WHAT manner of man was this Dominique Sarranti was about to see?

The monk put this question to himself as he set out for Vanvres; but it seemed to be answered satisfactorily long before he reached his mansion. Every one *did* know M. Gervais Gérard, and every one had a good word for him. He was bountiful to the poor, a Good Samaritan to the homeless, a man whose whole life appeared to be spent in doing good with his vast wealth. A man, questionless, with a face as benevolent as his actions were. Such was the Monsieur Gérard that the Dominican monk imagined he should see. What really met his gaze on entering the sick room at Vanvres was a cadaverous face the very opposite to everything the monk had conjured up. He beheld in the dying man, who welcomed his coming with feverish eagerness, one with a most repulsive face, in which the vilest passions had seemingly flourished only to die out and leave their emaciating marks indelibly behind them. The confession which M. Gérard made to the monk horrified him, albeit it was of vital interest to him. The fortune which M. Gérard had lavished with so free a hand was his, through a most infamous murder.

M. GERARD'S CONFESSION.

"Where was the woman?" M. Jackal would have inquired.

The woman was housekeeper in the country-house of Monsieur Jacques Tardieu, Gérard Tardieu's brother, a wealthy Brazilian merchant, who had returned in broken health with his two motherless children, to spend the remainder of his days in France.

Orsola Poutaé was one of the most insidious fiends ever seen in the shape of woman. She did not play her game till the death of Monsieur Jacques Tardieu. He died not long after he had installed himself with his two children in his mansion at Viry-sur-Orge. He left a handsome income for his brother, and bequeathed the rest of his fortune to his little boy and girl, with Gérard as trustee, and as sole heir in the event of the children's death.

"My little nephew and niece, continued the dying man, "were left to the care of a tutor, Monsieur Gaëtano Sarranti——"

"Sarranti!" exclaimed the young monk, moved from his religious calm, and the blood rushing tumultuously into his pale face. "I am his son, Dominique Sarranti! And it was you, then, who had the villany to accuse my innocent father of assassination and robbery!"

Dominique, the feelings of a son overpowering those of the monk, would have rushed from the presence of Gérard Tardieu, had not a pitiful moan detained him.

"Stop! stop! Providence has led you here. Remain, and God may let me make some reparation before I die."

The dying supplicant then fell back, exhausted with his appeal, and would have remained speechless had not Dominique, restraining his passions by a violent effort, handed him some medicine. He then gained fresh strength to continue his confession.

M. Gaetano Sarranti entrusted to the care of Gérard's notary the sum of a hundred thousand crowns, which he might want to have back at a day's notice. Dominique listened to all that concerned his father with bated breath, for he thought he might see the means to clear his father's name from the stigma that had so long been attached to it. He did not learn, however, the part this sum played in Orsola Poutaé's plan of treachery till later. Little by little this Lucrezia Borgia on a small scale gained a mastery over the weak mind of Gérard Tardieu. She fascinated him, played upon his passions, submitted to become his mistress in secret, and so worked upon his mind that he grew to be a mere tool in her hands. By a cunning and infamous trick she at length contrived to make him the innocent cause of a death. The children's faithful nurse, Gertrude, being very ill one night, Orsola got him to take a glass of something to relieve her sufferings; and the poor woman was so effectually relieved of her sufferings that she died the next morning—from poison. Intimidating her master by the threat that he would be convicted of the murder unless he kept the secret to himself, Orsola's supremacy over him became complete. There was now only one person to be removed to enable her to carry out her indomitable purpose—M. Sarranti.

Stay; the orphans had one more true friend in Brésil, the faithful dog—half Newfoundland, half St. Bernard—which had been brought with them from the Brazils. Orsola was one day on the point of punishing Léonie, the little girl, for some petty fault, when Brésil sprang upon her, bit her arm, and would have injured her further had not M. Sarranti rushed into the garden and dragged the dog away. Not long did M. Sarranti stand in her way after that. She learnt that he was involved in a Bonapartist plot; that the hundred thousand crowns left by him with the notary had been given to him by Napoleon I. himself at St. Helena to foment a conspiracy on behalf of the Emperor's young son, the Duke of Reichstadt. She denounced him to the Government. Sarranti was warned in time to fly the country, taking with him the money entrusted to him by Napoleon. The night of his flight Orsola conceived the villanous idea of murdering the children, so that the entire property would be Gérard's, and, therefore, hers as well; and then to accuse Sarranti of the crime, and to point to his flight as convincing evidence against him. Like a jaguar crouching for its prey, Orsola waited for her youthful victims. It was a dark night. The two children were playing in the grounds. Victor, the boy, was induced to follow his uncle on a shooting expedition. The girl was led indoors by Orsola. Gérard leapt with his nephew into a boat, and was soon skimming over the lake, which formed so conspicuous a feature of the estate. A terrible cry reached his ears when they were in the middle of the lake. Orsola had done *her* work, thought Gérard; and the thought had no sooner entered his mind than he seized Victor, threw him into the lake, left him to drown, and rowed quickly to the banks.

Had Orsola been as successful? He searched the château, but could find her nowhere till he entered an outhouse in the garden. There, lying before him near the door, was the dead body of Orsola in a pool of blood! She had evidently dragged Léonie there to murder her, and the child's cries for help had clearly attracted the faithful dog, who with one bound must have sprung through the window, seized Orsola by the throat with his teeth, and strangled her. The little girl disappeared entirely from that day. The dog was discovered by Gérard on that same fatal night of the 19th of August, 1820, at the edge of the lake, mourning over the corpse of his young master and friend, whom he had rescued from the lake. Gérard, on the opposite side of the lake, was in an agony of fear lest the body should be discovered. He fired. The dog was wounded. Yelping with pain, Brésil dashed into the woods; and, after a time, Gérard mustered up courage enough to walk round the lake, lift the corpse in his arms, and hurry to bury it in a spot hidden away in the woods where he imagined no one would be likely to seek it. Such, in brief, was the confession Monsieur Gérard made to the monk, whose eyes were bright with a strange light when the dying man handed him a written copy of the confession which proved Monsieur Sarranti innocent and Gérard Tardie guilty of the crime laid to his charge.

Chapter XXVI.—Justin's Quest.

Leaving Dominique Sarranti, let us return to Justin, whom we last saw riding at full gallop on the road to Versailles.

The demand now made on all the energy he could put forth seemed to have entirely changed Justin's nature. Quietly the deep river of his life had run on, while "Suffer and be strong" was the motto of his self-sacrificing existence. Indignant at the outrage offered to Mina, Justin showed the latent power and force of his character by the firm resolution stamped upon his face as he rode at topmost speed towards the *pensionnat* of Madame Desmarets. It was half-past eight when he leapt from his saddle and rang the bell of the Versailles boarding-school.

Taken by surprise at so early a visit, Madame Desmarets sent down a message to Justin begging him to wait a quarter of an hour whilst she finished her toilet. But Justin replied that the business that had brought him to Versailles would not admit of a moment's delay. He, therefore, requested the schoolmistress to see him at once.

Justin followed the servant upstairs with impatient steps, and, greeting Madame Desmarets directly she came out of her room, he startled her by his mortal paleness and altered demeanour. Her surprise was not diminished when he took her hand, and, leading her back into her room, closed the door behind them, in order to question her privately.

"*Mon Dieu!* What has happened?" Madame Desmarets stammered out.

"A grave misfortune, Madame," answered Justin.

"To you or to Mina?"

"To both of us, Madame."

"Am I to call Mina, then; or do you wish to see her alone?"

"Mina is no longer in this house."

"No longer in this house! Where is she, then?"

"She has been carried off during the night, Madame."

"But I accompanied Mina myself to her room last night, and left her there with Mademoiselle Suzanne de Valgeneuse, her bosom friend."

"Still, that has not prevented her abduction, Madame."

And Justin showed to the schoolmistress the pencilled message brought him by Babolin:—

> I am being taken away by force. I am a prisoner. They are taking me I know not whither. Save me, Justin! Save me, brother! or avenge me, husband!
> MINA.

Madame Desmarets rapidly read the note. She recognized the young girl's handwriting, and the next moment realised the peril Mina was placed in. Her heart failed her. She staggered, and would have fallen, had not Justin supported her.

"If this sad news is true," she said, a few moments after, in a sorrow-stricken tone, the genuineness of which Justin could not doubt, "it is on my knees that I ought to ask your forgiveness for the terrible misfortune of which I have been the cause."

"Will you give me your best help, Madame, to bring the villain to justice?" demanded Justin.

"With all my heart, Monsieur. What had I better do first?"

"Quietly wait for the police, and see, meanwhile, that no one enters the garden or Mina's room."

There was silence for a few minutes. The schoolmistress feared the coming visit of the police might occasion the loss of all her pupils; but a natural delicacy forbade her from obtruding her selfish fears on the young man in his grief. She ventured, however, to ask Justin,

"You conclude from the letter that Mina was carried off by force?"

"Unquestionably."

"But I must confess I cannot see how that could be possible. The walls are high, the windows are always securely fastened, and, besides, Mina would have cried out."

"Madame, there are ladders as high as walls; there are pincers to open windows with; a gag will stifle any voice."

Acting on a natural impulse, Madame Desmarets would have hastened to Mina's room and to the garden to see how the abduction could have been effected; but she was prevented by Justin, who was determined to observe the instructions of Salvator faithfully.

They had only another half-hour to wait. A carriage then drove up to the door, which Justin flew downstairs to open.

The light of hope shone in his eyes as he saw Salvator and another person alight. Salvator was soon by Justin's side. Grasping his hand, the Commissionnaire, full of the sad tragedy fatal to Colomban at Bas Meudon, said,

"Courage, Monsieur Corby! Believe me, there are misfortunes even greater than yours."

Monsieur Jackal then saluted Justin, and inquired whether any one had been allowed to enter the garden or Mina's room.

"No one, Monsieur," answered Justin.

"We'll see," said Jackal, with a business air, at the same time taking a good pinch of snuff.

CHAPTER XXVII.—M. JACKAL ON THE TRAIL.

"WHERE's the woman—where's the schoolmistress, I mean?" was M. Jackal's next inquiry.

"I am at your service," answered Madame Desmarets, reappearing at that moment.

"The gentleman I expected from Paris," said Justin, by way of introduction.

"Did you know anything of the disappearance of Mademoiselle Mina before the arrival of Monsieur Corby?" demanded the Chief Commissioner of Police of the trembling schoolmistress.

"No, Monsieur. I am not even sure that she is gone, since I have been forbidden to see whether she is in her room."

"We will visit her room all in good time. Make your mind easy on that point," coolly rejoined M. Jackal.

And, dropping his spectacles on to his nose, he put the poor schoolmistress through the ordeal of a searching scrutiny, in accordance with his custom on seeing any one for the first time. Then, replacing the glasses on his brow, he shook his head and enjoyed another pinch of snuff.

"If you like, gentlemen, we will step into the drawing-room; it will be better than this parlour," urged Madame Desmarets, seeking relief from the embarrassing pause.

"No, thank you," promptly replied M. Jackal, throwing a quick glance around the room, and noting that he had instinctively, like a good general, posted himself in the best possible position. Then, returning to the charge, he added, "May I ask you, Madame, whether you are fully aware of the responsibility a schoolmistress incurs when one of her pupils is carried off from her establishment? Let me caution you to think well before you answer any of my questions."

"Oh, Monsieur, whatever happens, I cannot feel more sorrow than I do," murmured Madame Desmarets. "As for weighing my words, and thinking before I reply to you, that would be useless, as I have nothing to conceal, and shall tell you nothing but the truth."

The Chief Commissioner of Police nodded his satisfaction at this frank answer, and continued,

"At what hour do your pupils retire to bed, Madame?"

"At eight o'clock in winter, Monsieur."

"And the governesses?"

"At nine o'clock."

"Do some stay up later than the others?"

"Only one."

"And what time does she retire?"

"At about half-past eleven or twelve."

"Where does she sleep?"

"On the first floor."

"Above Mademoiselle Mina's room?"

"No; my assistant sleeps in a room facing the dormitory, and looking on the street; whilst poor Mina's room looks on the garden."

"And may I ask where you sleep, Madame?"

"In the room next the drawing-room on the first floor, which also looks on the street."

"Then none of your rooms, save Mina's, faces the garden?"

"None, except also my dressing-room."

"Can you tell me about what time you went to sleep last night?"

"About eleven o'clock, I fancy."

"Ah!" said M. Jackal. "Now, let me look round the house. Come with me, Monsieur Salvator. Monsieur Justin will remain to keep Madame company."

"That woman has had no hand in the affair," muttered the Chief of the Police to Salvator, as he closed the front door behind him and once more gained the street.

"What makes you come to that conclusion?"

"Her tears; the guilty tremble, but never weep."

M. Jackal then gave himself up to a close examination of the exterior of the house, which was situated at the corner of a little street leading from the main road.

He was now like a bloodhound scenting his game from afar.

The garden wall was the object of greatest scrutiny to him. It enclosed the recreation-ground of the girls, and ran some fifty yards down the afore-mentioned little street, which was as quiet and deserted as any runaway lovers could desire.

"The very spot for the purpose!" exclaimed M. Jackal, stooping down and picking up two or three bits of plaster, which had evidently recently fallen from the wall.

He examined them carefully, and then wrapped them with infinite pains in his handkerchief.

There remained one piece of plaster on the pavement. This he threw over the wall into the garden.

"Is that where they scaled the wall?" asked Salvator.

"I'll answer that question presently. Let us go in again now."

M. Jackal and Salvator found Justin and Madame Desmarets in the same place in which they had left them.

"Well?" demanded Justin eagerly.

"We're getting warm," replied M. Jackal. "But follow me into the garden, young man. The key of the garden door, if you please, Madame."

The schoolmistress handed the key to the Chief of the Police, and as they passed along the passage pointed out the door of Mina's room to them. Justin begged hard that it might be searched at once.

"One thing at a time," was the answer of the methodical Chief of the Police. "The garden first: the room afterwards."

M. Jackal thereupon opened the garden door. He paused a moment to scan the garden with a sweeping look, which surveyed the whole scene in an instant.

"Good!" he said. "We must use every precaution here. Follow me in this order: Monsieur Salvator after me, Monsieur Justin third, and Madame Desmarets last."

M. Jackal clearly made for that part of the wall which he had already examined from the outside. Only, instead of proceeding straight to the spot, he kept strictly to the path which led close by the side of the wall.

Suddenly he looked up at Mina's window, and elevated his eyebrows a little as he saw that the Persian blinds were closed.

The path was covered with yellow sand, but nothing fresh arrested his attention till he caught sight of the piece of plaster he had thrown over the wall. As he picked it up a smile of professional satisfaction crept over his face.

"Here we are," the Chief of the Police remarked to Salvator, pointing out a fresh mark on the border at their feet, and attracting the attention of Justin and Madame Desmarets at the same time.

"Then you think the poor girl was carried off just here?" queried Salvator.

"There's no doubt about it."

"Mon Dieu! mon Dieu! An abduction from my house!" broke in Madame Desmarets.

"Monsieur, in Heaven's name give us proofs, not words!" appealed poor Justin.

M. Jackal, who felt sure he was on the right scent, thereupon had recourse to his snuff-box for further inspiration.

"Can you see any trace yet?" demanded Justin, impatiently, seeing that M. Jackal regarded the ground very attentively.

"Yes! those two holes in the soil joined by a deep line," replied the Chief of the Police.

"Don't you see? It's the imprint of a ladder," added Salvator.

"But what formed that cross-line?" asked Justin.

"The first rung of the ladder, of course," was Salvator's response.

"Now we must find out how many persons it took to drive the ladder so far into the soil," said M. Jackal.

"Let's see by the footmarks," suggested Salvator.

"Oh! the footmarks are too confused here. Besides, the rascals may have followed in the leader's footsteps."

Turning to Madame Desmarets, M. Jackal added,

"Is there a ladder in the house?"

"There's the gardener's."

"Where's that?"

"In the outhouse, most likely."

"And which is the outhouse?"

"There—that little thatch-covered building."

"Don't stir! I'll get it myself." And M. Jackal accordingly leapt lightly over the plot of ground whereon the footmarks were so confused, and, leaving this trail to be examined afterwards, soon found the ladder, and quickly returned with it.

"Let us make certain of one thing first," he said, placing the ladder against the wall, and adding, after a moment's pause, "Good! Here's one bit of circumstantial evidence. This is, probably, the very ladder they made use of. You see it fits into the holes exactly."

"But you said you were going to ascertain how many men took part in the abduction," broke in Justin.

"That's the very thing I'm doing at this moment."

So saying, M. Jackal lifted the ladder from the original holes, and placed it against the wall a short distance off. Then he mounted five or six steps, stopping at each rung to see how far into the earth the ladder sank.

"Only three inches!" he exclaimed, when half-way up the ladder. Therefrom he could command the whole garden, and he soon perceived a man in the doorway regarding them with some curiosity.

It was the gardener.

M. Jackal called the new comer, and was soon satisfied as to his honesty and utter ignorance of the abduction.

"Now, my friend," said the Chief of the Police, familiarly, to the gardener; "be good enough to come upon this ladder."

When the gardener gained the second rung, M. Jackal threw an inquiring look at Salvator.

"It has sunk a little more, but not so far as the first rung," said Salvator, in answer to the look.

"You can get off now," resumed M. Jackal. "Just take Madame Desmarets in your arms for a moment."

"I dare not, Monsieur!" protested the gardener.

"And I should not think of permitting such liberty, Pierre!" indignantly added the good lady.

M. Jackal jumped to the ground himself, and bade the gardener mount as high as he had mounted. That accomplished, the Chief of the Police placed his arms round the schoolmistress, and lifted her from the ground before she had time to resist.

"Monsieur! Monsieur!" cried Madame Desmarets, at last. "What are you doing?"

"Just suppose for the moment that I am passionately in love with you, and am carrying you off!" pleaded the gallant M. Jackal.

"A supposition, indeed!" laughed Pierre from his perch on the ladder.

"But, Monsieur! Monsieur!" cried out Madame Desmarets, more vigorously still.

"Be calm, Madame! As Pierre rightly remarks, it is only a supposition," said M. Jackal, reassuringly.

Then, retaining the protesting schoolmistress in his arms, he gained the fourth rung of the ladder.

"It's sinking?" called out Salvator.

"As far as the first rung, yet?" demanded M. Jackal.

"Not quite."

"Just place your foot, then, on the second step," added M. Jackal. Salvator obeyed the command.

"Now," said Justin, "the ladder has sunk just as much as it must have sunk before.

"Good!" answered the Chief of the Police. "Down we all go now."

Depositing Madame Desmarets safely on terra firma as if nothing had happened, M. Jackal next lifted the ladder up, and revealed two holes and a deep line between them exactly corresponding to the marks that had first attracted his attention.

"Good!" repeated M. Jackal. "My dear Monsieur Justin, you will understand that Madame Desmarets is in all probability rather heavier than Mademoiselle Mina, while I am very likely a little lighter than the man who carried off your *fiancée*."

"And you conclude?"

"That Mademoiselle Mina has been carried off by three men."

There remained to examine the footmarks. Breaking off a twig from one of the trees, this astutest detective in Paris measured the footmarks, and found, to his surprise, that they were all the same size. This puzzled him.

"The shoes were the same length and the same breadth, but were not identical," said Salvator at length. "Don't you see that the nails vary in shape !"

"True," exclaimed M. Jackal.

"Besides," added Salvator, "it is clear that one of the men was lame; one of his shoes was trodden down at the heel very much."

"Right again !" said M. Jackal. "One would think you were a shoemaker."

"Oh, I used to indulge in a little hunting and sport formerly," laughingly replied Salvator, in explanation of his keenness of sight.

"Ah ! here's the third man at last," broke in M. Jackal. "Evidently a swell, from the smallness of his boots and the lightness of his tread. Moreover, I see the prick of his spurs here and there !"

Below Mina's window the footmarks were more numerous and were imprinted more deeply in the soil.

Reaching up, M. Jackal found he could not pull the Persian blinds open as easily as he anticipated.

"Clever dogs, evidently !" he muttered. "I only know two men able to get out of a room, and leave the door and window fastened behind them ; and if one was not at Brest and the other at Toulon, I should say Robichon or Gibassier had had a finger in this pie."

"Let's return to the house now, Madame, and examine Mademoiselle Mina's room," added M. Jackal, leading the way himself.

Chapter XXVIII.—Mina's Sanctuary.

M. Jackal found the door of Mina's room locked, as he expected.

"You have a duplicate key for each room, haven't you ?" he demanded of Madame Desmarets.

"Yes; but what use would that be if the door has been bolted ?"

"Bring the key, and let us try," was the cool response.

Madame Desmarets disappeared for a minute or so, and then returned with the key in question.

M. Jackal slid it into the keyhole, and found that another key had been left in the lock inside the room.

"And yet it has evidently been locked from the outside !" he said to himself.

"But, if the ruffians locked the door outside," inquired Salvator, "how could they also bolt it inside ?"

"That's an invention of Gibassier's," replied the Chief of the Police. "He ought to have been sentenced to five instead of ten years' of hard labour for that ingenious idea. Let that pass, however. Send for a locksmith, Madame !"

The locksmith soon arrived with his implements, and forced the door open.

M. Jackal spread out both his arms, and prevented them from rushing into the room.

"Gently, gently!" he said. "Everything depends on the first inspection. Discovery hangs on a thread!"

The Chief of the Police smiled as he uttered the last sentence. Entering alone, he smiled again, and his smile became more marked as he pounced on something almost invisible on the lock, and held it up triumphantly.

"You see I spoke the truth," he exclaimed, "when I said our discovery hung upon a thread. Here's the very thread in question!"

On looking closely, they saw that M. Jackal held a long piece of silk thread, fastened to the bolt and to the door.

"Can the door have been fastened with that?" asked Salvator, almost incredulously.

"Yes," replied M. Jackal, with a smile. "It is done in this way. You double a piece of thread in two, fasten one end on the catch of the bolt, and bring the two other ends outside the room with you. Still holding these two ends, you close the door, then pull the thread, and the door is bolted. Only, there is this chance: that a certain M. Jackal may arrive, and, finding a part of the thread hanging from the bolt, may discover Gibassier's little trick."

"Monsieur Jackal," appealed Justin, filled only with anxious thoughts of Mina, and inattentive to this exhibition of professional skill, "pray let us enter."

Permission being accorded, they one and all followed M. Jackal into Mina's sanctuary.

"Ah! Footmarks from the door to the bed, and from the bed to the window!" exclaimed M. Jackal, ever on the alert. Then, casting a quick glance at the table and the bed, he added,

"Good! She had been reading some letters, and then went to bed, extinguishing the light first."

The Chief of the Police now regarded the footmarks on the carpet afresh.

"A woman's step!" he cried. "Did I not say, Monsieur Salvator, always look for the woman? Parbleu! She must have been a determined woman, too! No walking on tiptoe for her! See! her footmarks are plain and distinct enough!"

"Yet she is clearly a woman who is not careless where she walks," added Salvator; "for, look! you can see the sand deposited from her shoes, showing that she carefully kept to the garden walk last night!"

"Monsieur Salvator," cried the Chief of the Police, "what a pity you are not one of us! With your keen eyes your fortune would soon be made."

M. Jackal abruptly left them, hurried back to the garden, and returned saying that Salvator was right beyond doubt.

"I see as clearly as can be," he added, "how it all happened—as clearly as if I had been present and saw the abduction taking place before my eyes. Mademoiselle Mina retired at the usual hour, sad and tearful, naturally enough when we come to think of how much she must have suffered in being separated from our young friend here on what was to have been their wedding morn. By-and-by she blew out her light. The moment the light was extinguished some one knocked at the door——"

"Who?" demanded Madame Desmarets.

"Ah! you want to know more than I do, Madame. Who? Perhaps we shall know before long. At any rate, the woman——"

"The woman!" broke in the anxious schoolmistress again.

"Yes, the woman!" repeated M. Jackal, impatiently. "Mother, daughter, which I care not. Woman is sufficient, since there *is* a woman in the case, as there is in every case. . . . The woman, then, knocked at the door. Mina rose and let in her friend. Close behind the friend came the young spark with the spurs, and after him came his hireling—Gibassier, probably, as I said before. Then, they lost not a moment in gagging the poor girl with a handkerchief, and in enveloping her in the sheet or a shawl, and in carrying her off by way of the window. It is plain enough she was not given time to dress; for look! there are her clothes on the chair at the foot of the bed!"

"But why did they escape through the window?" asked Justin.

"Why? Because Mademoiselle Mina might have made a noise in being carried through the house, and then all the house might have been roused. So the poor victim was borne across the garden, and over the wall by means of the ladder, as you have already seen. Mina's friend then put the ladder back in its place, returned to Mina's room to close the Persian blinds and bolt the door, *à la* Gibassier, and finally went to bed to sleep tranquilly the rest of the night!"

"But she must have been seen either in quitting or returning to the dormitory!" objected Madame Desmarets.

"Has no other pupil of yours but Mina a separate room, then?" asked M. Jackal.

"Only one."

"Be sure that one is the guilty one, Madame," replied M. Jackal, with emphasis. "My dear Monsieur Salvator, the woman's found at last."

"What! Do you really imagine Mina's bosom friend can have been base enough to have been concerned in the abduction?" answered Madame Desmarets.

"Madame, *I* have no doubt it is she who is answerable for it," said Justin, warmly. "The first time I saw her I had a presentiment that I should have cause to regret Mina's friendship for her. Let her be brought before M. Jackal at once, that she may be accused of her treachery before her face."

"Stop!" said M. Jackal. "It will be more prudent to go straight to her apartment. Will you lead the way, Madame?"

Following the schoolmistress, they soon reached Mademoiselle Suzanne's room. No answer came to their knock. M. Jackal entered, and found proof conclusive of her complicity in the abduction. A single glance at the shoes at the bedside proved that they must be the very same shoes which had left the sand-marks in Mina's room, inasmuch as their soles were coated with sand.

"Where's Madame Suzanne at this moment?" M. Jackal abruptly inquired of the schoolmistress, carefully replacing the shoes where he had found them.

"In the garden, probably."

"And which of your rooms looks upon the garden?"

"The drawing-room."

"Good!" answered M. Jackal. "We'll just step down, and be looking, quite by chance, out of the drawing-room window; whilst you tell this formidable young conspirator that some one wishes to see her.

CHAPTER XXIX.—MINA'S BOSOM FRIEND.

M. JACKAL was, a minute later, scrutinising the young lady he desired to be face to face with from the drawing-room window.

She was walking alone in the garden, apparently in deep thought. From her day-dream she was roused, however, by hearing her name called.

Looking round, she saw it was Madame Desmarets, standing on the steps, who wanted her.

Mademoiselle Suzanne returned to the house slowly, and with a somewhat disdainful air.

Justin smiled bitterly as he recognised her cold, regular features.

"It's very singular; but that face seems not unfamiliar to me!" was the exclamation that involuntarily escaped from Salvator.

"What do you think of her," asked the Chief of the Police.

"Wicked to the very marrow," answered Salvator.

"So think I. Her mouth is so thin and firm and hard, her eyes are so cold-blooded, her whole expression is so repulsive, fine though her features are, that she *must* be wicked," was the stronger opinion of M. Jackal.

With the same air of indifference, the young lady joined Madame Desmarets, and, at her request, followed her into the drawing-room. Perceiving Justin and the two gentlemen with him, she could not repress a slight start; but her cold face remained impassive, and she soon recovered her sangfroid.

The Chief of the Police saw the resolute nature he had to deal with, so, without delay, introduced himself and his business.

"Mademoiselle, I regret to say that it is my duty to question you, on behalf of the law, as to the disappearance of Mademoiselle Mina, your intimate friend, from this house last night. I have reason to believe ——"

"What can I, Suzanne de Valgeneuse, know of the disappearance, since I was not aware of it till this moment?" answered the young lady, in her most imperious tone.

"Mademoiselle de Valgeneuse!" cried M. Jackal, in affright, as though he had committed himself, and thrown suspicion upon one whom he ought to have deemed above suspicion.

"Yes, Monsieur," she replied, following up her advantage, "De Valgeneuse is my name. I am the daughter of the Marquis Denis-René de Valgeneuse and the sister of the Comte Lorédan de Valgeneuse, and yet I am made to suffer this indignity."

"Suzanne de Valgeneuse!" exclaimed Salvator in his turn, regarding her with a look of menace and curiosity at the same time.

"Pardon, Mademoiselle; I was ignorant of your name," stammered M. Jackal, bending with the greatest deference.

Poor Justin could not comprehend the change which had been effected in a moment. His heart sank as the now humbled Chief of the Police bowed himself out of Mademoiselle Suzanne's presence with profuse excuses, and whispered to Madame Desmarets that she must regard his visit as if it had never taken place.

How could *he* hope to struggle against rank and wealth when the very Chief of the Police was impotent against their influence?

Salvator gave him one word of consolation. Ere he joined M. Jackal in his carriage, he whispered cheeringly in Justin's ear,

"Courage! In less than twenty-four hours I undertake to bring you good or bad news—good, I hope, Justin—of Mina!"

Chapter XXX.—Dead or Living?

Hopeful though Salvator's last words were, Justin felt irresistibly impelled to make one final appeal to the Chief of the Police before his departure. Hence he followed Salvator to the carriage door, and, addressing M. Jackal, said,

"One moment, Monsieur! Did you not ask, 'Where's the woman?' and answer the question yourself by proving that Mademoiselle Suzanne de Valgeneuse aided in the abduction?"

M. Jackal had recourse to his snuff-box. He was plainly taken aback for a moment. On the one hand, he had committed himself too far to retreat from the search for Mina's abductor; on the other the relatives of Mina's treacherous friend were too high in office for even the Chief of the Police to offend. He got out of his difficulty by replying,

"Come and see me, Monsieur Justin, to-morrow morning, at eight o'clock, in the Rue de Jérusalem. Then I may have some news for you. Depend upon it, I will put some of my best men on the scent directly I get back."

"To Paris!" added M. Jackal to the coachman, evidently anxious to rid himself of Justin and his embarrassment at the same time.

The carriage bearing M. Jackal and Salvator was rapidly whirled away from the Versailles *pensionnat*.

The Chief of the Police sank back into the corner with a sigh of relief, and would gladly have been left to ruminate in silence on the sudden check which Mademoiselle Suzanne de Valgeneuse had given him at the very juncture when he felt sure he was about to discover the secret of Mina's mysterious disappearance. He reckoned, however, without Salvator.

"May I ask you what made you change your opinion so suddenly just now, Monsieur Jackal?" questioned the young Commissionnaire in a tone of raillery.

"Certainly. You're a man of common sense; you're not in love——"

"How do you know that?"

"Not in love with a girl who's been carried off, then. So I may venture to tell you that when I heard the name of Valgeneuse a shiver ran through me."

"But I thought the first article of the code was: ALL MEN ARE EQUAL BEFORE THE LAW!"

"My dear Monsieur Salvator, that sort of thing appears in all codes, just as they put on all Royal proclamations, 'Charles by the Grace of God, King of France and Navarre!' Louis XVI. used the same formula, and yet he lost his head!"

"You mean, I suppose, that these Valgeneuses are very powerful?"

"I should think so. First, there's the Marquis, who is in the King's confidence. The Cardinal has the ear of the Pope. The Lieutenant——"

"Has the ear of the deuce. Just so! And therefore, it would be a matter of risk for you to run counter to this powerful family?"

"Yes."

"Let me see, Monsieur Jackal; the head of the family died five or six years ago childless, and so the fortune went to his brother, didn't it?"

"Yes; the first Marquis de Valgeneuse did not marry."

"I remember now. But was there not some story of a natural son who was to have been adopted or recognised, and was not?"

"How did you know that?" inquired M. Jackal, regarding Salvator with one of his keenest glances.

"Oh! In my business," replied the Commissionnaire, "one learns many things by being observant. I once carried some letters from a lady to a certain Monsieur Conrad de Valgeneuse living in the Rue de Bac, at the same house, by-the-way, which the present Marquis inhabits. But the story I allude to was a rather obscure one."

"Not to everybody!" answered M. Jackal, with an air of self-satisfaction.

"Not to those who found out the woman?" retorted Salvator.

"Strange to say," replied the Chief of the Police, "there was no woman in this affair at all."

"No? What occasioned his sudden disappearance, then? I am not unnaturally curious on the point, M. Jackal; one cannot help being anxious as to the fate of a young man, handsome, rich, and happy, whom one formerly knew."

"Justly; and I can tell you nearly the whole story."

"Nearly! Can't you divulge all?"

"I said 'nearly,' Monsieur Salvator, because the confidential nature of our business prevents me sometimes from telling all I know."

"And sometimes you may not know all," added Salvator, with a quiet laugh.

"Be that as it may," said M. Jackal, scrutinising Salvator over his spectacles, "I'll tell you what I know about the affair; and then you can tell me all I don't know."

"Agreed!"

"Good! What I know is soon told: The head of the family, the Marquis Charles Emmanuel de Valgeneuse, who inherited an immense fortune from an uncle on his mother's side, made up his mind never to marry. Yet, by-and-by, the Marquis adopted a certain Monsieur Conrad, who gradually became known as Monsieur Conrad de Valgeneuse."

"Wasn't that his real name?"

"Not exactly. It appeared he was a natural son, of whom his father grew to be passionately fond."

"But how came it that the Marquis, loving the young man as you say he did, left all his fortune to his brother, his nephew and his niece, whilst the young man was allowed to die in misery?"

"Ah! That may have been because his father loved him too much. You know there's a proverb which says, 'Excess in anything is a fault.'"

"Explain your parable."

"Well, you must know that there are, according to the law, two modes of dealing with a natural son. The first, which is simple enough, is to declare that one is the father of the child directly he is registered; or, if anything should prevent that formality, the father may later sign a deed of recognition before a notary; but, in that case, you can only leave the child the fifth part of your fortune. The second mode is to wait till one is fifty, and then to formally adopt the child before a notary. Then the adopted child can receive not only your name, but all your fortune. It was this last course that the Marquis preferred. The very day he attained his fiftieth year he summoned a notary, the deed of adoption was prepared, but the moment he took the pen in his hand to sign it he was seized with a fit of apoplexy."

"The moment he took the pen in his hand to sign the deed, or the moment after he had signed it?" demanded Salvator.

"*Ma foi!* Monsieur Salvator, if you can tell that you know more than I do, and more than all the world does. Was the deed signed or not signed? *That is the question*, as Hamlet says. The poor Marquis could not solve the riddle, for though he survived three days, he never once regained his consciousness."

"What is your private opinion, Monsieur Jackal?"

"My opinion is," answered the wary Chief of the Police, avoiding a direct reply, "that the family was rather hard upon poor Monsieur Conrad."

"Rather hard! Bah! The moment it was known that the deed was not signed, or, at least, that the notary affirmed it was not signed, what claim could a natural son have had on the family?"

"It was generally known that Monsieur Conrad *did* stand in that unfortunate relation to the Marquis."

"Yes; but, if the family admitted that, they would have had to surrender to him at least a fifth part of the fortune which was theirs entirely, provided he was not recognised: and the fifth of the fortune would have amounted to two millions of francs! Better disown him altogether, and so inherit the title and money intact, without any blot on the family escutcheon. Wasn't that the counsel they acted on, Monsieur Jackal?"

"It was. The young man was sent adrift without a sou. He seemed to bear his ill-luck bravely enough. He left his horses in their stables and the carriages in the coach-house; and he even left his bank-notes in his desk, only carrying away with him some two thousand francs which he might well have deemed his, seeing that he won them at écarté."

"A young fellow accustomed to live in luxury as Monsieur Conrad was, couldn't have made two thousand francs go far!" interrupted Salvator.

"You make a mistake there, my dear Monsieur. With those two thousand francs he lived nearly fifteen months. He tried every honest means of earning a living, but he could neither succeed as a music nor a drawing master, nor as a teacher of languages. Losing heart at last, he determined to give up the struggle for existence. He bought a pistol at Lepage's, wrote a letter detailing the misery he had undergone to the Commissioner of Police, and then shot himself!"

"*Ma foi!* Monsieur Jackal, you're as lucid as a police reporter!"

"Oh! it's not surprising that I know the details. It was I who made out the *procès-verbal* of Monsieur Conrad's suicide."

"Really! Then the poor young fellow was indebted to you for the last attentions paid him and for certifying his death?"

"It was not difficult to certify to that. The pistol had done its work only too well. Part of the face was blown away, and what was left was burnt. It was by the letter more than by recognition that he was identified."

"I presume the Valgeneuses were informed of the affair?"

"I took the news to them myself, with a duplicate of the *procès-verbal.*"

"Of course, the intelligence startled them?"

"Yes, my dear Monsieur Salvator; they were rather surprised—agreeably surprised."

"I understand. The existence of the young man had been a source of trouble to them?"

"Yes; they desired me to see that the burial was properly and effectually performed, and gave me five hundred francs for my trouble."

"Very noble of them!"

"So anxious were they that no formality should be neglected, that they bade me deliver to them the certificate of the burial."

"And you did so, I hope, Monsieur Jackal?"

"Yes; I conscientiously carried out all my instructions—accompanied the hearse to Père la Chaise cemetery, saw the coffin lowered, ordered a stone with CONRAD cut on it, to be placed above the grave——"

"And the Valgeneuses believe that Conrad rests there to this day?"

"Without doubt. Why shouldn't they?"

"Why, because extraordinary things happen sometimes, Monsieur Jackal," was the enigmatical answer of Salvator.

"What on earth could happen?"

Salvator avoided this question as the Chief of the Police avoided a leading question of his a little while before, and exclaimed,

"Here we are at Bas-Meudon, Monsieur Jackal. Will you tell the coachman to stop?"

A moment later Salvator opened the door and jumped out.

"Pardon me!" said M. Jackal, "you have not given me an answer."

"To what?"

"To my simple question, 'What on earth could happen?'"

"To Conrad?"

"Yes."

"Oh! it might have happened, my dear Monsieur Jackal, that *Conrad did not die, and that the Marquis de Valgeneuse may yet meet him alive in this world!* Adieu! Monsieur Jackal."

Quickly shutting the door, Salvator left the Chief of the Police so astounded by his mysterious speech that it was the Commissionaire, and not the Commissioner, who had to give the order,

"Coachman! To the Rue de Jérusalem."

CHAPTER XXXI.—LUDOVIC'S PRESCRIPTION.

IT was in vain M. Jackal tried to solve the riddle Salvator had puzzled him with. Even pinch after pinch of snuff did not aid the Chief of the Police, who at length leant back in the corner of his carriage, folded his arms, and plunged into a most perplexing reverie as he was being whirled back to Paris.

Salvator, smiling to himself, entered the cottage, thinking to find Ludovic. But the young doctor had left. He had seen Dominique depart with the body of Colomban for Penhoël. He had seen Carmélite show the first signs of returning reason. He was then called upon to use all his science and skill for the restoration of another patient.

Ludovic took the route through Vanvres on his way home. The village was still lamenting, for there seemed to be no hope of M. Gérard's recovery. Would Monsieur see him? The young doctor could not resist the earnest entreaties. He was soon by the sufferer's bedside, where he found a veteran army surgeon of the old school, M. Pilloy, one who had through many campaigns prescribed heroic remedies, which had sometimes succeeded, but which had oftener failed. His treatment was plainly the wrong one in this case, Ludovic soon discovered. It was pneumonia M. Gérard was suffering from; and the old surgeon was hastening his death by prescribing for a totally different disease. Despite the opposition of M. Pilloy,

Ludovic prescribed an emetic. He then returned to Paris, promising to be back in a few hours to see the effects of the prescription. In less time than that he was again in the sick-room. As he entered he overheard M. Pilloy exclaim,

"He is lost, beyond a doubt!"

Ludovic, paying no heed to these alarming words from his obtuse confrère, regarded the patient earnestly for a minute, and then felt his pulse.

He looked up with an air of relief.

"He's progressing capitally," said the young doctor.

"What!" cried M. Pilloy, stupefied.

"His pulse beats more regularly."

"But, my dear young man, he has vomited, and he is lost!"

"On the contrary, he is saved," replied Ludovic, calmly.

"Do *you* answer for the life of my best friend, then?" demanded M. Pilloy, furious at Ludovic's assumption of superior knowledge and unruffled demeanour.

"Yes, Monsieur, I do!"

The old surgeon put on his hat and bounced out of the room with the air of an arithmetician whom some one had sought to convince that two and two make five.

Ludovic wrote another prescription, and, handing it to the nurse, said,

"Madame, I take the responsibility on myself. Let my directions be followed to the letter, and Monsieur Gérard will be saved!"

There escaped from the patient a cry of joy. He rose and seized the young doctor's hand, and pressed it to his lips.

Then a look of extreme terror spread over his livid face.

"*But the monk! the monk!*" he gasped out, falling back exhausted on the bed.

Chapter XXXII.—Love at First Sight.

PETRUS now claims our attention. It will be remembered that on leaving Ludovic and the merry Carnival bevy of blanchisseuses at the door of Bordier's cabaret Pétrus excused himself on the plea that he was due at a sitting that morning.

Who the fair sitter was to be will soon be found in the one romance the young painter treasured in his heart of hearts.

One word about Pétrus himself. Reckless, pleasure-loving though he may have seemed during the night of Carnival revelry at the cabaret, it was merely a careless assumption of gaiety—a vain effort to drown an impossible hope which he had dared to cherish. He was naturally frank, pure, and simple. He had the very heart of a true artist. If you had seen him at work in his studio, you would have pronounced him a perfect realisation of Vandyke—an embodiment of grace and manly beauty—in face and in dress the very personification of the famous Flemish painter.

The first time Pétrus saw the fair ideal of his life was towards the close of a beautiful summer's day.

It was in that favourite promenade with the Parisians of the Faubourgs Saint-Jacques and Saint-Germain, running from the barrier of Grenelle to the barrier of the Gare.

The young painter had stopped in the middle of the thoroughfare to admire a fine sunset effect, when he had to move quickly on one side to allow a lady and a gentleman on horseback to pass by.

The lady was another Diana Vernon in the charm of her beauty, in her buoyant brightness, and in the wondrous ease with which she rode while she unconcernedly conversed with her companion, a middle-aged gentleman of military bearing.

Thenceforth the heart of Pétrus was not his own. Fruitless were his endeavours to paint till he came to picture one image, one and ever the same sweet face, on his canvas. He lived on the memory of the fair amazon, from whom he gained inspiration. He longed for the blissful intoxication of another view of his ideal; but months flew by before he was to be fascinated afresh.

It was in winter when Pétrus next beheld her. He recognised her in a closed carriage. She was now in mourning, and by her side there sat an old lady dozing or asleep. He followed the carriage, and saw it disappear down the Rue Plumet from the Boulevard des Invalides. The Rue Plumet became haunted by him. One morning he was rewarded by seeing the carriage drive into the courtyard of Marshal de Lamothe-Houdan's mansion in the Rue Plumet; and he was not long in ascertaining that the young lady was Mademoiselle Régina de Lamothe-Houdan, whom the reader has seen at the bedside of her Carmélite.

Worshipping her in secret as his ideal, Pétrus became more and more inspired, and his canvasses glowed with a mellow, ravishing beauty almost worthy of the original to whose loveliness they owed their sunny colouring.

The flame of love was destined to burn still more brightly in the young painter's breast.

The studio of Pétrus was situated in the Rue de l'Ouest; and he was about to enter it one day when he was surprised to observe a carriage at the door. His heart beat fast, indeed, for he recognised by the arms on the panel that it was Mademoiselle de Lamothe-Houdan herself, or some member of the family, who had honoured him with a visit.

Pétrus arrived just in time to hear a sweet voice asking of the concierge,

"Monsieur Pétrus Herbel lives here, does he not?"

Pétrus felt the blood rushing to his face as he recognised his divinity in the fair questioner, who was accompanied, however, by a chaperon whose hauteur was to speedily recall the young artist to his senses.

"Here *is* Monsieur Herbel, Madame," said the concierge.

The ladies both turned, and Pétrus saluted them with marked respect.

"Oh! you are Monsieur Pétrus Herbel?" demanded the elder lady somewhat haughtily.

"Yes, Madame," said Pétrus coldly in return.

The young lady, remarking the hauteur of her companion, made amends by addressing Pétrus, with a winning smile,

"You are the painter of a portrait in the last Exhibition, numbered 309, are you not, Monsieur?"

"I am, Mademoiselle," answered Pétrus, with a polite bow, charmed more than ever by the bright beauty and sweet voice of the young lady.

"If I am not mistaken, it was your own portrait, was it not, Monsieur?"

"Yes, Mademoiselle," replied the young painter, blushing as he spoke.

"Well, Monsieur, I wish to have my portrait taken in the same way. I was quite charmed with the tone. Mother or aunt has had eight or ten portraits of me already done, but not one of them pleases me. Will you, in your turn, try to satisfy so capricious a sitter?"

"I will try my best with pleasure, Mademoiselle; and I shall deem it a great honour to paint the portrait of Mademoiselle de Lamothe-Houdan."

"As you know my niece's name, Monsieur," said the elder lady, in a rather softer voice, "it only remains to give you our address and to see what hour will suit you for the sitting."

"My time is at your disposal, Madame," replied Pétrus, graciously in his turn, now the chaperon had thawed a little. "As for the address of the Princesse de Lamothe-Houdan, all the world knows her mansion in the Rue Plumet."

"Very well, Monsieur," answered the young girl, reddening faintly at the compliments implied rather than spoken, "let us say to-morrow, at twelve, if that will suit you."

"At twelve to-morrow I shall be at your service, Mesdames," said Pétrus, the bright light in his eyes betraying the eager gladness with which he made the appointment.

Chapter XXXIII.—The Painter's Paradise.

Pétrus mounted to his studio joyous in the extreme, and it was, perhaps, well for him that the idol of his dreams did not also ascend; for there was on his easel as faithful a portrait of the Princess as she could desire, albeit it was painted from memory only; and some twenty other likenesses of the same fair Princess adorned his walls, appearing as the heroine of each picture he had painted since he had first made Mademoiselle Régina de Lamothe-Houdan his ideal of all that was lovely and beautiful.

The glowing canvasses appeared dull enough to Pétrus, fresh from the presence of his goddess, who had now become a living reality to him, and whose gentle graciousness and winsome loveliness were to charm him for many a delightful day to come. What a thrill it sent through his heart simply to recall her fair form in a waking dream! To see her in fancy spring lightly from her carriage, or float like a cloud of lace and velvet and ermine, was to send the love-stream pulsing through his veins with the rare rush of ecstacy which a man only feels once in his life.

There was but one way to give vent to the deep gladness which filled his being. His trembling hands stole over the keys of the pianoforte, and music, with its enchanted voice, with its tender vibrations to which Heaven must have given birth for the solace of the earth—music alone gave adequate expression to the pleasurable emotions that made his heart beat with delicious rapidity.

The day and the night flew by as a vision. But one name, but one being, haunted him, and that was Régina.

Long before the appointed hour the next day, Pétrus was at the door of Marshal de Lamothe-Houdan's handsome mansion in the Rue Plumet (now the Rue Oudinot).

Régina awaited the young painter with a certain curiosity, though not with the impatience which characterised him. She had caused the conservatory to be made into an impromptu studio. This little floral palace was situated in the garden—a veritable oasis in the desert of Paris—and was beautiful alike with palms and ferns and rare exotics and with the most graceful sculpture.

Pétrus could not restrain an exclamation of admiration when he was about to enter this fairy bower. The taste with which it was adorned appealed directly to the artistic instincts of his nature. Viewed from the threshold, the scene was, indeed, one to awaken the keenest delight of an artist, for the dream of the warmest imagination could not transcend the glory of that fascinating actuality. Gazing with unconcealed admiration at the marvels of art—the Graces of Germain Pilou, the Nymphs of Jean Goujon, the Loves of Jean of Bologna—partially veiled by the wonders of nature from every quarter of the world—a virgin forest in miniature, with a wealth of camellias, magnolias, orchids, roses and innumerable other fragrant and luxuriant plants—Pétrus stood spell-bound, scarce venturing to take a step further into this sanctuary of Flora.

It was Régina who at length brought him to his senses—only to make admiration give way to secret adoration, however.

"Come in, Monsieur," she smilingly said, in the frank manner and sweet voice peculiarly her own.

"Forgive me, Mademoiselle," was his gallant reply; "but a poor mortal may be allowed to hesitate on the threshold of Paradise."

Régina, seemingly not ill-pleased at the compliment, answered by calling the painter's attention to the easel and canvas, palette and colours, ready for him in the centre of the studio. Pétrus saw that the materials had been arranged by no unskilful hand, and at once replied,

"Now, Mademoiselle, have the goodness to sit wherever you please, and just as seems most easy and natural to you."

Régina took her seat on the sofa near Pétrus, and naturally assumed, without effort, the most graceful of poses.

The painter seized a brush, and, with the dexterity of a master of his art, quickly sketched the outline of the portrait. Coming to the features of the sweet face, now spread like a mirror before him,

Pétrus felt that a little liveliness was wanting in his fair sitter to give that vitality which he wished to embody in his likeness.

"May I suggest that we should have a little conversation upon some topic agreeable to you, Mademoiselle?" he ventured to ask. "It is my desire to combine the idealisation of Scheffer with the colour of Décamp; and you will, therefore, excuse me if I wish to call up a look of greater animation in your face."

"Certainly, I will do as you wish, Monsieur," answered Régina, with a smile; "and if you would like my face to wear its habitual expression whilst I am enjoying the happiest moments of the day, will you kindly ring the bell?"

Pétrus rang.

"Will you tell Abeille I want her?" Régina said to the servant who answered the bell.

A few minutes after a young girl of about ten or eleven bounded into the studio, and nestled on a cushion at the foot of Régina. This fragile little elf, with golden curls and with cheeks like rose leaves, was a fresh source of admiration for Pétrus, and he noted with pleasure the loving light which shone in Régina's eyes, and the loving smile that played in dimples round her rosy mouth as she questioned Abeille.

"Why, you're quite hot and breathless, child! Where have you been?"

"In the salle d'armes, fencing with father."

"Ah! Father is more of a child than you, Abeille."

"But father says, Régina, it is fencing which has given you such a beautiful figure; and I want to be as tall and beautiful as you are. . . . Ah!" added Abeille, in an undertone, "is this the gentleman who is to paint your portrait?"

"Yes," whispered Régina.

"Will he do mine also?"

"I should be delighted to do so, Mademoiselle," was the prompt response of Pétrus, who had overheard Abeille's last question; "and especially posed as you are at this moment."

"You hear, Abeille?" said Régina, fondling her little sister, still nestling on the cushion at her feet. "In return, you must tell us a nice little story."

"Willingly," replied Abeille, regarding Pétrus with a look which implied that the little narrator had no doubt her story would be of particular interest to him.

Little imagining what a revelation of the charitable life of Régina he was about to hear, Pétrus proceeded industriously with his work, charmed more than ever with the ravishing expression of intelligent interest which now lit up the face of Régina.

CHAPTER XXXIV.—THE FAIRY CARITA.

"ONCE upon a time," began Abeille, "there lived a Princess, endowed with incomparable beauty and virtue. She was born at Bagdad, and lived under the reign of the Caliph Haroun-al-Raschid.

THE FAIRY CARITA.   97

"Her father, one of the Caliph's most illustrious Marshals, finding no vent for his valour, gave in his resignation to the good Haroun-al-Raschid, in order to devote himself to the education of Zuleyma. The Caliph, though loth to lose so brave a General, sanctioned his retirement when he learnt the cause, and even offered him for Régina —I beg pardon, sister; I should have said for Zuleyma—the very masters who had taught his own daughter.

"So the Marshal retired into private life, occupying a fine house in one of the faubourgs of the city, surrounded, just like our own dwelling in the Rue Plumet, with fine gardens.

"There numberless masters taught Zuleyma every art and science, every grace and accomplishment under the sun; and she profited so much by their instructions, that at the age of eighteen it was generally acknowledged that she was one of the most talented as well as lovely—"

"Abeille," interrupted Régina, not relishing the turn the fable was taking, "your story is not very interesting this morning. Can you not tell us something else?"

"The story may not be amusing, but it has the merit of being true," was the ready reply; "and the truth of a story is its best recommendation, is it not, Monsieur?"

"I must confess I am of your opinion, Mademoiselle," answered Pétrus, secretly rejoicing at the idea that he was going to hear some of the details of Régina's life disclosed in her sister's fable. "And I would humbly beg of Mademoiselle to allow you to continue."

Régina's face flushed as red as the camellias above her head, but she offered no further opposition to the continuance of the story.

"I will not enlarge on the good qualities of the Princess," resumed Abeille. "I will only say that the good women of Bagdad never saw her pass through the streets without exclaiming, 'There goes the most charitable Princess that has ever been seen, and ever will be seen.'

"The Princess gained the name of the Fairy Carita, by her relief of a poor Savoyard, who sought her kind help by crying, 'Carita, Carita, Principessa! Carita!'

"Without dwelling on the thousand and one good actions by which the Fairy Carita proved that she was well entitled to the name the people had given her, I come to one, and my sister Carita—no, Zuleyma; no, Régina—ah! I keep on making mistakes; but I appeal to my sister to assure you, Monsieur, that what I have told you is a fact.

"Well, one day the Princess was riding on horseback with her father, as was her custom; but saw something which caused her to rein in her steed. This was a poor girl in rags, about twelve or thirteen years old, sitting shivering on the pavement, though it was a warm day. Four or five young dogs were caressing her, and a crow was perched on her shoulder. The young girl shook, and her teeth chattered, as if it were winter; and yet it was in August last—what am I saying!"

Pétrus smiled.

"What are you saying, indeed!" exclaimed Régina. "You speak

of the Caliph Haroun-al-Raschid and of last year in one breath. You say the scene of the story is in Bagdad, and yet you introduce a Savoyard! You're not yourself to-day, Abeille. Tell me the rest some other day!"

"Shall I stop?" asked Abeille, of the painter.

"No; I beg you will continue, Mademoiselle," said Pétrus, eagerly. "The story interests me so much that I am illustrating it while you proceed. I have already drawn the poor girl, and am now about to sketch the Princess Carita."

"Oh! let me see!" said Abeille.

"No, no!" answered Pétrus, hiding the paper; "not till it is finished. By the time you have finished your story, Mademoiselle, I shall have finished my drawing."

"Where was I, then?" inquired Abeille.

"You had arrived at August, last year, Mademoiselle."

"Laugh as you like," said the young girl; "I made a slight mistake in saying last year, that's all. It couldn't have been last year, because my story goes back to the reign of the Caliph Haroun-al-Raschid; and every one knows that he died in 809, five years before Charlemagne.

"What I should have said was this—that about that time the heat was as stifling in Bagdad as it was in Paris last August. Well, Princess Carita dismounted, and soon placed her soft hand upon the girl's trembling shoulder. She found the girl was suffering from fever. She obtained her father's permission to see what sort of a home the poor girl had. Rose-de-Noël was her name. She lived with a hideous old woman, *la Brocante*, in one of the most miserable streets of Bagdad.

"'Who is *la Brocante?*' asked the Fairy Carita of the little girl.

"'A ragpicker, who has brought me up,' she answered.

"'Have you no mother, no father, then?'

"'No; I am all alone in the world,' said the poor thing, trembling more than ever.

"'All alone!' repeated the Fairy Carita, pitifully. 'How far do you live from here?'

"'Not more than ten minutes walk, Fairy Carita.'

"'Very well, then; we will carry you home, and see that you are well attended to.'

"And, so saying, this resolute Fairy lifted the child in her arms, and placed her gently on her father's saddle, bidding him hold fast his precious charge till he reached their destination."

Continuing her recital, Abeille, with many a speaking glance at Pétrus, related how that *la Brocante* was as ugly as Rose-de-Noël was pretty, how that the Caliph had to use threats to bring her to take proper care of her young patient, how that the Fairy Carita spent many days and nights by the bedside of the little sufferer, till she recovered from the brain fever, and the Princess herself had to return, worn out with nursing, to her palace, to indulge in a long rest to save herself from falling ill.

"From that moment," added Abeille, "the little girl recovered; and, if you doubt the veracity of my story, you have only to inquire for Rose-de-Noël, at *la Brocante's*, 11, Rue Triperet, and you will soon learn that it is true enough, Monsieur."

The story of the Fairy Carita was finished.

Abeille looked up at the painter, but he held a large piece of grey paper before his face.

The young raconteur then turned towards her sister, but only to see that Régina had hidden her face behind a large palm-leaf to conceal her embarrassment.

Astonished at the effect of her story, and not perceiving that each of her listeners guarded some secret closely, Abeille gave expression to her wonderment, and frankly asked,

"What makes you play at bee-bow? . . . My tale is at an end: is your drawing done, Monsieur?"

"It is, Mademoiselle," replied Pétrus, putting one last touch to his sketch, and then handing it to Abeille, from whom there escaped an exclamation of girlish pleasure at the sight of a vivid crayon picture of the very scene she had described—her sister as the Fairy Carita, and her father as Caliph, acting the good Samaritans in relieving Rose-de-Noël, whilst Abeille was looking on as the historian of the benevolent deed.

"Oh! look at this beautiful drawing!" cried Abeille to her sister.

Régina regarded it long and attentively, and the surprise she felt at its fidelity was plainly expressed in her face. It appeared almost incredible to her that Pétrus should have been able, from the simple words of Abeille, to depict the very scene which was impressed so clearly on her mind. Her conjectures were in vain. She did not know then of the painter's secret love for her. She did not know that the portraits of herself and her father in the picture were the counterfeit presentments which Pétrus had treasured most dearly in his memory ever since he first beheld them riding on horseback on that never-to-be-forgotten summer's eve. It was, therefore, with nothing but a natural admiration of the painter's seemingly wondrous skill that Régina at length said, throwing a witching glance at the anxious painter at the same moment,

"Abeille, you asked me at the Louvre the other day to point to you the design of some great master: You have one now before you, dear, in this drawing."

Pétrus blushed with pride and pleasure. The first sitting at an end, and an appointment having been made for the following day, the young painter left the studio intoxicated with love for the Fairy Carita, of whose goodness of heart, as well as peerless beauty and graciousness, he had now had so convincing a proof.

CHAPTER XXXV.—COMTE HERBEL'S CAREER.

THE prologue to the play is at an end. The reader has been made acquainted with the major part of the characters who will perform the chief rôles in the drama, and he has seen how the most diverse, as well as the most sympathetic, natures have been brought together until they form one human current to flow on through a city turbulent with dark and hidden crimes.

The task before us is to paint the Society of the Restoration from its highest summit to its deepest abyss. Each personage in this romance will be not simply an imaginary creation, but a type studied and drawn straight from nature : the incarnation of a vice or of a virtue, of a passion or of some heroism ; and these vices, virtues, passions, and heroisms will collectively represent the Society of the Restoration at large just as each of our heroes will represent one of its members.

Pétrus felt his passion for Régina growing more and more irrepressible as each fresh sitting opened her mind and heart to him more and more. Even if she could return his love (and the unfailing warmth of the greeting which the fascinating young Princess ever accorded to the young painter gave him some little hope), yet there was the apparently insurmountable barrier of family pride to prevent their being united, however affectionately they might be attached to each other. There was Marshal de Lamothe-Houdan, in the first place. An old soldier of the Empire, although of a noble French stock, and subsequently a soldier of the King in 1823, when he rose to the rank of Marshal in the Royalist army, Régina's father regarded Pétrus as he regarded his valet, or his gardener, or his footman.

Then the Marquise de la Tournelle (whose contempt for the vocation of Pétrus had not lessened much since her first interview with him) was in frequent attendance upon her niece at the studio, and became more assiduous in her visits as she deemed it necessary to plead the cause of her protégé, Comte Rappt, more vigorously to Régina. Nor could Pétrus hope for countenance from Régina's mother, for she was the daughter of a Russian Prince, and it was from her, therefore, that her daughter obtained the title of Princess by courtesy. But, on the other hand, Pétrus felt he could count upon one nobleman in his family—Comte Herbel de Courtenay, the eldest brother of the young painter's father.

Comte Herbel lived in the Rue de Varennes. His career had been an eventful one. Born at St. Malo, he offered his services to Louis XVI. in 1789. Two years after the Legislative Assembly abolished the throne, and called upon the officers and privates of the army to take an oath of allegiance from which the king's name was omitted. Comte Herbel refused. He remained true to the King's cause. He crossed the Atlantic with several comrades, and was in New Orleans when the voice of the dying King seemed to summon him and them from exile to a spot nearer the heart of France. He joined the staff of the Prince de Condé at Coblentz, figured bravely on many battlefields, but was taken prisoner on July 19, 1793, by a Republican soldier. Grievously wounded, General Comte Herbel was about to be despatched unceremoniously by his captor, who first demanded, however, whether his prisoner cried for quarter.

"We always grant quarter, but never ask for quarter," replied Comte Herbel, bluffly.

"You ought to be a Republican!" was the admiring answer.

At that moment three more Royalist prisoners were brought in and were soon led away, with Comte Herbel, to the wood to be shot. It was by a mere chance that they escaped. The Republican who captured Comte Herbel knew him to be a Breton by his voice, and, a Breton himself, resolved to save him. If the Comte would but cry, "Vive la République!" he should be released, said the Breton. This the Comte would not do; and he would at once have been executed with his comrades had not his Breton friend called upon them, as a last hope, to cry with him, "*Vive la France!*"

"*Vive la France!*" shouted the Royalists, accordingly, with all their might, and were released.

On the 13th of October in the same year, after the capture of Lauterbourg and Wissenbourg, at which Comte Herbel took three redoubts in succession, at the head of his battalion, capturing twelve cannon and five standards, the Commander-in-Chief himself warmly complimented him before the army, and the Prince de Condé made him a present of his own sword. Civil war against his fellow-countrymen grew more and more repugnant, however, to Comte Herbel, notwithstanding his stanch fidelity to the Royalist cause. When the Prince de Condé's army was dissolved, on May 1, 1801, Comte Herbel became an exile, like the majority of the Royalist officers. He fled to England, and took up his abode in London. He was long without the means of living, till one day he observed a boy cutting out boats for sale in the streets. It at once occurred to him that he had been handy at this very same thing when a boy at St. Malo. He began cutting out boats and vessels with the same energy and skill with which he had before then captured redoubts. He obtained a ready sale for them, such admirable models were they. He became quite famous as a constructor of miniature craft, and was led to take a shop in the Strand, where his sign attracted no little attention and custom:—

GENERAL COMTE HERBEL DE COURTENAY,
Descendant of the Emperors of Constantinople,
Turner in Wood.

He amassed a snug little fortune in this shop, remaining in London until the year 1818, when he returned to France and received from the King's Government twelve hundred thousand francs as his share of the indemnity. Rich as anyone could desire, Comte Herbel was then found worthy by his fellow citizens to represent them in the Chamber of Deputies, to which he was, accordingly, elected, and in which he took his place among the deputies of the Left Centre.

Such, in a few words, was the eventful career of General Comte Herbel, who, on the morning the reader is introduced to him, was deep in the study of one of his favourite classic authors when he was interrupted by Franz, a faithful Austrian servant, who had followed his master for some years. The Comte looked up from his book with manifest impatience to hear the message Franz brought.

"Didn't I tell you not to interrupt me till dinner-time, Franz?" he demanded, with a stern voice.

"Yes, General," replied the servant, starting back at the rebuff; "but someone wishes to see you, General."

"But didn't I tell you I would see no one, man?"

"Yes, General; but," answered Franz, instinctively closing one eye and allowing a half-fearful smile to crease his face, "it is a woman, General."

CHAPTER XXXVI.—A DELICATE MISSION.

FRANZ ushered in a moment later the haughty Marquise whom we have met before as the chaperon of Régina.

The General, smothering the rage he felt at being interrupted so near his dinner-hour, rose and received the Marquise with every mark of courtesy. Leading her to the arm-chair he had just vacated, he inquired, with a gracious smile,

"May I ask what has given me the honour of a visit from you in person, my dear Marquise?"

"Ah! my dear general," answered the Marquise de la Tournelle, with a sigh and a modest drooping of her eyelids, "I have a great service to ask of you; but the sight of you recalls old times and fills me with confusion for the moment."

"Surely, the love-making of forty years ago——"

"Ah, it seems but yesterday to me!"

"But it was not to revive those remembrances, my dear Marquise," interrupted the General, not relishing the turn the conversation was taking; "it was to give me the pleasure of being of some service to you that you called, wasn't it? What service?"

"Can you not guess?"

"Not in the least."

"Well, General, I have come to invite you to my ball to-morrow."

"You are going to give a ball?"

"Yes."

"At your house?"

"No; at my brother's."

"That is to say, that your brother gives the ball."

"Well, it is the same thing."

"Not as far as I am concerned. He and I have no romantic recollections in common——"

"Will you come?"

"Can you be serious in asking me? Your brother calls me the 'Old man of the Mountain,' because I belong to the Left Centre, and because I vote against the Jesuits. Why doesn't he call me regicide at once? What was he doing all the time I was cutting out boats in the Strand? Why, he did just what my brigand of a brother did—he served Monsieur Bonaparte; only my pirate of a brother served him on the sea, whilst your brother served him on land. That was the only difference. So, I repeat, are you serious in giving me this invitation?"

"Quite serious."

"The plain invites the mountain."

"The plain does as Mahomet did, my dear General; the mountain would not go to Mahomet——"

"So Mahomet went to the mountain. Quite so. But Mahomet was an ambitious man, and did many things an honest man would not care to do."

"What! You will not consent to come, my dear General, when the ball is to be given in honour of the coming marriage of my niece Régina with my dear son, Comte Rappt?"

"Isn't that marriage a little risky, my dear Marquise?"

"What objection can there be?"

"Your niece is only seventeen: isn't that somewhat too young for a man of forty-one?"

"Oh, General! What of that little disparity, if they love one another?"

"If? . . . But, surely, my dear Marquise, you have not taken the trouble to come all the way from the Rue Plumet to the Rue de Varennes to obtain a grey-headed recruit for a cotillon?"

"For what should I have come then?"

"Well, you know they say the pith of a lady's thoughts always comes out in her postscript."

"So you wish to come to the postscript of my visit? Ah! little did I think at one time that *you* would ever have found a visit from me too long."

"Peste! Madame la Marquise, we are no longer in our green youth!" responded the General, fairly irritated by her ladyship's circumlocution. "This is the third time I have seen you for the last eighteen months, and each time you have bothered me about something in which your scapegrace of a son has been concerned."

"Is it not natural for a mother——"

"Yes; but not for me! I'm not his father!"

"Ah! it is clear you have driven from your mind the vows you once whispered to me, my dear General!"

"And it is clear they did not trouble your mind for many, many years, Madame la Marquise, till I happened to come into an indemnity of twelve hundred thousand francs! Let me tell you, once for all, that it is either my corsair of a brother or my nephew Pétrus, unworthy though either may be of the honour, who will inherit my title and fortune. Does that satisfy you Madame la Marquise?"

"No, General; for I didn't come to hear that."

"Then what, in heaven's name, have you come for? Do you wish me to marry you?"

"Without answering that question directly, General, you must confess that at one time you loved me well enough to warrant my hoping we might become united."

7

"Be that as it may; let me beg of you to come to the point, Madame la Marquise."

"Very well. You have, doubtless, heard that Comte Rappt——"

"Still harping on the Comte!"

"Let me finish. . . . No doubt you have heard that he has been sent for by the King."

"I have."

"Do you know what for?"

"Proceed as if I were in utter ignorance of the reason."

"Well; he is to join the government; but his Majesty put a very important question to him about you, General."

"About me!"

"Yes; the king remarked that you were the sole man capable of succeeding the present minister of war, and——"

"Madame la Marquise, it is of no use to go further. I expect my nephew at dinner at six, sharp, and, unless you will do us the honour to take dinner with us——"

"You are very kind, my dear General; but it is imperative that I should dine with my brother, for to-day the marriage contract between Régina and——"

"Your precious son will be drawn up. Very well; I'll not keep you. Let me only add that I am quite aware that Comte Rappt will become a minister if the bill should pass; but in order that it may become law thirty or forty votes are needed, and the real purport of your visit is to ask for mine and my party's."

"And, supposing that was the prime object of my visit, what is your answer?"

"My answer is that I heartily regret I have not a hundred, five hundred—nay, a thousand votes to give against the bill, which I consider abominable, infamous, and, what is much worse, absurd!"

"You will vote with the Liberals, then! Do you know that, should another revolution break out, the roughs, the Jacobins, the sans-culottes will make you play the role of Monsieur de la Fayette? Oh! if the Courtenays of old could only revisit this world, what would they say to see their name borne by a Jacobin, a pirate, and a painter!"

"Marquise!" exclaimed the General, roused to anger by this parting shot.

"I will leave you now, General; but you'll be calmer after a night's reflection, and I hope to hear you have thought better of it to-morrow."

"Monsieur Pétrus Herbel!" announced Franz at this moment.

"Come in, Pétrus," said the general. "You have just come in time!"

Observing that the Marquise greeted Pétrus as though he were not altogether unknown to her, the General added,

"What! Do you know my nephew, Marquise?"

"Yes; his success has even reached our ears, and my niece is having her portrait painted by him. You ought to be proud, General, to have so talented an artist in your family!"

Bending low as she uttered these words in a sneering tone, the Marquise de la Tournelle took her departure. The moment her carriage had driven off the General pulled the bell violently, and shouted to the trembling Franz when he reappeared,

"Whenever that woman comes to see me again, tell her I am at the Champ de Mars!"

Chapter XXXVII.—A Love Confession.

"The visit of the Marquise has caused you some annoyance, uncle, hasn't it?" Pétrus ventured to ask when the General's equanimity had been somewhat restored.

"You have but a slight knowledge of her, I see, Pétrus. Whereever she goes there is the deuce to pay afterwards."

"Yet they do say in society, uncle, that you were once greatly smitten with the Marquise."

"*They* say! Morbleu! if you pay heed to all my enemies say, Pétrus, you'll have enough to remember. Let us change the subject. Any news from your pirate of a father?"

"I heard from him three days ago."

"And how is the old corsair?"

"Well and hearty, uncle; and he sends his love to you."

"General! The dinner is served," announced Franz in a joyous tone.

"Then let us fall to," said the General, rising and bidding Pétrus follow him to the dining-room. "Morbleu! I can well understand that hunger may cause revolutions."

The General, seated face to face with his nephew, lost no time in satisfying the cravings of his appetite. It was the dinner of an epicure, and the host relished it like another Brillat-Savarin, disturbed only by the evident pre-occupation which made Pétrus drain a glass of the rarest madeira as if it were vin-ordinaire.

"Franz!" cried the General, testily; "give Monsieur Pétrus a bottle of marsala, for he doesn't know the difference 'twixt that and madeira!"

Pétrus accepted the rebuke with profound indifference. His thoughts were elsewhere, and he had soon offended his uncle by another inadvertence.

"Pétrus!" exclaimed the General, in a tone which suggested that nothing less than sacrilege had been committed. "Do you know what you have done, ignoramus? I poured you out a glass of haut-lafitte, which has been in the cellar of the Tuileries since 1812, the comet year, a wine worth twelve francs a bottle anywhere, but simply valueless now it has been under my care, and you drink water with it!"

There was a pause, during which the look of blank wonderment that came over the General's face gave eloquent expression to his sense of the enormity of the offence committed by his nephew. Then, in a tone of mild remonstrance, the General added, "Pétrus, remember this, my boy! Men drink, animals absorb."

"Pray excuse me this time, uncle," pleaded Pétrus, urging his preoccupation as a reason.

"But you should not be preoccupied, my boy. In society you should do as society does. And, by-the-way, if you want to get on in the world, Pétrus, you must go out more than you do. No individual can get on without the world, whilst the world can get on well enough without the individual."

"That truth is incontestable, uncle."

"What of that? Incontestable truths have ever been the most warmly contested. Witness Colombus, against whom the world contested the existence of America, and ungratefully named the continent subsequently after Americus; Galileo, against whom the world contested the revolution of the earth; Harvey, against whom the whole world contested the circulation of the blood; Jenner, against whom the world contested the efficacy of vaccination; and Fulton, against whom the world contested the power of steam!"

"You overwhelm me with your argument, uncle; but I know what it is leading to: you wish to see me married; and I must repeat that I cannot!"

"You're right, Pétrus. I *was* coming to your marriage, and marriage will come to you, my boy, sooner or later. Just think how unthankful you are! I find you a young girl full of spirit, who is ready to throw herself into your arms, and ten hundred thousand francs to boot, and you actually refuse her! Whom are you waiting for? The Queen of Sheba?"

"But the young lady was ugly! It would be impossible to live with her!"

"Well, well; I must find you another heiress then!"

"It will be of no use. I couldn't marry any girl for her fortune."

"Not bad for the son of a pirate. Then *I* must give you a dowry. Look here, Pétrus! I'll give you a hundred thousand francs—nay, two hundred thousand—three hundred thousand—half my fortune, there! if it is necessary."

Pétrus silently acknowledged this generous offer by a warm pressure of the General's hand. His hopeless love for Régina must now be revealed, he thought, to the one relative who now stood as father to him.

"Your overpowering kindness, uncle," the young painter said, "claims my fullest confidence."

"Ah! Coming to the point at last!" exclaimed the General, adding, in a tender tone of encouragement, as he eyed the ruby wine through his glass, "Proceed my boy!"

"Well, for the last six months I have conceived one of those grand passions which a man only feels once in his life, but which, in my case, can have but one result."

"If you love in vain, my boy, then the six months has been so much lost time—that's all."

"No; the time has been no more lost than was the passion of Dante for Beatrice, of Petrarch for Laura, of Tasso for Eleanor."

"But what masterpiece do you owe to your Beatrice, Laura, or Eleanor?"

"You know my picture of the Crusader?"

"Yes; your best—especially since you re-touched it."

"What did you think of the face of the girl at the fountain?"

"I liked it very much."

"You did! That is *her* image."

"*Her* image! Whose image?"

"If I mention her name, bear in mind that I have not the least pretension, the least hope, to be her acknowledged lover."

"There can be no reason for withholding her name. Who is she?"

"Mademoiselle Régina——"

"De Lamothe-Houdan!"

"Yes."

"Bravo, my boy!" exclaimed the General with unfeigned delight. "If the table were not between us I could embrace you."

"Why?"

"Why, because you will be my avenger now."

"How can that be?"

"My dear fellow, ask me any favour you please. You have just given me the greatest pleasure that I ever had in my life."

"But why should my love for Mademoiselle de Lamothe-Houdan make you so glad?"

"I'll tell you that by-and-by. Let me enjoy my coffee first. May be, now I've dined, I see everything *couleur de rose*. Yet I heartily and sincerely compliment you on your taste, Pétrus."

"You think her pretty, then?"

"Think her pretty! I should be difficult to please indeed if I didn't, my boy. Why, she's one of the most lovely creatures in all Paris. I congratulate you from the bottom of my heart, Pétrus, for your love for the young lady will be the severest blow my greatest enemy can receive. But there is one thing you have omitted to mention."

"What is that?"

"Does she love you?"

"I never ventured to ask that," answered Pétrus, the flush that mounted to his face indicating how closely the question touched him. "Yet, although I cannot say for certain that she feels the same sentiment for me that I entertain for her, still I think she sees me with pleasure."

"But do you think that, if you were to ask Mademoiselle de Lamothe Houdan in marriage as a descendant of the Courtenays and as my heir, she would accept you?"

"She would," replied Pétrus, with eagerness, at the same time looking his gratitude to the impulsive General.

"But I say the young lady would not."

"Why?"

"Because the law forbids a woman to marry two husbands at the same time; and, in a fortnight's time, Mademoiselle de Lamothe-Houdan will be married to Colonel Comte Rappt."

"Married to Comte Rappt! Are you sure of this, uncle?" demanded Pétrus, plunged into an abyss of misery by the sudden shock.

"Ask the young lady herself at her next sitting."

"Adieu! I *will* learn it from her own lips."

CHAPTER XXXVIII.—ROSE-DE-NOEL'S PORTRAIT.

THE story of the Fairy Carita turned the thoughts of Pétrus into a brighter channel the next morning. No sooner had he recalled this simple instance of Régina's true charity than he felt impelled to pay a visit to Rose-de-Noël. He wished to include a lifelike sketch of the poor girl in his imaginary drawing of Régina relieving Rose-de-Noël. The painter had little difficulty in finding the Rue Triperet, and less difficulty in hitting upon the wretched abode of *la Brocante*. He simply entered the dingiest house in one of the most squalid streets of Paris.

"Who's there?" was the question which greeted him in a soft voice when he knocked at *la Brocante's* door.

"Someone from the Fairy Carita," said Pétrus.

The door was opened in the twinkling of an eye. He had hit upon the right password. There stood before him, barefooted and in rags, but beaming with gratitude and pleasure, the young girl whom he at once recognised to be Rose-de-Noël. His errand was soon explained; and, unperceived, he rapidly sketched her sweet face and figure, even whilst he was begging her to sit for her portrait. If *la Brocante* would but grant her consent, Pétrus had Rose-de-Noël's full permission to use her as a model all day, particularly as her portrait was for the Fairy Carita. But *la Brocante* would be sure to object. There was but one person who could persuade her—Monsieur Salvator."

"Monsieur Salvator!" said Pétrus. "Do you mean the Commissionnaire of the Rue aux Fers?"

"The same, Monsieur."

"Do you know him, then?"

"He is my best friend."

"And if he wishes me to take your portrait, will *la Brocante* have no objection?"

"*La Brocante* always agrees to everything Monsieur Salvator agrees to."

"Then I will arrange it with him, my dear," replied Pétrus, pressing her thin hand, and giving a last look at her poetical figure.

It struck twelve as he left *la Brocante's* miserable den. Thence he strolled to the Marshal de Lamothe-Houdan's, his heart leaping with joy when he comforted himself with the idea that the General's intelligence might prove untrue, and his depression being equally great when he feared the worst. Whatever was to happen, he was fated not to know that day whether the idol of his heart was engaged to be married or not to Comte Rappt. He learnt that Mademoiselle Régina had been suddenly summoned out of Paris that morning to the death-bed of a friend.

In the evening, however, there came from Régina a polite little note, begging the young painter to forgive her absence, and asking him to come the next morning, when she would be present without fail. Whither she had gone Pétrus heard the same night from his friend Jean Robert, who had recognised Régina, it may be remembered, among the group at Carmélite's bedside. With all a poet's fervour Jean Robert described that pathetic scene for the benefit of his friend; and Pétrus, loving to dwell in fancy wherever his ideal princess might have been, with all a painter's skill, drew the picture that Jean Robert's words had conjured up.

CHAPTER XXXIX.—THE FINISHED PORTRAIT.

REGINA stood on the threshold of the pavilion, anxiously awaiting the arrival of Pétrus the following morning, and nervously playing with the fair curls of her young sister.

Pétrus almost felt her presence before he caught sight of her. There ran through him that electric shock which told him too well how dearly he loved her. There was a quick interchange of glances as he courteously bent before his divinity; and it seemed as if each sought to divine the innermost thoughts of the other's mind.

"Come, Régina," said Abeille, drawing her sister after her; "you know your portrait must be finished to-day."

"*Must* it be finished to-day, Mademoiselle?" asked Pétrus, with sad emphasis.

"Pay no attention to Abeille, Monsieur," answered Régina, her colour coming and going with feverish quickness. "She simply overheard someone say it would be convenient for the portrait to be finished to-day, and she repeated what she heard. Abeille, I am thirsty; get me a glass of water."

The little blonde fairy hastened to obey her sister's order. The silence that ensued was more irksome than even the idle words of the child. Régina was the first to break it. "May I ask, Monsieur, where you went yesterday, as you could not proceed with my portrait?"

"I took the liberty of paying a visit to Rose-de-Noël, Mademoiselle; and then I made a water-colour drawing."

"Of Rose-de-Noël?" said Régina, eagerly.

"No; from fancy."

"What was the subject?"

"A very sad one: a young girl and her lover sought death together."

"Did they succeed?"

"Only one: the lover. I have chosen the moment when, her senses slowly returning, she sees three of her bosom friends praying for her recovery. Here is the picture."

Whilst Régina gazed at the picture in deepest wonder at the apparently clairvoyant power of the young artist to whom she seemed to be drawn by some magnetic attraction, Abeille came in with the glass of water. She drank it at a draught. Then Pétrus, trembling, said, "I should also tell you, Mademoiselle, that I heard yesterday that you were engaged to be married to Comte Rappt."

"It is true," Régina answered, in a tone so hopeless, and with a look of such blank despair in her pale face, that Pétrus felt he now knew all he should know.

The truth was not so bitter to him, learning it as he did. There was a mute eloquence that spoke in her softened gaze, and betrayed how deep was the feeling she entertained for him. A moment their souls communed in silence. The sweet spell was broken by the Marquise de la Tournelle, who entered the pavilion and abruptly demanded of Pétrus, after recognising him with a hasty nod,

"Oh ! how much longer will Count Rappt's portrait take, Monsieur ?"

"If you allude to this portrait of Mademoiselle de Lamothe-Houdan, Madame la Marquise——?" stammered Pétrus.

"I will explain myself better," answered the Marquise, airily. "I venture to allude to Régina's portrait here as Comte Rappt's, because it is destined to be the chief ornament of his nuptial chamber."

Pétrus staggered at these words, and grew pale as death. The Marquise turned to her niece to point out the young painter's pallor to her, but saw that Régina was quite as white as he was. Thorough woman of the world, the Marquise instantly divined what was passing in both their minds. Taking Abeille by the hand, she said significantly to Régina,

"I have learnt what I wanted, my niece."

The Marquise then left the pavilion with Abeille. Hardly was she out of sight when Pétrus unclasped his knife and ripped the canvas from top to bottom, utterly destroying the likeness he had painted with such infinite pains and tender love.

"I may be the victim of the Comte's happiness, but I will not be the innocent means of enhancing it," Pétrus exclaimed in his agony.

The rent in the canvas was at once the cause of a pang and a joy to Régina; for, while it signified to her the sundering of all friendship with Pétrus, it also revealed to her the very depths of his passionate love for her. With an irresistible impulse she held out her hand to him, and there escaped from her lips a sad, sweet farewell :

"Thank you, Pétrus ! That is how I would be loved !"

"Adieu for ever !" he cried.

Then, pressing his lips in one last wild kiss on her fair hand, he fled. A sigh was all that followed him. Régina fell back consciousless on the sofa, in a death-like faint.

CHAPTER XL.—ROSINA'S BENEFIT.

THE plot of our romance renders it necessary that we should now transport the reader for a very little while from Paris to Vienna—from the troubled love-making of Pétrus to the romantic passion of an illustrious exile—from the pavilion of Régina to the theatre of the reigning beauty of the Austrian capital.

Never was the Théâtre Impérial of Vienna more densely thronged by the fashionable world than it was on the night of the Mardi Gras, 1827; for the celebrated danseuse, Rosina Engel, took her farewell benefit on that night, and princes, and nobles, and millionaires vied with each other in paying homage to the grace, and beauty, and virtue of the popular favourite. The theatre resembled the interior of an Arabian palace, resplendent with diamonds, pearls, lace, flowers, and lovely faces—the cream of the cream of society. But what attracted most attention before the curtain rose was neither the cluster of blonde beauties in the Imperial box, nor the equally fair bevy of princesses in the Royal box of Bavaria, nor the flashing brilliants, nor the beauteous wreaths. There was one particular feature which stamped the scene as being more like a dream or souvenir of the "Thousand-and-One Nights" than anything else. The personages to whom every eye was directed were in the *loge* facing the stage. They were an Indian Rajah and suite. The Rajah was attired in more than Indian splendour—precious stones and gold glittering from his snowy cashmere robes; a plume of emeralds, fixed by a lustrous diamond, rising from his turban; and a beauteous fan adding to the Oriental splendour of his appearance, which was enhanced by the simple costume of the four young Indian girls who were with him, and who were clad in cashmere robes of virgin white. To the right hand of the stranger, whom everyone regarded as an Indian Prince, stood a Frenchman in civilian attire, whose face, however, was not whiter than the Rajah's. Each wore, moreover, the ribbon of the *Légion d'honneur*. No one knew them. Their sudden appearance in Vienna was a mystery none could solve.

"*Ma foi !*" said the Rajah to his friend in the Delhi dialect, which both appeared to speak with the ease of natives; "I can't see him; can you, Gaëtano?"

"No; but some one very well informed assured me that, visible or not, he would be certain to be present to-night."

"May not illness detain him?"

"With his iron will, what illness would keep him away? He is sure not to fail. Is not this the last performance of one to whom he is passionately attached?"

"You're right, Gaëtano. He is either here now incognito, or he will be here. Have you heard anything fresh about Rosina?"

"Yes, General."

"Does it agree with what we learnt before?"

"Quite."

"She loves him?"

"She adores him."

"Purely out of love?"

"Purely, my dear General."

"What is the girl's history?".

"Strange enough. Her mother—or, rather, the woman who passed as her mother—took little care of her as a child. The budding beauty of the girl at length made her take interest in her. But Rosina ran away, and joined a band of gipsies, who taught her every Spanish dance. She soon danced into fame. At thirteen she made her début on the stage at Grenada with such success that she got engagements at the theatres of Seville and Madrid. Recommended by the Austrian Ambassador at Madrid, she came to Vienna. Her life has been stainless. She is as good as she is beautiful."

"If you are persuaded of that, Gaëtano, I am satisfied. I have already written the letter. It is in this purse. The only thing I wish to be certain of is whether her mind is large enough to grasp the overwhelming importance of our mission."

"Women understand with their hearts, General. She loves him. She must, therefore, wish for the glory, the renown, the greatness of her lover. So she will not fail to understand!"

"But how can she gain access to him?"

"At Schönbrunn. She only sees him there, you know; and she is introduced by the gardener of the castle as his niece."

"That seems simple and natural enough on the face of it. But how can *you* find your way to him?"

"Ah! I know a secret way of getting inside the castle from the garden. You will remember that I spent a little time at Schönbrunn with the Emperor in 1809. Besides, I have the plan he gave me at St. Helena."

The overture to Mozart's "Don Juan" interrupted this whispered conversation; but the Rajah did not relax his scrutiny of each tier during the whole of the opera.

Whom did he look for so earnestly?

As the reader will probably already have guessed, it was that unfortunate young exile who received the title of King of Rome from his infancy, and to whom the Emperor Francis II. had given the title of Duc de Reichstadt.

The secret mission of the Indian Prince and his intimate friend was to raise the frail heir of the great Napoleon to the Imperial throne of France; and, as the Duc de Reichstadt was passionately fond of Rosina Engel, the danseuse was chosen by them as the fittest instrument by which to gain the ear of the young Duc.

Rosina Engel! She soon glided on to the stage like some enchanting fairy from "The Arabian Nights." The ballet in which she delighted her numberless admirers almost seemed to have been produced in honour of the Indian Prince, whose brilliant box had been the centre of attraction until Rosina absorbed universal attention. Beneath a sky of cerulean blue there shone the glowing pagodas of an Indian village on the banks of the golden Ganges. There entered, to the tune of a bewitching melody, a circle of Indian maidens, garbed in long flowing robes of white, undulating, floating, rushing, as it were, like playful waves on a golden strand.

The snowy circle swayed, while their voices rose with a voluptuous swell; and in their midst appeared, springing up like a bouquet from an alabaster vase, a score or so of *almées*, clad in skirts of rainbow hues, the centre flower, the Queen, being a goddess of beauty and grace, the incarnation of all that was lovely in woman, la Signora Rosina Engel.

A mighty shout of welcome greeted her. Then the most hearty

and vociferous cheers broke forth, and a shower of bouquets and wreaths was rained down on the stage, whence their divinity smiled her sweetest.

The ballet at length proceeded. From that moment to the end the theatre had no existence for the two thousand people held spellbound by the magic of Rosina. They were fascinated and led away to the captivating realms of fancy, willingly allowing themselves to be transported to the most glowing scenes of the Orient by the divinity whom they worshipped. The curtain fell at last amid a tempest of applause, but soon rose again in response to the enthusiastic shouts for Rosina.

She appeared. It was not a shower simply, but a torrent, an avalanche, a deluge of flowers, which was now poured at her feet. Bouquets of every form fell around her like a perfumed fountain. Yet, amid all those floral offerings at her shrine; amid the most splendid floricultural designs, the sole bouquet which Rosina appeared to notice, the only one that she deigned to gather from that enchanted garden, was a small bouquet of violets with a white rosebud in the centre—the offering of a soul as tender and pure as it was true.

So thought Rosina, evidently. She pressed the violets to her lips, and sent a world of love in the soft look of gratitude she directed towards the centre box from which the bouquet of her choice had come.

"He *is* here!" said the Rajah, in French, to the friend at his side.

"Yes," was the response, in Hindostanee; "he is clearly in that box; but, for goodness' sake, speak Hindostanee, General!"

"You are right," replied the stranger attired as an Indian Prince, and added, "It is time we flung our *nazzer* at la Signora, is it not?"

The General's *nazzer* consisted of a bag of musk, made from the skin of the animal, an Indian rarity, round which he entwined a bracelet of diamonds of the first water.

Seeing this brilliant offering fall at the feet of Rosina, exceeding a thousandfold their most precious gifts, the enraptured spectators could not repress an exclamation of surprise.

What did the *nazzer* contain?

This was a question which piqued the curiosity of Rosina even more than it did her admirers.

She solved it for herself directly she gained her dressing-room. After an involuntary gaze of admiration at the flashing diamonds, Rosina opened the perfumed bag, took thence a letter, read it twice, refolded it and replaced it, and then remained lost in thought for some moments.

CHAPTER XLI.—"SHE COMES! SHE COMES!"

IT was a moonlight night, and the reader who could have stood on one of the heights overlooking Schönbrunn would have rejoiced in the sight of the panorama at his feet. But before arriving at the village of Meidling, his attention might have been drawn to a lonely figure standing on one of the balconies of the castle. It was a young man in the white uniform of an Austrian officer. He was fair, and his blue eyes were wondrously soft and dreamy. His tall figure stood out plainly in the moonlight. He, too, might have been admiring the scenery. Vienna and her suburbs lay at his feet. Through the clear atmosphere he could see the city with all its towers and steeples, and myriad lights, surrounded by the black rampart, whilst beyond, the Danube meandered until it was lost to sight in the plains of Aspern, Essling, and Wagram.

An impatient gesture which escaped the young man now and again seemed to show that it was not the beauty of the scene that had led him to brave the cold night air. He was eagerly awaiting someone, and that someone was the bewitching danseuse; whilst he was the Duc de Reichstadt, her infatuated lover.

He had escaped from his Imperial prison to attend Rosina's benefit, had thrown at her feet his humble bouquet of violets, only to see it eclipsed by the brilliant offering of diamonds, and he had then fled home in despair. Had he not, however, one sweet consolation? Was he not to see Rosina at Schönbrunn that night?

A look of deep pleasure soon lit up his pale face. He leant over the balcony to listen. He heard the clatter of horses' hoofs galloping on the road from Vienna to Schönbrunn. He next discerned the two flashing lights of the approaching carriage.

A moment later all doubt was at an end.

"She comes! she comes!" he exclaimed, in a tone of rapture, which plainly told how much his heart was absorbed by this first passion of his young life.

CHAPTER XLII.—LOVE AND LOYALTY.

THE young prince withdrew from the balcony and regained his room with a light heart and with cheeks aflame. For a minute or two he waited, motionless as a statue. A bright smile then lit up his face. He heard a light, familiar step ascending the stairs. The door opened.

"Rosina! Dearest Rosina!" he cried, as he clasped to his heart a young girl in a picturesque Tyrolean costume.

It was the lovely danseuse, whose triumphant farewell all that was noble in Vienna had honoured that same night. Rosina had slipped on the Tyrolean dress in order to escape the notice of her many admirers in her ride from her Vienna hotel to Schönbrunn; and she obtained ready access to the castle by passing as the niece of Hans, the head gardener, whom the two lovers had won over to countenance their secret meetings.

What need to repeat the lovers' vows which passed for the hundredth time between the young prince and his winsome inamorata? Assured over and over again of Rosina's constancy, he was yet troubled by some jealous doubts which her frankness soon set at rest. The Prince, having expressed a fear that she would not come that night, she brightly answered,

"Not come, when I had to thank you for your sweet bouquet!"

"But where is it?"

"Where? Why here," replied the young girl, plucking from her bosom the cherished bunch of violets, crushed, but with the fragrant scent still clinging to the flowers. "Ah, if these violets could only speak, they would tell you how truly my heart has beaten for you!"

She kissed the flowers as this confession escaped her, in a low, sweet voice; and the Prince snatched the bouquet from her to press his lips against the petals bedewed by her delicious kisses.

Suddenly his attention was drawn to the sparkling bracelet of diamonds which Rosina wore, and his thoughts reverted to the mysterious sachet round which the brilliant jewels had been entwined, and once more he felt the jealous pangs which arose in his breast when he saw this priceless present flung at the charming danseuse's feet.

"Now, you are thinking ill of me, I see," said Rosina, reading his thoughts in his face. "A penny for your thoughts!"

"Well, Rosina, I am jealous."

"Jealous!" exclaimed the young girl, with a captivating air of coquetry. "Of whom?"

"Oh! I'm jealous of all the world in general, and of somebody in particular."

"That somebody must be your shadow, then; for I love but you in the whole world."

"But the somebody I mean was at the theatre to-night, Rosina."

"At the theatre! Oh! I must confess you had a rival there."

"You know it, then?"

"Mon Dieu! Yes. I have received declarations of love in every imaginable form from the rival in question."

"Then you know his name?"

"Yes; it is the Public, Monseigneur!"

"Oh! I know that only too well. The whole city is in love with you. But I refer now to a man who regarded you with such a passionate gaze that I longed to pick a quarrel with him."

"You allude to the Indian?" said Rosina, with a smile.

"Yes? His eyes were fixed on you all the time you were on the stage; and, at the end, he made my bouquet seem small, indeed, by the side of his magnificent gift."

"You say that, Monseigneur, when you know how near my heart the violets rested! Ah! you will learn presently that it was pure loyalty to *you* that prompted the Indian's handsome offering. You will learn it from this letter!"

Sinking on one knee, the young girl drew the letter from the perfumed sachet, and presented it to the Duc de Reichstadt, adding,

"It is not my beloved Franz that I address now; it is Napoleon, King of Rome! I have the honour to hand you the letter from one of the most illustrious generals of your father."

The Prince involuntarily rose to the full height of his figure, as Rosina's speech made him realise the greatness of the name he had inherited. Then, bending, with a deprecating gesture, as if implying that a loving heart was worth more than all the greatness of the world put together, he gently raised Rosina to her feet, and took the letter from her.

One extract will give the pith of this important missive:—

"It was four thousand leagues from here that I first formed the idea of changing his name from Franz to Napoleon. Let me hope that you will grant me your aid to place the father's imperial crown on the brow of his son. I am ready to devote my life to this work; and, if a million of men are needed for the purpose, I know the means to find them. A man who followed Napoleon in his exile at the Island of Elba and the Island of St. Helena—a man whose name is the symbol of fidelity and devotion—Gaëtano Sarranti, my companion, my friend, has been intrusted by the father with a message to the son. He knows all my projects. You have the entry into the castle of Schönbrunn. It is to you I appeal to procure for Gaëtano Sarranti an interview with Napoleon II. If the Prince consents to receive him to-morrow, let the signal be this: wave the light three times before the third window in the left wing of the castle, which looks towards Meidling.

"GENERAL COMTE LEBASTARD DE PREMONT."

An exclamation of surprise escaped the Prince when he came to the signature, for he recognized the name as that of one of Napoleon's bravest generals. He next experienced a thrill of deepest gratitude for the devoted loyalty these two men had shown to the memory of his father in venturing all that distance to serve him. His eyes glistened as he thought of the warmth of their attachment, which he yet felt himself too weak to repay in the one way that would be most acceptable to them.

Proud of the confidence that had been placed in her, grateful for the general's selection of herself as his ambassadress, Rosina felt the strongest desire to second his wishes. She knew that the slightest false step on the part of either the Duc de Reichstadt or herself, the slightest revelation to the authorities, might cause the two faithful Napoleonists to be plunged into the dungeons of Spielburg, the dreaded state prison of Austria. Nevertheless, her warm heart was full of the enthusiasm which animated the letter; and she roused the Prince from the reverie in which he seemed lost by a leading question.

"Do you remember anything of your father or of France, Monseigneur?" asked Rosina.

"Yes; I have one recollection, but only one, of my father. I was asleep in my cradle one night, when I was awakened by a kiss. My eyes rested on my mother and father. The kiss was my father's, but it seemed the kiss of a statue."

"Yet you still have a remembrance of the kiss?"

"I shall remember it and him who gave it while I live. He departed for that grand and glorious campaign of 1814, where all the glory was on the side of the vanquished. Often have I compared my father to Hannibal beaten by Scipio, and yet more famous with posterity than his victor."

"More famous than Scipio!" repeated Rosina, with enthusiasm.

"Greater than Cæsar, greater than Charlemagne, greater than all! What an example to follow, Monseigneur!"

"Overwhelming! What could I do after such a man? Ah, Rosina, I have not the strength to be great!"

The young girl smiled to herself. Monsieur Sarranti, she thought, will succeed where I have failed.

"No," continued the Prince; "I have a presentiment that I shall never see the Tuileries again."

"But you shall!" answered Rosina, with animation.

She ran to the window—to the third window in the left wing of the castle, looking towards Meidling—and, pulling aside the curtain with one hand, she waved a light three times with the other.

The Prince made an effort to detain her, but was not in time to prevent the signal from being given.

"Well, everyone must fulfil his destiny!" was the remark he consoled himself with.

Five minutes later, a horse might have been heard galloping at full speed on the high road from Meidling to Vienna.

CHAPTER XLIII.—SARRANTI'S MISSION.

THE following evening—or, rather, the night of the same day—saw the Duc de Reichstadt awaiting Gaëtano Sarranti in his private apartments in the Castle of Schönbrunn.

It was near midnight, the hour the Prince expected his visitor. How could he enter the castle unperceived? The Prince walked impatiently up and down the room, asking himself this question. He was in ignorance of the secret staircase and door leading into the adjoining dressing-room.

There was the first stroke of midnight, and yet Sarranti had not arrived.

The Prince stopped and leant against the chimneypiece. An indefinable fear seized him. His legs trembled under him.

As he stood, the door of the salon was to his left, and the door of his dressing-room to his right.

His eyes were naturally fixed upon the door to the left, for the dressing-room had no separate entrance, that was visible at least.

As the twelfth stroke of the hour was still vibrating, the Prince turned suddenly and looked towards the door of his dressing-room, whence a strange cracking noise proceeded, followed by the creaking sound of footsteps.

He instinctively placed his hand on his sword, and stepped forward to meet the intruder. Ere he gained the door the curtains which separated the salon from the dressing-room were parted, and there stood before the Duc de Reichstadt the sombre figure of a man.

"Who are you?" demanded the Duc, deftly drawing his sword from its scabbard at the same moment.

The stranger drew back. Not seeming to fear the blade pointed threateningly towards him, he yet sank on one knee, and, bending his head, respectfully, said,

"I am Gaëtano Sarranti, your majesty."

"Speak lower, lower," replied the Prince, looking round suspiciously, and offering his hand to Sarranti. "And don't use the word 'majesty.'"

"By what title, then, may I be permitted to call the heir of Napoleon, the son of my Emperor?" humbly asked Sarranti, kissing the proffered hand with profound devotion.

"Call me prince or monseigneur, whichever you please. Call me by the name I bear here. But how, in heaven's name, did you gain access to my rooms?"

"I will tell you directly, Monseigneur; but first let me prove that I really come from your father."

Sarranti thereupon took from his pocket a packet, and handed it to the Prince, who removed the envelope and unfolded the letter within, disclosing a curl of black silky hair. Tears fell from the young man's eyes on this simple souvenir of his father, who had written the following brief note to his son, under the lock of hair:—

"MY BELOVED SON,—The person who will hand you this letter and souvenir from me is M. Sarranti. He has been a comrade in the battle-field, a friend in exile. I confidently entrust him with the execution of my most secret wishes and my dearest hopes. Listen to him as you would to your father; and, whatever counsels he may give you, follow them as if they were mine.

"Your father, who only lives for you,

"NAPOLEON."

The young Prince embraced his father's trusted follower with warmth.

"Yes," he said, with eager enthusiasm, "I promise to faithfully obey your counsels and follow your advice, as if I were counselled and advised by my father himself."

"But again let me ask you, Monsieur Sarranti," he added, after a pause, "how did you manage to penetrate into my apartments?"

"You are aware, Monseigneur," answered Sarranti, "that you occupy the same rooms that your father formerly occupied."

"Yes."

"Have the goodness to follow me, then," continued Sarranti, leading the way into the dressing-room.

Holding up a light, he pointed out to the Prince a spring, artfully concealed in the moulding of a mirror let into the wall.

He touched the spring. The whole panel opened, revealing to the Prince the secret staircase by means of which Sarranti had reached the room without being seen by the Imperial servants, who guarded the castle like a prison.

Replying to the Prince's look of astonishment, Sarranti said,

"This secret way was made by order of the Emperor Napoleon in 1809. He often made use of it to escape from the fawning attentions of the courtiers, ever ready to bore a conqueror with their homage. May not what served your father also serve you one day?"

SARRANTI'S MISSION.

It would take too long to give the eloquent arguments by which Sarranti tried his utmost to persuade the Duc de Reichstadt to enter heart and soul into the plot to succeed to the Imperial throne of France; how that General Lebastard de Prémont was first despatched by Napoleon to India to gain that knowledge and power which the emperor counted upon for the fulfilment of his most ambitious dream —the conquest of India; and how that the exile of St. Helena at last sent Sarranti to join the general in India to conspire together for his son.

Vainly did Sarranti appeal to his filial love, his ambition, his patriotism.

"France does not desire the empire," said the Prince.

"France does! France would substitute the empire for the existing government!" persisted Sarranti. "No one doubts that."

"Excepting me," replied the Prince; "and you must allow I count for something in the affair!"

"Monseigneur," answered Sarranti, "I am but your father's echo. The emperor bade me 'Deliver my son from the hands of the man who betrayed me;' and I am here to deliver you. 'Place my crown on the brow of my son,' he said; and that is why I repeat, 'Sire return to the well-beloved city of Paris, which you should never have quitted!'"

"Sarranti," came the response, in a firm tone, which indicated that the young Prince had determined on one course, and would not alter it, "before I consent to follow your advice I must weigh well all you have said in private. Give me till to-morrow to think over it. Between now and then I will try to put on the armour of my father, and you will find, I hope, a man in the place of the youth you leave to-night."

CHAPTER XLIV.—JEAN TAUREAU'S REVENGE.

WE must now return to Paris, leaving Rosina to her dream of love, the Duc de Reichstadt to his dream of ambition, and Sarranti and General Lebastard de Prémont to their conspiracy to restore the imperial crown of France to the heir of Napoleon.

It was Sunday, March 23, 1827; and the Coquille d'Or—a cabaret noted for the excellence of its oysters—was the scene of a noisy orgie, in which Barthélemy Lelong—the Jean Taureau of our opening chapters—was carousing with his fickle mistress, Mademoiselle Fifine and his two boon companions, Father Gibélotte and Croc-en-Jambe.

The carpenter, unappeased by the presence of his charmer, was fuming and threatening because of her persistent fickleness.

A creature utterly without heart, and living for the mere sensual enjoyment of the moment, Mademoiselle Fifine did but answer his complaints by jeers and scoffs. If she had one passion it was for the theatre and actors, and her latest fancy was a worthy low comedian of one of the open-aired boulevard theatres, Fafiou by name. She quite persecuted the poor young comedian with her attentions, but her persecution was utterly fruitless. Not the slightest encouragement did the woman ever receive from him. Yet Fafiou was ever on her lips. This fact made Jean Taureau terribly jealous of the comedian.

"Mon Dieu!" the infuriated carpenter exclaimed. "If you only saw this Fafiou, Gibélotte, you would say with me he's not worthy the name of man."

"Tastes differ," retorted Mademoiselle Fifine.

Jean Taureau's reply was a blow with his fist on the table and a sulky start from his seat. He strode angrily to the door of the cabaret, which a thin, lean slip of a youth was about to enter.

"Fafiou!" exclaimed Jean Taureau, enraged at the sight of the meek-looking young man, "You have come just in the nick of time. We'll let Mademoiselle Fifine see what you're made of."

The lusty carpenter seized Fafiou by the collar, lifted him close to the table at which his companions were still drinking, and shook the poor fellow within an inch of his life.

"Now, tell me why you've come sneaking after Mademoiselle Fifine?" shouted Jean Taureau, when he had almost shaken all the breath from the young actor's body.

"I assure you I had not the least idea *she* was here, Monsieur!" gasped Fafiou.

"Who *were* you looking for then?"

"For Monsieur Salvator."

"It's a lie!"

"Hold! You will strangle me! Help! help!"

"Say who were you looking for. Tell the truth, and I'll let you go!"

"For Monsieur Salvator, I repeat."

Jean Taureau was about to indulge in a fresh shake of his victim, when a calm voice stopped him.

"It is quite true he came to see me," said the voice. "Leave go!"

Jean Taureau turned round, and recognised Monsieur Salvator himself.

"Has he really told the truth?" he demanded, submissively.

"Leave go! I command you!" was the stern reply. "You know *I* never lie?"

"Mon Dieu!" answered Jean Taureau, releasing Fafiou, with a gesture of disdain. "You've come not a moment too soon, Monsieur Salvator. I was on the point of strangling the little wretch; and then that infernal quack, Monsieur Galileo Copernicus, would have had to do his fooling without his clown to-night."

Fafiou was glad enough to hasten out of the cabaret, under the protection of M. Salvator.

"How can I repay you, M. Salvator?" he exclaimed, in grateful tones. "This is the second time you have saved my life. Would that I could only do you some service in return!"

"You can, Fafiou."

"How?"

"You still love Musette?"

"With all my heart."

"Well, you shall have the means to marry her if you will only consent to do me a service this very evening."

"I'll do it willingly, whatever it is."

"Oh! the task will not be difficult. It will be simply to repay Monsieur Copernicus what he gives you every day."

"Monsieur Copernicus? *He* gives me nothing!"

"Pardon! At the end of each performance he invariably gives you a kick in the same place."

"Yes—behind! that's true!"

"Very well! When he gives you the kick this evening I want you to return it."

"What!" cried Fafiou, in alarm.

"To return it."

"To kick Monsieur Copernicus back! What if he should object? What if he shows me the door?"

"Well, in that unlikely eventuality I'll engage you myself, and give you thirty francs a month."

"Why, then I could marry Musette! Oh! depend on me! I'll do what you ask of me, Monsieur, even though I break one of the fundamental clauses of my engagement."

Chapter XLV.—Salvator's Signal.

THE booth of Galileo Copernicus was situated on the Boulevard du Temple, between Madame Saqui's theatre, now the Théâtre des Fumanbules, and the Cirque Impériale, formerly known as the Cirque Franconi. It was a mountebank's theatre of the ordinary kind, possessing a platform outside, whereon Galileo and Fafiou were wont to go through a little fooling to draw the spectators inside, and displaying a gaudy expanse of canvas on which were painted colossal women, giants, white negroes, dwarfs, and all the monstrosities likely to awaken the wonderment of the gaping crowd.

The idlers and holiday-makers assembled early that afternoon before the booth, for four o'clock was the hour of the first performance. But five o'clock came, and no performers. The flaring naphtha-lamps above the platform were lit. Still, no one was forthcoming. At last the vast throng began to hiss, and hisses grew into threatening shouts. Then the manager thought it prudent to appear in person to allay the excitement.

Galileo Copernicus considered apparently that the multitude would be calm at the mere sight of his majestic figure, clad as he was for the part of Cassandra, and yet deigning to wear a conciliatory smile on his face. In point of fact, however, he was greeted with a perfect volley of hisses, catcalls, and angry cries. But the manager was not to be condemned unheard. He placed a large key to his lips, and out-whistled the shrillest whistle of the crowd. This quieted the mob; and Galileo Copernicus took immediate advantage of the lull to address his constituents.

"My Lords and Gentlemen," he said, after saluting them with an air of supreme dignity, "I imagine that it was not to me those hisses were addressed——"

"Yes, it was! To you and Fafiou!" shouted some of the leading malcontents in reply. "Down with Copernicus! Down with Fafiou!"

"My Lords and Gentlemen," pleaded the mountebank, "it would be unjust to hold me responsible for the delay you complain of. At four o'clock exactly I had assumed the robes of Cassandra, and was ready to appear before you."

"Why didn't you, then?" was the ready shout in response.

"What was the cause of this mysterious delay, my Lords and Gentlemen? Shall I venture to tell you?"

"Yes, yes! Speak out, man!"

"Well, my Lords and Gentlemen, since you drag it from me, the delay arose from an immense, a dreadful misfortune which happened to your favourite artiste, to our dear comrade, to Phœnix Fafiou, in short, the moment he was about to appear before you in his popular rôle of valet!"

From the movement of lively sympathy with which this announcement was received, it seemed plain that Fafiou was really a great favourite with the people.

"What is this lamentable misfortune which has occurred to our friend Fafiou? That is the question I know you all ask me with one voice," continued Galileo Copernicus in his grandiloquent manner. "My Lords and Gentlemen, a misfortune has happened to him, as it may happen to you, to me, to Monsieur, to Madame, to our friends, to our enemies, for we are all mortal—as the Prince de Metternich one day confidentially remarked to me."

The curiosity of the crowd was piqued afresh.

"Yes, my Lords and Gentlemen," added Copernicus, profiting by the sensation he had caused, and resolved to obtain a quiet hearing by a masterpiece of oratorical effect, "yes, poor Fafiou was on the point of death but a short while ago."

A murmur of pity rose from his listeners; and he thanked them for their sympathy with a graceful wave of the hand.

"My Lords and Gentlemen," he continued, having now secured their closest attention and absolute silence, "the facts are simply these, to relate them without circumlocution and in all their grand simplicity:—

"For some time past it has been remarked with no little inquietude that Fafiou was getting thin, sad, and hollow-eyed; that his hair grew redder and redder; that his teeth fell out; that his chin day by day approached nearer his nose, which, like the nose of the unfortunate Father Aubrey, whom I knew on the borders of the Mississippi, pointed mournfully towards the tomb.

"What was the matter with Fafiou? What poignant grief filled the breast of your cherished favourite, rendering it desolate? Ah! what indeed?

"Was it misery that pursued him? Was it misery that drove him into the streets of Paris bareheaded, shoeless, and in his shirt-sleeves?

"No. You are yourselves ocular witnesses of the fact that he had a new hat, a new vest, and new shoes—which I myself authorised him to select from among my old clothes.

"Had Fafiou to lament the loss of a dear relative? Had his uncle died without leaving him anything? Or had his nephew departed leaving him to pay his debts?

"No, my Lords and Gentlemen. Fafiou has neither father nor mother; Fafiou had no uncle; Fafiou had no nephew; Fafiou had no relatives whatever.

"But you will, perhaps, ask me, my Lords and Gentlemen, what *was* the affliction of Fafiou?"

"Yes, yes! Come to the point!" was the impatient answer.

"He suffered, my Lords and Gentlemen," continued Galileo Copernicus, his voice sinking to a confidential stage-whisper, "he suffered, alas! from what, sooner or later, we are all alike—rich and poor, tall and short, fat and lean—subject to. The cause of Fafiou's misery was an affection of the heart. Fafiou was in love—stark, staring, mad in love!

"That was the secret cause of Fafiou's thinness and melancholy. What were his innermost thoughts? What, think you, occurred to his mind at that dreadful moment of temptation?

"I cannot think of it without a shiver, and cannot confide it to you without a shiver. He thought of committing self-destruction by water, by gunpowder, by fire, by a rope, or by poison.

"The means of accomplishing this terrible resolve were not lacking. On the contrary, Fafiou was embarrassed at the choice, for there are means *and* means—as Monsieur le Comte de Nesselrode, by-the-way, confidentially remarked to me.

First, there was the river. He might have thrown himself into the Seine from Notre-Dame bridge, but suddenly remembering with terror that he could swim, and simultaneously finding that it registered ten degrees of cold, it occurred to him that he could not drown himself, and that, if he did, he would only catch his death of cold.

"Firearms became the next resource. He could still blow out his brains; but Fafiou found, on reflection, that the report of a gun always frightened him so much that he would inevitably start off before the detonation reached his ears, and so send the ball harmlessly up into the air.

"Fire next. He could have enjoyed, like Sardanapalus, his last breakfast, dinner, or supper on a pile of wood; could have set a light to it, and thus have been consumed whilst he was himself consuming. Recollecting, however, that his name was *Phœnix* Fafiou, and that he had read in Pliny or Herodotus that the phœnix rose from its own ashes, it appeared to him perfectly useless to die on a Sunday simply in order to be born again on Monday or Tuesday.

"The rope! Why not hang himself? Why, because he thought of the countless people he would render happy by leaving them a rope to be divided into souvenirs of himself, and, with a misanthropic smile, he resolved to deprive them of that pleasure.

"There remained poison, the sombre, fatal poison; for, my Lords and Gentlemen, whether it be the poison of Mithridates, the poison of Hannibal, the poison of Lucrezia Borgia, the poison of the Médicis, or the poison of the Marquise de Brinvilliers, it is clear as day that poison is always poison—as Monsieur le Prince de Talleyrand one day remarked to me in confidence.

"He had recourse, then, to poison—to the sombre, fatal poison! and when I beheld him but a short while ago, pale, disfigured, panting, hideous, my limbs trembled beneath me, and I divined with half an eye that he had committed suicide. Yet I asked him—in that friendly and affectionate manner I ever use with Fafiou—

"'Why have you kept the public and me waiting an hour, Fafiou?'

"'Monsieur Copernicus,' replied Fafiou, as well as he could, poor fellow, 'I have put an end to my life!'

"His frankness touched me. But, at the same time, I must confess that one thing astounded me; that was that he should be able miraculously to tell me himself of his own death! Still, as I have in my lifetime come across things a hundred times more surprising than that, I continued my inquiries:

"'In what way,' I asked him, with a voice as full of emotion as my age and position would permit—'in what way did you put an end to your life?'

"'By poisoning myself,' Fafiou replied.

"'With what?'

"'With poison.'

"Let me confess that this answer appeared to me full of the most amazing logic and grandeur.

"'And where did you find the poison?' I pursued.

"'In your bedroom cupboard,' was Fafiou's cavernous response.

"At those words my peruke stood on end, and my beard, which I had just shaved, started out afresh. I felt pale from head to foot, and I oscillated on my base.

"'Miserable wretch!' I cried, in a broken voice, 'did I not forbid you to go to that cupboard?'

"'True, Monsieur Copernicus,' he answered; 'but I saw you put away two pots inside the cupboard.'

"'But did I not warn you,' I continued, 'that those two pots contained the arsenic marmalade which the Shah of Persia, whose head doctor I am, had ordered me to prepare to rid himself of the rats which infested his palace?'

"'I know it,' Fafiou said.

"'And you have put away one?'

"'I have eaten two.'

"'Pots and all?'

"'No, Monsieur; only their contents.'

"My Lords and Gentlemen, it was this sad calamity, and the tears which Fafiou's suicide drew from the eyes of his comrades, that occasioned all this delay, which, I assure you, I most sincerely regret. If you are not pitiless—if an emotion of sympathy has sprung up amongst you for the victim of this tragedy, you will pardon me this time, for the sake of the deceased, and you will allow me to perform this evening, in accordance with our announcement, the little comedy of 'Two Letters—Very Urgent,' in which Phœnix Fafiou will take the part of Gille, while your obedient servant fills the rôle of Cassandra.

"But you may naturally ask me how it is that Fafiou will be able to play his part this evening. The answer is easy, my Lords and Gentlemen; and I have replied to queries of a more puzzling character put to me in some of the greatest Courts in Europe. Some of you are probably aware of the gormandising propensities of Fafiou. He was mad after such delicacies as prunes, peaches, chestnuts, and the like. His epicureanism became a disease, and his health bade fair to be ruined by it. What was the best remedy? This was the question I put to myself, and it did not remain long without a solution, for one has not drunk white wine with the most distinguished diplomatists of the Continent without having preserved some reflection of that astuteness and perspicacity for which they are famous. A foreign Princess, whose life I had the honour and happiness to save after she had been abandoned by every doctor in her native land, sent me, at the end of last autumn, two pots of preserved pears, a preserve for which I had avowed to her my weakness. Now, knowing Fafiou's love for sweets, and not wishing to be deprived of the enjoyment of those two pots of preserve myself, I confided to him, under the seal of secresy, the fact that they contained a special arsenic marmalade which I had prepared for the Shah of Persia. Fafiou had no idea then of putting an end to his life. So he shunned the two pots as he would a viper. But when the madness of love overcame him, he had recourse to what he conceived to be the arsenic marmalade, and swallowed the contents of both pots. The first symptoms were those of poisoning. I applied prompt remedies; and I have now the satisfaction to inform you that the popular favourite, Phœnix Fafiou, is now out of danger, as you shall see for yourselves in a few minutes, my Lords and Gentlemen. Play up musicians!"

The eloquent mountebank brought his long explanation to a close with a stately bow, and as he retired within the booth the noise of the trombone, the clarionet, and the big drum set the crowd hoping that the word of Galileo Copernicus would now be kept to the letter.

The moment after he had disappeared, a close observer might have noticed a sudden and simultaneous increase in the throng, now thoroughly restored to good humour by the recital of Cassandra.

The new-comers were all clad in the long brown cloaks then in fashion; and one remarkable thing was that they exchanged some mysterious watchword with one another.

When Copernicus and Fafiou at length appeared together, they were received with shouts of laughter prolonged for ten minutes. The performances then took place, and the personages in the long cloaks appeared to be as much interested as the ouvriers with whom they freely intermingled. Without dwelling on the various incidents of the little piece, we may briefly state that Galileo Copernicus enacted with characteristic aplomb the rôle of the father whose daughter was beloved by, and was in love with, his servant, played by Fafiou. Galileo in the end dismissed Gille from his service instead of accepting him as his son-in-law, the comedy concluding thus :

Cassandra : " I dismiss you, then, Gille."

Gille : " Without giving me anything ?"

Cassandra : " No, Gille, you will not find me ungenerous. Every labourer is worthy of his hire !"

Gille : " Then you will give me something ?"

Cassandra : " Yes, Gille."

Suiting the action to the word, Galileo Copernicus gave Fafiou the usual kick at this juncture, and there the play generally ended. Cassandra followed up his kick by a low bow to the crowd ; but he was suddenly precipitated on to the heads of the people by a vigorous return kick from Gille, who shouted after him the quite unusual retort,

" Short reckonings make long friends, master."

There was then a great movement in the throng. The strangers in the brown cloaks withdrew, whispering to one another,

" *He returned the kick ! The meeting is for to-night, then.*"

They one and all then set off at a good pace, some proceeding down the Rue du Temple and the Rue Saint-Martin, others by way of the Rue Saint-Denis and the Rue Poissionière, but all in the direction of the Seine, as though they were to meet later at a common rendezvous.

CHAPTER XLVI.—THE MYSTERIOUS HOUSE.

AT nine o'clock the same evening there seemed to be something mysterious going on in the Rue des Postes. The centre of mystery was a small house, one story high, with only a door and a window facing the street. The night was fine enough to account for any number of Parisians being out and about to enjoy the first fine weather of the early spring. Clearly, however, it was not the enjoyment of the balmy air and the bright moonlight that took one person down the Rue des Postes. He stopped a moment, as if to listen for any sound which might come up from the low house, then turned back, walked up the street, and said to a second person whom he met,

" Nothing yet !"

The man to whom this enigmatical message was given next drew near the house, listened an instant, went on his round until he was stopped by the third man in the Rue du Puits-qui-parle, to whom he said, in his turn, " Nothing yet !"

The same manœuvre was repeated by this third personage, who whispered the same words in the ear of another comrade at the corner of the Rue d'Um. The first comer, who appeared to regard the Rue des Postes as his beat, by-and-by observed a number of men in long brown cloaks enter the mysterious house one by one. He every now and then walked down the street, whistling a popular air nonchalantly, when a fresh stranger in a brown cloak was about to enter; but, listen as he would, he could not catch the pass-word which each new arrival had to pronounce before he was let in. It was "*Lammas.*"

Sixty persons had thus entered the mysterious house in the house of two hours. At eleven o'clock their watcher-in-chief seemed satisfied that all had assembled, and that the company was complete. He whistled another air, this time a very lively one. In a few seconds he was joined by seven men.

"Attention!" he cried, in the martial tone of one used to authority.

"Papillon," he said, "you post yourself behind the house. Carmagnole, you look after the right wing. Vol-au-Vent will guard the left. Longue-Avoine and the rest will remain near me. You are all well armed?"

"Yes," was the unanimous reply.

"Then to your posts at once."

The three men addressed as Papillon, Carmagnole, and Vol-au-Vent disappeared with a celerity which proved they fully deserved their sobriquets.

"As for us, Longue-Avoine," added their chief in the brown overcoat, "let us continue our walk like peaceful and loyal citizens."

Having taken a good pinch of snuff from a rococo snuffbox, and having wiped his spectacles with his handkerchief, and deposited them carefully on his nose again, Monsieur Jackal (for it was the Chief Commissioner of the Police) stepped out leisurely with his patrol, muttering to himself, "Sixty men marching like one! *Ma foi!* they may be conspirators drilling!"

CHAPTER XLVII.—THE MYSTERY.

THE Chief Commissioner of Police halted at the corner of the Rue du Puits-qui-parle, and dispersed the remainder of his men, except Longue-Avoine, in various quarters close at hand.

M. Jackal remained with Longue-Avoine at the corner, whence they could command a good view of the house of mystery in the Rue des Postes.

"Now, then," said M. Jackal, abruptly, to his trusted emissary, "tell me how you first came to hear of this dark affair. It is a serious matter that sixty people should meet in this clandestine fashion in Paris and the Chief Commissioner of the Police should not know the reason of their meeting."

"It was through la Barbette that I first heard of it, Monsieur—la Barbette, who lives in the very house Carmagnole entered a minute ago. One night she heard strange noises coming from the next house. She fancied she could make out the voices and steps of many men. I dropped in to see la Barbette that same night about eleven, when she told me that for two hours and a half she had heard what appeared to her the tramp, tramp of an entire regiment. Of course, I listened with all my might on my next visit, which took place earlier in the evening. The same noise struck my ears, Monsieur. But when I came to listen at the door of the mysterious house itself, not a sound could I hear. I found out nothing further till a fortnight ago, when I watched and saw sixty men enter the house, two at a time, just as we saw them enter to-night, Monsieur."

"And what do you think is the object of their meeting, Longue-Avoine?"

"First, I thought they must be conspirators. Now, I think they may be Jesuits."

"Why?"

"Because I overheard them utter some Latin words now and then."

"You're a fool, Longue-Avoine! What should the Jesuits want with a secret meeting place, when they have the Tuileries?"

"What *can* they be, then?"

"Well, I have an idea we shall not remain much longer in the dark, for here comes Carmagnole."

A thin man with an olive-coloured face glided rather than walked up to M. Jackal at that moment.

"Well, Carmagnole! What news?" demanded the Chief Commissioner of the Police.

"The news is that the hole is almost made. Another blow with the mattock, and I could effect an entrance."

"Good! Go back to la Barbette. Don't stir. Wait for me!"

Carmagnole disappeared as quickly and noiselessly as he came. Scarcely had he re-entered la Barbette's residence, when a shrill whistle came apparently from the roof of the suspected house. M. Jackal hurried down the street, and, placing his hands round his mouth in the form of an O, shouted out to the man he saw on the roof,

"Is that you, Vol-au-Vent?"

"Yes."

"Can you get in?"

"Easily."

"Then do so in ten minutes' time."

"Good!" repeated M. Jackal to himself. "Carmagnole watches them on the left, Papillon in the rear, and Vol-au-Vent is ready to drop down upon them. Now's the moment to strike!"

A whistle from him brought fifteen men running as rapidly as they could towards their chief, two of them carrying torches, and all of them armed to the teeth. Taking a life-preserver from his pocket, M. Jackal led his men silently down the Rue des Postes. He stopped at the door of the mysterious house and knocked three times, calling out as he knocked. "Open, in the name of the law!" No answer came. The same formula was repeated, with the same result. There was not even a breath to prevent M. Jackal from hearing the slightest noise within; his men were mute and still as statues; yet not a single footfall—not the faintest echo of a voice—proceeded from the house which had been entered by sixty men only an hour or two previously. After the third and final summons, M. Jackal impatiently exclaimed,

"Since no one will open the door, we must open it ourselves."

The Chief of the Police thereupon took a key from his pocket and quickly opened the door. Leaving two men outside, he boldly stepped in first, followed by the rest. By the fitful light of the two torches they could see they were now in a spacious hall, and that a strong oaken door had yet to be opened ere they could penetrate further. This oaken door was also proof against M. Jackal's impressive summons. It refused to fly open even at the bidding of the law. It was equally obdurate when key after key was turned in its lock. M. Jackal had recourse to a pinch of snuff, his enjoyment of which was interrupted first by a cry which rose from the interior, and then by the sound of one falling heavily to the ground from a great height.

"Poor devil! He's dead!" muttered M. Jackal.

"Who?" asked Longue-Avoine.

"Who? Why, Vol-au-Vent, of course! That was his cry, He has probably fallen through the skylight!"

A sinister silence ensued, followed by the noise of another fall, but a lighter one this time. The next moment a voice was heard the other side of the oaken door.

"Are you there, Monsieur Jackal?" asked the voice.

"I am. Is that you, Carmagnole?" replied the Chief of the Police.

"Yes."

"Open the door, then. You have your nightingales, haven't you?"

"I'm never without my birds, Monsieur."

The noise of someone picking a lock was then heard. Still, the door would not move.

"Well, what now?" demanded M. Jackal.

"Oh, here's two bolts, I see," replied Carmagnole, drawing them back as he spoke. "And a bar—padlocked."

"Haven't you a file?"

"No."

"Take mine, then," said M. Jackal, pushing the thinnest of files under the door.

The grating of the file lasted a minute. The bar then fell heavily to the ground, and the door flew open.

"Ah, Monsieur!" exclaimed Carmagnole, as the Chief of the Police entered. "We've found their hole at last, but not without some difficulty."

M. Jackal replied by casting a piercing glance round a spacious rotunda, which was but dimly lit by the torches borne by his followers. It seemed empty at first sight. A second look, however, revealed a dark heap in the centre.

"It is as I thought," said M. Jackal phlegmatically, pointing to the dark mass.

"You guessed it was Vol-au-Vent then?" answered Carmagnole.

"Yes. It is Vol-au-Vent, isn't it?"

"It was, Monsieur. The poor fellow's dead now."

"That means a pension of two hundred francs to his wife," said M. Jackal to himself. He added aloud, "Let us lose not a moment in examining the rotunda."

The white circular wall of the rotunda was most carefully scrutinised, and the floor was examined with equal care; but not a trace could be discovered of any secret door or trap-door by which the sixty men could have escaped. The only opening for escape (save by the inaccessible skylight, sixty feet above the corpse of Vol-au-Vent) was the hole in the wall by which Carmagnole had effected his entrance from la Barbette's dwelling; but Carmagnole could vouch for it that not a soul had departed by that route.

"Vanished like phantoms!" exclaimed M. Jackal, in a tone of great perplexity.

An hour more was spent in sounding the walls and the flooring. Lost time. M. Jackal and his myrmidons of the Rue de Jérusalem found the mystery even greater than when they entered the mysterious house. Still M. Jackal was a man who never despaired.

CHAPTER XLVIII.—M. JACKAL'S ADVENTURE.

THE Chief Commissioner of the Police left six men on guard in the rotunda, despatched two others to the Rue de Jérusalem with the body of Vol-au-Vent, and quitted the house with Carmagnole and the rest of his company. One or two more men were intrusted to patrol the Rue des Postes. M. Jackal, apparently buried in thought, then led the way to the Rue du Puits-qui-parle—the Street of the Speaking Wells. The street, on this night at least, amply deserved its title. M. Jackal was presently roused from his reverie by a series of dismal moans, seemingly coming from the bowels of the earth. There was a well close by. He drew near its mouth, and heard the cries much more distinctly. The look of intelligence which flashed from his eyes might almost have indicated that the voice of the man in distress was not strange to him.

"Here! Tie this rope round my waist, Carmagnole," M. Jackal said. "That'll do. Now let me down carefully. This is a little bit of business I must investigate myself."

So saying, he lightly leapt on to the circular wall which inclosed the mouth of the unused well, and was slowly let down by Carmagnole and Longue-Avoine.

"It's Gibassier, as I'm alive!" M. Jackal muttered, as the prayers and groans of the man he was about to rescue grew plainer and plainer.

Hardly had he reached the bed of the well when he was grasped by trembling hands and a tremulous, husky voice saluted him with the following outburst of gratitude, "You have saved my life, Monsieur! You have delivered me from certain death! Let me devote myself to you body and soul in return!"

CHAPTER XLIX.—GIBASSIER'S ESCAPE.

"HALLO, up there!" shouted the Chief Commissioner of Police from the bottom of the well. "Wait where you are until you get another signal from me!"

"All right, Monsieur!" was the answer that came echoing down the well in the voice of Carmagnole.

"And now," said M. Jackal to the man whose cries for help had caused him to make the descent by means of the rope, "having sufficiently thanked me, tell me, first of all, how you came to be down here."

"I was robbed, half killed, and then thrown down this well, Monsieur."

"Do you know the would-be assassins?"

"Yes, Monsieur."

"Then you can have them arrested!"

"Alas! no, Monsieur. They are friends."

"Friends! Ah! only friends of your own kidney would serve you so, Gibassier."

"You know me, then!"

"Know you! I should think so. You are one of my oldest acquaintances, Gibassier."

"Well, I will be equally frank, Monsieur Jackal: I recognised your voice almost before you began your timely descent down the well."

"Now we're on even terms, then, perhaps you'll tell me how long it is since you left the prison at Toulon?"

"Certainly. I can keep no secret from my saviour. I left there about a month ago."

"And how did you effect your escape?" pursued M. Jackal, touching a spring in his stout walking-stick, and making it form a kind of camp-stool, on which he sat with the air of a man in no hurry to leave his present quarters, damp though they were. "Tell me in as few words as you can, for this apartment is not the most pleasant in the world."

"Why not tell you above, then, Monsieur Jackal?"

"Oh, other ears would hear your story up there; and you wouldn't particularly care for that, would you, Gibassier?"

"No—no, Monsieur. It will be best told here. To begin with, Monsieur Jackal, I was heartily tired of the convict prison. It was not as if it had been my first visit. Then it had all the charms of a sweetheart for me, as it were. The second time I soon became sated and blasé, for living in the prison seemed like living with a legitimate spouse after all the fire of novelty had died out. Brest would have been preferable to Toulon, as Brest would have been new to me. Brest might probably have rejuvenised me. But I had to bear my chains and my ennui at Toulon, where I should doubtless have remained till my last hour if the enthusiasm of a young comrade in misfortune had not infused into my heart the hope that we might both obtain our liberty. My companion in chains, Gabriel, was a fair young fellow of about twenty-three. Fresh as a daisy, he had gained the sobriquet of 'The Angel Gabriel.' Not only by our iron bracelets were we linked together; the warmest friendship sprang up between us. One common thought animated us—Escape! That was the one desire which filled our minds, sleeping and waking."

"What was Gabriel's term of imprisonment, and what crime was he convicted for?" interrupted M. Jackal, with professional interest, and refreshing himself at the same time with an enormous pinch of snuff.

"Oh! he was sent to Toulon for five years for a mere escapade—the folly of a young man; but when we came to call him the 'Angel Gabriel,' he was struck with an idea. 'If I'm an angel,' he said, 'I must have wings. Why shouldn't I fly out of bondage, then?'"

"Why, you're quite a poet," said M. Jackal.

"I was President of the Academy at Toulon," modestly answered the escaped convict.

"Proceed!"

"I will, Monsieur Jackal. When once the determination to escape had been resolved upon, I saw little difficulty in the way, though I had first to answer the vain and simple idea entertained by Gabriel.

"'I wish to recover my liberty,' he whispered to me one day, in reply to a question I addressed to him, 'but I trust to Providence to provide the means.'

"'Providence!' said I, not without a little contempt, I fear. 'Providence is simply an old usurer, who only lends to the rich. The best of old proverbs says, "Heaven helps those who help themselves." Who would be free themselves must strike the blow. But let our blow be a secret one. I intend to enjoy the Carnival in Paris. It comes off in a fortnight's time. Would you accompany me? Yes? Well, first of all, rub yourself with that herb you see yonder. It is an herb of wonderful qualities. The first application may seem to you like striking a hundred thousand needles into your skin. Never mind the pain. Rub away, and you will be smothered with angry pimples. They will think you are suffering from an attack of fever, or erysipelas, or some other malady, the technical name of which I forget. What will follow? Why, prompt removal to the hospital, of course. Once there, you are saved!'

"'Saved!' Gabriel exclaimed.

"'Yes; for one of the hospital attendants is an intimate friend of mine.'"

M. Jackal hereupon interrupted with the remark,

"I must confess, Gibassier, that I can't see how escape from the hospital was easy, even with the aid of your friend. Surely, the hospital was guarded well enough to render an evasion a matter of peril and difficulty!"

"You're as impatient as Gabriel was, Monsieur Jackal. Listen a few minutes longer, and you shall hear the dénoûment. Well, Gabriel rubbed himself with the herb with such good effect that in a couple of hours he was covered with pimples from head to foot. Forthwith he was conveyed to the hospital, and the doctor pronounced that he was suffering from a severe attack of erysipelas. Next day I was seized with the same symptoms. In a few hours I was in a bed not far from Gabriel's.

"My trusty friend, the hospital attendant, then performed his part of the play with a perfection which would have brought down the house at any theatre. One morning he told me all was ready, and that we could fly in the night.

"How? Easily enough. At one end of the hospital ward in which both Gabriel and I were lodged was a small room, used as a mortuary. When night came we slipped from our beds in obedience to my friend's instructions. The other patients were all sleeping heavily. We gained the little room on tiptoe. When we were safely inside, Gabriel, to my disgust, leant against the wall, and trembled like an aspen leaf. It may have been the associations conjured up in his mind by his presence in the still, dead room. At any rate, I was put out.

"'En route, Gabriel!' I whispered. 'Everything favours us. Let's leave this.'

"'Impossible,' he replied. 'Courage fails me. I don't seem to have any command over my limbs.'

"'Thousand thunders!' I exclaimed in anger. 'You *must* come.'

"'You escape by yourself!'

"'Never!'

"I thereupon pushed Gabriel under one of the black marble tables. He saw the hole in the flooring through which we were to escape, and he seemed to take heart at the sight. Untwining the sheet he had wrapped round his waist in bed, Gabriel silently gave me one end to hold. He seized the other end, and I lowered him through the hole down to the marine store-room beneath the hospital. I then tied my end of the sheet to the iron leg of the table, and safely descended myself.

"We were now in the store-room, on the ground floor. It was pitch dark. I lit my dark lantern, and searched for the stone under which my friend had hidden our disguises. The stone soon caught my eye: it was considerably marked with my initial, G. I lifted the stone, but found one disguise only—that of a gendarme, with full equipment, and arms, and everything complete. Only one suit! I was in despair. Gabriel nobly offered to remain; and this time it was not fear, but pure friendship, which prompted the offer.

"'Courage, Gabriel!' I said, a happy idea striking me. 'Help me to get on my uniform, and all will go well yet!'

"'But how can I escape in my convict's dress?' he asked.

"'You'll see presently. Let me fasten your hands.'

"'I haven't the least idea of your plan yet.'

"'Yes, you have. Why, I'm a gendarme with a prisoner—a convict, whom I'm taking from one prison to another. Don't you twig now?'

"'Yes, yes; I see now!' he exclaimed, in his bright, taking way.

"Well, we stopped in our hiding-place till the first light of morning, dreadfully anxious lest the hole above should be discovered. Directly the cannon announced the opening of the arsenal, we made our way out of the store-room, unobserved, and marched straight to the gate, by which the workmen were thronging in. I held Gabriel fast; and, luckily, we were taken for what we pretended to be. In less than ten minutes we had traversed the town and were on the road to Beausset.

"A few gunshots from Toulon was a wood. We plunged into the very heart of this wood. Three thundering reports then reached our ears. That was the signal that a convict had escaped; and the cannon warned the villages round Toulon of the tact. We sought a secluded nook, covered ourselves as well as we could with branches, and remained motionless, resolved not to continue our journey to Beausset till nightfall.

"Happily for us, a violent rainstorm came on just as the gendarmes began to search the wood. They actually came within twenty paces of our place of concealment, but they were so much occupied in cursing the weather, and talking longingly of the nearest cabaret, that they utterly failed to see us; and it was with no little gratification that we heard their voices growing fainter and fainter in the distance.

"We were saved! I need not detain you, Monsieur Jackal, with the details of our flight to Paris. Suffice it to say that, with the exception of a stab or two and numberless bruises, I am at the present moment in the best of health."

"A wonderfully clever escape," said M. Jackal. "If I were only Préfet of Police I would give you a ticket-of-leave as a reward for your ingenuity, Gibassier. Unfortunately, I am not; and, however much my artistic instincts may have been gratified by your story, I fear my position as guardian of the public safety will not allow me to let you off scot-free. But you have yet to tell me how you came to be in your present unenviable position, Gibassier."

"Well, you must know, Monsieur Jackal, that I came into an inheritance of five thousand francs."

"That is to say, you have stolen five thousand francs."

"As true as you sit before me, Monsieur Jackal, I did not steal the money. I earned it, fairly and laboriously, by the sweat of my brow."

"Then it was you who had a hand in the Versailles business, Gibassier? I made certain it was you, from the skilful manner in which the door had been closed."

"What do you mean by the Versailles business?" demanded Gibassier, with all the innocence he could assume at a moment's notice.

"What were you doing on the night of Shrove Tuesday?" retorted M. Jackal.

"Is it imperative that I should lift the veil of my private life in Paris, Monsieur?"

"Confess you *were* at Versailles on that night, Gibassier."

"Well, I confess I was, then."

"What took you to Versailles?" pursued M. Jackal, a slight smile of satisfaction playing round his lips. "You were not alone, were you?"

"Who is ever alone on this earth?" was Gibassier's evasive reply.

"I have no time to play upon words, Gibassier. You were concerned in carrying off a young girl from the boarding-school of Madame Desmarets?"

"I was."

"And you received the five thousand francs as your reward?"

"You see now I did not steal the coin, Monsieur Jackal."

"What has Monsieur Lorédan de Valgeneuse done with the girl?"

"Monsieur Jackal," answered Gibassier, opening his eyes wide with wonder at the omniscience of the Commissioner of Police, "I assure you I am entirely ignorant of her whereabouts. When I had lifted her safely over the garden wall and placed her in the carriage, my work was done. What became of the happy couple afterwards I didn't trouble my head about."

"What has been your occupation since then?" continued M. Jackal.

"Stockbroker, Monsieur. First, I initiated myself into the secrets of the rise and fall of stocks; and I was wild with myself to think that all my life I had been running the risk of being imprisoned or hanged, when here was a means of gaining more money than I had ever dreamt of obtaining, with the utmost safety, and with no dishonour. I speculated. I was rewarded with success. In a month I realised thirty thousand francs. With such a sum I naturally became an honest and respectable member of society."

"Then you should be changed beyond recognition," ironically answered M. Jackal, lighting a small lantern he had taken from his pocket, and holding it before Gibassier, whom he now saw to be covered with mud and blood.

"No; your face has not changed a whit," said the Commissioner of Police. "The years have passed over your head as lightly as shadows. Apropos of shadows, be good enough to hold this light a moment, while I write a line or two."

Gibassier held the lantern; and M. Jackal produced from one of his bulky pockets a scrap of paper and a pencil. Whilst he wrote, he bade Gibassier finish his story.

"The finish is sad enough," resumed the escaped convict. "Being rich, I gained friends. Having friends, I had enemies; and last night, on my return from the banker's, I was seized by the collar, felled to the ground, plundered, and, finally, thrown down this abandoned well."

M. Jackal rose, seized the end of the rope by which he had descended, fastened the pencilled note to it with a pin, and shouted to his men,

"Pull up the rope!"

The paper fluttered like a butterfly in the darkness for a moment, and then vanished from their sight. The note was soon in the hands of Carmagnole, who unfolded it, and read what follows:—

> "I am about to send up to you a man whom you must guard with the utmost care. He is worth his weight in gold!
>
> "Take him to the hospital, four of you; and never lose sight of him for a moment."

M. Jackal then turned to Gibassier, and said.

"Your history is very touching; but, after such stormy experiences, you must need repose. You'll find a safe refuge above. This rope will draw you from the well. You go first. I'll follow."

Gibassier made a loop at the end of the rope with the dexterity of a practised hand, placed his feet in the loop, caught hold of the rope with both hands, and cried out,

"Ready!"

"Bon voyage!" called out M. Jackal, watching the ascent with interest. "Good!" he added, as Gibassier's form swung out of sight. "It will be my turn when the rope comes down again."

CHAPTER L.—M. JACKAL DISCOVERS A CONSPIRACY.

"SEND the rope down as quickly as you can. It's confoundedly damp at the bottom of this well!" shouted out M. Jackal, impatiently, a minute later. The end of the rope touched his hand almost before the last word had left his lips.

"Pull steadily, men!" the Commissioner of Police called up, as soon as he had fastened the rope to his belt.

He had hardly ascended half a dozen yards when he cried, "Stop!"

"Where the deuce does this light come from?" M. Jackal muttered to himself, as he paused in the ascent and swayed to and fro with the rope, like a living pendulum.

Well may he have been puzzled. There was something especially weird and fantastic about the glimmer which revealed to him the entrance to what was apparently a deep vault or cave. Through this narrow opening in the side of the well he could see a long vista of gloom and shafts of light, ending in a spacious vault, illuminated by a dozen torches jutting from the pillars, flaring fitfully on a meeting of some sixty men, whose attention was absorbed by one of their number, evidently addressing them with great animation and earnestness.

"Hallo! I must see further into this," said M. Jackal to himself. "Who are these men, I wonder; and what's their business in this out of the world place?"

Thanks to the reflections of the torches and the keenness of his vision, the astute Chief of the Police could make out that every member of this secret assembly was watching the speaker and listening to him with marked intensity and complete silence. Clearly, the orator had absolute power over their hearts, and moved them all at will. Whether it was that the leader was designedly speaking in a low key, or that M. Jackal was at too great a distance to overhear what was said, one thing was certain—after five minutes of the closest listening he could not hear a single word of the discourse which stirred the hearts of this nocturnal meeting so strongly. As he looked and looked, it seemed to him at length that not a few were familiar figures to him—comfortable bourgeois, whom he had seen at the doors of their shops bearing the most peaceful aspect. The majority, however, were plainly old military men, from their grey moustaches and soldier-like bearing. All wore brown or blue overcoats buttoned up to their chins. The sombre air of secrecy which surrounded them accorded well with the gloom of the vast vault in which they were assembled.

"*Mordieu!* I see!" exclaimed M. Jackal, at length. "Of course, these are our sixty missing conspirators of the Rue des Postes! They gave us the slip by descending to the catacombs. But chance has put me on their track again, and it will be hard if I let them slip this time without learning their little game."

The Guardian of the Public Safety was right. The vault before him was a part of the immense subterranean gallery extending from Montrouge to the Seine, and from the Jardin des Plantes to Grenelle. The moment M. Jackal made this discovery there stole into his ears the echoes of bravos and applause, and of a ringing shout which was seditious enough at that epoch:

"*Vive l'Empereur!*"

"*Vive l'Empereur!*" repeated M. Jackal, innocently joining in the seditious cry. "What fools they are! The Emperor Napoleon has been dead six years."

The same shout, nevertheless, was re-echoed, and this time mo.e energetically than before.

"I would willingly join in your devoted cry," chuckled M. Jackal, "but, I repeat, the Emperor's dead. Monsieur de Béranger has even written a song on the event."

A third shout of "*Vive l'Empereur!*" came echoing into his ears. There was then a movement among the sixty, and another speaker stood forth to address them, exciting the curiosity of M. Jackal so much that he determined to make an effort to get near enough to hear the subject of the speech.

"Lower the rope a foot or two!"

The command was no sooner uttered than it was obeyed. A momentum was given to the rope at the same time by M. Jackal; and a few seconds after he was standing safely on the threshold of the long passage leading to the vault. Bidding his men at the mouth of the well not to budge until they received his next order, the Chief of the Police let go the rope, and started along the passage with the agility of the animal whose name he aptly bore. The tunnel grew wider and wider as he noiselessly threaded his way between the huge stones which obstructed his path. He kept carefully to the dark side. When he had proceeded about a hundred paces, what was the moment before but the murmur of a distant voice rose into articulate speech, and the words that reached his ears made him accelerate his pace. He was now within a dozen yards of the lofty vault. It was pitch dark where he stood, but a broad shaft of light shot between him and a colossal pillar, behind which he thought he might see and hear without being seen himself. Crouching down, M. Jackal made a spring across the shaft of light and gained a jutting boulder, which, together with the wide pillar, formed a hiding-place as safe as he could desire, seeing that the conspirators would to a certainty make their exit from another quarter of the vault. He arrived in the nick of time.

"Brothers," said the speaker, in a clear sonorous voice, "I have come to give you an account of my visit to Vienna. I returned to Paris last night, and you have been called together by the orders of our chief to hear a piece of news of the highest importance. Two men whose glorious devotion to our cause is well known to you, General Lebastard de Prémont and Monsieur Sarranti, arrived in Vienna two months ago——"

"Sarranti! Sarranti!" communed M. Jackal with himself. "Why, it must be Sarranti back from India! Poor Monsieur Gérard will be glad for one, to hear tidings of the assassin of his nephew and niece!"

The orator meantime continued, "Both have returned to Europe to throw their whole hearts, and souls, and fortunes into our cause; and Monsieur Sarranti has been charged by the King of Rome to arrange his flight!"

The meeting greeted this announcement with joyful acclamations.

"*Ma foi!*" murmured M. Jackal. "This grows interesting. I must not miss a word!"

"Our project," resumed the speaker, "is to deliver the Prince from his prison, to conduct him in safety to Paris, to get up a rising in the streets simultaneously with his arrival, to spread his powerful and popular name far and wide, and thus unite all those faithful hearts which yet beat truly towards the son and heir of Napoleon!"

"It is clear these men are not such fools as I imagined they were when they shouted 'Vive l'Empereur!'" So ran the thoughts of M. Jackal at this juncture.

"You all know the Prince lives in the Château de Schönbrunn, or rather, is imprisoned there. But Monsieur Sarranti will be able to deliver him from that prison, let the Austrian soldiers guard the palace as closely as they may. Monsieur Sarranti's plan was suggested by the Emperor himself, and it has received the sanction of the Prince. Every day the Prince goes out on horseback for two or three hours. On a day which remains to be fixed, the Prince will set out in the morning, as usual; but instead of returning to Schönbrunn, he will join General Lebastard de Prémont, who will be waiting for him at the foot of Mont Vert with the requisite number of horses and carriages, and twenty trusty men, all well armed. Along the whole line of route from Vienna to Paris relays will be prepared for the envoy of Runjeet Singh. Gold will give wings to the horses. The hour is near, brothers. Monsieur Sarranti will precede the Prince by twenty-four hours; so Monsieur Sarranti's arrival in Paris must be the signal of a simultaneous rising throughout France!"

M. Jackal scarcely dared to breathe, so bent was he on learning every detail of the Bonapartist plot.

"Before another week is over, Monsieur Sarranti will probably be in Paris," added the orator, impressively. "The loss of a day, an hour, a minute, may spoil all. Let us act at once, then. You have to-night to choose a delegate for the central committee, which meets in another part of the catacombs."

"*Mordieu!* muttered the Commissioner of Police. "These cata-

M. JACKAL DISCOVERS A CONSPIRACY.

combs are nothing better than so many mines, all ready to explode for the benefit of the poor King!"

M. Jackal, motionless as the granite pillar which sheltered him, kept a sharp eye on what followed. He saw the conspirators gather more closely round the two men who had addressed them. The one whom M. Jackal had first seen speaking, and who appeared to be the president of the meeting, beckoned the second orator, and said a few words to him in too low a voice for the anxious Commissioner of Police to hear. The sense of what had been said, however, was soon obvious to the trained mind of M. Jackal. The second speaker gave a gesture of thanks to his comrades, seized a torch, and then disappeared through a small grotto in the wall of the vault. It was clear, then, that he had himself been elected as the delegate to the central committee. Half an hour of confusion ensued—men talking one against the other and all at once, with a superabundance of shrugs, gesticulations, and waving of torches. Silence was restored in a moment. Every voice was hushed as their delegate reappeared and uttered one pregnant word, "Agreed!"

Three ringing shouts of "*Vive l'Empereur !*" were given in reply, The meeting then broke up, each of the sixty making his exit through the grotto ; and five minutes later the silence and darkness of death reigned in the vault which had echoed and re-echoed their cries. M. Jackal, who did not feel inspired with fresh courage by the darkness which now surrounded him, relit his lantern, and made the best of his way back to the well. He found the rope dangling where he had left it. Attaching the end afresh to his belt, he lustily called out, "Hallo, up there ! Will the rope still bear me ?"

"Yes, yes, Monsieur Jackal," shouted half a dozen voices at once.

"Pull away, then, lads."

The venturesome Chief of the Police was pulled up with a will which plainly told how glad his men were to be released from their tiresome post.

"Ah ! it was high time I touched terra firma," cried M. Jackal, as he leapt on to the pavement of his Majesty Charles X. "Another quarter of an hour, and I should have been eaten by the rats which infest that cursed well."

"Where's Gibassier ?" suddenly asked M. Jackal of Longue-Avoine.

"At the Hôtel-Dieu, with Carmagnole, who has been charged not to lose sight of him, Monsieur."

"Good ! *En marche*, my men ! Meet me at the Préfecture in half an hour."

M. Jackal then set out briskly for the Rue de Jérusalem, musing to himself as he went,

"It is rather droll to think that if I were not to move in the matter we should probably have the empire restored by next week. And yet these idiots of Jesuits still fancy themselves the absolute masters of the kingdom ! And our honest king hunts on in happy ignorance that he may be on the point of being chased off the throne !"

CHAPTER LI.—GIBASSIER'S MISSION.

It struck four by Notre-Dame as M. Jackal entered the Hôtel-Dieu. He went straight to the dormitory in which Gibassier had been sleeping since two o'clock the same morning, and, dismissing Carmagnole, sat down by the bedside of the escaped convict. Gibassier was the very man M. Jackal needed at this crisis. His ingenuity, readiness of resource, fluency of speech, and audacity could not be matched on the staff of the Chief of the Police. Wherefore M. Jackal was resolved to try all his art to win Gibassier into his service. He did not dally. Frankness, he knew, would be his safest card. Accordingly, after the first few formal words had been interchanged, he plunged at once into the subject.

"My dear Gibassier," he said, "I see you fear I shall send you back to Toulon. Nothing's further from my thoughts. You are free. When you are well enough to quit this hospital you will be at liberty to roam where you like."

"Thank you—thank you, Monsieur Jackal! But what could I do? Remember the straits you found me in. In Paris I should always be at their mercy. Besides, I should run such risks. Who knows that I might not be tempted to join some plot against the king? I *have been* tempted, I can assure you."

"Keep out of danger and enter my service, then," said M. Jackal, eagerly.

"Become a police spy! Are you serious, Monsieur Jackal?"

"Perfectly so, Gibassier. Here's my hand in token of good faith."

"What is the service you require of me? I know there's plenty of work for the police in Paris. Why, only yesterday my poor comrade, 'the angel Gabriel,' was taken off to prison for helping himself to a loaf of bread when he was dying with hunger, whilst all the time the police left untouched the nest of conspirators plotting the downfall of the king in the catacombs."

"Ah! Gibassier, the 'speaking well' has spoken to you as well as to me, I see. This is the very duty I want you for. Your friend Gabriel shall be released at once. Will you join my service?"

"Willingly, Monsieur Jackal. You saved my life, do what you please with it."

"Will you be able to leave your bed in twenty-four hours?"

"In less than that."

"To-morrow morning, then, you must start for Kehl, where you will put up at the Auberge de la Poste. A man from Vienna will pass there in a post-chaise: forty-eight, dark eyes, grey moustache, five feet seven inches. His name is Sarranti, but he'll travel under an assumed name. Don't lose sight of him. Here's an order for a thousand crowns. Twelve thousand francs shall be yours if you carry out my instructions to the letter, Gibassier."

"Count upon me, Monsieur Jackal. Ah! I knew true merit would be recognised one day, and the day has come!"

"Adieu, and good luck," answered the Chief of the Police, quitting the room and joining Carmagnole and Longue-Avoine outside.

Near Notre-Dame a carriage with four horses and postillions awaited M. Jackal. He gave a whispered message to Longue-Avoine, bade Carmagnole jump up outside, sprang inside the carriage himself, and called out to the coachman,

"Take the road to Belgium, and drive as fast as your horses will go."

CHAPTER LII.—ROLAND'S RECOGNITION.

LEAVING M. Jackal and Carmagnole en route to intercept the Bonapartist conspirators, let us return to the Rue de l'Ouest, and enter the studio of Pétrus Herbel. It was a magnificent workshop—at once the studio of a painter, a musician, and a poet: fit atélier for a Raphael of the modern school. Its luxurious furniture and adornments charmed and astonished one at the same time. Every sense was gratified—the heart-moving notes of an organ saluting the ear, fragrant incense perfuming the air, fine-art gems pleasing the eye. The musician was Justin. He was improvising an air to wed with the sweet poem Jean Robert had just transcribed from the German of Goethe to accompany the dancing figure of Mignon, for which Rose-de-Noël was sitting to Pétrus. The painting was nearly finished. It was a masterpiece of colouring and vivid power. The artist had put his whole soul into it. Mignon was a perfect portrait of Rose-de-Noël, and yet there was in the face an indefinable likeness of Princesse Régina's fair features. The reason was that while Rose-de-Noël was the model that Pétrus had before his eyes, the one being who occupied his heart and mind was the Princesse de Lamothe-Houdan. Another little "Mohican of Paris," Babolin, reclined beside Rose-de-Noël, and was included in the life-like painting to which Pétrus was giving the finishing touches, and which represented Mignon dancing with marvellous grace before Wilhelm Meister. Pétrus himself seemed a prey to the deepest gloom and sorrow. For a while his palette rested idle on his knee; the brush hung listlessly in his hand. His thoughts had flown to the pavilion of Régina, where the sweetest hours of his life had been passed—where she whom he loved with a hopeless love might at that very moment be meditating on the cruel fate which was so soon to bestow her hand on the man she most detested, for the morrow was to be her wedding day. The young painter was roused from his reverie by a familiar knock at the door.

"It's Salvator!" exclaimed Pétrus. His face turned pale, whilst his eyes were filled with a momentary gleam of hope, as he eagerly said, "Come in!"

"Lie down, Roland!" said a clear, ringing voice. The door then opened, and Salvator entered in his garb of Commissionaire.

"Well, any news!" asked Pétrus, advancing to meet Salvator.

"Yes," replied his friend in a low voice. "I have a message to give you in private."

"Excuse us a moment, friends," said Pétrus to Jean Robert and Justin, at the same time leading the way to his private room, Salvator following after giving Justin, Jean Robert, and the two children a nod of recognition.

"Pardon my anxiety, Salvator," cried Pétrus in an agitated voice, as he shut the door behind him, and found himself alone with his friend. "Is the message from *her?* Can it be that on the eve of her wedding she has deigned to think of me?"

"Read for yourself," answered Salvator, handing him a note addressed in a lady's handwriting.

"A letter? Tell me: is it from the Princesse de Lamothe-Houdan?"

"That I can't tell you."

"But who gave it you?"

"A chambermaid from Marshal de Lamothe-Houdan's. She gave it to me as I was the only commissionaire in sight; and I have brought it as quickly as I could to Monsieur Pétrus Herbel, to whom it is addressed, you see."

Pétrus tore the note open, glanced at its contents, and then grew white as death.

"A letter—from her—to me—on the eve of her wedding!" he exclaimed in a bewildered tone; for there seemed a veil of blood before his eyes, and he could not at first believe in the reality of the words that had met his astonished gaze.

The very moment of his deepest despair, when he had given up all hope of his sweet dream of love being realised, when it had seemed to him inevitable as fate that the idol of his soul would be wedded to another, there had been brought to him from Régina herself this note, which, if he could credit his senses, ought to make life a joy to him again. Calming himself, with a great effort, Pétrus handed the note to Salvator.

"Read it for me, Salvator," he said; "and tell me whether I've read aright, or whether I've lost my senses."

"If you deem me worthy to share your secret," replied the Commissionaire, taking back the note, "I will accept the trust."

Salvator then read aloud the words traced in the delicate handwriting of the Princesse de Lamothe-Houdan:—

"My marriage with Comte Rappt will not take place.

"Be at the door at eleven o'clock to-night, when some one will be waiting to conduct you to my pavilion.

"Heaven only knows how devoutly thankful I am to have escaped the doom of being that man's wife!   "REGINA."

"It *is* true, then!" exclaimed Pétrus, who had listened to each hopeful word with the close attention with which one condemned to death must listen to the merciful words of a reprieve. "The marriage will not take place. Thank Heaven! . . . Salvator, my true friend, do me another service. Make my excuses to Jean Robert and Justin, and see Rose-de-Noël and Babolin safely in a cab for me. Let me enjoy the joyful news you have brought me alone."

Salvator shook Pétrus heartily by the hand, in token of warmest sympathy, and then left to fulfil his bidding.

ROLAND'S RECOGNITION.

As Salvator re-entered the studio, Roland, tired probably of waiting for his master, gave an uneasy whine outside the door. The whine became a plaintive howl, and the dog scratched at the door, as the organ pealed forth at the same moment the melodious notes Justin had composed to give musical expression to Goethe's verse.

"Isn't that Roland?" asked Jean Robert.

"Yes," answered Salvator.

"Let him come in, then."

"Yes; do let him come in, Monsieur Salvator!" appealed Rose-de-Noël. "I should so much like to see him. Babolin, open the door."

Babolin, only too delighted to make the acquaintance of Salvator's faithful dog, ran to the door and let Roland in.

The dog made two bounds, and was by his master's side.

Roland was then about to favour Salvator with his customary caresses, when he suddenly stopped and gazed earnestly at Rose-de-Noël.

"What's the matter, Roland?" said his master. "And you, Rose-de-Noël, do you know Roland?"

The girl and the dog continued to look at each other in mute astonishment and perplexity. Then, as if the recognition was mutually complete, Rose-de-Noël raised her arms towards Roland, and he bounded joyfully to her side. An affectionate cry escaped from the dog as Rose-de-Noël threw her arms round his neck; and there ensued loving caresses as from friends long parted.

"Come here, Roland!" shouted Salvator, for he feared the dog, in his boisterousness, was growing wild, and would hurt Rose-de-Noël.

"Oh, let him stay! Brésil won't harm me!" was the reassuring albeit puzzling reply of the young girl, whom the dog, moreover, appeared to have no intention of leaving yet awhile, for he skipped around her, betraying the exuberance of his gladness by a series of barks, which drew Pétrus wonderingly from the next room for a moment.

"Good Brésil! Have we met again at last, then?" murmured Rose-de-Noël, fondling the dog afresh, and submitting anew to his caresses.

"You're mistaken, Rose-de-Noël," hereupon said Salvator; "my dog's name is not Brésil, but Roland."

"Yes. Yet you see he knows *me* as Brésil; don't you, Brésil?"

There could be no doubt, from the dog's joyful answer, that the girl and he were fast friends at one time. But when? This was the question Salvator asked himself now. Puzzling his brain for a solution of the riddle, he at last bethought himself of *la Brocante's* account of her discovery of Rose-de-Noël. He recollected that she had found the poor girl one night flying, as if for her very life, from the wood of Juvisy, blood streaming down her white dress, from a wound in her neck. He then remembered that it must have been about the same time that he had found Roland lying wounded in a ditch near the same neighbourhood.

"And *where* did you know him as Brésil?" asked Salvator, continuing his conversation with Rose-de-Noël.

"That I can never, never tell you," answered the young girl, shrinking back and turning pale, as if from fear.

"But I can tell you," said Salvator, suddenly recollecting that once, when he had caught *la Brocante* in the act of ill-treating her, the poor girl had cried out, "Oh! don't kill me, Madame Gérard!"

"It was at Madame Gérard's," hazarded Salvator, at a guess.

Rose-de-Noël almost fainted away at these words, and the dog gave forth a most lugubrious howl. Salvator, alarmed at the effect of his allusion to Madame Gérard, begged Jean Robert and Justin to see Rose-de-Noël and Babolin safely home. His friends at once consented, Justin appealing to Salvator, as he left with the still trembling girl, "Pray remember that the heart of one of your friends is still suffering. Don't forget that Mina has not yet been restored to us!"

"Courage, Justin!" answered Salvator; "Mina has not been out of my mind for a moment. Keep up your heart a little longer. We may be able to rescue her sooner than you think!"

Roland, or Brésil, would have rushed after Rose-de-Noël, and leapt into the cab with her, had not Salvator held him fast.

"Quiet, Brésil!" said Salvator. "You must remain with me, and help me to unravel the mystery which surrounds Rose-de-Noël."

The dog appeared to thoroughly comprehend his master. He made no fresh effort to follow Rose-de-Noël, contenting himself with sending a sympathetic whine after her.

CHAPTER LIII.—SALVATOR AT HOME.

ABOUT ten minutes later Salvator had reached his apartments in the Rue Mâcon. There he was greeted with the ever-loving welcome of Fragola.

"We mustn't lose much time over dinner, love," said Salvator; "for I have a little journey to make to-night."

"A journey!" exclaimed the fair girl, in a tone of disappointment, yet of resignation.

"Yes; but don't be uneasy, dear. I shall not be away long. We shall be back in the morning, sha'n't we, Roland?"

"Oh, if Roland's going with you I know you'll be safe. And now I've given *you* permission, you must give *me* permission to spend the evening out."

"Certainly, dearest! This is Liberty Hall, you know."

"I want to keep Carmélite company, that's all. Poor girl! Lydie, Régina, and I, thought she would be less sad in Paris than at Bas-Meudon. So we have found a comfortable lodging for her in the Rue Tournon."

"Just like your dear, considerate self, Fragola. Go, by all means, and brighten her with your sunshiny presence!"

The fair girl glanced up inquiringly in Salvator's face, as if she would ask yet another favour of him.

"Well?" said Salvator, smilingly answering her mute inquiry. "What's next?"

"Well, you know Carmélite is sometimes so sad that nothing

seems to awaken her from her grief; and so I thought that if I were to tell her a story almost as sad as her own—even sadder at the beginning, but ending very, very happily—she might be consoled somewhat."

"And whose history would you relate to your poor friend, Fragola?"

"My own."

"Relate it, dearest; and, while you are doing so, angels will listen to you. But what will the poor girl do for a living?"

"You know she has a magnificent voice."

"And she would cultivate it! Luckily, I know the very man who will teach her admirably."

"That news will cheer poor Carmélite immensely. Surely you are Fortunatus himself, Salvator, or you possess his wonderful purse, and can produce from it anything the heart can desire."

"Then tell me what you desire, Fragola."

"Oh! you know very well I wish for nothing but your love."

"And as you have every bit of that——"

"I only desire one thing—to keep it."

Fragola emphasised her last word with a sweet kiss, and then hastened to serve the dinner, Salvator meantime hieing to the inner room, whence he quickly re-issued, fully attired in his shooting costume.

Accustomed to his irregular hours and mysterious life, Fragola made little further remark on Salvator's secret journey. She put implicit faith in him, and trusted him with the full confidence of true love.

During dinner Salvator paid particular attention to Roland, whom he involuntarily called "Brésil" now and again.

"Brésil?" cried Fragola, with an air of surprise, the first time she heard his new name.

"Yes, 'Brésil' is right," answered Salvator. "I've heard news of Roland's early days. Before he was christened 'Roland' he was called 'Brésil,' just as I went by another name before I became Salvator. Like master, like dog, you see! Are you ready, Brésil?"

The dog replied by bounding to the door, standing on his hind legs, and knocking against the panels.

"You see, love," said Salvator, "the dog only waits for me. Till to-morrow, Fragola. Fulfil your mission of consolation. As for me, I may be able to do my duty as an avenger."

CHAPTER LIV.—THE PHANTOM IN THE WOOD.

NOTRE-DAME struck seven as Salvator set out with Roland at his heels. He made straight for the Place of the Palace of Justice. There, for five francs, he arranged to be taken to Juvisy by the one public vehicle going there that evening. It was a slow and tiresome journey to the little village in the suburbs of Paris. They did not reach Juvisy till half-past ten. Roland, anticipating his master, sprang from the carriage in advance. The object of the journey seemed to be as interesting to Roland as to Salvator. The dog even took the lead, his master following with the utmost confidence. They kept the main road, passed the fountains of la Cour-de-France, emerged on the common, cut across the fields, and thus gained the ditch wherein, seven years previously, Salvator had found Roland wounded and bleeding. Roland came to a full stop at the ditch. A touching whine escaped him. He looked up in his master's face, as much as to say, "I remember my wound, and I'll never forget my saviour."

"Poor Roland! Yes, it was here I found you, wasn't it?" answered Salvator, as the dog gratefully licked his hand. "But it is not to renew our acquaintance with this ditch we have come to-night, is it, Roland?"

Roland thereupon sprang forward, and once more became Salvator's guide. Now and then the intelligent dog appeared at fault for a moment; but he was soon on the scent again. Their way lay across a little bridge on two arches, and then down a pathway with apple-trees in blossom on each side. Darkness veiled the snowy blossoms, but the air was impregnated with their sweet odour, fresh as spring. Roland led the way surely and without hesitation from this fragrant alley into the roadway. The moon shone out from a mountain of sombre clouds at that moment, and Salvator saw by the moonlight that they were now in front of the high gates of a large park. A dismal moan escaped from the dog and mingled with the weird soughing of the wind through the gaunt trees that towered above.

"Yes, Roland," said Salvator, patting the dog sympathetically, "it was another such a night as this, wasn't it, when you were driven from your home inside there?"

The dog remained stationary for a little while, peering intently through the gates at the house visible within the park. Satisfied with his inspection, Roland tried, but tried vainly, to effect an entrance through the iron bars. He then ran impatiently to and fro alongside the park wall, but could find no breach, and so looked up appealingly to Salvator.

"You want my help, do you, at last, Roland? Well, you shall have it. I am as anxious as you are to inspect the park, for I have a fancy that I shall discover some important secret there."

Roland's acquiescing growl strengthened Salvator in his suspicions. He resolved not to lose another minute. With his powerful arms Salvator found it easy enough to lift Roland as high as was necessary to enable him, by springing from his master's shoulders, to leap over. Nor was Salvator long in following. He gave a good jump, caught hold of the top of the wall with his hands, raised himself by a great muscular effort, and rested awhile on the summit. The gallop of an approaching horse then reached Salvator's ears, and he could see the rider was clad in a long cloak. The horseman was plainly coming along the high road, and would, therefore, in a few moments pass by the park wall. Salvator let himself down quickly on the park side of the wall, but did not leave go his hold. He could, therefore, still peer over the wall in safety, for his face was in the shadow of a giant tree. The moon shone full in the face of the horseman as he passed by. Salvator recognised him. Dropping lightly on the turf, he threw himself down by the side of Roland, and exclaimed, in a tone of astonishment, "Lorédan de Valgeneuse! What the deuce is my dear cousin doing here?"

Salvator waited till the gallop was quite out of hearing. Rising and looking around him, he found himself in the most thickly-wooded part of a huge park. Roland apparently only needed a signal from his master to continue the search which had brought them so far that night. This was given directly the moon retired behind the clouds. The dog went stealthily forward, as if fully aware that the greatest caution and quietness were now necessary. Unslinging his gun and satisfying himself that it was loaded, Salvator followed Roland, keeping a sharp eye on every tree and bush they glided by, and holding his firearm firmly in his right hand. A rabbit or a hare would now and then rustle past Salvator, startling him at first. Gaining confidence as he proceeded, still following Roland's lead, Salvator soon found himself by the bank of a pond, into which his dog had the greatest desire to plunge.

But the château was visible from this miniature lake; and the light which shone from one of the windows proved to Salvator that the place was still inhabited, despite the wild and neglected state of the park. Restraining Roland till he gained the shelter of a convenient thicket, Salvator assured himself that the one light had been extinguished, and then let the dog go, encouraging him with the words, "Find it, Roland!"

The dog disappeared an instant in the reeds which fringed the pond, sprang into the water, and swam for the centre. He dived, but brought nothing with him to the surface the first time. He dived a second and a third time with the like results. He left the pond on the opposite side to Salvator, shook the water from his coat, took two or three steps up the bank, then turned and gave a doleful howl, as if bidding Salvator to follow him. His master did follow him. Roland led the way back to the wood. They marched in silence for some minutes. Roland, guided by his unerring scent or instinct, crossed the wood, penetrated a dense thicket, and stopped at a spot where there was a large accumulation of dead leaves and withered branches at the foot of a giant elm. These he soon tossed aside. Smelling with all his might at the turf, he gave a low growl, and then began to furiously paw away at the soil. A hole was soon hollowed out, but it was not yet deep enough. Encouraged by the stimulating cries of Salvator, Roland dug with fresh energy. At the end of ten minutes the dog leapt suddenly out of the pit and crouched shudderingly at his master's feet. Salvator endeavoured to see what it was that had filled Roland with fright, but the darkness prevented him. He then knelt down and touched the bottom with his hand, but withdrew it shiveringly. It was soft, silken human hair that he had touched! Salvator felt a thrill of horror dart through him. He had discovered at last a clue to the horrible crime that had been committed there. Whilst Salvator shivered again at the thought of the dread deed Roland had brought to light, the poor dog's teeth chattered with an almost human sympathy.

"What is it, Brésil?" whispered Salvator.

The dog looked round with fresh agitation, not hearkening to his master's voice, for a wonder, but directing his gaze fearfully towards the nearest pathway. Salvator looked in the same direction, but saw nothing. Placing his ear to the ground he could hear, however, the sound of approaching footsteps. Looking up again, Salvator saw what seemed a phantom girl gliding along the pathway. The dog would have sprung upon the figure that looked so ghastly in the moonlight, but was forcibly held back by the strong hand of Salvator, who crouched down by the side of Roland. Salvator instinctively held his breath with awe. In the superstition of the moment, he imagined that it might be the ghost of the human being murdered so near where the phantom took her walks at midnight. As a breath of wind merely did this morbid fancy pass through his mind. He had heard substantial footsteps, and a ghostly shadow would not be weighty enough to crush even dead leaves, much less to break the dry branches which strewed the path. The château clock struck the hour of midnight. The phantom started, and Salvator satisfied himself that his fancied phantom was a bright young girl of sixteen or seventeen. She passed near enough for him to notice that she was fair as Fragola, with eyes as blue, but with eyes filled with tears that rolled down her cheeks as she looked heavenwards, her tremulous lips moving in prayer.

"Mina!"

The name of Justin's betrothed, uttered in the distance, filled Salvator with a desire to spring to his feet, and hasten at once to the rescue of the young girl.

"Mina! Mina!" was called again in a man's voice.

A moment's reflection told Salvator that his most prudent course would be to wait and listen. The cry was echoed and re-echoed through the wood, and each time the young girl heard it she looked round like a startled fawn, as if she would willingly have fled, could she but gain her liberty.

"It is useless, I am his prisoner," she sighed to herself, as she sank wearily on a garden seat.

A rapid step was then heard approaching by the same path. A young man passed by, and Salvator recognised in him the horseman whom he had previously seen that night.

"Thank Heaven, if this is really our Mina!" murmured Salvator to himself.

Chapter LV.—Mina at Bay.

Salvator pressed his hand on the dog's mouth to bid him maintain strict silence, and then crept forward in the shadow till he could plainly see, through a gap in the thicket, every movement of the young girl who had flung herself down on the rustic seat in despair at the approach of Lorédan de Valgeneuse, the man who had brought her thither by force and kept her prisoner.

"Mina! I have found you at last!" exclaimed the young man in a tone of protest. "What has brought you out alone in the wood at this late hour of the night?"

"And you, Monsieur, what brings you here at this hour," demanded the young girl, "when I thought it was an understanding between us, that you would never come again at night-time?"

"Mina, forgive me! I could not resist the desire to see you. Ah! if you only knew how fondly I love you! Have pity on me! Even if you cannot return my love, pray let us be friends!"

Simultaneously with this appeal he made an attempt to clasp her hand.

"You know very well, Monsieur Lorédan," coldly answered Mina, withdrawing her hand, "that there can be no friendship between a gaoler and his prisoner."

"At least tell me why you have sought this gloomy spot at midnight," said the young man impatiently.

"Why? Why, because I was warned of your treachery."

"Treachery, Mina?"

"Yes. I was asleep. Yet as plainly as I see you stand before me at this moment, I saw you open the door of my bed-room with a duplicate key and enter. I awoke. I found I was alone. But I took it as a warning that you *would* come to-night. So I fled to this wood, and my vision has come true. Did you *not* enter my room?"

"Mina, pardon me!"

"Pardon you!" exclaimed the young girl with disdain. "What need have you of my pardon? Am I not kept a prisoner here? Am I not bound here by a cruel spell? You know I remain because, if I were to escape, you assure me the liberty and even the life of Justin would be menaced. But there were conditions you agreed to, and you have broken them, Monsieur Lorédan."

"Mina, it is impossible you could really have been forewarned in this superstitious manner of my coming."

"But I *was*, I repeat; and that warning has, perhaps, spared you from a life-long remorse, if you could ever feel any remorse in this life."

"What do you mean, Mina?"

"I mean," answered the young girl resolutely, drawing a small dagger from her waistband, "that if I had really seen you enter my room I would have killed myself with this blade!"

"Enough of this nonsense!" cried the young man, in anger, seizing by a rapid motion the hand in which Mina held the dagger. "I'll take care that you shall not commit that crime!"

"Simply by snatching this bit of steel from me? But this is only one means of death. Ten other ways of avoiding dishonour are before me. Is there not the lake in front of the château? Is not my window a dangerous height from the ground? Oh, rest assured that my honour is safe; for it is guarded by death, Monsieur de Lorédan!"

"Mina, Mina! you would never dare to carry out these threats!"

"Not dare! As true as I hate you, as true as I mistrust you, as true as I love Justin with all my heart and soul, and as true as I will never, never love anyone but Justin, I will deprive myself of life the moment I am unworthy of Justin's love!"

"Mina," answered the young man, releasing her hand and restraining his mortification and rage with a great effort, "let me beg of you to listen to reason so far as to return with me to the house."

"Whilst you remain in the château I'll stop here," replied Mina, firmly.

"I assure you, on my honour, that if you will but let me accompany you to the door I will depart immediately after."

"On *your* honour! That I'll never trust. The moment I know for certain that you have left the château I will return by myself."

"Very well. I will go, since you drive me from your side. Adieu, Mina! If Justin is in peril, you will have only yourself to thank for it, mind!"

Salvator overheard no answer to the adieu, but saw Lorédan de Valgeneuse flash past him in the moonlight, and listened till his footsteps were lost in the distance. Mina remained motionless as a statue till her persecutor was out of sight. When she believed herself to be overlooked by no one, she seemed to realise her utter loneliness and weakness in this solitary retreat. Alone and friendless in her place of captivity, where could she hope for succour? Sinking on her knees, she sent up to Heaven a prayer for strength to withstand her sore trial, and beseeched that Justin might be protected from the perils with which he was threatened. In her misery and despair she added,

"Seigneur! Seigneur! are you too far off to hear my prayer?"

"No, Mina," said a firm, clear voice, as if in answer to her appeal. "He has heard you, and has sent me to help you."

"Grand Dieu!" exclaimed Mina, looking round, "who was it that spoke to me?"

"A friend of Justin. You need have no fear, Mina."

But, notwithstanding these reassuring words, Mina could not repress a cry of alarm at the sight of a man and an immense dog suddenly making their appearance from the thicket close by. The young girl vainly sought to account for this alarming interruption. Yet, by an indefinable instinct, she moved towards the stranger, and, in spite of herself, seemed impelled to murmur, "Welcome, whoever you may be!"

CHAPTER LVI.—SALVATOR AND MINA.

MINA needed but a glance at Salvator's frank face to assure her that it was, indeed, a friend that had almost miraculously come to her aid.

"May I ask whom I have the honour of speaking to, Monsieur?" she said in a voice free from the slightest touch of fear.

"A devoted friend, Mademoiselle."

"A friend! That's the second time you have mentioned that sacred name, Monsieur; but still I don't know you."

"True, Mademoiselle; but in a few moments you will——"

"First," interrupted Mina, "tell me if you have been here long."
"Since twelve."
"Then you heard——"
"All. I did not lose a word that you spoke to Monsieur Lorédan de Valgeneuse. I heard every word he had to say in reply; and my admiration for your heroism and my contempt for his baseness grew with every sentence that reached me."
"Ah! Monsieur, Providence must have conducted you here to help the helpless. Pray tell me your name, that I may know whom I have to thank."
"What good would it be to tell you who I am? I am a riddle, and the answer is in the hands of God. As for my name, I can tell you that which I am known by. I am called Salvator. Accept that name as of good augury: it means Saviour."
"Salvator!" repeated Mina. "A noble name! I feel I can fully trust you, Monsieur."
"There's another name that would give you deeper pleasure."
"Justin's?"
"Yes."
"Do you know Justin, then?" asked Mina, with trembling eagerness.
"Well. I was with him this very afternoon."
"Oh, Monsieur, tell me—tell me—does he love me still?"
"Love you? He adores you!"
"Thank Heaven, *he* has not lost confidence in me. You will tell him for me that I love him better than I ever did before; that I will never love anyone but him, that I would die rather than wed another."
"I will deliver your sweet message, word for word, Mademoiselle Mina. Moreover, Justin shall know all that passed between you and Monsieur Lorédan de Valgeneuse to-night. But we have not a moment to lose now. It almost seems providential that in searching for the trace of a crime committed in this park years ago I should have unwittingly found out where the betrothed of my friend was kept prisoner. Let us profit by this providential coincidence. We have a hundred explanations to give to one another, haven't we?"
"Oh, yes, Monsieur," answered Mina, making room for Salvator beside her on the seat which she had resumed. "Tell me, first of all, how poor Justin bore the news of my disappearance from school at Versailles."
Salvator fraternally pressed the hand which Mina offered him as a sign of her entire trust in his good faith. He then related every incident of the drama with which the reader is familiar: how that he and Jean Robert were first attracted by Justin's violoncello; how that Babolin had rushed in just as they were leaving with the hurried note in which Mina begged Justin to hasten to her rescue; and how that, finally, he, Salvator, had hied with Monsieur Jackal and Justin to the *pensionnat* of Madame Desmaret's, only to trace out, bit by bit, the daring way in which Mina had been carried off by force.
Mina's story was but a realisation of what the acute mind of Mon-

sieur Jackal at once concluded to be the means used for her abduction. As the Chief Commissioner of Police proved step by step, Mina was abducted through the treachery of the young lady whom she took to be a friend; was blindfolded, gagged, and bound fast in her bed-room; was carried off by way of the garden; and was left in a carriage with M. Lorédan de Valgeneuse. The details of her journey through Paris to Juvisy were alone new to Salvator; and he could with difficulty restrain his indignation when he learnt how the young girl in her agony came to write the note which first told Justin of her abduction, and how she had been insidiously tempted by her captor from time to time. The note had been written by her during a temporary stoppage at the Paris residence of M. Lorédan de Valgeneuse. En route in the carriage again, she managed secretly to slip her watch inside the note and to wrap the watch chain round it, so that she might aim her missive—addressed to Justin—at any likely looking messenger she might see before they left the streets of Paris. The opportunity came. She saw *la Brocante*, the ragpicker. Unperceived by M. de Valgeneuse, she threw the note at her feet. Until that hour, however, she had remained ignorant of whether her missive had reached Justin. Mina next explained how it came that fear kept her a prisoner in the chateau. The very morning after her arrival there M. de Valgeneuse, irritated by the scorn and contempt with which she met his advances, informed her of the power he held over Justin. He showed her the passages in the Code by which it seemed that penal servitude would be the punishment of any man marrying a young girl without the consent of her parents or her guardians. He then said that the gates of the château would be left open every day, so that Mina would be free to fly if she pleased; but the moment he heard of her flight he threatened her that Justin should be arrested for connivance at her flight.

"He thereupon took from his pocket," said Mina to Salvator, "an official warrant—a large parchment warrant in which I saw the name of Justin already filled in. 'What is that?' I asked.

"'Oh, nothing,' he said lightly, 'merely a warrant for the arrest of Monsieur Justin. His liberty, you see, is in your hands. An hour after your flight from here your lover will be in gaol.'"

"And that is why I am kept a voluntary prisoner here against my will, Monsieur Salvator. That is why I have not even ventured to write to Justin."

"You have acted wisely, Mademoiselle."

"I have waited, hoped, prayed. My prayers have been answered. Thank Heaven for sending me a friend of Justin. You will give him my message?"

"Rest assured of that."

"But when shall I hear of him again?"

"To-morrow, at this same hour and at this same spot."

"A thousand thanks, Monsieur Salvator. But hide yourself. I hear footsteps approaching. You will be discovered unless you conceal yourself in that thicket. Adieu! Adieu!"

Salvator quickly regained his place of concealment behind the thicket with Roland. The young girl, with light steps, then hastened towards the house; and Salvator heard the servant who was seeking her say to Mina,

"Mademoiselle, Monsieur le Comte has just left the chateau and returned to Paris; and he directed me to tell you the night air would harm you, and to beg of you to come in."

Chapter LVII.—Saved on the Wedding Eve.

In that floral pavilion wherein Pétrus painted the portrait of the beauteous Princess whose loveliness had taken his heart captive, Mademoiselle de Lamothe-Houdan awaited her lover. She was pale and cold as marble. The dress she wore was one of the white costumes prepared for her bridal trousseau. She looked the picture of Despair. It appeared rather the eve of a funeral than a wedding. She listlessly gazed at a pile of letters scattered at her feet. From her reverie—from the utter hopelessness which seemed to have taken possession of her very soul—she was roused by the sound of approaching footsteps.

"He *has* come!" she murmured gladly to herself, at the same time hurriedly placing the letters in a little cabinet.

A moment more and Pétrus was by her side. The love-light involuntarily flashed from her eyes as she greeted him and thanked him for coming.

"You are curious to know," she added, "what has happened to prevent my marriage with Comte Rappt to-morrow. You know that it was a match arranged by my parents. In France, alas! we poor maidens are allowed no choice. Our husbands are chosen for us, and whomsoever we may love, we must marry the men our parents have selected for us. But, thank Heaven! I have had a revelation this day which saves me from being joined to a man I detest. Pétrus, you know I love but you. Conceal yourself for a moment behind that curtain there, and you shall learn the power I have over Comte Rappt."

Even as Pétrus, after snatching one sweet kiss from Régina, hid himself in the veiled alcove, the door of the pavilion was again opened, and Comte Rappt entered, cold and self-possessed as ever. He had not long to wait for his fate.

"I asked for this interview, Monsieur le Comte, to tell you that our marriage cannot take place," said Régina, with the enforced calm of one who had schooled herself to unburden her mind of the painful thoughts weighing upon her.

"Cannot take place!" exclaimed the Comte, with mingled surprise and indignation. "Mademoiselle, you are trifling with me!"

"No, Monsieur le Comte; *I* am in earnest. I leave trifling to those who would trifle with the affections of their best friends' wives. See here!" continued Régina, snatching one of the letters from the cabinet, and opening it, before the Comte.

"Do you recognise this writing?"

The Comte sank down on the sofa like one paralysed.

"You do! Then you *were* base enough to try by every vile art to win my mother's heart away from my father when she was but a young bride! Thank heaven, you could not succeed! These letters clearly tell me *that!* What a mercy they have fallen into my hands! Shall I tell you how I became possessed of these *billets-doux* of yours, Monsieur le Comte? It was Abeille that found them. The key had been left in my mother's private cabinet. Abeille seized the opportunity, and searched it. She found these letters and brought them to me. I saw they were in your handwriting. I have read them, and now know how wickedly you would have repaid the trust my father reposed in you."

Comte Rappt shrank from Régina as though she were his judge.

"What would you wish me to do?" he faintly asked, not daring to meet Régina's scornful glance.

"Release me from my engagement. Do that, and for my poor mother's sake I will keep her secret. Refuse, and I will hand these letters to my father."

"But how could I explain my withdrawal from my engagement?" stammered the Comte.

"That I leave to you, Monsieur le Comte. Could you not be suddenly called away to Hungary to-night, and send the letter to my father to-morrow morning?"

Whether it was that a demand was about to be made upon the diplomatic powers he fancied he possessed, and this turned his thoughts into a less humiliating channel, or whether it was that he was glad to escape from the presence of the indignant girl who had thus narrowly escaped an alliance with him, Comte Rappt rose at this juncture, and, bowing low, said,

"It shall be as you wish, Mademoiselle Régina. Some excuse for breaking off our marriage, and terminating our engagement shall be found by me before the morning, since you insist upon it. But let me, in parting, ask you to take my ready compliance with your desire as entitling me to be less harshly judged by you."

"I wish you good-night, Monsieur le Comte," answered Régina, as he paused with his hand on the handle of the door; "but I cannot promise you anything before I see your letter in the morning."

"Adieu, then, Mademoiselle Régina."

* * * * *

A few minutes later Pétrus was kneeling at the feet of Régina, repaying her for her constancy by an eloquent declaration of his love for her. Clasping her hands with the fervour of a young lover, he poured into her ears all his pent-up passion; and Régina, yielding to the seductive joy of the moment, felt a tremor of delight steal over her as she realised the icy fate she had escaped and the rapturous pleasure she had gained in winning the ardent lover whose first warm embrace sent an ecstatic thrill through her veins.

Chapter LVIII.—Mina and Justin.

Salvator was with Justin early enough the next morning; and it need scarcely be said that Justin was almost overwhelmed with joy at Salvator's discovery of Mina. Still more did he rejoice when he learnt that that very night he might be favoured with a sight of his beloved, nor was his ardour damped at the precautions Salvator thought it wise to enforce, lest Justin, in the blindness of his love, should fall into any trap M. Lorédan de Valgeneuse might have set for him. Warned, therefore, of the danger that would attend any rash attempt to rescue Mina, Justin set out with Salvator in the evening for Viry-sur-Orge, the village nearest the château which was Mina's prison. It was eleven o'clock by the time they reached the château. Salvator and Justin crept as silently as shadows alongside the wall till they gained the spot where Salvator had climbed over into the park on the previous night. As he helped Roland to escalade the wall on the former occasion, so he helped Justin now. In the twinkling of an eye Salvator had joined his friend on the other side. Avoiding the detour to the lake which he and Roland had made, Salvator led Justin straight to the wood in which Mina had at first appeared to him in the light of a phantom.

"There's the seat," whispered Salvator to Justin. "Keep quiet, and hide yourself in that thicket. I hear the rustling of a dress."

"Is it Mina?" whispered back Justin.

"Probably. But let me speak with her first. She might not be able to bear your sudden appearance, Justin. Make haste. Conceal yourself. She's close at hand."

It was Mina. She looked round anxiously when she had reached the rustic seat, and started when she heard the branches near her cracking.

"Fear nothing. It is I, Mademoiselle," said Salvator, revealing himself.

"Ah! I am so happy to see you again! Have you brought me any news of Justin?"

"Yes. He was overwhelmed with joy to hear I had at last found you."

"Dear Justin! Did you tell him where I was?"

"Yes."

"And then——"

"And then, of course, he wanted to see you at once."

"Naturally."

"So I promised to conduct him hither."

"When?"

"One of these fine nights."

"One of these fine nights!" exclaimed the young girl with an impatient sigh. "And did he consent to wait?"

"No; he wished to come at once."

"And he has——"

"And he has come, and is here now!"

"Ah, Monsieur, I thought I overheard you both talking together a little while ago. It was to him you were speaking, wasn't it?"

"Yes, Mademoiselle. He would have rushed up to you at once, but I prevented him."

"Oh! I should have died with joy if I had met him then!"

"You hear, Justin?" said Salvator, giving him a preconcerted signal.

Justin answered by pushing his way through the thicket, and by clasping Mina to his heart.

"Mina!" and "Justin!" the two words that escaped them, were almost inaudible from the rapturous kisses the young man showered on the sweet lips of his beloved.

Gratitude to Salvator was the mutual feeling they next felt and gave hearty expression to.

"Justin," replied Salvator, "you know it was by chance only that I found Mina. You know I was led here for a far different purpose. Let me pursue my search. Enjoy an hour of happiness with Mina. Meanwhile I'll watch and see that you are not interrupted."

Chapter LIX.—A Race to Paris.

WHILST Justin's heart was rejoiced at the clandestine meeting with his lost love, how fared it with Gibassier, whom M. Jackal had despatched to Kehl in search of M. Sarranti? The mission was one just suited to the genius of the escaped convict. Witness how he fulfilled it. In the early morning of March 27, two post-chaises rattled through the main street of Kehl with such velocity that mine host of the Frederick the Great Inn not unnaturally feared that his hostelry would lose two good customers, and that the travellers would, as a punishment for their haste, be precipitated into the Rhine directly they ventured on the bridge of boats connecting the French with the German frontier. Happily, however, the two post-chaises relaxed their speed midway in the High-street, and the landlord of the foremost inn of Kehl felt reassured by seeing both vehicles stop short at his hospitable doors. A man of about fifty years of age leapt from the first carriage. He wore a blue overcoat, buttoned up to his chin. His upright bearing and commanding air proclaimed him a military man.

From the second chaise a man enveloped in a gorgeous Hungarian cloak descended with an assumption of dignity. He looked at first sight like some rich Hospodar from Bucharest or a well-to-do Magyar from Pesth. His whiskers and moustaches were most ample. That costume and manner were put on it would not have been difficult for a keen observer to see. In fact, as the reader has doubtless already surmised, the pseudo Hospodar or Magyar was no other than Gibassier, whilst the stranger in the blue great coat was M. Sarranti. It will be remembered that the Chief Commissioner of the Paris police dispatched Gibassier to Kehl, there to await further instructions. To Kehl Gibassier accordingly journeyed. Thither he was subsequently joined by Carmagnole, who brought him word that M. Sarranti would reach Kehl on March 26, but that Gibassier was to hasten to Steinbach, where he would find a post-chaise, in which, after assuming the disguise therein deposited, he would have to follow closely in the wake of M. Sarranti on his journey to Paris. Gibassier was now in his element. He sped to Steinbach, full of ardour for the chase. He donned with glee the strange dress prepared for him. In inaction he then had to spend a day or so; for the 26th passed by, but no M. Sarranti was among the travellers journeying through Steinbach. Towards two o'clock on the following morning, however, the man he was so anxiously awaiting arrived. The moment he heard the horses pulled up at the Sun Hotel he hurried to the yard and got his chaise ready, and set off for Kehl in the twinkling of an eye. Promptitude was necessary. Ten minutes later M. Sarranti, who had only stopped to change horses, and snatch a hasty meal, resumed his journey. Two leagues from Steinbach he caught up to Gibassier. A rule of the road, however, prevented him from passing the leading post-chaise without obtaining the first traveller's permission. This was asked; and was granted with so much courtesy and readiness that M. Sarranti shouted out his hearty thanks. This done, his post-chaise disappeared in a cloud of dust; but Gibassier, not put out in the least by the incident, bade his postillion follow as closely as he could. The postillion did his duty so well that both vehicles, as we have seen, entered Kehl almost together, and stopped at the same time at the inn of Frederick the Great. The travellers exchanged cordial salutes on alighting, and both made straight for the *salle à manger*, where they demanded breakfast, and discussed that meal in silence. Gibassier did not rise till M. Sarranti had finished. Still, without exchanging a word, they regained their seats, and started afresh on the route to Paris, Gibassier whispering to his postillion to continue to keep M. Sarranti's post-chaise in sight. M. Sarranti's post-chaise led the way at a furious pace. The postillion had personal reasons for reaching Nancy at the earliest possible moment. "Best man" at his cousin's wedding, he was naturally desirous to lead off the ball that evening with the first bridesmaid. Using spurs and whip freely, therefore, he urged the steeds on at a tremendous gallop, which ended, however, in a way little anticipated by the postillion. As night drew on they were rapidly nearing Nancy. Going down hill with undiminished speed, the chaise cannoned against the hedge, the horses were jerked to the ground, and traveller and postillion alike were pitched out into the roadway. Gibassier was profuse in his commiseration when he drove up and found M. Sarranti stamping with impatience, though he had escaped with a sound skin, unlike the rider, who had severely contused his shoulder, and received such injuries on his knees that dancing at his cousin's wedding that night was quite out of the question. One of the horses was stunned, the other lamed, and the chaise had lost a wheel. Providence, it seemed to M. Sarranti, came to his rescue under these unfortunate circumstances, in the person of the stranger, who luckily happened to be travelling along the same route himself. In a language which sounded half French, half German, Gibassier, in the guise of the Magyar, offered the belated traveller a seat in his vehicle. The offer was at once gladly accepted; the luggage was lifted in after M. Sarranti; the luckless postillion, who had so sadly realised the truth of the "more haste the less speed" adage, was promised prompt succour; and Gibassier was soon speeding towards Nancy with the man he was hunting sitting face to face with him, little suspecting his benefactor to be the acutest police-spy M. Jackal could have selected from all Paris. There was first a mutual interchange of compliments natural to the occasion. Then Gibassier (whose knowledge of German was very slight, and who feared that M. Sarranti, Corsican though he was, might be familiar with that language) carefully avoided being enticed into any conversation, contenting himself with simply replying in monosyllables to the questions of his companion, who could scarcely have avoided noticing that his every "Yes" and "No" sounded more and more French to his ears. Arrived at Nancy, they put up at the Grand Stanislas Hotel, the posting-house of the town. M. Sarranti renewed his thanks to the stranger who had so opportunely befriended him, and would have entered the hotel alone.

"Excuse me, Monsieur," said Gibassier, "but it is evidently your object to reach Paris as speedily as horses can carry you; and, as your carriage is hors-de-combat for a day, at least, I fear you will be sadly retarded. Pray retain your seat in my chaise."

"Thank you," answered M. Sarranti, with a certain air of reserve. "The mishap vexes me all the more since a similar accident happened as I was leaving Ratisbonne, and delayed me twenty-four hours."

Gibassier now knew the cause of M. Sarranti's late arrival at Steinbach.

"But," continued M. Sarranti, "I shall not wait until the post-chaise is repaired. I must buy another one. Here, landlord, get me the best carriage you can at a moment's notice. Anything on wheels will do, so long as it will take me safely and quickly to Paris."

Gibassier, concluding that there would be time to enjoy dinner in peace ere M. Sarranti was satisfied, took his seat at the table, but was surprised to find that M. Sarranti sat in the chair opposite, and called out simultaneously with him—

"*Garçon un dîner!*"

The fact was, certain vague suspicions began to fill M. Sarranti's mind with regard to his chance acquaintance, a Magyar, who, singularly enough, seemed equally ignorant of German and French, as far as speaking those languages went, and yet could apparently readily understand every French sentence that was addressed to him, although he invariably replied with a laconic "*ja*" or "*nein.*" Why should he be so anxious to fasten himself upon him? M. Sarranti silently answered this question by resolving to disembarrass himself of this obliging but reticent fellow-traveller, and so it was that he declined to continue the journey to Paris in Gibassier's post-chaise, and ordered a fresh carriage to be brought to the door without loss of time. Gibassier was too cunning not to perceive that M.

Sarranti regarded him with suspicion. It would now be a war of wits, he felt. Giving as an excuse that the Austrian ambassador was anxiously waiting him in Paris, Gibassier accordingly ordered fresh horses to be put to the post-chaise during dinner. The meal over, he gave a profound salute to M. Sarranti, hastened back to his carriage, and, as the horses broke into a smart gallop, pondered over the difficulty that faced him—which route would M. Sarranti take? Pressed as he was, the Bonapartist agent would doubtless pursue the high road as far as Ligny. There he would probably leave Bar-le-Duc on his right, and reach Sainte-Dizier and Vitry-le-Français by way of Aucerville. From Vitry-le-Français, however, would he proceed to Châlons, or would he keep on the straight route through Fère-Champenoise, Coulommiers, Crécy, and Ligny? This was a question which could only be decided at Vitry. Half a league, therefore, from that town, Gibassier held a short conference with his postillion, which resulted in the chaise being overturned as if by the accidental snapping of the front axletree. The belated traveller quietly waited half an hour in the unfortunate position with which M. Sarranti was more familiar than he was. He was then impelled into sudden activity. He heard the welcome sound of approaching wheels; he guessed it was M. Sarranti, and he made sure that one whom he had relieved would hasten to assist him. The post-chaise drew up, and M. Sarranti, putting his head out of the window, saw that it was Gibassier, who was fruitlessly endeavouring to repair the mischief done to his carriage. To have left the distressed Magyar alone in his difficulty M. Sarranti felt would have been churlish and ungrateful.

A seat in M. Sarranti's chaise was no sooner offered than it was accepted with remarkable alacrity by Gibassier, who protested, however, that he would not trouble his "Excellency Monsieur de Bornis" (the name assumed by M. Sarranti) beyond Vitry. Twenty minutes after the post-chaise rattled through the streets of Vitry-le-Français. At the posting-house an old cabriolet was found that suited Gibassier; and "M. de Bornis" took leave once again of the Magyar, giving the order, as Gibassier fancied, "Follow the route through Fère-Champenoise."

Gibassier soon started on the same road. He promised the postillion five francs directly he should catch sight of the carriage he was pursuing. The horses were urged on at their very highest turn of speed; the clatter of their hoofs rang through the night air. The hedges flew by. Still no sign of M. Sarranti's vehicle. Gibassier sprang to the ground the moment the next posting-house was gained, and learnt that no post-chaise had passed there that night. It was clear, then, that M. Sarranti had eluded him. He had uttered the command "to Fère-Champenoise" in his hearing on purpose to throw him off the scent. He must in reality have gone by way of Châlons. There remained the chance of reaching Meaux before M. Sarranti. Should he not be able to do so, Gibassier felt that he must certainly fail in the very first commission M. Jackal had given him. Quick as thought, Gibassier resolved to give up the cabriolet. From his box he took the complete livery of a courier in blue and gold, and donned it with the celerity of one well used to disguises, pulled off his false whiskers and moustache, strapped the despatch-bag to his shoulders, and mounted the horse which had been saddled meantime. There was not a moment to lose. A spirited steed was under him. Gibassier did not spare spur or whip, nor did he abate his speed till thirty leagues had been covered, and he was fairly inside the gate of Meaux.

No post-chaise answering Gibassier's description had passed through Meaux. He drew a deep breath of relief, and sat down, half-famished, to a meal which was breakfast and dinner rolled into one, having first taken the precaution to order a fresh horse to be saddled and kept in readiness for him. It was night by the time the traveller he so anxiously awaited arrived; and M. Sarranti was evidently determined to profit by the start he imagined he had secured of that leech of a Magyar whom it had been so difficult to throw off. He simply ordered a basin of soup to be brought to him in the chaise, and directed the postillion to continue the route to Paris through Claye. This was enough for Gibassier. He knew he could not be mistaken this time. Springing into the saddle, he gave his horse the reins, and let him canter easily along the high road to Paris. He had but a short while to wait, for, in about ten minutes, on looking back, he saw the lamps of M. Sarranti's post-chaise flashing behind him. These brilliant lights he could see without being seen himself, and he now took care that he should not be heard either. He kept about a kilomètre in advance, and thus he galloped into Bondy. There another metamorphosis took place. The courier was tranformed in the twinkling of an eye into a postillion, and the transference of five francs from his pocket to the pocket of the postillion on duty secured for Gibassier the next vacant saddle. M. Sarranti thought it not worth while to alight now he was so near Paris. He contented himself with ordering a fresh relay. The horses—the fleetest pair in the stables—were harnessed by Gibassier, who wore his postillion's disguise with the aplomb of a true comedian, and who, with unabashed reliance on the total change he had effected in his appearance, put his head in at the window, and exclaimed, in an unmistakable French patois, "Ready Monsieur! Where shall you put up at in Paris?"

"Grand Turc Hôtel, Place Saint-André-des-Arcs," answered the unsuspecting M. Sarranti.

"Good!" said Gibassier; "we shall be there in no time, Monsieur."

"En route, then. Ten francs for yourself, if we're there in an hour!"

"Done, monsieur," replied Gibassier, mounting and chuckling to himself at the double meaning of his words.

The barriers were soon gained; there was a formal inspection of the luggage, and M. Sarranti, who seven years previously had fled from Paris by the barrier of Fontainebleau, returned to the city through that of Petite-Vilette. The post chaise rattled safely into the court-yard of the Grand Turc Hôtel in another quarter of an hour, and M. Sarranti was tracked to his destination by the wily agent of M. Jackal.

CHAPTER LX.—THE SPY'S DISCOVERY.

THE hotel had but two rooms vacant, Nos. 6 and 11, both on the same floor, the doors facing each other. M. Sarranti chose No. 6. By what ruse could Gibassier secure No. 11? The astute postillion remained quiet till the garçon had done waiting on M. Sarranti. As soon as he could have a word with the busy waiter, Gibassier demanded if he knew M. Poirier.

"What Monsieur Poirier?" said the garçon.

"What Monsieur Poirier! Why, our Monsieur Poirier—the great farmer who has a flock of four hundred sheep. He will be here by eleven, and he commissioned me to engage a room for him at this hotel. He said to me, 'Charpillon'— that's my name, 'Charpillon,' you know— 'Charpillon,' he said, said he, 'give the chambermaid at the Grand Turc this hundred sous, and she will be sure to reserve a room for me. Where is the chambermaid, garçon?"

"Oh, if that's all you want, Monsieur Charpillon," returned the waiter, "I can engage the room as well as the chambermaid."

"Can you? Here's the hundred sous, then. You'll not forget Monsieur Poirier?"

"Oh, no, if he only mentions his name."

"He'll be sure to mention that. By-the-way, you had better get a good supper ready for him, with a good bottle of bordeaux, with the chill taken off, you know."

Satisfied that his instructions would be obeyed to the letter, Gibassier left the hotel, but only to return a quarter of an hour afterwards as the portly M. Poirier from Plât-d'Étain. The garçon at once conducted him to room No. 11, where an excellent supper awaited him, together with the bottle of bordeaux, placed a proper distance from the fire to acquire that degree of warmth which brings the true flavour out of the wine. M. Poirier was not to be tempted from duty even by the savoury meal spread for him. He patiently waited till he heard the door of M. Sarranti's room opened. His own door being ajar, he could distinctly hear his fellow-traveller tell the chambermaid, as he was leaving, that he should return in an hour or two. Where could M. Sarranti be bound for at so late an hour? Gibassier determined to find out. He quickly descended the stairs of the hotel, and was soon dogging the footsteps of the Bonapartist agent afresh. The Rue de Bussy, the market of Saint-Germain, the Place Saint-Sulpice, and the Rue du Pot-de-Fer were traversed by the spy in pursuit. M. Sarranti just called in for a minute at No. 28, Rue du Pot-de-Fer. Therefrom he was followed by Gibassier to the mysterious house in the Rue des Postes, which was the source of so much trouble to M. Jackal. M. Sarranti paused at the door until he should be joined by the four confederates, who (as M. Jackal told Gibassier) would have to put in their appearance before admission to the secret rendezvous could be gained. Only three came. Gibassier could plainly see that M. Sarranti was getting impatient. His natural daring suggested a venturesome ruse. The ex-convict walked boldly up to the group, was welcomed as the one conspirator for whom they had been waiting, and, thanks to the initiation of the Commissioner of Police, was enabled to give the sign of freemasonry which would admit him, without exciting their suspicion in the faintest degree. The Bonapartist conspirators, little suspecting that they had a police spy in their midst, were soon in the middle of the rotunda. It was an assemblage of leaders to hear the news M. Sarranti had to impart; and the important intelligence he brought was that in less than three days the Duc de Reichstadt, the heir of Napoleon, their future Emperor, would be at Saint-Leu-Taverny, where he would remain incognito until the moment came for him to be welcomed by the French people. It was a settled plan of all the affiliated secret societies to take advantage of any assemblage of their leaders to appoint a general meeting of the members; and in accordance with this practice, M. Sarranti appointed the next day for a general meeting, the Church of the Assumption being the rendezvous, as there would unfailingly be large numbers of the public there to do honour to the memory of the Duc de la Rochefoucauld, whose funeral was fixed for that morning, and the strength of the Napoleonic gathering would, therefore, not be noticed. So the Bonapartist chiefs left the mysterious house at one o'clock, with the understanding that they would meet again in the morning at the Church of the Assumption.

CHAPTER LXI.—THE POLICE EMEUTE.

GIBASSIER did ample justice to the supper awaiting him in Room No. 11 of the Grand Turc Hôtel, when he returned thither close at the heels of M. Sarranti. Sure of his man in the morning, M. Jackal's faithful spy departed with a light heart at an early hour to inform his chief of the success of his chase from Kehl. He was received with open arms by the Chief Commissioner of Police at the Rue de Jérusalem.

"Welcome, welcome, my dear Gibassier!" said M. Jackal, effusively. "You see I have returned to Paris as soon as you have. Join me at breakfast, and tell me what has befallen you."

The whole story of his adventures since leaving Kehl was then recounted with animation by Gibassier, to the huge delight of his chief, who overwhelmed him with praise, but did not allow him to linger long over the déjeûner, for he had a new task ready for him.

"This very morning, opportunely enough," said M. Jackal, "we are about to have an émeute in honour of the funeral of the Duc de la Rochefoucauld, and it will be hard if we can't manage to start the disturbance in the very nick of time to arrest this Monsieur Sarranti, and so stop the Bonapartists' little game. That, however, shall be our last resource. First, you and Carmagnole shall have the duty of arresting M. Sarranti in the church. You will find him, at midday, leaning against the third pillar to the left. His son will join him there. You cannot make a mistake. Do this job as well as you have done the last and you shall be well rewarded. Luck attend you, Gibassier!"

* * * * * *

At the hour named by M. Jackal, M. Sarranti was to be seen at the very spot mentioned by the Commissioner of Police. He had been identified by Gibassier and Carmagnole, both of whom were disguised. They were about to act upon M. Jackal's orders, and arrest the determined-looking Bonapartist, when a monk glided up to M. Sarranti and knelt at his feet with an air of profound reverence. That very moment M. Sarranti must have received some caution or signal, for he disappeared in the midst of the dense crowd that thronged the church, and the police spies could see him nowhere. All Paris seemed in an uproar outside the church. The students were out. They marched in a large, compact body, and showed their reverence for the patriotic statesman whose funeral was taking place by soliciting that some of their representatives should be pall-bearers. The relatives of the Duc de la Rochefoucauld readily granted permission; but the Government authorities refused to allow it. Murmurs grew into threats. The military, with bayonets drawn, drove back the students. Blood was spilt. In a moment the émeute organised by M. Jackal broke forth, and life-preservers were wielded so recklessly that heads were broken open, and a revolution was almost provoked. M. Sarranti, discovered in the crowd by the lynx-eyed Commissioner of Police, was now pounced upon, irritated to defend himself, and then overpowered by superior numbers, and made a prisoner of. Another incident that happened to a conspicuous personage in this story was an attack upon Jean Taureau, who was about to wreak his vengeance on the innocent head of Fañou, the mountebank, who chanced to be standing near, when his amazonian mistress wrenched a life-preserver from the hand of one of the *mouchards*, and brought it down with a vigorous crack on the temples of Jean Taureau.

Chapter LXII.—M. Sarranti's Arrest.

INTERESTED eye-witnesses of the riot which raged round the Church of the Assumption were Salvator, Jean Robert, Ludovic, Pétrus, and Justin. The Commissionaire, their leader, had forewarned them of the émeute, and had cautioned them on no account to join in the fray provoked by the police. All save one obeyed Salvator implicitly. That one was Justin, the youngest and most susceptible. He, like his friends, had been sworn in as a member of the Carbonari of Paris; and, prompted by vengeance against the Comte de Valgeneuse and his orde for the violent abduction of Mina, whose rescue he was prevented by powerful reasons from effecting yet awhile, and impelled to action by a more than usually brutal attack by a mouchard on a mere lad, Justin acted upon the generous impulse of the moment, and pushed the police-agent away from the prostrate form of the boy he was punishing. Out of revenge for his comrade's repulse, another police emissary was about to play upon Justin's skull with his heavily-loaded life-preserver, when Salvator, quick as thought, interposed his arm ; but, to his surprise, the weapon was stopped in its descent, and a well-known voice whispered in his ear,

"Well met, Monsieur Salvator! How glad I am to meet you again!"

It was the Chief Commissioner of Police himself. M. Jackal followed up his friendly greeting by a significant gesture of command to his men not to interfere with our heroes, but, at the same time, he thought it necessary to give them a warning.

"My dear Monsieur Salvator," said the Commissioner of Police, confidentially, to Salvator, as he lifted his dark spectacles from his eyes, in order to see the better, "let me advise you and your friends to make the best of your way out of this."

"Why? Is there any danger?"

"One never knows how far an émeute may spread."

"But suppose we wish to see the fun?" replied Salvator.

"Oh! that is another matter. You know the risk you run."

"Rest assured, Monsieur Jackal, *we* shall not run the same risk as that gentleman who is struggling with your men yonder!"

"Where?" asked the Commissioner of Police, feigning not to have seen the arrest of M. Sarranti, and looking in another direction.

"Why, over there; a few steps from that noble-looking monk. Surely it must be the Abbé Dominique, the faithful friend of poor Colomban, and my saviour! I thought he was at the Château de Penhoël, in Brittany."

"He was; but he returned this morning," answered M. Jackal, unable to resist the temptation to show his omniscience. "And, *ma foi!* I see now. They *have* arrested some one in whom he seems singularly interested. I sincerely pity the poor citizen, whoever he may be."

"You don't know him then?"

"No."

"Nor the men with whom he is wrestling so pluckily?"

"I wish my sight was better," replied M. Jackal, adjusting the glasses on the bridge of his nose. "Yes, surely I know the fellows who have seized our citizen by the collar. But where can I have seen them?"

Not deeming it prudent to remain longer under the fire of Salvator's examination, the dapper Commissioner of Police bade him farewell and hastened towards Gibassier and Carmagnole, who found it an almost impossible task to prevent their prisoner escaping.

"I arrest you, in the name of the king!" These words, muttered harshly in his ears by Gibassier and Carmagnole at the same moment, had been the first inkling M. Sarranti had had of the danger he was in after he had left the Church of the Assumption.

"Arrest me! What for?" he had indignantly exclaimed.

"We want no noise. You are known to us, Monsieur Dubreuil," answered Carmagnole, acting under the instructions of M. Jackal, and mentioning the name under which M. Sarranti had written to announce his arrival to his son. The Abbé Dominique involuntarily stepped forward to aid his father when he witnessed the arrest, but was kept back by a sign from M. Sarranti.

"Pray don't concern yourself with my arrest, monsieur," he said to the monk. "I am the victim of a mistake. To-morrow I am sure I shall be set at liberty."

The monk bent his head as if in reverence to one in authority, and turned to make his way out of the seething crowd.

"And now," continued M. Sarranti, addressing Gibassier and Carmagnole in a haughty tone, "tell me why I have been arrested and what authority you have to arrest me here."

"We can easily satisfy you on those points," answered Gibassier. "In the first place we have a warrant to arrest Monsieur Dubreuil. In the second place we have been on the look-out for you ever since you left your hotel in the Place Saint-André-des-Arcs this morning, and this is the first opportunity we have had of seizing you since."

The moment Gibassier mentioned the name of his hotel, a thought flashed like lightning through the mind of M. Sarranti. He seemed to recognise the voice of Gibassier, and to find something familiar in his features. Then all became clear to him--the sham Hungarian, the courier, the postillion, and Gibassier, he instinctively felt to be one and the same person.

"Miserable spy!" exclaimed M. Sarranti, pale as death, impulsively drawing a dagger from a hidden sheath.

Gibassier saw the cold steel flash above him, and death would in all probability have followed the flash as quickly as the thunder follows the lightning, if Carmagnole had not seized the up-lifted arm with both hands just as the fatal blow was about to be dealt to his comrade. It was at this juncture that M. Sarranti, filled with rage at being dogged and entrapped thus, had made that supreme effort to escape which had attracted the attention of the Chief Commissioner of Police himself, and had caused him to leave Salvator so abruptly. The prisoner, with a mighty effort, tore himself from the grasp of Gibassier and Carmagnole, and bounded off, dagger still in hand, shouting in the voice of one used to command, "Clear the way!"

But the two police emissaries darted after their prey, and, by a preconcerted signal, drew a number of other sleuth-hounds to join in the chase. In an instant M. Sarranti was surrounded by an insurmountable circle, and a score of life-preservers were in the act of settling his fate when the weapons fell harmlessly to the sides of the mouchards at a command, uttered in a tone they knew only too well, "Stop! Take him alive!"

There ensued an indescribable mêlée. One against twenty, M. Sarranti yet fought with a vigour and a courage that soon put some of the mouchards hors-de-combat. He hurled his assailants off with lion-like valour. They, knowing the conflict was taking place under the eyes of their chief, returned to the assault; and, strengthened by ever-increasing numbers, at last overpowered M. Sarranti, handcuffed him, and held him prisoner again with iron grasps. Dominique watched this conflict in terrible anguish. Monk though he was, Dominique felt himself drawn by an irresistible impulse to the aid of his father, but was separated from him by an angry torrent of people, rushing in a panic from the bayonets of the military. An eddy in this furious torrent, as it were, the group of which M. Sarranti was the centre soon became lost to the view of the despairing monk.

CHAPTER LXIII.—SALVATOR'S SAVIOUR.

ON the morrow of March 30, 1827, Paris awoke indignant at the police émeute of the previous day, and angered against the Government for the vexatious interference with the funeral of the national benefactor, the Duc de la Rochefoucald-Liancourt. Eye-witnesses of the outrage done to the memory of the illustrious dead fed the flame of popular indignation, which was fanned by the violent remonstrances of the opposition press, and even spread to the two Chambers. What was the defence of the Government? It simply made the Bonapartist party responsible for the disturbances. An official communication to the Ministerial journals thus credited one of the principal personages of this history with being the real cause of the émeute :—

"The hydra of anarchy has lifted its head. The Altar and the Throne, the King and the Church, have been threatened. Happily, the Préfet of Police has discovered the conspiracy in time to render it abortive. The chief conspirator has been arrested. He is no other than the celebrated Corsican, Sarranti, who, a fugitive from France a few years ago, when he was accused of the double crime of robbery and murder, had returned to Paris to place the Duc de Reichstadt on the throne of his Majesty. It may be remembered that the village of Viry-sur-Orge was, in the year 1820, the scene of a fearful crime. One of the most respected men in the county found, on returning home one evening, that his safe had been burst open and rifled, his wife assassinated, and that his young nephew and niece, with their tutor, had disappeared.

"That tutor was M. Sarranti.

"He will be at once tried on the capital charge."

The agitation into which Dominique Sarranti had been thrown by the arrest of his father was the cause of this startling accusation escaping his attention. A dream had revealed to him during the night that in this emergency he would find his greatest friend in Salvator. Awaking in the morning, the monk was irresistibly led to put faith in the dream, for he suddenly remembered that he had observed Salvator in conversation with M. Jackal during the émeute, and therefore felt strengthened in the hope that help might be forthcoming from the Commissionaire. Leaving his journal unread, his breakfast untasted, Dominique accordingly lost not another moment in hieing to Salvator's dwelling. With a gesture at once respectful and cordial, our hero welcomed him, and introduced him to Fragola.

"I owe my life to this noble monk, Fragola. Love him as a brother. In that terrible hour of misery, years ago, I heard Father

Dominique preach in Saint-Roch. His compassionate words saved me. I was in such stress that I had resolved to blow out my brains. The sympathetic sermon gave me a new love of life. So I owe my life to him. Let him do what he will with it."

"I have remembered your promise," answered the monk with a sad smile; "and I have come to seek your aid."

"It is granted with all my heart."

The monk pressed Salvator's hand with a feverish grasp, and continued, "A man for whom I entertain the deepest affection was arrested by the police yesterday during the émeute in the Rue Saint-Honoré, and was spirited away before I could haste to his succour."

"I saw the arrest, and noticed that he made a vigorous resistance before he was captured."

"Yes," replied the monk, with a sigh; "and I fear that resistance, legitimate though it was, will but tell against him. But what I ask of you now is to learn for me the nature of the offence he is charged with."

"Is that all? What is the name of your friend?"

"Dubreuil."

"His profession?"

"An officer on the retired list."

"I'll just slip on my overcoat," replied Salvator; "and gather the information you require in no time."

CHAPTER LXIV.—CARMELITE'S DEBUT.

A SOIREE at the Hôtel de Marande was one of the most brilliant sights in Paris. The lovely wife of one of the richest bankers in the city had drawn around her all that was brightest and gayest in the fashionable world. Her salons were famous. It is but a glimpse of the charming abode of Madame de Marande that need be given now. As one of the four heroines of this story, Lydia de Marande will appear again and again, but never more beautiful than she was on the night when she proved the constancy of her love and friendship for Carmélite, and gave the soirée especially devoted to the launching of Carmélite in the world of fashion as a singer of whom Paris might well be proud. There were gathered that night in the luxurious drawing-room of Madame de Marande some of her most trusted friends, with a sprinkling of acquaintances whose influence would be of use to her portégée. The Princesse de Lamothe-Houdan enjoyed an hour of intoxicating delight with her lover, Pétrus. Jean Robert hovered admiringly around the fascinating hostess, to whom assiduous court was also paid by Comte Lorédan de Valgeneuse. The latter Lydia de Marande felt an instinctive but (to her) unaccountable prejudice against, and so gladly listened to the witty gossip of Jean Robert and to the frank converse of General Comte de Herbel. The sad heart-history of Carmélite was known to all these, save De Valgeneuse. It was, consequently, with no little contempt for her betrayer that Jean Robert and Pétrus saw Camille de Rozan enter with his young wife the moment Carmélite, seated at the pianoforte, was pouring forth, as if from the very depths of her soul, some of the most heart-stirring strains of the opera of "Otello." Her grand contralto voice swayed the emotions of her audience as she listed. Her melodious notes spoke to the mind as well as the ear. Carmélite made captive all her hearers except one. The one listener whose shallow mind was not reached by her transcendant genius, but whose ear was simply tickled by the magic of the music, was Camille de Rozan. He had just arrived in Paris from Louisiana on his honeymoon trip, and was invited by Monsieur de Marande as an act of courtesy to a gentleman who had brought influential letters of introduction to his bank. With graceful courtesy, Madame de Marande had taken charge of his young wife on her entrance; and he, finding himself near Pétrus, ventured to utter a few empty compliments as to the talent of the singer, and as to his preference of Rossini to Mozart.

"That was not the opinion of your late friend, Monsieur Colomban, I believe," answered Pétrus coolly.

"Late friend!" echoed Camille, involuntarily shrinking at the mention of the friend he had so basely betrayed. "Can Colomban be dead?"

"Yes, Monsieur," replied Pétrus, with a frigid bow; "he died from asphyxia. He committed suicide in order that he might not be *untrue to the trust of his friend.*"

Camille, sensitive as he was vain and heartless, shuddered at this unexpected intelligence of Colomban's death; and, seized with a transitory fit of remorse, buried his face in his hands as he realised the tragedy of which his treachery was the cause.

CHAPTER LXV.—THE BONAPARTIST FIASCO.

SALVATOR found the Chief Commissioner of Police absent from the Préfecture. Whether from his close knowledge of M. Jackal, however, or from the instinct of a conspirator, he guessed where he would find him. Salvator rightly imagined he would find the jackal he was in quest of where there was the greatest likelihood of pouncing on his prey: on the scene of the previous day's émeute. Appointing the quay corner of the Place Saint-Germain-l'Auxerreois as a rendezvous with Dominique Sarranti, our hero, accordingly, set out briskly in the direction of the Rue Saint-Honoré. He was hastening across the Pont Neuf when a hand was waved to him from a carriage, which was suddenly brought to a full stop. Salvator paused to look at the man who had beckoned him, and recognised General la Fayette. Saluting the General with profound respect, he at once complied with his request, and accepted a seat by his side.

"You are Monsieur Salvator, are you not?" demanded the General, as the carriage started off again at a slow pace.

"Yes, General; and I have twice had the honour to be associated with you as a delegate."

"I thought so. You are the chief of your lodge, are you not?"

"Yes, General."

"How many men have you? Two hundred—three hundred?"

"General," answered Salvator, smiling, "the day you need us you'll find us three thousand strong."

"The more you have the greater the reason you should know the news."

"What news?"

"The Vienna business has failed."

"I feared so, and cautioned my men not to join in yesterday's movement. But is your information absolutely certain?"

"I had it from Monsieur de Marande, who had it direct from the Duc d'Orleans."

"Then the plot had been discovered?"

"Yes; but it is uncertain whether the failure is due to the activity of the police or to one of those accidents which maintain or break up a kingdom. You know all was ripe for the departure of the Duc de Reichstadt from Vienna for Paris. March 24 was the day fixed upon. The Duke himself was not found wanting. Throwing a cloak over his shoulders, he readily managed by a bribe to pass the guard at the gates of Schönbrunn. At the foot of Mont Vert a carriage and an escort of four men on horseback awaited him, and he was soon en route, the horses going at a gallop. The chief of his escort was General Lebastard de Prémont, and he had the satisfaction to see that they dashed through Baumgarten and Hutteldorf in safety. A bridge crosses the river at Weidlingen. On this bridge a market cart loaded with calves had been upset either by mishap or design. The bridge was impassable.

"'Clear the road!' shouted the General to his three companions. Whilst they galloped forward to obey his command, his quick eyes saw the flash of an officer's helmet, and the next instant he saw General Houdon coming out of the neighbouring roadside inn at the head of twenty men.

"'Turn back!' exclaimed General de Prémont to the postillion, who, seeing the urgency of the situation at a glance, wheeled his horses swiftly right about to carry out the direction. Just then they heard the clatter of a troop of cavalry approaching by the very route they were about to pursue.

"'Fly, General!' cried the Duc. 'We are betrayed!'

"'But you, Monseigneur?'

"'Oh! fear nothing for me. They will not harm me. But you —— Fly! In my father's name, I order you to save yourself!'

"'In the Emperor's name, stop!' cried a loud voice at this juncture.

"General de Prémont hesitated no longer. He bent down and kissed the young Duc's hand; put spurs to his horse; and leapt boldly over the parapet of the bridge. The noise of a great splash in the river was heard, and that was all. The night was too dark to let them see what had become of him. Besides, they were anxious to escort the Duc to Vienna, where he was once again imprisoned in the Emperor's palace."

"It cannot have been mere chance that upset the market-cart, and led the soldiers to Weidlingen?" interrogated Salvator.

"No. The Duc d'Orleans is of opinion that the police of Monsieur de Metternich were warned by the French police. In any case, it is a warning for you. Be cautious!"

General la Fayette again stopped his carriage as he uttered this warning, and Salvator bade him farewell with the respectful obeisance due to the illustrious patriot.

Salvator then made straight for the Rue Saint-Honoré. It was encumbered with people, as he anticipated ; and he overheard no gentle words used towards the police for provoking the breach of the peace. With numberless men in the crowd he exchanged a secret sign ; but not a word passed between them—simply a gesture, which was meant to signify, "Not yet !"

Here, amidst these thousands of people drawn thither by the news of the émeute, Salvator at length found M. Jackal, disguised as a worthy citizen, and one of the most voluble in disparaging the police. Not the least disconcerted at being discovered in this guise, M. Jackal bade Salvator follow him, and led the way into an adjacent courtyard, where they could converse without being observed.

"And now of what service can I be to you?" demanded the Commissioner of Police, when Salvator had explained that, not finding him at the Préfecture, he had sought him there.

"Well, I want you to be good enough to inform me on what charge Monsieur Dubreuil was arrested yesterday. You will remember him when I tell you he was the man whose arrest I pointed out to you at the time. I am anxious to know, because he is the friend of a friend of mine."

"I am sorry I can't answer you at this moment. You could scarcely expect I could, Monsieur Salvator, taking me by surprise like this."

"Take *you* by surprise, Monsieur Jackal ! Impossible !"

"Ah ! I see you're just like the rest. You *will* see an analogy in my name : because I happen to be called jackal you take me to be as cunning as a fox."

"That is certainly your reputation," laughingly answered Salvator.

"Reputation belies me, then."

"Do you mean to make me believe, then, that you ordered the arrest of a certain man without knowing the charge on which he was arrested?"

"To hear you speak, one would think I was King of France."

"No ! King of Jerusalem," retorted Salvator on the astute chief of the Rue de Jérusalem. "And the King of Jerusalem declines to tell me the why and wherefore of Monsieur Dubreuil's arrest ?"

"But I assure you I have not the least idea why this Monsieur Dubreuil has been arrested. Perhaps he was taken up by mistake."

"Do the police ever make mistakes?"

"Oh, as for that, you know it's only the Pope who's infallible."

"At all events, the charge against Monsieur Dubreuil cannot be a grave one, since you are ignorant of it."

"Make your mind easy on that point. There is no such name as Dubreuil in my black-book."

"Then I have only to wish you good-day, Monsieur Jackal," replied Salvator, bowing to the Commissioner of Police, and taking his departure.

Joining the monk at the rendezvous, Salvator grasped his hand with sympathetic warmth as he said,

"Your friend's position is very serious."

"The Chief of the Police has told you all, then?"

"On the contrary, he would tell me nothing. That is what alarms me. He doesn't know your friend's face. The name of Dubreuil seemed unfamiliar to him. He is ignorant of the cause of his arrest. All the more reason to fear your friend is in grave peril."

"In grave peril!" exclaimed the monk, his voice trembling with emotion. "Forgive me, my friend, for not telling you all. His real name is not Dubreuil, but Sarranti, and he is my father!"

"Sarranti!" repeated Salvator, in a tone of the deepest pity, as the name reminded him of the grave charges made public against the Bonapartist conspirator that very morning. "You have need of all your friends' help now. Count on me, for I'll work for you heart and soul; but we must not be seen together. Adieu!"

"Adieu, true friend!" replied Dominique Sarranti, with grateful warmth. "Rest assured that, whatever my father is charged with, he has been guilty of nothing base or ignoble."

Leaving Salvator to pursue his way with rapid steps towards the Rue de Rivoli, the monk crossed the Pont de la Concorde, and soon gained the Church of Saint-Germain-des-Prés. There he sent up a humble prayer to the Father of all Mercies, and appealed for Divine protection; everything around him, the sombreness of the old church, with its eighth-century air, and the solemn hush of its sober aisles, seeming to sanctify the mournful cry which went up from his heart. Just returned from a visit of consolation and condolence to the aged Count de Penhoël in Brittany, whither he had accompanied the remains of Colomban to their last resting place, Dominique was himself thus plunged into a sea of sorest troubles. His heart sank within him as he drank of the cup of sorrow, and he did well to call for help on high; for the time was nigh when he would have to drain it to the dregs. Homewards he then went, animated by a vague hope that his father might have been released from custody, for some unforeseen reason, and might be awaiting him at the Rue du Pot-de-Fer. So it was that the first question put by the monk to his concièrge was,

"Has anyone called for me?"

"Yes, Father," answered the concièrge. "A gentleman has called twice."

"His name?"

"He did not mention it."

"Was it the gentleman who brought that letter for me the day before yesterday?"

"Oh, no! I should have recognised him at once. He had one of the gloomiest faces in all Paris."

"Poor father!" murmured Dominique to himself, as he slowly mounted to his room.

"But, Monsieur l'Abbé," called the concièrge after him, in a voice of concern, "you have not breakfasted yet, and it is evening. You must let me bring you up a good basin of soup and a couple of cutlets."

Dominique gave a listless sign of assent. According to his custom on entering his room, he opened the window looking on the gardens of the Luxembourg. The setting sun was gilding the branches of the trees, the buds of which were just bursting, and that sweet violet haze which heralds the approach of spring filled the evening air. Trilling out their chirping notes with heart-rejoicing gaiety, the birds were joyously singing their gladsome even-song. All Nature seemed cheerful and bright with liberty, whilst the monk remained buried in sombre reflections as to the fate of his father. Even when his savoury meal had been most temptingly spread on the snowiest of tablecloths, he left it untasted; and, absent-mindedly, glanced over his morning journal—glanced with the apathy of despair—till there met his eyes the official charges against Monsieur Sarranti, accusing his father with being prime mover in the abortive Bonapartist plot, and (Dominique's heart sank deeper still when he read this) reviving the old indictments of murder and robbery which had been so long suspended over his head. The monk seemed as if struck by a thunderbolt when the full force of this terrible blow was realised by him. Recovering from the paralysing effects of the news, Dominique leapt to his feet, and sprang to his writing-desk, crying,

"Heaven be praised! Here I have the means of refuting the murderous calumny!"

So saying, Dominique drew from a drawer the confession which Monsieur Gérard had made to him when he imagined he was on his deathbed; and the monk clasped the paper to his heart with a great joy, for he knew it contained a revelation that would save the life of his father—nay, more than his life—his honour. With a sigh of heartfelt relief, he placed the treasure in his breast-pocket, and descended the stairs with a bounding pulse. A man was coming up as Dominique Sarranti was hastily going down. The monk paid no heed to him. One thought only filled his mind—the release of his father. Dominique was in the act of passing this stranger, when he felt himself held fast by his robe.

"Pardon me, Monsieur l'Abbé," said a voice which sent a strange thrill through Dominique, "I wish to speak to you."

"I must beg you to call again," answered the monk; "I have business which will not admit of a moment's delay."

"And so have I," said the same strangely familiar voice to Dominique, who, at the same moment, felt his arm in an iron grip.

"Who are you, and what do you want with me?" asked the monk, impatiently, as he endeavoured to release himself, and tried in vain to recognise in the obscurity the face of the man who held him.

"I am Monsieur Gérard," was the dread answer; "and I have come to demand that paper which you have in your possession."

Dominique knew his worst fears were realised. The man in him triumphed over the monk for the moment. He seized M. Gérard in his turn, drew him up to the landing by main force, and did not relax his grasp till the light from the window had proved to him that it was, indeed, the man he thought to be dead who stood before him.

"Have you satisfied yourself that I am still alive now?" demanded M. Gérard. "You see Heaven forgave me for my repentance, and sent me a clever young doctor, who saved me."

"And was it you who called to see me twice before to-day?" gasped Dominique, instinctively pressing his hand to his breast to guard the precious document upon which the safety of his father depended.

"It was. And I have come a third time, you see, to demand the restoration of that paper. You have read the news, and will understand that it is of vital importance to me. Besides, as I am alive, my confession is null."

"Null?" repeated the monk, mechanically, the cold sweat of agony bedewing his brows.

"Yes. Are not priests forbidden by the Holy Church to reveal a confession without the consent of the penitent?"

"You gave me that permission," answered the monk, coldly.

"Yes, in case of my death; but now I have recovered, I recall it."

"Villain! And my poor father?"

"He can defend himself. He may accuse me. He may be proved innocent. But you, confessor, must keep silence."

"Be it so!" exclaimed Dominique, with the calmness of despair, as he felt himself helpless against one of the fundamental dogmas of the Roman Catholic Church. "*I will be silent whilst you live!*"

"But you must deliver up the paper!" cried the assassin, impatiently.

"That I will never do," said Dominique, firmly. "As I am a priest, I must keep my vow. As I am a man, I will guard your confession with my life, for who knows that Heaven may not be merciful, and call you from this world during the trial of my father, and enable me to prove his innocence?"

Dominique freed himself from the murderer's grasp as he finished, and re-entered his room, locking the door after him, before Gérard could follow him.

Chapter LXVI.—The Sarranti Trial.

The main features of a trial have so great a family resemblance that it will be unnecessary to expatiate on the formal proceedings inaugurating the *affaire Sarranti*. It will be sufficient to say that all Paris seemed to feel the intensest interest on the night of April 29 to know the result. The Palais de Justice was besieged by an army of anxious Parisians; thousands lining the quays, and every approach to the court being thronged by citizens who would fain have gained admission to watch every incident of the great case. The court itself was crowded to excess. Dimly lit by the puny lamps and candles, the interior of the Palais de Justice had a weird and Dantesque aspect that night, suitable to the gloomy occasion. The Attorney-General, a dry-parchment-faced advocate, had closed his speech for the Crown; but his subtle, cold-blooded argument—irresistibly pointing to Monsieur Sarranti as the man who had beyond a doubt murdered Madame Gérard, abducted the young nephew and niece of Monsieur Gérard, and absconded with a large sum of money—did not make the calm, noble-looking prisoner flinch in the least. On the contrary, it was Monsieur Gérard who trembled and shrank back as the apparently fatal chain of reasoning and evidence was wound round Monsieur Sarranti, for there opposite him sat the prisoner's son, piercing him to the soul with his cold, implacable gaze. The prisoner was accused of having committed the crimes laid to his charge on Aug. 20, 1820; and the counsel for M. Gérard had concluded that he would embarrass M. Sarranti greatly by demanding of him why he had so suddenly quitted the château at Viry if he did not fly for fear of arrest. But a clear and straightforward answer was forthcoming. The prisoner frankly avowed that he fled to India in order to mature that conspiracy for the restoration of the Napoleon dynasty to France which had been the main cause of his arrest. For complicity in that conspiracy—a conspiracy for which M. Sarranti was ready to be a martyr—Government were afraid to put him on his trial, thundered out his young and eloquent counsel, amid the cheers of the Court. They preferred to overwhelm a political opponent with dishonour, and so revived these monstrous charges against him. What! Was it possible that a man who had freely shed his blood for France on many a battle-field, and had lived to be the confidential friend of Napoleon, the friend to whom he intrusted his dearest hopes for his only son, the friend who had devoted his life to the cause of the Duc de Reichstadt—was it possible that such a man would stoop to commit the terrible charges in the indictment? "No," concluded the eloquent young orator, Emanuel Richard; "if the prisoner at the bar had been the guilty wretch you say he is, the man with the eagle's glance, the man who could read the hearts of those who served him, Napoleon, would never have taken him by the hand, called him friend, and confided to him the most cherished desire of his soul. Convict Monsieur Sarranti, if you like, then, of a life-long devotion to the cause of the late Emperor; but do not dishonour his name by finding him guilty of these base crimes, which Heaven will prove him innocent of in its own good time!"

An electric thrill of sympathy for M. Sarranti ran through the court as his counsel sat down, and received the grateful glances of the prisoner and a warm pressure of the hand from Dominique; and this palpable feeling did but add to the agony of M. Gérard, on whose brow stood beads of sweat. Unimpeded, however, was the course of the trial by the popular sentiment. The judge's summing-up, admirably impartial, left the issue yet in doubt. The jury then deliberated for ten minutes. The verdict was "Guilty." The prisoner was sentenced to death.

"Monsieur," added the judge to M. Sarranti, addressing him with exceptional courtesy, "have you any request to make to the court?"

"Only that I may be allowed to see my son in prison, that he may, as a priest, prepare me for the scaffold!"

"Father, the scaffold shall never be mounted by you!" cried the son, adding, to himself, "If any one perishes there it shall be I!"

CHAPTER LXVII.—FRAGOLA'S MISSION.

ANYONE who had been present at that memorable trial at the Palace of Justice, who had seen the feeble lamp light grow paler and paler as day dawned, who had heard the sentence of death pronounced on M. Sarranti, who had been witness of the menacing murmur and threatening movement of the throngs inside and outside the Court, and who had then been suddenly transported to the charming nest which formed the dwelling of Salvator and Fragola, would have experienced a similar sensation of sweetness and freshness to that which a roysterer must feel in inhaling the pure air of a bright May morning after a night of dissipation. He would have seen first of all that artistic little dining-room, the walls of which seemed the facsimiles of Pompeian interiors; then Salvator and Fragola, seated one on each side the table, the fair mistress having before her the prettiest of breakfast sets in white porcelain, spread on a table-cloth of snowy damask. At a glance he would have seen that the young couple were all in all to each other; that their lives were bound fast in loving links; that theirs was the purest and happiest of existences; that mutual sympathy and confidence knit them heart to heart. Yes, all these evidences of perfect love might have been patent to a common observer, although their brows were evidently clouded by some deep anxiety. The frank and candid face of Fragola—a sweet flower of spring time opening its petals to the April sun—bore this transient cloud even when she stole faint glances at the hero of her life, whilst Salvator, on his part, every now and then seemed buried in the saddest of reveries. The trouble which filled both their hearts with pity and sympathy was the supreme sorrow which had fallen upon Dominique Sarranti, for Salvator had brought home to Fragola the sad news of M. Sarranti's conviction of the murders and other crimes laid to his charge. In one of his reveries Salvator found his thoughts going back to the night on which he and Roland had escaladed the wall of the Château de Viry, and on which the dog had conducted him first to the lake and then to the spot in which the remains of a dead body had been brought to light by Roland's sagacity. But what connection could that discovery have with M. Sarranti? Would it not rather tell against than for him? And then Mina—would not one incautious step in the matter alarm the Comte de Valgeneuse, and cause him to spirit his captive away to some new and inaccessible retreat? How Salvator's heart would have leapt for joy could he have foreseen how Destiny had interwoven the fates of M. Sarranti and Mina, and how soon he was to take part in the rescue of Justin's betrothed. A movement on the part of Roland aroused Salvator.

The dog had lifted his intelligent head, and sprung to his feet at the sound of the bell.

"Who's there—a friend, Roland?" asked Salvator.

The dog appeared to fully understand his master. He walked slowly to the door, wagging his tail—sure sign of friendliness. Salvator smilingly opened the door, and, seeing Dominique, pale, grief-stricken, and weary, standing before him, said, with all his heart in his voice,

"Welcome to my poor abode! We were thinking of your terrible sorrow. How I wish I could help you with more than barren words, my poor friend!"

The monk pressed the two hands warmly proffered by Salvator and Fragola, and answered,

"You once before promised to do your utmost to help me, Monsieur Salvator, and you nobly fulfilled your promise by doing what was in your power. Let me first ask you now—do you believe my father to be innocent?"

"Yes, with all my heart. And Heaven may enable me to aid you in bringing to light the proof of his innocence!"

"I possess the proof," replied the monk.

"You hope to save him, then?"

"I am certain of it, if I can but obtain audience of the King; but, influential though you are, it is, doubtless, beyond your power to procure for me that privilege."

Salvator turned smilingly towards Fragola.

"Dove," he said, "fly from the ark and bring back the olive branch."

Fragola, without replying, at once retired to the inner room, and quickly donned bonnet and veil and mantle. She received a whispered message from Salvator, and, with a loving *au revoir* to him and a respectful obeisance to Dominique, she sped on her errand of mercy.

"Take a seat, Father," said Salvator to the monk. "In an hour you will receive an answer, either granting you audience of his Majesty for to-day, or to-morrow at the latest."

Dominique sat down, and regarded Salvator with an air of the greatest astonishment.

"Who are you, Monsieur?" he asked, in a tone of wonderment, "that you live in so humble a sphere, and yet have so much influence with the highest authorities in France?"

"The hour has not yet come when I can reveal the secret of my life to you, Father," replied Salvator. "Rest satisfied with the assurance that I am devoted to you heart and soul, and that I may be able to help you in proving Monsieur Sarranti's innocence in a way you little expect."

* * * * *

Salvator's dove flew to the floral boudoir of a bosom friend at a timely moment.

The charming conservatory of the Princesse de Lamothe-Houdan happened that morning to be the rendezvous of our four heroines;

FRAGOLA'S MISSION.

Régina herself, Lydia de Marande, Carmélite, and Fragola, firm and fast friends ever since they had been drawn together by the silken bands of a warm attachment in their schooldays at Saint-Denis. All save Fragola were daughters of officers in the Imperial army. How came it, the reader may ask, that the daughter of a simple trumpeter was admitted to so select a circle as the Imperial School at Saint-Denis? The question may be soon answered. At the battle of Waterloo there was a supreme crisis when Napoleon thought that victory was in his grasp. It was imperative at this juncture that he should send an order to General Comte de Lobau. But not a single Aide-de-Camp was at hand; they were all engaged in delivering orders to the other divisions of the Imperial army. Napoleon saw a trumpeter near him, and called him to his side.

"Quick," said Napoleon. "Ride with this order to General Lobau by the shortest road. Don't lose a second. It is urgent!"

The trumpeter threw a hasty glance along the cannon-raked course he would have to pursue, and answered,

"'Tis rather warm yonder."

"Are you afraid?" replied the Emperor.

"Afraid! A Chevalier of the Légion d'Honneur afraid!"

"En route, then! Here's the order."

"If am killed, the Emperor will grant me one favour?"

"Yes. Be quick. Name it."

"Should I fall, I wish that my little girl, Athénais Ponray, living with her mother at 17, Rue des Amandières, Paris, should be brought up at the Saint-Denis college as the daughter of an officer."

"Granted," said Napoleon.

"Vive l'Empéreur!" cried the trumpeter, darting off at a gallop.

The fearless rider had to pierce to the very thickest of the fight. His precious message was for the valiant Young Guards of Napoleon. Ponray galloped scatheless through showers of bullets, and reached General Lobau in safety; but the very moment the General took the order from his hand the brave trumpeter fell from his horse, shot dead through the lungs. Nothing more was heard of the poor trumpeter. But Napoleon, though he fled to Paris crushed by the loss of the Empire, did not forget his promise. The Emperor at once gave the requisite order that little Athénais Ponray should be educated at Saint-Denis. Thus it came that the daughter of the humble but gallant trumpeter had the opportunity of winning the hearts of her true friends, Régina, Lydia, and Carmélite; and it was of the sincere friendship of Régina that Fragola (as Salvator rechristened Athénais) availed herself on behalf of Dominique Sarranti. Fragola received a warm welcome when she was ushered into the florescent boudoir of the Princesse de Lamothe-Houdan.

"We see nothing of you now, dear," protested Régina and Madame de Marande; whilst Carmélite, whose tender and attentive nurse Fragola had been, pressed her hand with fondest gratitude.

"Oh! You are the Princesses and I am only poor Cinderella, and must therefore keep to my hearth," replied Fragola, smilingly.

"That is," she added, recalling the urgency of her mission, "except when I want to ask a favour of one of my Princesses."

"You know you have only to mention it, Fragola," answered Régina. "Is it not our compact that whenever one of us needs the assistance of her friends she is bound to seek our help? You look grave, dear. I hope no misfortune has befallen you, Fragola."

"Neither to me nor Salvator, thank Heaven! but to a friend."

"What friend?"

"Dominique Sarranti."

"Ah, yes," answered Carmélite in a tone of deepest pity, as she remembered how good a friend the Abbé had been to Colomban; "his father——"

"Has been sentenced to death," said Fragola.

"Can we not obtain his pardon?" asked Régina, with quick sympathy. "You know my father has some influence with the King."

"Ah! I knew I could count on your aid, Régina. The Abbé does not venture to solicit a pardon for his father. He simply wishes to gain an audience of his Majesty. Can you obtain it, Régina?"

"For what day?"

"This very morning."

"I will do my best, dear," said Régina, touching a bell, and directing the servant who answered the summons to have the carriage ready for her as quickly as possible.

"You'll excuse me for a little while, I know," added Régina, pausing at the door amid the earnest thanks of Fragola. "I must hasten to the Tuileries and prevail upon my good friend, the Duchesse de Berry, to get me the King's permission. It is now eleven o'clock. At twelve I will be back with his Majesty's letter for your friend, Fragola."

The hour soon sped by in the interchange of confidences. At twelve, true to her word, the Princesse de Lamothe-Houdan returned, and handed the Royal missive to the overjoyed Fragola. The audience was fixed for half-past two that very afternoon. Fragola, having thus not a moment to lose, bade an affectionate farewell to Régina and Carmélite, and gladly accepted a seat in Lydia de Marande's carriage, in order to gain the Rue de Mâcon the more speedily. So, with the olive-branch in the shape of the King's letter, the dove flew back to the ark, and filled the monk's heart with the balm of hope.

CHAPTER LXVIII.—AN INTERVIEW WITH THE KING.

THE King was not in the best of humours on April 30, 1827. The affront offered to his Majesty's Ministers by those free speaking National Guards after the review of the previous day had led to the publication of a Royal order in the *Moniteur* dissolving the *Garde Nationale*. And yet Paris was not satisfied. What will satisfy Paris? the King asked himself in despair. The Revolution of July was destined to tell him what the people wanted. But the present, without any thought for the future, sufficed to darken the King's brow with a sombre frown not at all habitual to him. His Majesty was attired in his usual uniform of blue and silver, in which Horace Vernet has painted him; and on his breast he wore the order of the Saint-Esprit, which Victor Hugo was destined to see later, when the King came to prohibit the performance of "Marion Delorme"—prohibition impotent enough, for the poet's "Marion Delorme" will live for ever, whilst Charles X. is already forgotten. The Abbé Dominique Sarranti had been announced; and the King hastily read a written paper, open before him on the desk, and then bade the usher to admit Dominique to his audience. The Abbé bent low on the threshold of the Royal chamber in deference to his Majesty, and the King bowed in recognition of his priestly office.

"Monsieur l'Abbé," said the King, as Dominique was emboldened to enter the Royal chamber, "the readiness with which I granted you this interview will prove to you, I hope, the high estimation in which I hold ministers of religion."

"That is one of the glories of your Majesty's reign," replied Dominique, "and one that has won for you the love of your people."

"I am anxious to learn the object of your visit," was the kingly response.

"Sire," said Dominique, "my father has just been condemned to death."

"I know it, Monsieur; and I have the deepest pity for you."

"But my father was innocent of the crimes for which he was condemned——"

"Excuse me, Monsieur," interrupted the King, "but that was not the opinion of the jury."

"Sire, the jury are but men, and, being but mortals, may be deceived by appearances."

"I grant that, Monsieur; but still, as far as justice can be administered by human hands, full justice seems to have been done your father by the jury."

"Sire, I have the proof of my father's innocence."

"You have the proof?" repeated Charles X., with astonishment. "Then why did you not produce it before your father was sentenced to death?"

"It was impossible, Sire."

"Very well! Happily, there is time now. Give me the proof."

"Give it to you, Sire! Alas! that is as impossible now as it was yesterday and will be to-morrow."

"But whatever motive can a man have in keeping back the proof of his father's innocence?"

"Sire, I dare not inform you. Heaven knows that I tell you the truth when I affirm from my soul that my father *is* innocent, and that one day I shall be able clearly to prove his innocence before your Majesty."

"Monsieur," replied the King, with a sympathy that well became his Majesty, "you speak as a son. I honour the sentiment which prompts your earnestness. Permit me to answer as your King. If the crime for which your father was condemned did but concern me only ; if, in a word, it had been a political offence, an attempt against the safety of the State, or even an attempt against my life which had ended as fatally as did the blow with which Louvel struck down my poor son, I would have done what my dying son did. Monsieur, out of respect for your piety, which I honour, my last act would have been to pardon your father. But his crime was not political. He was condemned for robbery, abduction, and assassination——"

"Sire ! Sire !" cried the humbled Dominique.

"I know these things must be terribly painful to hear : but, since I am compelled to refuse your prayer, would it be just to myself to keep back the reasons for my refusal? It was not the King, then, who was menaced by these crimes, nor the State ; it was Society ; and the Law must run its course, and Society be avenged——"

"Sire," broke in Dominique, impetuously, "it is not as a son that I address you. It is as a man convinced of the innocence of a man whom the scaffold claims that I implore you to step in before it is too late. Sire, if you refuse my last prayer, the guilty will escape unpunished, and the innocent will suffer instead. Sire, grant my father a respite of fifty days, and I will undertake to prove his innocence beyond doubt."

"Be it so! I freely accord the respite. But the law must not be broken. Your father must appeal to the Court of Appeal against the sentence. Tell me, too, why you want so long a respite as fifty days."

"Sire," answered Dominique, in grateful tones, "I have a journey of three hundred and fifty leagues to make."

"On foot?"

"Yes, on foot, Sire, because it was thus the pilgrims of old journeyed who had a favour to ask of God."

"But, if I defray the expenses of the journey out of my purse——"

"Sire, I cannot tell you how sincerely grateful I am for your Majesty's clemency and generosity ; but I have made a vow to make the journey on foot, and barefooted."

There was a moistness in the king's eyes at the filial devotion of the young Abbé, and, in his heart of hearts, he felt half convinced of the righteousness of Dominique's fervent belief in the guiltlessness of M. Sarranti.

"Sire, continued Dominique, "may I beg you to grant me the means of gaining an audience of your Majesty directly I return, at any hour of the day or night?"

"Willingly," replied the king, ringing the bell at the same moment.

"You see Monsieur l'Abbé," said his Majesty to the usher who appeared at the door. "Look at him well, and remember that he is to be admitted to my presence at any hour of the night or day he may wish to see me. Instruct the servants to that effect. Adieu ! Monsieur l'Abbé," added the king, graciously, as Dominique made his farewell obeisance, with a heart overflowing with gratitude and hopefulness.

Chapter LXIX.—Dominique's Pilgrimage.

Let us not linger over the painful interview that followed between Dominique and his father in prison. The son, after long hours of argument, prevailed upon the condemned man to appeal for another trial, and to accept the respite granted him by the king.

At the gate of the Conciérgerie Dominique found Salvator waiting for him.

"What is to be your next step?" asked Salvator of his friend, seeking to divert his thoughts from the sad parting which had evidently just taken place 'twixt father and son.

"I start for Rome."

"When?"

"At once."

"But you must have a passport first. We are close by the Préfecture. Let us get one without losing another moment."

On the threshold of the Préfecture they met Monsieur Jackal, who had been informed by the Ministry of Dominique's coming departure, and who had already procured the necessary passport, making certain, with his usual penetration, that it would be for Rome. There seemed to be nothing but frank good-nature in his face when he presented the Abbé with the passport. Yet Salvator fancied he detected a flash of triumph in the small, foxy eyes of M. Jackal when Dominique accepted the paper in perfect trust; and, when they reached the Rue Mâcon, and Salvator found himself safe in his Pompeian sanctum again, he borrowed the passport from his friend, held it up to the light, and detected an ominous

$$S$$

visible only as a water-mark when thus closely inspected.

"Suspected! A trap, as I thought," exclaimed Salvator, pointing the letter out to Dominique, and then indignantly tearing the paper to pieces. "The authorities are plainly anxious to thwart you, Dominique. But we will dupe *them!* See here!"

Salvator thereupon drew from his desk a signed and viséd passport for Turin, with blank spaces left for the names. These he filled in, and, handing it to Dominique, added, "This will frank you to Turin. At Turin you can get it viséd for Rome. So we shall foil them yet."

"How can I repay you for this devotion?" said the Abbé, with trembling lips.

The same question was repeated by Dominique with greater intensity at sunset that evening, when Salvator bade him farewell, after accompanying him some distance outside the barriers. There was a luminous streak of light in the west, and, pointing to this good omen in the heavens, Salvator said, "Let that sign cheer you on your long pilgrimage, Dominique. As for me, you know I owe you my life; and it shall be devoted to you and yours while you are away. Adieu! Adieu!"

Chapter LXX.—Hope for Mina.

Let us leave Dominique Sarranti to accomplish his long and painful pilgrimage to Rome, and let us see what took place about three weeks after his departure in the park of a deserted mansion in one of the most populous faubourgs of Paris.

Imagine a strip of virgin forest abounding in luxuriant plane and chestnut, fir and linden trees, acacias and sycamores, with their branches and parasites intermingled in inextricable confusion, and conceive this wealth of vegetation to be transplanted into the heart of a great city. This is what passers-by must have conjured up in glancing through the rusty iron bars of the gloomy gate in the Rue d'Enfer, which was so rarely opened to allow a closer inspection of this mysterious wood.

When darkness fell upon the city, and pale rays shone down from the silver diadem of the Queen of Night, and weird shadows were cast through the lonesome park, and the ruined deserted house in the centre looked a fit haunt for ghosts, it was with fear that anyone snatched a hasty glimpse through the iron gate; for tales were current of mystic noises rising from the patch of wild forest, and strange forms were said to flit 'twixt the trees at midnight. Nor were these rumours without foundation.

At midnight on Monday, May 21, twenty masked men assembled in the most secluded part of this park. They were carbonari.

Why had the conspirators pitched upon this fresh meeting-place? Why, to be out of hearing of the omnipresent Chief Commissioner of Police. M. Jackal, it will be remembered, discovered their rendezvous in the catacombs at a most critical juncture. But he had not yet found out that those same catacombs had an outlet into this wild piece of ground, thanks to the ingenuity of one of the conspirators, who had burrowed a hole through the earth by way of which the carbonari could gain their new rendezvous in secret.

The main object of this nocturnal meeting was to scheme how the elections and public opinion might best be influenced in accordance with the views of the carbonari. They had reached the very height of the discussion. It was one o'clock in the morning, when there occurred an interruption which made each instinctively grasp the poniard hidden inside his cloak.

The dead branches which strewed the ground crackled as if beneath a heavy tread. A dark figure advanced towards them. It was the charcoal-burner, whose blackness had gained for him the nickname of Toussaint Louverture. Concièrge of the deserted park and mansion, Toussaint was himself a member of the carbonari, and therefore fulfilled the double duty of guarding the estate from interlopers and his fellow conspirators from surprise.

"What is it?" demanded one of the chiefs of the dusky concièrge.

"A foreign associate, who wishes to speak with you."

"Are you certain he is a member?"

"He made all the signs."

"Where is he from?"

"Trieste."

The carbonari consulted for a minute. The leader who had before acted as spokesman then answered Toussaint.

"Introduce our foreign brother, but with the usual precautions."

Toussaint thereupon disappeared, and returned in a few moments leading a blindfolded man, whom he left in the midst of his superiors, and then retired to keep watch once more.

"Who are you, and what is the object of your visit?" demanded the voice we have before heard of the stranger, whose eyes were still kept bandaged.

"I am General Comte Lebastard de Prémont," replied the new-comer, firmly and frankly. "I have arrived from Trieste, where I embarked after the failure of our Vienna enterprise; and I have come to Paris to save my friend and confederate, Monsieur Sarranti."

A confused murmur rose from the lips of the carbonari at this bold declaration.

"You can take off your bandage now, General," continued the leader. "You are amongst brothers."

Each hand was cordially held forth to welcome him as he tore the handkerchief from his eyes, and all saw his noble countenance, and recalled the long years he had spent in maturing the fruitless plot for placing Napoleon's son on the Imperial throne of France.

"Brothers," said the General, "You are all aware how our venture failed at Vienna. I fled to Trieste, where I was concealed by one of our brethren. There I first learned that Monsieur Sarranti was condemned to death. Then as I have already told you, I at once set out for Paris to share the fate of my friend : to live if he should live, to die if he should die, for, accomplices in the same crime, it is but just we should bear the same penalty."

A cold silence was the sole response to this confession.

"I know brothers," resumed the General, "that our opinions are not the same. I know that among you are Republicans and Orleanists; but Republicans and Orleanists surely wish, with me, for the deliverance of the country, for the glory of France, for the honour of the nation.

"Well, I have known Monsieur Sarranti for six years intimately, and I answer with my life for his bravery, his truth, his honour, his fidelity. Let me, therefore, beg of you, in the name of our wronged brother and in my own name, to help me to do what it would be impossible for me alone to accomplish. Let us spare one of our brethren an ignominious death. Let us free Monsieur Sarranti from prison. I have two good arms for the enterprise. I have millions of francs for the sinews of war. Brothers, I await your reply. Will you grant me your aid, and restore to me my friend, unjustly sentenced to the scaffold?"

The carbonari preserved the same frigid silence till their spokesman broke it.

"Brothers," he said, "every urgent request of a comrade claims consideration according to our rules, and must be complied with or rejected as the majority wills. Let us deliberate then, on the General's appeal."

General de Prémont, familiar with these formalities, felt a shiver of anxiety run through him as the twenty carbonari retired out of ear-shot to decide what he felt was a matter of life or death for his friend. He awaited their decision with greater agitation even than M. Sarranti himself awaited the fateful decision of the jury. For five minutes he could hear the murmur of earnest voices. The murmur was succeeded by a dead pause. The foreman of this secret Court of Appeal then advanced and delivered the verdict.

"General," he said, "I speak in the name of the majority of the members present, and this is the answer I am deputed to give you. Cæsar said that Cæsar's wife should be above suspicion. Liberty is a matron who should be equally chaste, equally immaculate. So— and it is with sincere regret that I say it—failing irrefutable, clear, and patent proofs of M. Sarranti's innocence, the opinion of the majority is that we cannot take part in an attempt to save from the supreme penalty of the law a man whom the law has justly condemned; I say '*justly*,' brother, believe me, simply from the lack of evidence on his behalf. Our warmest sympathies were with Monsieur Sarranti, during the whole of the trial. Our hearts bled when the verdict was pronounced. It only remains for me to add, General, —prove the innocence of Monsieur Sarranti, and not only two arms, but the hundred thousand arms of our association will be lifted to restore your friend to liberty."

"General," added the speaker, "have you brought us any proof of Monsieur Sarranti's innocence?"

"Alas!" replied General de Prémont, "I have no other proof than innate conviction."

"In that case," answered the chief carbonaro, "we have nothing more to say."

"Brothers," continued the General, raising his voice in one last appeal, "I have no alternative but to submit to the voice of the majority. I see I cannot hope for your help as a body; yet let me appeal to the one sympathetic soul in your midst who may share in my belief of my poor friend's guiltlessness. Let me beseech him to grant me his aid; and we two may be able to accomplish the great task before us."

"Comrades," replied the previous speaker, "if there be among you any one who believes in the innocence of Monsieur Sarranti, he is perfectly at liberty to join General de Prémont in his humane enterprise."

One of the twenty advanced, placed his left hand on the shoulder of the General, and with his right hand raised his mask.

"I am with you heart and soul," he said.

"Salvator!" exclaimed his comrades, in astonishment, as they recognised him.

One by one the nineteen carbonari then disappeared amid the

trees and dispersed, leaving General Comte Lebastard de Prémont alone with Salvator.

"Monsieur," said the General warmly to his new friend, "I only know you by name, which I have just heard for the first time. It is a name of happy augury, however. Accept my heartfelt thanks for your noble offer. May we together be able to save my friend!"

"I trust so," answered Salvator.

"Do you know Monsieur Sarranti?"

"No, Monsieur; but I am the intimate and devoted friend of his son. I owe him my life. And, as I said to you before, General, I am ready to work heart and soul for the liberty of his father, whom I hope, moreover, to be able to clear from the terrible crimes for the alleged committal of which he is under sentence of death. I am not yet in possession of any proofs positive; but——"

"But?"

"I feel certain I am on the track."

"On the track!" cried the General, his keen eyes beaming with hope and gratitude. "Oh! explain, my dear Monsieur!"

"I will, General. You are aware that Monsieur Sarranti was tutor at a Monsieur Gérard's at the time these crimes were committed?"

"Yes."

"The Château de Viry was the name of this Gérard's house. The château is situated in a park; and in that park I discovered a little while ago, a proof that one of the children Monsieur Sarranti has been found guilty of abducting was murdered!"

"But will not that fact tell against my friend still?" remarked General de Prémont.

"Monsieur, when we wish to arrive at the truth every grain of evidence should be scrupulously examined, even if one particular piece of evidence should appear to tell against him whose interests we have most at heart. Let but the light of truth pour down on this mystery and I am convinced that Monsieur Sarranti will be set free and the real murderer revealed."

"Be it so! But how came you to fall across this proof you speak of, Monsieur Salvator?"

"One night I was wandering with my dog in the park of Viry for a very different purpose from that which now occupies us. At the foot of an oak my dog began pawing up the soil. He soon made a large hole, and gave a most doleful howl as he came across some object. I knelt down to see what it was, and found the skeleton of a child."

"And you believe those were the remains of one of the children who disappeared so strangely the very night my friend seems to have quitted Viry?"

"It is more than probable."

"And the other child?"

"I believe I have found her also."

"Thanks to your dog?"

"Yes; thanks to Roland. The poor girl lives, happily. From

this double discovery, I hope to be able to arrive at a complete knowledge of the history of the sad tragedy."

"If you have found the little girl, and she still lives, as you say, surely she will remember——"

"The night of the crime? Yes, but the slightest reference to that night nearly turns her sensitive brain. The horrors she suffered must have been frightful. Her recollection of them is too vivid, even after this lapse of time, for her to be examined in safety yet. She would lose her reason. And of what use to us would be the evidence of a young girl out of her senses?"

"Let us return to the dead, then. If the living cannot speak, may not the dead?"

"Yes, promptly enough, if we could act openly in the matter."

"What prevents us from doing so? Go to the Prosecutor-General. Inform him of the whole affair. Let it be the task of Justice to cast upon these crimes the light of truth which you invoke."

"Yes, and the police in one night could obliterate all traces of what we might offer as evidence. Why, the Government, and therefore the police, have the greatest interest in disproving Monsieur Sarranti's innocence. For an obvious political reason, they wish him to appear a malefactor of the deepest dye."

"Let us act in your own way, then, Monsieur Salvator. You can regard the matter more coolly than I can. But let us begin at once, for my poor friend's days are numbered. Let us search every corner of the park of Viry for further proofs."

"Unfortunately, secrecy, and care, and much money are needed for that simple search, General."

"My fortune and life shall be devoted to it."

"Come under the shadow of these trees, General. The moon shines too brightly on us here. We have to speak of an undertaking in which we risk our lives not only on the scaffold, but at the angle of a wall—everywhere, in short; for we shall have the police against us as conspirators, and a rich and powerful noble as an unscrupulous enemy."

So saying, Salvator led General de Prémont to a spot where they were completely hidden, and satisfied himself that no one was lurking near to overhear the conversation.

"Now, to begin with, General," continued Salvator, "it will be necessary to make ourselves masters of the château and park of Viry."

"Nothing could be easier, if they're to be let."

"Unfortunately they're not."

"But a handsome sum may yet buy the estate. What is there money will not buy?"

"Alas! not the Château de Viry, General; for it is at present the scene of an outrage almost as gross and monstrous as the crimes you seek the proof of."

"The château is inhabited then?"

"Yes, by an influential and infamous man—Comte Lorédan de Valgeneuse."

"Stop! That name is familiar to me. Yes, I remember, now, it was the Marquis de Valgeneuse whom I knew; but I knew him as the soul of honour."

"The Marquis!" answered Salvator, a strange light glistening in his ardent eyes. "He, indeed, was a man of noble heart and mind."

"You knew him also, Monsieur? What has become of my old friend?"

"He is dead," replied Salvator, vainly endeavouring to suppress the sorrow filling his heart. "He died suddenly of an attack of apoplexy."

"But he had a son—a natural son, had he not? Is he not alive?"

"No. He died a year after his father."

"Dead! I knew him well when he was a child—a clever boy, far above his age in intelligence and firmness. . . . Dead! And how?"

"He blew his brains out," said Salvator, laconically.

"Poor fellow! Through some great misfortune, no doubt."

"No doubt," responded Salvator.

"Then, I suppose, it was the brother of the Marquis who bought the Château de Viry?"

"No; it is the son of that brother—Comte Lorédan—who has taken it on lease, not bought it."

"I hope he does not resemble his father?"

"The father, General, was the model of a gentleman compared to the son."

"And what use does the Comte Lorédan make of the Château de Viry?"

"He makes it the prison of a young girl of seventeen."

"A young girl! Seventeen! That is just the age my little one would be," murmured the General to himself.

"But if the Comte detains the young girl against her will," he resumed aloud, "why not denounce him to justice?"

"Because, General, there are some criminals, high in position, whom Government protects instead of punishing. We must be content to meet force with force, and craft with craft. A few words will make the position clear to you. About nine years ago a friend of mine found a little country girl sleeping in a field in the suburbs of Paris. He took pity on her, and made his humble home her home, educated her, and when she was budding from girlhood into womanhood he would have married her; but she was carried off by force from a boarding-school at Versailles, and disappeared, he knew not where, till chance led me to discover the retreat of her abductor at Viry, where, through the sagacity of my dog, I at the same time found the trace of the crime I have already mentioned to you. I made myself known to the poor girl as a friend of her lover; and she confessed to me that she was kept there, spell-bound, by the knowledge that the Comte held a warrant for the arrest of Justin——"

"Who is this Justin?" demanded the General, with an eagerness which showed the interest he took in Salvator's story.

"Justin is my friend, the affianced lover of the young girl; and it is this cursed warrant that the Comte holds against him that has kept me from taking the law into my own hands."

"The park is not inaccessible, I suppose," suggested the General.

"No, for I have been in it, and so has Justin, many times."

"Why did not her lover carry her off, then, in his turn?"

"Where could he have fled to?"

"Anywhere out of France."

"Poverty prevented him. Justin is only a poor schoolmaster with about five francs a day, on which he keeps his mother and sister, besides himself."

"Let me be his banker, then. Here are a hundred thousand francs for your friend. Let him fly with the girl of his choice."

"I have but one scruple. Suppose her friends should turn out to be noble and rich; would they not be indignant with Justin?"

"For bringing up the child they had abandoned, and for saving her from dishonour? Impossible!"

"I am satisfied now, General. In a week Justin and her fiancée shall be well out of France, and we shall have full liberty to investigate every nook of the château and park of Viry."

"Your hand, Monsieur," said the General, grasping Salvator heartily, as if to seal the compact between them. "Thank Heaven we have met, Monsieur Salvator, for something whispers to my heart that we shall not only succeed in saving my friend from death, but that you will also be the means of relieving my soul from another terrible anxiety."

CHAPTER LXXI.—JUSTIN'S JOY.

THE next morning was a busy one with Salvator. He had a host of calls to make in order to set in train the hazardous undertaking he was about to embark in with General Comte Lebastard de Prémont. It was late in the afternoon when he paid his visit to Justin to bid him prepare for the daring attempt which might end in the restoration of Mina to his arms. The door was opened by Justin's sister, Céleste, who greeted the ever-welcome visitor with brightening glances and the friendliest of smiles.

"I have a budget of good news for Justin," whispered Salvator; "but I had better deliver the message myself."

"What news?" asked a familiar voice.

Salvator looked up, and found that Justin himself had overheard the whisper, which had been delivered in a joyous tone.

"Justin," said Salvator, entering the room, and embracing his friend, "supposing you should hear that from to-day Mina would be free—free to escape—free to marry you; but that in order that she might gain her liberty it would be indispensable for you to leave both mother and sister—to quit France, even? What would be your reply?"

"I should not stop to reply, Salvator. I should hasten to the rescue of my beloved!"

"Then come. One bold move, and she is yours, Justin!"

"Alas! Salvator," stammered Justin, "on second thoughts, I could not leave Paris, even to save Mina, on those conditions. Mother and sister, and my young pupils—what would become of them without me?"

"Let me answer your question by another, Justin. What is the dearest wish of your mother and sister?"

"To have the means to pass their last days in the pure fresh air of their native province."

"How much would a cottage in the country cost?"

"Perhaps three or four thousand francs."

"And how much would the living cost?"

"Five hundred francs at the most."

"Then they could live comfortably for a thousand francs?" mused Salvator, taking some bank-notes from his pocket-book and handing them to Justin. "Here's enough to buy the cottage and to provide them with all the comforts of life for the next ten years."

"Salvator!" exclaimed Justin, in wonderment, as he felt the crisp bank-notes in his hand, though he could scarce believe his senses.

"And now," resumed Salvator, in a business-like air, "it will be only necessary to arrange with your good friend, Müller, to take your classes, and you will be at liberty to enjoy the happiness you so well deserve, Justin."

"Salvator, my friend, my brother, I cannot thank you as I should, now. My brain is in a whirl; but I know you would not delude me with false hopes. Decide everything. I will follow where you lead, my best of friends."

"Follow me, or rather accompany me, to-night to Viry. If all goes well, you shall carry off Mina in your turn."

"But whither could we fly for safety?"

"To Holland. There you could live a year, two years, ten years if needed, until you can return to France without risk. Here's the passport. Here are notes sufficient to maintain you both for some time."

"But who is the donor of all this money, Salvator?"

"I cannot explain now. Rely upon it he is a true friend. Providence has sent him to save Mina at the most opportune juncture."

CHAPTER LXXII.—THE RESCUE OF MINA.

OUR hero met Justin the same evening a little way outside the Barrière Croulebarbe, where a carriage and four and a postillion awaited them.

"Jump in!" cried Salvator. Crack went the postillion's whip, and off the carriage bearing the two friends started on the road to Fontainebleau, Roland keeping up with the horses notwithstanding they were going at a good pace.

Bernard, the postillion (whom Salvator could depend upon), reined in the horses a short distance from the village of Cour-de-France. There Justin and Salvator were joined by General de Prémont; and they were speedily en route again, Salvator presenting Justin to the

General, but not revealing to the anxious lover that the newcomer was his benefactor. The inn of the Grâce-de-Dieu at Châtillon was their next stopping-place. This was the rendezvous Salvator had given to Jean Taureau and Toussaint-Louverture, whose strong arms he thought would be of good service in case of any resistance being offered at Viry. The two Mohicans of Paris were at their post, and greeted Salvator from the door of the inn.

"Follow us," whispered Salvator to them when they were close to the carriage, "but do not come to my assistance till I cry 'Help!' Jean, this handkerchief may be useful to you. Toussaint, you stow this cord away in your pocket ready for use."

"Depend upon us, Monsieur Salvator," answered Jean Taureau for himself and comrade as well.

The horses were then wheeled round, and the carriage was driven back along the Fontainebleau road till the white wall of the Château de Viry came in sight. Giving the postillion instructions to drive the carriage down a little lane, so as not to be seen by any traveller on the high road, Salvator led General de Prémont and Justin to the spot whence he had previously escaladed the wall. The three were quickly joined by Jean Taureau and Toussaint and by Roland, the faithful dog having followed his master on foot unflaggingly all the way from Paris. One after the other they climbed and vaulted over the wall, Salvator being the last. No sooner had he gained the summit than he heard the gallop of an approaching horse. He bent back so as to be completely hidden in the shadows of an overhanging branch, and his heart failed him for the moment as the horseman dashed past, and, for the second time, he saw it was Comte Lorédan de Valgeneuse, who had chosen the very night of his visit to Viry in order to tempt Mina once more to forget her virtuous resolves. Salvator leapt lightly to the ground, crying, "We must make haste, or it will be too late."

Justin knew the way so well that he acted as guide to the spot where he was accustomed to meet Mina. The young girl rushed into her lover's arms with all the trustfulness and warmth of true love directly she saw Justin, but started, and grew pale, when she caught sight of the General.

"Fear nothing, love," said Justin; "it is a friend."

"Be alert!" exclaimed Salvator, "or the Comte will be here to detain his prisoner. The moment has come when Justin can deliver you from imprisonment, Mina."

"Mina!" cried the General, rushing forward to clasp the trembling girl in his arms. "That was the name of my daughter!"

"Silence and promptitude now!" interrupted Salvator. "Explanations can follow when Mina is safely in the carriage."

Salvator and Justin, with hurried steps, then escorted Mina to the wall. Justin and Salvator sprang to the summit; and the General lifted Mina, light as a feather, in his arms, imprinted a kiss on her fair face, and then held her up high enough for her lover and Salvator to reach her. Their strong arms grasped the young girl firmly round the waist, and Mina was speedily seated beside Justin. Her lover then leapt down on the other side and received her in his arms as Salvator carefully lowered her.

"Saved!" cried Salvator, with a sigh of relief.

"Not yet!" exclaimed a loud voice.

The next moment Justin and Mina looked up with a terrible fear, for the report of a fire-arm smote their ears, and their first thought was for Salvator's safety.

CHAPTER LXXIII.—ABDUCTION OF THE ABDUCTOR.

A CRY of agonising suspense from Mina reached Salvator's ears almost simultaneously with the report of the pistol.

"Save yourselves! Bon voyage!" shouted Salvator in reply.

He then sprang down from his perilous perch, and rushed nimbly over the soft turf of the park, past General de Prémont, who had instinctively hastened to the bush whence the strange voice and pistol-shot had come.

"The shot was meant for me," was the only excuse Salvator offered the General.

The next moment he found himself face to face with Lorédan de Valgeneuse.

"Ah! I missed you the first time," exclaimed De Valgeneuse, fiercely; "but you shall not escape this shot!"

With these words he levelled the barrel of his pistol point-blank at Salvator's breast. A second later our hero would inevitably have been shot dead; but at this critical juncture Roland sprang with the ferocity of a tiger at the throat of Lorédan de Valgeneuse, and, in doing so, jerked the would-be assassin's arm upwards just as the Vicomte's finger had touched the trigger, causing the ball to be fired harmlessly in the air.

"*Par ma foi!* My dear Monsieur Lorédan," said Salvator drily; "if it had not been for the timely help of my good dog, you would have killed your cousin."

The Vicomte de Valgeneuse had been thrown heavily by Roland, and the faithful dog would unfailingly have strangled him if Salvator had not mercifully cried, "Roland! Come here, sir!"

The dog evidently let go of his master's enemy with great regret. Growlingly, he took his station by Salvator's side, cautiously reclining, however, with his intelligent eyes fixed on the Vicomte, and ready for a fresh spring on so treacherous an opponent. Availing himself of his freedom, De Valgeneuse leapt to his feet and fled in the direction of the house, crying, "Help! help!"

But he was now stopped by General de Prémont, who presented a pistol at his head and said, "Monsieur, I give you my word of honour that if you make another step to escape, if you raise another cry for help, I will shoot you dead as I would a mad dog."

"Am I attacked by a band of brigands, then?" demanded De Valgeneuse.

"No," replied Salvator; "but by men of honour who have

sworn to wrest from your keeping the young girl whom you have so shamefully carried off."

The two Mohicans of Paris, Jean Taureau and Toussaint Louverture (who had glided from their place of concealment directly they heard the cry of "Help!"—the signal for their approach),—hereupon obeyed a signal from Salvator, and deftly gagged and bound the startled Vicomte. Whilst General de Prémont saw that the handkerchief was tied securely over the prisoner's mouth, and that his limbs were bound fast by the cord, Salvator disappeared for a few minutes. He soon returned, leading the Vicomte's horse with one hand, and holding in the other a large iron bar.

"Jean," said Salvator to the herculean carpenter, "you can now run and open the gates with this bar while we fasten your prisoner on horseback."

Toussaint lifted Lorédan de Valgeneuse in his arms, placed him on horseback, face upwards, and left it to Salvator to strap him securely in that position, *à la* Mazeppa. Thus was the abductor of Mina abducted from his own park. To Jean Taureau, who stood at the open gate awaiting his final instructions, Salvator said, "You know the little house by the river side?"

"Where we met a fortnight ago? I could find my way to it blindfolded."

"Very well. You will conduct the Vicomte thither, and keep him there for two days. You'll find plenty of meat, bread, and wine in the cupboard. Mind and keep a vigilant watch on him, you and Toussaint!"

"Depend upon us, Monsieur Salvator. And when do you wish the prisoner to be set free?"

"The day after to-morrow, at this very hour, his horse will be at the door ready saddled; and you may then set him at liberty."

"Be sure we will guard him well till then, Monsieur Salvator. So, *au revoir!* Monsieur."

The two Mohicans of Paris were in another moment out of sight with their charge.

"And now, General," added Salvator, shutting the park gates, "let us devote ourselves to the interests of Monsieur Sarranti."

"Roland!" called Salvator next; but the dog had fled in the direction of the lake.

A second time did his master call him, this time more urgently, using the name of "Brésil!"

Much against his will, seemingly, Roland now answered to the call, expostulating, however, with a growl as he ran up to Salvator.

"Quiet! Quiet, Brésil!" said his master, soothingly. "I know where you were bound for, and you shall return there all in good time. Meantime, follow us, there's a good dog."

The General, who appeared not to have noticed Salvator's conversation with the dog, mechanically walked after Salvator, evidently lost in thought. The oak and the bench (which had so often been the rendezvous of Justin and Mina during those blissful stolen meetings that were the source of such deep joy to the lovers) were passed, and the two men, with their sagacious companion, took the path leading to the chateau. They had not gone far when the General remarked, "You cannot imagine, Monsieur Salvator, the intensity of the emotion which seized me at the sight of that young girl."

"Isn't she charming?"

"Alas, I should have had a daughter of the same age and beauty had she lived!"

"Are you sure she is *not* still alive, General?"

"What struck me as a singular coincidence, M. Salvator," continued the General, pursuing his own train of thought, "was that you addressed Monsieur Justin's betrothed by the name of Mina. That was the name of my little girl. If God in his mercy has spared my Mina, I fervently hope I may find her as pure as your Mina!"

In silence they walked on again for some distance, till Salvator, to divert the General's desponding thoughts, observed, "We have but one difficulty now, General. The château was only inhabited by Mina and a housekeeper, who was virtually her gaoler. Now, the first thing we ought to discover is whether she heard her master's pistol-shots, and fled at the first alarm."

"And the only way to find that out," replied the General, "will be to search the château."

"Brésil will be indispensable to us in the search," was the response of Salvator.

"Brésil! Who is that?"

"My dog, to be sure. Roland is his present name; but he used to answer to the call of 'Brésil.' Do you observe how the keenness of his scent and his natural acuteness seem to increase the nearer we get to the château?"

Pricking up his ears, and clearly restraining himself from bounding forward with much difficulty, the dog did, indeed, appear marvellously aroused at this moment.

"Be sure Brésil will find the housekeeper if she is still in the château," added Salvator, as they gained the door, which had been fortunately left open by Mina.

Salvator took from his pocket a dark lantern, lit it, and then led the way into the hall, completely dark, save for the faint glimmer of the lantern light. Brésil frisked to and fro with the certainty and freedom of a dog quite at home, and at length sprang against a low door as if he wished to burst it open. Finding it resisted his attack, he bounded back to his master, held fast to Salvator's coat with his teeth, and drew him to the recalcitrant door. No sooner had Salvator opened it than the dog dashed along the sombre passage before him, descended some seven or eight steps at the end, and uttered a lugubrious howl which made even two strong men like Salvator and General de Prémont involuntarily shiver. They, nevertheless, quickly followed the dog, and found themselves in a kind of cellar or outhouse.

"Well, Brésil, what is it? asked Salvator of the dog. "Was it here that Rose-de-Noël——?"

As though he at once understood the question, Brésil gave a doleful whine and disappeared by the way he had come. Salvator and the General had not long to wait for an explanation of the sudden disappearance. Whilst they were wonderingly looking through the door by which he had made his exit a window looking on the park was shivered into bits and Brésil jumped in, his eyes all aflame, his red tongue pendent. Fiercely the dog raced round the cellar as if in search of some one to devour.

"Rose-de-Noël is in your thoughts, isn't she?" demanded Salvator.

Brésil howled in assent.

"It must have been here," murmured Salvator, "that they attempted to murder poor Rose-de-Noël!"

"Who is this Rose-de-Noël?" inquired the General.

"One of the two children Monsieur Sarranti was charged with abducting, but the one who happily escaped the would-be murderer, whoever he was."

"Escaped! That is the poor girl, then, whom you providentially came across, but who is not yet strong enough to answer any questions we might put to her?"

"The same. Luckily we have Brésil, who will answer in her stead. See with what fury he is pawing and biting the ground?"

"What interpretation do you put upon that action?"

"That Rose-de-Noël was on the point of being killed here by somebody when Brésil dashed through the window by which he has just leapt in, and rescued his little mistress, and probably flew at the assassin."

Salvator lowered his lantern, and let the light show what had so greatly excited the ire and roused the most terrible recollections of Brésil.

"*Mon Dieu!* Blood stains, sure enough!" exclaimed the General.

"Yes, General; and, as true as Monsieur Sarranti is innocent, the blood is the blood of the assassin."

"But who was the intended assassin?"

"I fancy now it must have been a woman. I have heard Rose-de-Noël, in some of her moments of derangement, cry "Don't kill me! Pray don't kill me, Madame Gérard!""

"What a fearful labyrinth of crime this is we seem to have entered upon!"

"Yes. But patience, and Brésil will furnish us with the key. First, however, let's find the housekeeper. Here, Brésil, Brésil!" called Salvator, as he led the way up the stairs and returned to the hall.

Close at his footsteps went the dog, as he and the General ascended to the first floor. Then Brésil rushed in advance again, traversing the first-floor corridor and stopping outside a door at the further end.

"Is that the housekeeper's room, think you?" asked the General.

"No; I think not. It is probably the bedroom of one of the poor children," answered Salvator, as he pushed open the door.

Brésil gave a joyous bark as he entered. Two little cots for children appeared to be the source of a wealth of glad reminiscences to him. He darted from one to the other; and proved by every affectionate demonstration in his power that not only was it, as Salvator supposed, sacred to him as the bed-room of one but of both the little friends he loved so well. It was hard, indeed, to tear the dog from this cherished sanctum. Faithful, however, to his present master, Brésil mounted with him to the second floor. At the landing an ominous growl escaped him, and all his fury returned. He continued growling until a small door facing him was pushed open by Salvator.

With unerring scent, Brésil flew to a small chest of drawers, and would not be appeased until his master had opened the drawers, one after another. The last evidently contained some terrible souvenir. It was simply a red bodice of linen. The dog snatched it from Salvator's hands with his teeth, and his ferocity was redoubled, and he would have torn the relic of Orsola's national costume to pieces had Salvator not wrested it from him.

"It was no mistake of mine," said Salvator, calling the General's attention to the scarlet bodice. "It *was* a woman who attempted the life of Rose-de-Noël. That woman was Orsola, or, rather, Madame Gérard; and this was a part of her dress."

The General looked thunderstruck at this intercommunication of ideas between the dog and his master. As for Brésil, he barked and growled as if the most savoury of bones had been wrenched from him by force, and leapt up to prevent Salvator from restoring the obnoxious bodice to the drawer.

"Down, Brésil! Down, Brésil!" commanded Salvator. "We'll return here all in good time. Help us to find the housekeeper now!"

The dog growled as he unwillingly quitted the room. Once on the second floor, however, a fresh object engaged his thoughts. He paused opposite a door and began barking loudly.

"We've found her at last, General," said Salvator, hastening towards the same door, and adding to the dog, "There's some one inside there, isn't there, Brésil?"

Handing the lantern to his companion, he produced from one of his pockets a white belt, which he fastened round his waist after the mode then in fashion with magistrates and commissioners of police.

"It is only reasonable," Salvator explained, "that if the police don't perform their duty, somebody else must do the duty of the police."

Thereupon he gave three raps at the door, and exclaimed, "Open, in the King's name!"

The door was promptly opened, and there stood before them a trembling woman, white as her night-dress, evidently filled with fright at the sight of the two men, one of whom she took by his belt to be a police official. It did not allay her fears when Salvator added, "In the King's name I arrest you!"

Her cry of terror was answered by a fierce growl from Brésil. Her ugly features became uglier still as her terror increased. She was a repulsive-looking woman of about sixty. Her appearance was hideous in the extreme. Beside her, la Brocante would have seemed a Venus of Milo.

Salvator reflected for a moment as to where he could have seen this hag before. Hideous though her face was, it did not appear altogether unfamiliar to him. He whispered to the General to throw the lantern light on her; and, that done, he murmured to himself, "'Tis she!"

"I swear to you I am an honest woman!" broke out the trembling hag with a harsh voice.

"You lie!" answered Salvator, sternly. "I know who you are. You are known as Mother Cagnote in Paris. Were you not the means of almost bringing a lovely young girl to ruin when she had unwittingly been led to a vile and infamous house? Did you not try your utmost to drive the poor girl to dishonour?"

"Monsieur, I protest——"

"Recall to mind, Athénais, and let me hear no more of your falsehoods," answered Salvator, indignantly.

Athénais was the Christian name of the daughter of the Trumpeter Ponray before Salvator re-christened the fair girl Fragola; and, in due course, it will be explained how our hero came to the rescue of Athénais in the time of her direst peril.

"Now," said Salvator to the Mother Cagnote, who had sunk on her knees before him, "answer my questions without equivocation."

"Monsieur——"

"Answer me directly; or I'll call my men and have you at once hurried off to prison."

"Monsieur, I promise to answer you truthfully."

"How long have you been here then?"

"Since last Shrove Tuesday."

"When did the young lady carried off by your master arrive?"

"The same night."

"Has Monsieur de Valgeneuse ever allowed his prisoner to leave the park?"

"Never."

"What means did he adopt to prevent her from leaving when she pleased?"

"He menaced her with a warrant which would send her lover to the hulks."

"And what was the name of her lover?"

"Justin Corby."

"How much did you receive per month for being the gaoler of the young girl?"

"Monsieur——"

"How much?" repeated Salvator, in an imperative tone.

"Five hundred francs."

Ceasing his questions for awhile, Salvator strode to a desk, in which he found papers, pens, and ink.

"Sit down here," he said to Mother Cagnote, "and write down what you have just told me, and sign it."

"I cannot write," pleaded the hag.

Salvator referred to his pocket-book, took out and opened a folded paper, and held it up before her eyes.

"If you can't write," he said, drily, "who wrote this?"

The woman read the following paper, and then dropped her head, as if it were utterly useless to contend against the occult power of Salvator:—

"If you don't send me fifty francs this evening, I will tell them where my daughter met you, and you will be expelled from the shop.

"Nov. 11, 1824." "LA GLOUETTE.

"You know you can write well enough when you want to for any nefarious purpose," continued Salvator. "Now, just let me see a specimen of your penmanship on behalf of justice. Write down, word for word, what you told us, I command you."

Much against her will, she sat before the desk, and, in the light of the lantern held by the General, wrote with much labour, and appended her signature to a connected account of what had a minute or so ago been elicited from her. The confession finished, Salvator folded it, and put it safely in his breast pocket.

"Now you can finish your night's sleep," he said; "and, as you have been an accomplice of Monsieur de Valgeneuse, who is in custody for forcibly carrying off the young girl against her will, I may as well lock you in, and leave a sentinel on the landing, and another outside the château, with directions to fire at you if you venture to open the door or window."

Leaving the trembling hag full of earnest promises that she would not disobey the instructions of "Monsieur le Commissaire," Salvator hastened from the room with the General and Brésil.

"Now, to complete our night's work!" added Salvator. "We need fear no interruption from *her*, I think, General! My only fear is that De Valgeneuse may contrive by craft to escape from his lusty custodians."

CHAPTER LXXIV.—THE ABDUCTOR'S RUSE.

MEANWHILE, how fared it with the two lovers, whose escape from the Château de Viry was so dashingly contrived by Salvator? It was naturally a moment of terrible suspense for Justin and Mina when they heard the first report of the pistol, and saw Salvator disappear. Was he wounded? The instant this doubt filled their hearts with fear, a joint prayer for his safety went up to Heaven from the fugitives. Justin's next impulse was to spring up, catch a firm hold of the top, and so regain his seat on the wall. From this coign of 'vantage he was an eyewitness of the struggle which ended in the capture of Mina's abductor, and his being led off, bound and gagged, on horseback. A deep sigh of relief escaped from Justin when he was assured of his friend's safety, and satisfied that he and Mina could continue their flight without being arrested by Lorédan de Valgeneuse. Anxiety was driven from their young minds by the ardour of love. They seemed to tread on air as, with bounding hearts and an exultant feeling of intense joy, they hastened past the park wall within which Mina had so long been imprisoned. Redolent with the sweet incense of spring was the fresh night air, insensibly adding to the deep pleasure the lovers drank in with every breath they took. His arm around her slender waist, and his pulses tingling with the rapturous tremor of true love, Justin did not slacken his pace till they had reached the lane wherein the carriage awaited them. The postillion recognised Justin. Seeing him accompanied by a young girl, Bernard at once divined his duty. Gallantly doffing his hat, he saw the two lovers comfortably seated, and remained uncovered till he had received his instructions.

"The road to the north!" said Justin.

With a willing "Oui, Monsieur!" Bernard leapt into his saddle with an alacrity that sufficiently proved that his heart was in his work In the twinkling of an eye the carriage had shot out into the high road, and was rattling back to Paris, which it was necessary to traverse, from the Barrier of Fontainebleau to the Barrier of Vilette. Wishing Justin and Mina *bon voyage* on their journey of love, let us now return to the prisoner whom Salvator delivered into the hands of the two Mohicans of Paris. Lorédan de Valgeneuse, securely bound and gagged, and strapped *à la* Mazeppa, was duly led to the riverside cabin; and, whilst the herculean Jean Taureau bore the elegant form of the young man of fashion inside on his atlantean shoulder, Toussaint-Louverture mounted the horse, and rode back to lodge the steed in the stables of the château. The master of Viry was unconscious. He felt mortally cold when Jean Taureau deposited him on a rude table in the one room of the cabin, and, after bolting the door, removed the bandage from the mouth of the captive Lothario, and freed his limbs from the cords that bound them. Not a breath seemed to come from his lips. His arms fell down by his side, apparently limp and lifeless. Jean Taureau, who was at first inclined to praise the admirable acting of the Viscount de Valgeneuse, and ironically complimented him upon the ability with which he feigned death, became at length alarmed at the continued silence of his prisoner. He lit a lamp, and the light gleamed on a face of deadly pallor.

"Sacrebleu!" cried Jean Taureau. "What the deuce does he mean by giving me this trouble? He has fainted, like a woman. Ah! I see something in the corner there which will bring my dandy to his senses!"

Thereupon the burly carpenter seized a ewer of water, tilted it a few feet above the head of Lorédan, and let a thin stream pour down on his pale forehead. This soon revived the Vicomte. He heaved a deep sigh, and Jean Taureau felt himself at once relieved from the grave responsibility which would have rested upon him had his prisoner breathed his last.

"Where am I?" faintly murmured the Vicomte de Valgeneuse, in a few seconds.

"Where are you?" repeated Jean Taureau, gaily, completely reassured now. "Why, you're in the country house of one of your most devoted friends; and, if you will only give yourself the trouble to move from that table, and take this stool, you'll be able to study your new abode at ease."

"New abode!" exclaimed Lorédan. "Am I a prisoner, and are you my gaoler, then?"

"Sacrebleu! You use plain words, Monsieur! Look upon me in the light of a companion, not gaoler. Reckon me and my comrade (whose knock I hear) as friends, and the time will pass not unpleasantly, I hope."

Unfastening the door, Jean Taureau let in Toussaint-Louverture, and explained to him the position of affairs in a whisper.

"Yes, let's be friends, Monsieur!" said Toussaint-Louverture, a grim smile spreading over his dusky face; "and let's pledge our friendship in some of the wine the master left for us in yon cupboard."

"A good idea!" answered Jean Taureau, slapping his comrade on the back with a rough heartiness that made their prisoner tremble again. Acting on the hint, Jean quickly produced a bottle and three glasses from the well-stocked cupboard, and added, with as much courtesy as he could command, "Monsieur, we may be gaolers, but we're not bears. You must be as thirsty as we are. Will you do us the honour to accept a glass of wine?"

"Thank you," replied the Vicomte de Valgeneuse, hiding his repugnance beneath a well-assumed mask of frankness, the better to carry out a ruse which suddenly occurred to him, and which would require all his cleverness and astuteness to carry out.

The celerity with which Jean Taureau and Toussaint-Louverture drank glass after glass of wine favoured his idea. As if determined to make the best of a bad job, the Vicomte joined in the toasts, and apparently drained his glass with as much zest as they unquestionably did. A second bottle was opened, and Lorédan, making, as he thought, a great concession to the two Mohicans of Paris, raising his glass to his lips, said, "I drink to your healths, Messieurs!"

"To yours, Monsieur le Comte!" cried Jean Taureau and Toussaint, not to be outdone in courtesy.

The two Mohicans of Paris, it might have been noted, emptied their tumblers at one large draught, whilst the Vicomte drank slowly, taking three or four draughts at each glass.

"Jove!" interjected Jean Taureau. "This liquor may not be Château-Lafitte nor choice Mâcon, but may I be shot if ever I wish to drink primer stuff."

"The wine is certainly not bad," answered the Vicomte, smacking his lips to hide a grimace; "but I have not tasted enough to give you my opinion yet, Messieurs."

"Oh, that can soon be remedied," said the burly carpenter, rising from his seat. "This cupboard holds at least fifty bottles more."

"How can we pass our time better than by discussing them?" responded the prisoner, with forced gaiety.

"Are you in earnest?" asked Jean Taureau, at once delighted and surprised at the convivial tone of the Vicomte.

"Try me."

"Bravo!" exclaimed Toussaint. "Spoken like a prince of prisoners."

As for Jean Taureau, he hastened to the cupboard and armed himself with eight fresh bottles, which he placed upon the table with an air that seemed to imply, "There, my fine fellow! Now we'll put you to the test."

The Vicomte de Valgeneuse smiled to himself, and secretly enjoyed the readiness with which the two Mohicans of Paris fell blindly into the snare he had laid for them. Not that it was at all difficult to set the trap. Given two men, each of whom was a very Bacchus in his love for wine, nothing was easier than to lead them to drink, drink, drink till they lost their reason. In pursuance of his scheme, therefore, the wily prisoner feigned a frank geniality as he clinked glasses, and continued the carouse with his hospitable and unsuspecting gaolers. Two more bottles were soon "down among the dead men," and two fresh ones were quickly uncorked by the Vicomte, now effusive in his praise of the wine, which was in truth harsh enough to his epicurean taste.

"Ah! you're getting on famously, comrade," said Jean Taureau, growing familiar as the wine opened his heart, and observing that Lorédan was enjoying his potations as zestfully as he and Toussaint were enjoying theirs.

"Yes, I am doing very well, thank you," was the response.

"You must bear in mind, however, that it is a treacherous wine, comrade," continued Jean Taureau, with a laugh.

"Think so?" replied the Vicomte, naively.

"I'm sure of it," broke in Toussaint-Louverture. "Let me but drink three bottles, and 'good-night!' Down I should roll under the table, senseless as a log of wood."

"Bah!" answered the Vicomte de Valgeneuse. "Not you!"

"I should—as true—as true as I've the honour of speaking to you, Monsieur. Three bottles, or three and a half at most, settle me. Jean Taureau, here, is Hercules himself. He can stand four bottles. No; no more, I tell you. And at the last glass his senses leave him; he is like a mad bull, and he will turn and break open the head of his best friend if he provokes him. Don't you, Jean?"

"So you say," replied the lusty carpenter.

"And *you'll* prove it," answered his friend.

This last bit of information was not altogether reassuring to the Vicomte de Valgeneuse, for it suggested a not improbable contingency, which might not be without peril to him. So, seeing that Jean Taureau, his face flushed and his eyes glistening, was in the act of opening the seventh bottle, he quietly spread his hand over his glass, and said, "Not another drop for me, thank you. I have drunk enough."

Now it happened that Jean Taureau was just getting into that obstinate mood which was one phase of intoxication with him.

"You have drunk enough!" he exclaimed, with a glare of surprise.

"Yes; I have satisfied my thirst."

"Bosh! As if one only drank when thirsty! Come, the cork is out, and you must help us to finish this bottle, at least."

"Fill my glass, then, since you insist upon it," said the prisoner, resignedly.

The glasses were accordingly replenished. The fumes were now working their mischief. The two gaolers had fallen into the trap laid for them, rather to the discomfort than the gratification, however, of their guest. They roughly bade him to dance or sing for their amusement. He pleaded that he knew neither accomplishment. Jean Taureau insisted upon his trying his best, and the rough handling in store for him might have been anticipated had not Toussaint-Louverture come to his rescue with the alternative, "If you won't sing, and if you can't dance, we know you can drink. So fill up again."

"With all the pleasure in the world," answered the Vicomte, with an alacrity which excited a vague suspicion in the clouded brain of Jean Taureau.

"Stop, Toussaint!" he called out. "We have drunk enough. Remember, we have a prisoner to watch."

"It was you who first challenged me, bear in mind," retorted the prisoner.

"*You* can drink till all is blue," replied Jean Taureau, pointedly, refilling the Vicomte's glass. "But *we* have a duty to perform."

"Be it so, then. Still, have one more glass to keep me in countenance."

"Done," said Jean, only partially filling his glass, however. As he raised it to his lips he closely scanned his prisoner, saw him grasp his glass so that he totally concealed its contents, saw him lift it to his lips, and replace it empty on the table after performing a singular movement.

The same moment Jean Taureau experienced a dampness about his feet. Quick as thought, he seized the lamp, looked under the table, and sprang to his feet with savage energy.

"You treacherous rascal!" he exclaimed, rushing towards the Vicomte with clenched fists.

But he was intercepted by Toussaint-Louverture, who, ignorant of the discovery made by his friend, seized him, and, holding him back with all his might, cried, "I told you how it would be. I warned you to beware of him in his cups. You have only yourself to thank for what may happen now."

The Vicomte needed not this reminder to put himself on the defensive. He armed himself with an empty bottle in each hand, and awaited the attack.

Jean Taureau lowered his head after the fashion of the animal that gave him so suitable a cognomen, burst from Toussaint's hold, seized a stool, and brandished it with fury over the head of his prisoner.

"Whatever is the matter, Jean?" persisted Toussaint.

"Look under the table, and see for yourself!" roared his comrade.

Toussaint looked, and saw what seemed a streak of red where the white wine had streamed over the brick floor.

"Is it blood?" he exclaimed.

"Blood!" shouted Jean Taureau, with a savage laugh. "If it was merely blood, that wouldn't matter; we could make fresh blood with a mouthful or two of bread. But wine! Wine's not to be made without grapes, and the vintage may be a failure this year. Why, 'tis a crime to spill good wine!"

"What! Is it his wine that he has spilt? In that case he is unpardonable. Deal with him as he deserves, Jean!"

"I intend to," replied Jean Taureau, with a loud oath and an aggressive gesture.

"A step further, and I'll break your head open!" cried the prisoner resolutely, poising a bottle in each hand.

"What! It's not enough to waste good wine! You wish to break the bottles also!"

"Strike, and settle him at once! Why do you pause, Jean?" said Toussaint.

"Because I've thought better of it," answered Jean, lowering his stool. "I'm cooler now, and I hope our convivial friend's the same."

The Vicomte readily agreed to the truce, and replaced the bottles on the table as his formidable antagonist let his stool fall from his hand.

"Confess now," said the sobered gaoler, "that your project was to see us overcome by wine, and then to make your escape."

"Force made me your prisoner," replied the Vicomte; "and my ruse was excusable; though I crave pardon for abusing your kindness and friendly hospitality."

"Pardon is granted. Let's forget the affair now!"

"But what shall we do, as you say we must not drink, Jean?" asked Toussaint.

A new idea flashed through the prisoner's mind. Would these men be proof against bribery? He tried them; gradually he approached the subject. At length he ventured to put the question.

"Will you set me at liberty, my brave fellows, if I give you fifty thousand francs between you?"

"No!" thundered Jean Taureau, shouting all the louder because the temptation so sorely tried him. "You rich think you can buy everything: honour, virtue, friendship. Bah! Were you twenty times as rich as you are, Monsieur le Comte, and were you to offer me a million to betray my trust, I would refuse you with as much contempt as I do now."

"I offer you a hundred thousand francs, instead of fifty thousand," persisted the Vicomte.

"Jean, Jean!" cried the half-yielding Toussaint. "Do you hear? Fifty thousand francs each! The wages of a lifetime in one night."

"Toussaint," answered the carpenter, "I believed you to be an honest man. Another word on the subject, and you're no longer friend of mine."

"But, Jean, it would be for your advantage as well as mine."

"How?"

"Your little one,—Fifine; she would be quite an heiress."

At this subtle mention of his little girl, Jean hesitated for one moment, but only for a moment. He drove the temptation from him by a powerful effort of will, and seized Toussaint by the collar and shook him as he would a boy, as he cried, "Silence! I command you, Toussaint!"

"But ——," the Vicomte added, when he was interrupted by Jean Taureau.

"If you tempt me further, either of you, I'll strangle you!"

There could be no doubting the earnestness of this threat. Thus, the first and second ruse of the Vicomte had failed. It remained to play his last trick. It was yet to be seen whether intimidation would succeed.

"Messieurs," he resumed, in a firm tone, "you know I shall be set free by your master's orders before long. I know your employer; and rest assured that the first thing I shall do after my release will be to denounce him to the police, and he will be arrested!"

"Monsieur Salvator arrested! Never!" exclaimed Jean Taureau.

"Salvator's his name, is it?" answered De Valgeneuse. "I didn't know him under that name. Whatever you may call him, however, depend upon it his arrest will soon follow my deposition. Then your turns will come, and the galleys will be your lot."

"The galleys! You're joking!" answered Jean Taureau, with a laugh.

"It may be a joke to you now; but as sure as I am Lorédan de Valgeneuse, two hours after I am at liberty all three of you will be in the hands of the police."

"Do you really mean it?"

"By my faith as a gentleman."

"Then we must prevent you."

With these words Jean Taureau rushed upon the Viscomte, and held him fast, whilst Toussaint rebound him with the cord and gagged him afresh.

"To the river with him now! Let us rid ourselves of this dangerous encumbrance, Toussaint!"

The Vicomte felt as if he were in the grasp of his executioner. So rapidly had Jean Taureau effected his last movement, that the prisoner had scarce time to protest. He was conscious, moreover, that he had brought this violence upon himself by his threat.

"Yes; to the river with him!" chimed in Toussaint, as Jean Taureau lifted the light form of the Vicomte in his arms and moved towards the door. "Dead men tell no tales."

Toussaint opened the door and was about to lead the way, when he stepped back suddenly, and an exclamation of surprise came from him. A man barred the way. He crossed the threshold, and, in a loud voice, cried, "Release your prisoner!"

Chapter LXXV.—Salvator Declares Himself.

"Diable! 'Tis Monsieur Salvator!" exclaimed Jean Taureau, recoiling at the imperative command to release the treacherous prisoner whom he had bound fast, and whom he was about to bear away to the river.

"Well! What does all this mean?" demanded Salvator, entering the room, and motioning to the stalwart carpenter to loosen the cords with which the Comte de Valgeneuse had been fastened.

"Oh, nothing!" answered Jean Taureau, surlily enough. "We were only going to put this fine gentleman out of harm's way."

"Yes; we were only going to drown him, Monsieur," chimed in Toussaint.

"But what for?" pursued their master, with severity.

"Oh! we had good reasons, Monsieur," replied Jean Taureau. "First, he tried to make us drunk, so that he might escape."

"Then he sought to bribe us," added Toussaint.

"Lastly, he would have intimidated us," continued Jean Taureau. "So you must allow we have had provocation enough. Pray let us pass, then, and we'll soon settle him."

"No! I bid you ungag him."

"What! Will *you* be merciful to him, when the coward has threatened to denounce you, and us also, to the police directly he is released?"

"Release him, I repeat; and leave him alone with me, my good fellows."

"Since that is your wish, Monsieur Salvator, I must obey," answered Jean Taureau, unwillingly freeing the prisoner's limbs and letting him breathe freely again; but warning Salvator, or rather De Valgeneuse, as he dragged Toussaint out of the cottage with him, that they would be within call in case of need. When the door had closed behind them, Salvator turned to the Comte de Valgeneuse, and courteously said,

"Do take a seat, cousin, for we have much to say to each other."

Lorédan de Valgeneuse looked at Salvator with wonderment.

"Look at me well, Lorédan," continued Salvator, calmly, "and assure yourself it *is* your cousin who stands before you!"

"Where the deuce do you spring from, M. Conrad?" asked Lorédan de Valgeneuse, with bated breath, after a pause. "'Pon my honour, we all thought you were dead! And, proof enough, hadn't we to pay for your burial?"

"Oh! my dear cousin, surely you don't regret the miserable sum of five hundred francs that my funeral cost you! Never was a sum better expended. Why, in return, for something like six years, you have netted no less than two hundred thousand francs a year. Don't distress yourself, pray, about the petty five hundred francs. Depend upon it, I'll return it when I come to settle accounts with you!"

"Settle accounts?" repeated Lorédan, with a sneer. "What accounts have we to settle?"

"Ah! what indeed?"

"You can't refer to the inheritance of the Marquis de Valgeneuse, my late uncle!"

"You might have added, Lorédan, '*and your father!*'"

"Well, there's no need of ceremony between us; so, since it is your pleasure, I will add, 'and your father.' And now, Monsieur Conrad, or Monsieur Salvator, whichever you prefer to be known as, for you seem to have many names, may I venture to inquire how it is that you are alive when we have for so many years concluded you were dead?"

"Would you like to hear the story?"

"With the greatest interest I should listen to it."

"It is soon told," answered Salvator. "You remember, my dear cousin, the sudden and unexpected nature of my father and your uncle's death?"

"Perfectly well."

"You may also recollect, then, that he would never recognise me—not because he deemed me unworthy to bear his name—but, on the contrary, because if he had recognised me as his son he could only have left me a fifth of his fortune."

"*Ma foi!* I never trouble myself about the law with regard to natural children. Being a legitimate son myself, why should I have given the subject a moment's thought?"

"*Mon Dieu*, Monsieur Lorédan, it was not myself, but my poor father, I was referring to at that moment. So entirely did the subject engross *his* thoughts that he sent for his notary the very day of his death, and the honest Monsieur Baratteau came."

"Yes, and it was never known what he was called in for. It is your belief, I presume, that Monsieur Baratteau received from the hands of your father a will in your favour?"

"I don't presume—I am certain of the fact!"

"You are certain?"

"Yes."

"How so?"

"Why, because the Marquis, as if he feared the impending attack, confided to me what he had done."

"Oh! I am as familiar with that episode as you are."

"Are you?"

"Oh, yes! The Marquis made a will; but either before or after he handed it to Monsieur Baratteau—that point has never been cleared up—your father was attacked by a fit of apoplexy, and fell down dead. Isn't that right?"

"Yes—with the exception of one detail."

"What was that?"

"It was that the Marquis, as a double precaution, made two wills!"

"Two wills!"

"Yes."

"In which he left you his name and fortune?"

"Precisely."

"What became of the wills, then?"

"It was intended that one should be deposited with the notary. The other was to be handed to me, but it was left in the interim in a secret drawer of a certain piece of furniture in his bedroom."

"I thought," said Lorédan, scrutinizing Salvator narrowly, "that you were ignorant of the whereabouts of that precious document?"

"I was; but to-day I am no longer in ignorance on that point."

"Indeed! This grows interesting. Proceed!"

"I will proceed in due order, my dear cousin. Things are always clearer related in their proper sequence. Let us now leave the two wills for a little while. I will not dwell on that interval when it was still uncertain whether I should be the heir to the name and fortune of my father, the Marquis de Valgeneuse, and when your father even thought it politic to make a match between your sister Suzanne and me. You will do me the justice to say that when, at last, your family refused to acknowledge any relationship with me, and bade me quit the family mansion in the Rue du Bac, I did not hesitate to obey?"

"True," responded Lorédan quickly; "but would you have left so readily if the famous will had been found!"

"Perhaps not. Human nature is weak; and when one is abruptly called upon to step all at once from riches to poverty, it is but natural that one should hesitate as some miners may before descending for the first time the deep shaft, at the bottom of which even virgin gold awaits them. And at the bottom of the gloomy gulf into which I plunged headlong I by-and-by found the pure metal, free from dross. But, first, what heart-struggles, what soul-killing misery, what hunger and wretchedness had I not to endure! The few accomplishments I had were insufficient to procure for me a living. Rather than prolong my misery I at length resolved to blow out my brains. The day arrived. The pistol was ready. My mind was made up. Chance led me through the Rue Saint-Honoré. People were crowding into Saint-Roch to hear a young preacher of note. A providential impulse bade me enter. I listened, and my soul was touched by the loving humanity that filled his sermon. The theme was suicide. I was awakened from my selfish, cowardly dream. Frère Dominique saved me. 'Work is prayer!' That was the noble motto he bade me strengthen my sinking heart with. Work I did with all my might as a Commissionaire."

"But how came it about that we buried you, if you were not dead?" inquired Lorédan de Valgeneuse, with a puzzled air.

"I will soon explain that. I had a trusty friend in an attendant at the Hôtel-Dieu, and prevailed upon him to sell me the very next suicide that should be brought to the hospital. The subject was soon forthcoming; and, as luck would have it, the poor fellow had so disfigured his face in discharging a pistol at his head that he was totally unrecognisable. He was, moreover, just about my age and size. It was, accordingly, the easiest thing imaginable to smuggle the dead body up into my room, clad it with a suit of my clothes, leave it on the bed, and take farewell of my lodging, first smashing a window pane to account for the disappearance of the pistol whereby the suicide had been effected. So it came, my dear cousin, that whilst I assumed the garb and employment of a Commissionnaire, you and yours were good enough to give a Christian burial to what you were led to believe were my remains."

"I compliment you, Monsieur," said Lorédan, "on the sensational nature of your confession. But you have left untold what has become of the last will of the Marquis, and how you intend to return me the five hundred francs which we so uselessly gave to Monsieur Jackal for your proper interment."

"Wait a moment, my dear cousin. Surely you didn't think I was such a fool as to confide the secret of my life to you without being certain beforehand of your discretion?"

"You intend to keep me here a prisoner, then, for ever?"

"How little you know me! At five o'clock to-morrow morning you shall be free."

"And you promise this in the face of what your men told you—that as soon as I am at liberty you will be denounced and arrested?"

"Oh, that threat doesn't frighten me! Where would you be at this moment if I hadn't made my appearance as you were being borne off on the shoulders of Jean Taureau? I am persuaded that you will reconsider the matter well, and that you will leave me tranquil in my quiet home in the Rue aux Fers, in order that you may rest undisturbed by me at your mansion in the Rue du Bac."

"May I venture to inquire how you could disturb me in any way when once I am free?"

"I have purposely kept that till the last, my dear cousin."

"I am all attention, then."

"Well, you know that last night I had the gratification to deliver a lovely maiden from the wicked knight who had carried her off."

A look of cold hatred and malignant vengeance was called up in the Comte's face by this allusion.

"I had just engaged the carriage yesterday for that delicate enterprise," continued Salvator, unmoved, "when my attention was drawn to something in the court-yard of the sale-rooms in the Rue des Jeûners. At the sight of a certain piece of furniture in the court-yard a cry of surprise escaped my lips. I recognised it as the one I had so often seen in my father's bed-room. I bought it for sixty francs, rejoiced in being able to take home the souvenir of the Marquis, and searched the drawers and every nook and corner of the rosewood cabinet. What do you think I at length found?"

Lorédan de Valgeneuse awaited to learn what was to follow with the utmost eagerness.

"You decline to guess? Very well, I discovered at last that the centre drawer—the one that served as cash-box—had a false bottom. Hidden away underneath was a paper ——"

"And that paper was ——"

"The same that we had so many years searched for in vain."

"The will! Impossible!" exclaimed Lorédan, striving to realise all that this startling announcement might portend.

"It was the will."

"The will of the Marquis?"

"The Marquis de Valgeneuse's will, leaving to his son Conrad all his household goods and fortune, on condition that he should take the title and arms as head of the house of Valgeneuse."

"I repeat it is an utter impossibility—a mere fable," protested Lorédan de Valgeneuse with as much warmth as his icy nature was capable of expressing.

"See for yourself," answered Salvator, producing a paper from his breast-pocket.

Lorédan instinctively thrust his hand forward to snatch the paper away.

"Oh, no, my dear cousin," said Salvator, quietly withdrawing the will. "It had better remain in the custody of him it will be most useful to. But I cannot deprive you of the pleasure of hearing its contents."

Salvator had not read far when his eager listener appeared fully satisfied that it was the duplicate will of the Marquis de Valgeneuse that had so strangely fallen into the hands of his cousin.

"And now," concluded Salvator, "shall it be peace or war between us? You are perfectly free, my dear cousin, to choose. Bear this in mind, however: if you set yourself up against me I will at once act upon this will, and ruin will stare you in the face directly. If, on the other hand, you let your late prisoner and her lover continue their flight unmolested, I promise to leave you unmolested. In accordance with my plans, I intend to retain my post of Commissionnaire a year, two years, it may be three years longer. During that time my five or six francs a day will do for me, and I shall not miss the income of two hundred thousand pounds. So take your choice: peace or war. Reflect for the rest of the night, and follow my advice, cousin."

Thereupon Salvator quitted his cowering kinsman, and, leaving the door a-jar, drew Jean Taureau and Toussaint-Louverture away with him, showing the Comte de Valgeneuse that he was perfectly at liberty to gain his freedom at once or later, whichever might please him best.

CHAPTER LXXVI.—ROSE-DE-NOEL'S LOVER.

RETURNING to Paris, let us see what happened a few day's later at No. 10, Rue d'Ulm, the new abode of la Brocante, Rose-de-Noël, Babolin, and the family of dogs.

The fortune-teller of the Rue d'Ulm had her canine favourite—the ugliest of the circle—Babylas by name; and she was petting Babylas, as usual, when a stranger unceremoniously entered the sorceress's apartment, which was partly a museum of curiosities, partly a dog-kennel, and partly furnished with the paraphernalia of necromancy.

The visitor wore an ample great coat, though the weather was anything but cold, had a pair of spectacles on his nose, and carried a cane.

"Are you la Brocante?" asked the stranger, brusquely.

"Yes, Monsieur!" answered the sorceress, not without the tremor which a harsh voice invariably called up in her now.

"You tell fortunes, then?"

"By the aid of my cards, Monsieur."

"Good! I've come to put your skill to the test," said her visitor, taking a pinch of snuff with satisfaction.

"Perhaps Monsieur wishes to know whether he will contract a good marriage?"

"No, no! Marriage being an evil in itself, what do I want with marriage?"

"Does Monsieur desire to know, then, whether he will be the heir of some rich relative?"

"Wrong again! I've only one relative in the world—an old aunt—and it is I who have had to settle upon her an income of six hundred pounds a year, worse luck! *Ma foi!* what I want to know is whether I shall go to Paradise?"

"Monsieur will have to pay thirty sous before the cards will answer."

"There's the money," said the stranger, throwing a piece of silver into la Brocante's lap with an air of lavish generosity. "Thirty sous are not much, to learn if one's destined for Paradise."

Now la Brocante had allowed Babylas to stray to the window, out of which he was looking with all his heart in his eyes, for he caught sight of a dainty canine love of his below, looking up at him with an expression irresistibly coquettish and captivating. The poor dog yielded to the spell. He sprang out of the window. The moment the fortune-teller saw the retreating form of her favourite, she also sprang up, and leapt out of the window in pursuit, followed by the faithful rook and the whole pack of dogs.

Babolin, the agile gamin de Paris, was about to dart after them when he felt himself held back by the stranger, who had clutched his blouse, and exclaimed,

"Stop, stop, my young friend! Here's five francs for you if—"

"If what, Monsieur?"

"If you'll let me speak with Rose-de-Noël for a few minutes."

"You mean no harm to her, I hope?" questioned the quick-eyed gamin, satisfying himself as to the genuineness of the coin, and pocketing it.

"Oh, no."

"Then follow me."

Babolin led the way up stairs to Rose-de-Noël's room, opened the door, and revealed the young girl seated at a little fancy table, the gift of Régina, and engaged in colouring a drawing of flowers.

"Rose-de-Noël," said Babolin, "this gentleman wishes to see you."

"To see me?" exclaimed Rose-de-Noël with surprise, looking up at the visitor.

"Yes, my dear young lady," answered the stranger, jerking his blue spectacles up over his brows.

Rose-de-Noël rose. She had grown marvellously since we last saw her. She was no longer the thin slip of a girl we knew at the Rue Triperet. She was pale and slender still, it is true, but her form had a girlish gracefulness and lissomness beautiful to see.

"Well, Monsieur," she said, her blue eyes opening wide with wonder as to the business of her visitor; "what can you have to say to me?"

"I am sent, my dear, by some friends who love you sincerely."

"By the Fairy Carita and Monsieur Pétrus?"

"No."

"By Monsieur Salvator, then?"

"Right, my dear!"

"If you are from Monsieur Salvator you are welcome," said Rose-de-Noël, moving a chair towards her visitor with instinctive courtesy.

As for Babolin, hearing that it was a friend of Monsieur Salvator who was Rose-de-Noël's guest, he left them alone with confidence, and went out to see what had become of la Brocante and her happy family.

"And now we are alone, my dear," said the stranger, sinking into the seat offered him, "permit me to put a few questions to you on behalf of Monsieur Salvator."

"With pleasure, Monsieur."

"To begin with, have you any recollection of your young days? Do you remember your father and mother?"

"I have a faint remembrance of my father," replied the young girl, looking searchingly into the face of her interrogator; "but I don't remember anything of my mother."

"Do you remember your uncle Gérard?"

"Yes," answered Rose-de-Noël tremulously, and turning pale as death. "Have you any news of him?"

"I have."

"Is he still alive?"

"He is my dear."

"And——"

The young girl trembled in every limb, and it was evident she had the greatest repugnance to put the next question which was uppermost in her thoughts.

"And Madame Gérard?" suggested the stranger.

On hearing this name, Rose-de-Noël uttered a fearful cry, and fell from her chair in a dead faint.

"Diable! Diable!" exclaimed the visitor, starting to his feet. "Who would have thought this girl was as sensitive as a Princess? The situation is growing embarrassing, too. Diable! I had better lift her on the bed, and vanish."

He did so; and then, quick as thought, took a wax impression of the lock of the door, and pocketed the wax, chuckling to himself,

"Voltaire was right. 'All *is* for the best in this best possible of worlds.'"

"And yet," he continued—an involuntary impulse of humanity detaining him—"I ought not to leave this poor girl insensible."

The door was opened as these words escaped him, and Ludovic entered the room.

"Bravo! bravo!" exclaimed Rose-de-Noël's visitor. "You have arrived in the nick of time, my gallant young doctor."

"Monsieur Jackal!" was all the astonished Ludovic could ejaculate in reply.

"At your service," said the Commissioner of Police, offering Ludovic his snuff-box.

But the young physician pushed M. Jackal's hand on one side and hastened to the bedside.

"Monsieur Jackal!" he exclaimed sternly, "perhaps you'll explain how I find Rose-de-Noël in this state?"

"Certainly. She is subject to spasms, it appears."

"There's no denying that. But you must have said something alarming to her to render the poor girl insensible."

"Diable! If you must know, Monsieur Ludovic, I did say a few words to her; but I never imagined her nerves were so weak as they seem to be. You should know that my jurisdiction extends over all Bohemians in Paris. La Brocante having disappeared from the Rue Triperet without informing me of her change of address, it became my duty to learn the reason why. So I came here to question her; but she abruptly left me; and I came up to see little Rose-de-Noël, and I had simply asked her if she remembered a certain Madame Gérard, when she fainted away!"

All was explained with such apparent frankness by the Commissioner of Police that Ludovic felt he could not doubt the truth of his words.

"But I see signs of returning consciousness, Monsieur Ludovic," added M. Jackal, "and as my presence may be a disturbing influence to the poor girl when she opens her eyes, I think I had better go. Good-day! Forgive me for being the innocent cause of so much trouble."

"Good-day, Monsieur Jackal," replied Ludovic, who had been bathing Rose-de-Noël's temples with cold water. "She will soon come round again."

Rose-de-Noël did awaken to consciousness a few moments after M. Jackal's departure. Her large blue eyes were, however, momentarily filled with fear till they rested upon Ludovic. Then, with a deep look of loving confidence welling up in the liquid azure of her eyes, she would at once have explained the cause of the fainting fit in which the doctor had found her. But Ludovic placed his hand on her sweet lips as a caution that she must not speak yet.

"Sleep for a while, little Rose," he whispered. "Take a short nap, and then you can tell me all when you feel yourself again."

"Yes," she murmured drowsily, almost falling off to sleep as she spoke.

What were the thoughts of Ludovic as he sat by the bedside and gazed at the pure, innocent face of the sleeping maiden?

A glance at the adorable beauty of Rose-de-Noël was a sufficient answer. She was Mignon personified. What would Jean Robert not have given for the privilege of embodying her budding charms in a poem? With what pride Pétrus would have painted this lovely realisation of innocent and guileless girlhood!

Rose-de-Noël's was equally the grave beauty of Goethe's and Airy Scheffer's Mignon. She was the idealisation of that fleeting moment when girlhood buds into womanhood, when the body receives a soul, when, in fine, love shafts are impelled and received with the strength of virgin youth.

Nor was Ludovic an unworthy Wilhelm Meister. He had hitherto struggled successfully against the arrows of Cupid. Love, he argued, was but a physical sensation, and beauty but skin deep, for Byron had disenchanted him in common with many more of his contemporaries. Led to the Rue d'Ulm by Pétrus as the trusty friend who could best prescribe for Rose-de-Noël, Ludovic had grown quite at home there; but it was not until this moment that the subtle beauty of the young girl penetrated into his soul, as it were, and proved to him what an all-powerful passion that of Love really was.

The source of that delicious tremor—the heart-tingling, soul-searching shiver of first love—was not to be revealed to him all in a moment. The sweet girl slept on. There was the slightest movement perceptible in the undulating beauty of her form, as her bosom rose and fell with each breath. He felt glad that his care and skill had preserved the life of so charming a creature. Then there stole into his brain the sweet consciousness that in Rose-de-Noël he had found his fate. At last he knew he loved her. Yes, he at length felt he loved the young girl with all the delightful strength of an untried passion.

"Sleep, dearest," he murmured. "You have taught me what life, what love is. Sleep on, for in your dreams you have stolen my heart away, and yet I rejoice at the loss——"

Rose-de-Noël opened her blue eyes at this moment, and a blush involuntarily rushed to Ludovic's face. The same instant there darted into the young girl's heart, there rushed tumultuously through her veins, a joyous pulsation, such as the spark of love only occasions. The pale cheeks of Mignon were flushed in their turn. She turned her face to hide her confusion and palpitating gladness.

"Rose, darling," her lover exclaimed, bending over her in alarm, fearing she had been seized with a fresh attack. "Rose, dearest, say you are no worse!"

The flushed face was turned towards his. Their breaths mingled. They read the love-light in each other's eyes. Their lips were silent, but heart spoke to heart, and their blissful enjoyment of the first moments of love was only interrupted when a young voice—that of Babolin—informed them through the open door,

"Good news, Rose-de-Noël! Babylas has been recovered, and la Brocante is happy!"

Chapter LXXVII.—M. Jackal's Ruse.

THE same day that Rose-de-Noël was visited by the Chief Commissioner of Police, the same day that she found a lover in Ludovic, honest Monsieur Gérard was seated comfortably in the luxurious drawing-room of his mansion at Vanvres, engaged in reading a newspaper, when he was interrupted by his valet.

"His Excellency General Triptolemus de Melun, of his Majesty's Household!" announced the valet, in a sonorous tone befitting the occasion.

M. Gérard turned crimson with pride. He started to his feet, and prepared to receive so illustrious a visitor with becoming homage and humility. Might he not be the bearer of some mark of honour from the King? With bowed head and body bent—a living note of interrogation, as it were—he waited for the first words of this eminent personage, who had followed the servant into the room with that supreme air of impertinence and haughty disdain which distinguishes the suite of Royalty from ordinary mortals.

His Excellency General Triptolemus de Melun as the new comer styled himself, was a tall, thin man. He wore a blonde wig, gold spectacles, and a Court costume. Maintaining the cool effrontery with which he had entered, he wheeled an arm-chair close to M. Gérard, motioned to him to be seated, helped himself to a pinch of snuff from a gold snuff-box, and sat down face to face with his host in the most unceremonious style possible.

"Monsieur," he at length said, "I am the bearer of a message from the King."

M. Gérard bent his head until his nose nearly touched his knee, to signify his sense of the great honour paid him by his Excellency. He could only stammer,

"From the King?"

"Yes; his Majesty has sent me to congratulate you upon the issue of your trial."

"The King honours me too much, your Excellency. I can scarcely believe it possible that his Majesty should interest himself——"

"The King is the father of his people," interrupted his Excellency, "and interests himself in all who suffer; and, aware of the terrible sufferings you must have endured since the loss of your poor nephew and niece, his Majesty condoles with you through me."

"Your Excellency, I am unworthy——"

"*You* unworthy! Oh, Monsieur! you wrong yourself. What! a man who has suffered as you have suffered, a man known far and wide for his charity, a man who must be worshipped here in Vanvres for his open-hearted liberality, a man regarded as the model of a philanthropist—such a man unworthy of the sympathy of his King! Monsieur Gérard, humility such as yours is but another proof of your goodness."

M. Gérard could not perceive the undercurrent of irony running through his Excellency's eulogium. He was overcome by this mark of Royal condescension. The one ambition of his later life had been to obtain the cross of the *légion d'honneur*. Was it possible, he asked himself in his heart of hearts, that this ambassador of the King was the bearer of this coveted insignia?

"Not only does the King fully sympathise with you," continued his Excellency, "but he would reward you."

"Reward me!" cried M. Gérard, in an exultant tone, which he regretted a moment after, and hastened to disguise by adding, "Duty's its own reward, you know, General."

"No doubt! No doubt!" replied his Excellency, his thin lips curling with an almost imperceptible smile. "I fully appreciate your just remark. No doubt, every good action brings with it its own recompense. But does not an accumulation of such good actions as yours merit public recognition? And is it not one of the proudest functions of the King, as the head of the State, to honour such deeds? His Majesty thinks it is, at any rate; and, in proof thereof, the King has commanded me to ask what honour you might be pleased to accept from his Majesty?"

"Oh," answered M. Gérard, again bending low in token of his abject humility, "if the King has deigned to honour me thus, I must confess there is one thing I do heartily desire, your Excellency."

"Name it."

"It is," said M. Gérard, pausing between each word, as if fearing he was asking too much, "it is—your Excellency—the cross—of the *légion d'honneur!*"

"Only the *légion d'honneur!* Is it possible that so eminent and virtuous a citizen as you can be satisfied with such a trifle as a bit of red ribbon in your buttonhole?"

"Yes, your Excellency," replied M. Gérard, eagerly. "That is really the summit of my ambition."

"Well, my dear Sir, you will be gratified to learn, then, that the cross of the *légion d'honneur* is the very order the King has bestowed upon you."

"Is it possible?" exclaimed M. Gérard, his face flushing with joy.

"Yes, Monsieur," replied his Excellency, rising as he spoke, and fumbling in his pocket as if he were searching for the order; "and his Majesty has deputed to me the honour of presenting the cross to the most honest of men."

"I feel overwhelmed by the King's kindness," murmured the expectant M. Gérard, sinking on one knee to receive the insignia of honour.

But, instead of drawing the coveted order from his pocket, his Excellency folded his arms, and, regarding the kneeling man with a look of supreme contempt, said,

"*Pardieu!* Monsieur, what a hypocritical scoundrel you are!"

M. Gérard sprang to his feet as though a viper had stung him.

"Look me straight in the face," continued his strange visitor.

"What is it that you wish to say to me?" stammered M. Gérard, his eyes dropping beneath the stern gaze of his interlocutor.

"I wish to say that Monsieur Sarranti is innocent; that it is you who are guilty of the crimes for which he is condemned to death; that the King never had the remotest idea of offering you the cross of the *légion d'honneur;* that my name is not General Triptolemus de Melun, but simply Monsieur Jackal, Chief of the Secret Police! And now, my dear Monsieur Gérard, let us talk like two friends, who know each other thoroughly, and listen to me with the profoundest attention, for I have something to communicate of the utmost importance to you!"

The first words of this unexpected declaration drew a cry of terror from M. Gérard; and his face turned ashy pale as he sank back, faint and sick with fear, into his chair.

"It is understood between us, then, that Monsieur Sarranti is innocent, and you are the guilty one?" continued M. Jackal, drawing his chair confidentially closer to his stricken listener.

"Mercy, Monsieur Jackal," was the pitiful answer.

The Chief of the Police regarded the craven wretch for an instant with a look of supreme disgust.

"Come, come," M. Jackal then added, "bear up, for I have come to save you."

"To save me!" muttered M. Gérard, whose white face betrayed the mingled emotions of hope and fear that his mind was a prey to.

"Yes, to save you; it *is* rather astonishing, isn't it, that anyone should lift a hand to save such a villian as you? The marvel is easily explained, however. The powers that be have determined that Sarranti shall go to the scaffold. It is not to save you, but to settle the fate of an innocent man, that you will be spared."

Now, M. Gérard was an assiduous reader of the newspapers of the day, and had already noticed with secret satisfaction, the persistent way in which the official press daily attacked M. Sarranti. Armed with this knowledge, he at once guessed the object of M. Jackal's visit, and breathed rather more freely.

"I think I understand, Monsieur," he said, with a faint attempt at a cunning smile.

"Good! Then tell me all the inns and outs of the affair."

"For what purpose?"

"In order that we may get rid of all trace of the crime."

"Traces! Is it possible any trace can be left?" demanded M. Gérard, terror again taking possession of him.

"I should think there is; and an undeniable trace, too. There's your niece!"

"My niece? Is she not dead?"

"No. Madame Gérard did not quite succeed in killing the poor girl. She lives and trembles whenever she hears the name of Orsola mentioned."

"She knows all, then!" muttered M. Gérard, a shiver passing through him at the mention of the dread name of his temptress.

"Most probably; and it is, therefore, all the more necessary for you to make me acquainted with all the details of the business."

M. Gérard felt that M. Jackal was an ally now, and so recounted to him the tragedy of the Château of Viry as freely as he had told it to the Abbé Dominique when he thought he was on his death-bed.

"I see it all now," said M. Jackal, with professional relish, at the end of the story.

"What! Was it not all known to you before you came here, then?"

"Oh, no, not all, by any means," replied M. Jackal.

"Poor Dominique!" murmured the Commissioner of Police to himself, after a pause; "I see now how he came to swear so earnestly that his father was innocent. I know now what the poor fellow alluded to in referring to the proof he possessed of Monsieur's Sarranti's innocence; and I guess the object of his pilgrimage to Rome."

"Has he left for Rome, then?" demanded M. Gérard. "What for?"

"My dear Monsieur Gérard, there is only one man who can release the Abbé Dominique from the oath of secresy with regard to your confession."

"Yes, the Pope."

"Well, he went to Rome to see the Pope for that purpose."

"Then I am lost!"

"Not at all. I know his Holiness. He is a jovial Pope, whose only anxiety is to leave the temporal and spiritual power of Rome just as he received it from his predecessor. Depend upon it, means will be found to prevent him from granting the poor Abbé's prayer. His Holiness has most likely already refused it. At any rate, the Abbé Dominique Sarranti will probably return to Paris in a fortnight, having made his pilgrimage in vain."

"But suppose he should reveal the secret without the Pope's permission?" suggested M. Gérard fearfully.

"Has he not sworn to you that he would not?"

"Yes, he swore he would not make use of the paper containing my confession until after my death."

"Then he will keep that oath, like a man of honour. Only you must take care of one thing."

"What?"

"That you don't die. If you do the Abbé will be released from his oath, and you know what must follow. So be careful of your precious life. Keep in doors as much as possible till my next visit. My interest in your affairs may lead me to make a trip to the Château de Viry, and I may want you as a companion. However, good-bye for the present, my dear Monsieur Gérard!"

With these words, uttered in a frigid tone of irony that made M. Gérard's blood run cold, the Commissioner of Police rose and took his leave as abruptly as he had entered.

"Where to, Monsieur?" demanded his coachman, as M. Jackal was about to enter his carriage.

"Return to Paris by the Barrière Vaugirard, and drive through the Rue aux Fers," replied M. Jackal, adding to himself, as he took his seat, "I must see if that troublesome young Monsieur Salvator is at his post. It strikes me somehow that he may have a hand in this Sarranti business, and may be of use to us."

CHAPTER LXXVIII.—LOVE'S BLOSSOMING.

LANGUAGE fails to adequately express the subtle joy, the calm delight, which all true lovers experience during those silent reveries they indulge in while lingering beneath the windows of their beloved ones. In the full vigour and strength of his early love for Rose-de-Noël, Ludovic was wont to enjoy sweet stolen meetings with his girl-love at midnight. Then the squalid Rue d'Ulm became etherealised. The light which streamed from Rose-de-Noël's chamber seemed a ray of light from Heaven, and the grey Persian blinds the gates of Paradise. The summer air was full of perfume, the sky an Italian blue, and the myriad stars sparkled with a softened beauty, as if keeping time to the beating of Ludovic's heart. There was no need of any appointment between this Paul and Virginia, of Paris. As sure as midnight came Rose-de-Noël knew she might count on the appearance of Ludovic beneath her window. This night, therefore, she extinguished her lamp, and pushed back the Persian blinds, as usual, with the sweet certainty that her heart would be rejoiced with the sight of her lover. Well might the roses that clung to the window have awakened and flushed a rosier red when Rose appeared. It made the tendrils of her lover's heart tingle with a delicious joy directly the delicate beauty of her pure sweet face met his enraptured gaze.

"Rose!" he murmured, in a loving tone, as he mounted a stone under the window, and snatched a kiss from her dainty hand.

"Ludovic!" was the sweet response of the gladdened maiden.

What need of words to interpret their mutual love? They pressed each other's hands, and an electric thrill rushed to their hearts. They gazed into the loving depths of each other's eyes, and mind spoke to mind in the silent language which both had learnt to read so well. Though absorbed in the ecstacy of the moment, Ludovic yet had ears for any sign of the least interruption. He heard the noise of approaching footsteps, and sprang into the shadow of a convenient angle of the wall, and Rose, taking the alarm, quickly closed her Persian blinds, and retired. Two men came down the street, looking about curiously, as if in search of some house. They stopped opposite the dwelling of la Brocante and Rose-de-Noël. Ludovic held his breath, and trembled as he overheard one of the strangers say, "This must be the place."

"Can Rose be in any danger?" thought Ludovic to himself.

Whatever the intentions of the two men might have been, they were clearly not prepared to carry them out that night, for they speedily disappeared by the way they had come, and left the two lovers to resume their caresses.

"What did those men want?" asked the young girl somewhat tremulously, as Ludovic regained his position beneath the open window.

"Nothing, nothing, Rosette," answered Ludovic, reassuringly. "They had only missed their way, I fancy."

"I felt instinctively afraid, I don't know why, directly they stopped," said Rose.

The bells of Val-de-Grâce, Saint-Jacques, and Saint-Etienne struck the hour; but Ludovic had now only ears for a distressing sound, a hacking cough which came from Rose-de-Noël. He had striven with Death and mastered him, and saved the fair patient he was destined thereafter to love with all his heart and soul. Yet this cough came to remind him that Rose was not yet out of danger, and that, balmy and sweet as the summer's night air was, it would be prudent for him to bring their stolen meeting to a close, and to awaken his love from the Midsummer Night's Dream in which she was wrapt. Loving vows were exchanged ; and, watched by adoring eyes, the young doctor left Rose-de-Noël to end the night in fresh dreams of her pure love.

Chapter LXXIX.—Love's Passion.

THE stolen meeting between Ludovic and Rose-de-Noël, though similar in some respects to that which took place about the same hour in the garden of General de Lamothe-Houdan, was in reality widely different. Love had but blossomed in the one case. In the other, Love had grown to the full height of its overwhelming passion. Which is love's most delicious moment? The moment of its birth, the *élan* of its youth, or the ripeness of its maturity? Let who will decide the problem. It is sufficient for ordinary mortals to gather the rosebuds as they may, and enjoy each varying phase of the divine passion to the full. There was this additional element in the meeting of our Mohican of Art, Pétrus, and the Princess Régina : farewell had to be said, and the pain of parting seemed to make the rapturous moments more precious to the two lovers. Pétrus, his heart beating as lovers' hearts will, had been admitted through the garden gate, as usual, by Nanon, the nurse, and had hastened to the rendezvous— the most secluded nook in the grounds, where huge trees towered above, their interlacing branches forming a roof to the most welcome arbour in all Paris for love-making. There he found Régina awaiting him—the fairy of the green glade, the Queen of Night, the mistress of his soul. Clasping her loved form to his heart, Pétrus was greeted by the sweet, dovelike murmurings so prized by lovers, and showered down upon her sweet lips a rain of kisses. The Princess was charmingly attired in white. There had been a soirée at her father's, but she had not stopped to change her dress. Throwing a light robe over her shoulders, she had hurried as she was to the rendezvous. A thread of pearls encircled her ivory neck, a diamond earring flashed from each ear, a river of brilliants sparkled in her hair, and bracelets of emeralds, sapphires, rubies, and gold glistened on her arms. No one could have appreciated the magnificence of the Princess's beauty, thus enhanced, better than her painter lover. Nor was his love any the less sincere that he could take in every detail of this perfect picture, as it were. With the eyes of an artist he admired her, with.the passion of a lover he adored her. There was a mossy bank close by, and on this the lovers sat, leaving their hearts to throb love's language as they remained locked in each other's arms. The jewels on Régina's arms proving embarrassing, she unclasped the bracelets, and a shower of rubies, sapphires, and emeralds fell at their feet. Then ensued a delightful interval, and each appeared too intoxicated with bliss to speak. Vows and sighs came all too quickly, however, for them. As the hour of departure drew near, Pétrus had so much to explain to Régina that words took the place of embraces. He had to tell her that his dream in Paris had at length come to an end. Luxuriously he had lived on, deeming himself possessed of a competency. Suddenly a letter had informed him that his father had impoverished himself to provide his son with the extravagancies of a man of fashion. His father had at last sold an estate for twenty five thousand francs to meet the wants of Pétrus; and Pétrus had resolved, directly he knew of these sacrifices, to give up his studio, sell off everything, and hasten into the country to repay his father, at least, a small portion of the money he had generously lavished on his son. Regina heard all her lover had to say with unconcealed interest, and simply answered, "You may make yourself as poor as you like, Pétrus, but you shall still be my true love, as I am yours."

CHAPTER LXXX.—THE RUE DE JERUSALEM.

THE day for the Abbé Dominique's return to Paris being close at hand, Salvator, fearing the worst, felt irresistibly impelled to seek the aid of the Chief Commissioner of Police. Once more, therefore, he found himself in the presence of M. Jackal, who was busy as ever in his office in the Rue de Jérusalem, early in the morning though it was.

"You may remember," said Salvator, coming without delay to the object of his visit, "that you authorised me to claim your help whenever I might have an injustice to repair."

"Perfectly, Monsieur Salvator, and I am ready to keep my word."

"Well, Monsieur, I have come about that unfortunate Sarranti affair. Supposing you were convinced of Monsieur Sarranti's innocence, would you do everything in your power to save him?"

"Naturally."

"Very well, I am in a position to convince you of his innocence. I can produce an indisputable proof that he is not guilty of the crimes for which he has been convicted."

"Can you? Why not produce it, then, my dear Monsieur Salvator?"

"That is precisely what I wish to do; only your assistance is necessary to throw the full light of day on this proof."

"I repeat I am at your service."

"To-night?"

M. Jackal darted a lightning-like glance at Salvator before he replied:

"No; not to-night, unfortunately."

"To-morrow night, then?"

"Yes. For how long?"

"Only a few hours."

"Shall we find the proof in Paris, or out of Paris?"

"A few miles from Paris."

"Good! At what hour shall I expect you?"

"At midnight."

"At midnight you'll find me quite ready."

Thanking M. Jackal for his prompt compliance with his request, Salvator quitted the Commissioner's room with a lighter heart, and scarcely noticed a man enveloped in a large overcoat whom he brushed past in the corridor. The appointed hour came, and with it Salvator. Our hero entered the snug bureau of M. Jackal at midnight on the following night, and was received with the affectation of cordial warmth habitual with the wily Chief of the Secret Police, in whom Salvator still placed implicit faith, although he had an indefinable repugnance to the man.

"You see I have kept my promise, Monsieur Salvator," said M. Jackal, instinctively letting his spectacles fall down over his nose. "In five minutes the horses will be harnessed and the carriage will be ready for us."

"I cannot thank you enough, Monsieur. But let me now give you the particulars I omitted to tell you yesterday."

"I am all attention, my dear Monsieur," answered M. Jackal, helping himself to a pinch of snuff.

Before Salvator had time to commence, however, the usher appeared with the announcement that the carriage awaited them.

"Let us resume out chat en route," said M. Jackal, rising and politely bowing, as a hint to Salvator to precede him.

"And now, where are we bound for?" added the Commissioner, when they were both seated in M. Jackal's private chariot.

"To Cour de France, on the road to Fontainebleau," replied Salvator.

M. Jackal's eyes twinkled with secret satisfaction as he repeated the order to the coachman.

"Let him drive through the Rue Mâcon," added the young man.

"Through the Rue Mâcon?" interrogated M. Jackal, with an air of surprise.

"Yes," answered Salvator; "I want to stop at my place to take up a companion."

"Rue Mâcon, No. 4, then!" called out M. Jackal.

Thither the carriage drew up a few seconds after. Salvator sprang out, opened the door with a key, and ran up stairs to his apartments. Fragola greeted him with the ever-welcome smile of trustful love; but a sigh involuntarily escaped her when she learnt that Salvator was to be absent from her side yet another night.

"Fear nothing! There will be no danger, dearest!" exclaimed Salvator, in reply to the sigh.

"Take Roland, then."

"I have just come for him. Roland, Roland!"

The dog jumped up with joyful alacrity, and bounded caressingly round his master in his gladness. There was then an ardent embrace between Salvator and Fragola. Sweet whispers and sweeter kisses were lovingly exchanged ; and, followed by his dog, the young man quickly rejoined M. Jackal, who seemed not a little astonished to find his companion was of the canine species.

"Follow us, Roland !" cried Salvator.

And, as if the dog divined their destination in a moment, he ran swiftly along well in advance of the carriage, leading the way by instinct to the spot which had for him such tragic associations.

Chapter LXXXI.—The Park of Viry.

The midnight travellers soon reached the bridge of Godeau. There the carriage was stopped by Salvator, and he alighted with the Chief of the Police.

"I fear you have lost your dog," said M. Jackal. "It will be a great pity if you have, for he appears to be very intelligent."

"Don't be uneasy about him," answered Salvator. "We shall come across him again directly, and you'll have a better opportunity to judge of his intelligence."

So saying, Salvator led the way to the Château de Viry, at the gate of which they found Roland stretched at full length, his head uplifted in the attitude of an Egyptian sphinx.

"This is our destination," said Salvator.

"A fine estate !" answered M. Jackal, looking through the gate. "But how can we gain an entrance ?"

"Oh ! with the utmost ease imaginable, as you'll see presently. Up ! Brésil !"

The dog instantly leapt to his feet.

"I thought you called your dog Roland ?" remarked M. Jackal, inquiringly.

"So I do in town," responded Salvator ; "but in the country I call him Brésil. His is a curious history. One day I'll tell it you. Here, Brésil !"

Salvator, followed by the dog and M. Jackal, moved from the gate to the spot, whence he had been in the habit of escalading the wall. With the agility of an acrobat, Brésil now obeyed a sign from Salvator, and sprang on to his master's shoulders, from which he could just reach the top of the wall with his fore-paws.

"Over you go !" cried Salvator.

The dog made another spring and disappeared on the other side of the wall.

"Clever dog !" exclaimed M. Jackal. "He leads where we must follow, I suppose ?"

"Exactly. It is our turn now," was the answer of Salvator, who leapt up and firmly grasped the summit, and then drew himself bodily up, as usual, until he could jerk one leg over, and so sit astride the wall.

"Let me help you," he said, bending down, and offering one of his muscular arms to the Chief of the Police.

"Oh ! I'll manage by myself, thank you," was the independent rejoinder, as M. Jackal raised himself to the level of Salvator with the celerity and ease of a practised gymnast.

In another moment he once again followed the example of his young companion, and leapt down beside him on the turf of the park.

"Do you know where we are now?" demanded Salvator.

"No; but I hope you will be good enough to inform me."

"We are in the park of Viry."

"Viry, Viry? I am still in the dark, Monsieur Salvator."

"Let me freshen your memory. The park of Viry, once the abode of honest Monsieur Gérard!"

"The honest Monsieur Gérard! That name seems familiar to me."

"I should think it was. It is the estate he has not resided upon for many years. It is the estate he leased to Monsieur Lorédan de Valgeneuse as a retreat or prison for Mina."

"Mina! What Mina?"

"Why, the young girl whom De Valgeneuse abducted from Versailles. Surely you recollect that?"

"Yes, yes! I remember now. What has become of her?"

"Will you allow me to tell you a little anecdote, Monsieur Jackal?" answered Salvator, avoiding a direct reply.

"With pleasure."

"Well, a friend of mine in Russia—it was at St. Petersburg—was indulging in rather high play at a nobleman's house on night, when he imprudently left his diamond snuff-box on the table, and was very much put out by losing it, because, in addition to its great value, he prized it on account of its being a present from a friend."

"I can well understand that," remarked M. Jackal, emphasising his agreement with a huge pinch of snuff.

"Well, he naturally mentioned his loss to the master of the house, wrapping his communication up, of course, with as much circumlocution as he had at his command, for it was anything but pleasant to tell a friend that he had been entertaining a thief under his roof.

"'Give me an exact description of your snuff-box,' was the host's answer. My friend did so.

"'Good,' added the host; 'I will endeavour to get it restored to you.'

"'You will communicate the affair to the police?'

"'Not at all. If I were to, you would never see your snuff-box again. On the contrary, don't mention a word of the robbery to anyone.'

"At the end of eight days," continued Salvator, "the nobleman called on my friend.

"'Is this your snuff-box?' he asked, producing one flashing with diamonds.

"'It is,' said my friend, not a little delighted to find it safe in his hands again.

"'Take my advice, then, and never leave it on a gaming-table in future. It is well worth stealing: its value must be ten thousand francs, at least.'

"'But how the deuce did you recover it?'

"'It was one of my friends who stole it from you: Comte So-and-So.'

"'And had you the moral courage to ask him for it?'

"'Not I. He would have felt hurt. I followed his lead and stole it from him.'"

"I follow your parable so far, Monsieur Salvator," replied M. Jackal. "Monsieur De Valgeneuse stole Mina from Justin."

"And I stole Mina from Monsieur de Valgeneuse," added Salvator.

"Strange! I heard nothing of that! How was it Monsieur de Valgeneuse did not bring his complaint before me?"

"Owing to a certain little arrangement between us, Monsieur Jackal. But neither Mina nor De Valgeneuse now claims our attention. Honest Monsieur Gérard will engross us for the rest of the night."

"As you will, my dear Monsieur Salvator. You know I am quite at your disposal."

"To return to Monsieur Gérard, then. No doubt the fact that Monsieur Gérard lived for some time at the Château de Viry has quite recurred to your memory by this time."

"Quite so. I remember now that it came out during the trial that Gérard lived here some time after the robbery committed by Sarranti, and after the disappearance of Gérard's little nephew and niece."

"Has the cause of that disappearance come to your knowledge?"

"No. Don't you know that Monsieur Sarranti persisted in denying he had anything to do with their flight?"

"And he only said the truth in holding fast to his denial, for both children were alive in the château at his departure."

"So he affirmed, that is to say."

"And so I affirm, Monsieur Jackal. I know what became of the poor children."

"Take pity on me, then, my dear Monsieur Salvator, and let me into your secret."

"The girl was stabbed by Madame Gérard, and the boy was drowned by Monsieur Gérard."

"What could be their inducement?"

"The reason was plain enough. He succeeded to the children's inheritance."

"Can you prove these facts?"

"This moment, if you'll follow me."

"Isn't that what I have come for, my dear Monsieur Salvator! Lead on, and I'll follow."

The two men then walked on in silence across the park to the château, Salvator having great difficulty in holding back his dog, which appeared to be drawn by some invisible power to the wood wherein Mina and Justin had enjoyed so many blissful stolen meetings.

The château was sombre and silent. Not a light glimmered in any of its windows. It was patent that it was deserted.

"Let us stop here awhile," said Salvator, when they were close to the house, "and I shall be able to explain to you in a few words how the affair happened."

"According to your conjecture?"

"Nay; I mean how it happened to a certitude. You see the lake yonder; therein the boy was drowned. You see this cellar here; it was the scene of Madame Gérard's conflict with the poor girl."

As General Lebastard de Prémont was enlightened on the night of Mina's flight, so was M. Jackal now enlightened by Salvator and Roland as to the crime perpetrated and attempted in the Château de Viry years ago by the "honest Monsieur Gérard" and his subtle temptress, Orsola. The Chief of the Police could not restrain a burst of professional praise as Orsola's attack on Rose-de-Noël and the child's gallant rescue by the dog were made clear to his understanding link by link. And a certain secret assurance he kept hid in his own breast induced him to enter into the spirit of the adventure without any hampering fear as to Salvator's crowning discovery interfering with the settled purpose of the Government to spare the guilty man and send the innocent Monsieur Sarranti to the scaffold.

"Ah! Monsieur Salvator, what a pity you're an honest man!" exclaimed M. Jackal, when his guide informed him of the mode of reasoning by which he had, through the instrumentality of Roland, satisfied himself that M. Gérard had first drowned the boy in the lake, and then, when the dog had dived to the bottom and brought his young master ashore dead, had wounded the faithful Roland, and hastened to bury the body of his nephew in one of the most secluded nooks of the wood.

"You thoroughly understand the miserable business now, then?" responded Salvator.

"Yes; I must do you the credit to say you have told a most closely connected story. But there's one thing I should like to see——"

"The boy's remains?"

M. Jackal nodded an affirmative.

"This way then!"

We know the path they took. Preceded by Brésil they gained the wood.

At the foot of the old familiar tree the dog paused, and gave an inquiring and puzzled look round him. Instead of running up to the well-known spot, nose to the ground; instead of pawing up the earth with impatience as heretofore, Brésil stood stock still, looking singularly inquiet, and giving utterance to an ominous growl. Salvator, who had the power of reading the dog's thoughts, saw that something unusual had happened. He followed the dog's gaze, and, looking suddenly into M. Jackal's face, detected a cynical smile upon his lips.

"Is this the spot?" demanded M. Jackal.

"It is," answered Salvator. "Find it, Brésil!"

A lugubrious howl was the dog's sole response.

"Come, search and find it, Brésil, there's a good dog!" cried Salvator impatiently.

But Brésil shook his head, as if to intimate that search would be useless. Salvator, wondering at the dog's obstinacy, thereupon knelt down himself and removed the earth without difficulty, the turf having apparently been disturbed by some one since his last visit to Viry.

"Well?" ejaculated M. Jackal, coolly looking down in the pit Salvator had made.

"The skeleton has disappeared!" answered Salvator, in dismay.

"What a pity! What a pity!" replied the Chief of the Police. "It would have been an indubitable proof. Search the hole thoroughly."

In spite of the repugnance Salvator felt at bringing his hands into contact with the soil which had been touched by a murderer's hand, he plunged his arm boldly in up to the shoulder, but withdrawing it after an interval, exclaimed a second time, with amazement stamped on his pale face, "Mon Dieu! The skeleton has disappeared!"

"Who can have removed it?"

"The man most interested in its disappearance."

"But are you certain there *was* a skeleton here, Monsieur Salvator?"

"Absolutely certain. As I have already told you, I was led here by Brésil or Roland, whichever you like to call him; and it was at this spot, beyond a doubt, that I saw the remains of little Victor. Wasn't it, Roland?"

"What was the last time you saw it here?"

"The day before yesterday. It must have been, therefore, last night that it was removed."

"What a pity! What a pity!" repeated M. Jackal.

Salvator again scrutinised the face of the unmoved Chief of the Police, and felt impelled to retort, "Confess that you knew all the time we should not find it here. Confess you suspect who has removed it!"

"But I assure you, my dear Monsieur Salvator, I knew nothing of the kind—nor do I suspect anyone, I pledge you my word."

"It could not have been Monsieur Sarranti, for he's in prison."

"No; but may it not have been his accomplices? For who is to prove that Monsieur Sarranti did not bury the boy here?"

"I will. But, Mon Dieu! how can I prove his innocence? Stay! Let us find out poor Victor's new grave first. That may lead us on the track of the murderer. Find it! Find it, Roland!"

The dog instantly obeyed the command. Nose to earth, he dashed off as if on a trail. His keen scent followed the track of a weird figure who entered the park the previous night like a ghost, and bearing a fearful burden in his arms, glided, phantom-like, through the wood, skirted the lake, and left the park by way of the iron gate.

"See!" said Salvator, when the two men had followed the dog some distance along the highway. "A vehicle took him up here, and he evidently drove off somewhere with the skeleton still in his possession."

"What then?"

"It remains for me now to find out his destination."

M. Jackal shook his head discouragingly as he followed Salvator to the carriage awaiting to drive them back to Paris. Discouraging though the check he had received was, however, Salvator regained his sangfroid during the return journey. And he had need of all his fortitude. The thanks he gave M. Jackal were formal enough when the Chief of the Police dropped him at his house in the Rue Mâcon.

"Demon!" muttered Salvator to himself. "I suspect you know well enough where the remains of that poor child have been removed to. Never mind. Rose-de-Noël remains."

But with Fragola he found a woman whose appearance filled him with new fears. The woman was la Brocante. Wringing her hands, the sorceress exclaimed, the moment she saw Salvator,

"Rose-de-Noël! Rose-de-Noël! This morning when I entered her room, Monsieur Salvator, I found the poor girl had gone, and the open window told me the way she had disappeared!"

"Ah!" cried Salvator, with a groan. "They have done their work effectually. First the brother, and now the sister, have been borne off by the monsters!"

Chapter LXXXII.—The Stolen Love-Letters.

LOVE, and a singular turn of fortune's wheel, held Pétrus still spellbound in Paris. A billet-doux bearing the beloved signature of Régina chained him to his studio. It came the morning after their rapturous meeting in the garden. It begged him to give up all thought of quitting Paris. It infused new life and energy into his heart by urging him to labour hard at his art to pay the great debt he owed his father. The crowning argument employed by the Princess was a commission to paint a portrait of her little sister Abeille, who was to be accompanied on each visit to the studio of Pétrus by Régina herself. His heart beat hopefully again at the prospect of receiving the idol of his soul in his atélier. The one thing that caused him a pang of regret was the coming sale, that would sweep his walls clear of the choice paintings, curious shields and arms, and rich ornaments and luxurious curtains with which they were adorned, and which he would fain have retained, in order to do honour to the Princess whom he adored. Clearly, his star seemed in the ascendant. The day his studio was thrown open to the inspection of possible purchasers of his pictures there was one particular amateur, rustic enough in appearance, yet quite demonstrative in his admiration of the paintings made by Pétrus himself. He appeared to be a connoisseur of pictures, and he delivered his criticism in the loud and unrestrained voice of one who had shouted himself hoarse at sea. Evincing the greatest curiosity to see Monsieur Pétrus Herbel, the stranger was no sooner gratified by the sight of the young painter than he conducted himself in a more demonstrative manner than ever. He embraced Pétrus, and was profuse in his exclamations of pleasure at seeing the son of his old friend again.

"What! not know me, my boy? Not know Captain Pierre Berthaud Monte-Hauban? Well, well! You were but a little one when you saw your old godfather last,"

No. Pétrus had no recollection of Captain Pierre. The captain, however, showed he was so familiar with the leading events of Captain Herbel's life, and seemed so frank and sincere in his rough protestations of friendship, that Pétrus at length believed him, and was made to accept a loan of ten thousand francs to extricate himself from his embarrassments. Thus the home of Pétrus became the home of his soi-disant godfather, who, to do him justice, lost no time in making himself at home. Let us glance at this model god-father, as day was breaking on the first morning of his stay with Pétrus. An early riser, the gallant captain had already sprang from his bed, plucked from his head the bandanna that served as nightcap, dressed himself with celerity, and thrust open the window to breathe the fresh air of morning. His blue dress smacked of the sea as much as his free talk and open manner with Pétrus did. His head was crowned with a forest of red hair. He looked a man of about fifty, and he carried his years well. Captain Monte-Hauban heard the light-hearted chirping of the sparrows as they bathed themselves in the sparkling dew of dawn, and fluttered among the verdant branches that formed their summer dwelling, but the cheerful matinade of the birds seemed to have little charm for him, for he soon shut the window, and in a tone of ennui muttered,

"By Bacchus! How thirsty I am!"

A moment's reflection suggested the remedy.

"What, ho, captain!" he laughingly exclaimed to himself. "Here you've been a whole night in port, and haven't visited your godson's wine-cellar yet!"

Resolved not to delay another minute, he opened the bed-room door, slipped quietly out, and went noiselessly down-stairs. His eyes twinkled with delight when the cellar door yielded to his pressure, and he beheld, by means of a dark lantern which he always carried with him, the well-stocked bins of Pétrus. Pocketing two bottles of choice claret, he regained his room as noiselessly as he had left it.

"Leave us old sea-dogs alone to know a good glass of wine when we find it!" chuckled the captain to himself, smacking his lips to give emphasis to his appreciation of the Bordeaux he was discussing with such zest.

An hour passed in the quiet enjoyment of the claret. The "old sea-dog" was now thoroughly awakened, and ready for a little search he had determined to make before breakfast.

"I must be careful not to wake Pétrus," said the captain to himself, considerately kicking off his slippers and mounting the stairs on tiptoe to the studio.

The key was in the studio door, and, as the captain turned it and entered the studio, his thoughts again found tongue. "Youth! youth! Imprudent youth! Never mind! Sleep on, Pétrus, and dream golden dreams of love, my boy! Let your old sea-dog of a god-father enjoy himself in his way!"

Captain Monte-Hauban's way of enjoying himself at this moment might have been described, in any other than an affectionate godfather, as indulgence in the most prying curiosity. Every cabinet, every article of furniture, was scrutinised by him most closely. He minutely examined an old Louis XV. writing-table, opened each drawer, and gave a smart rap with his knuckles to see whether there was a false bottom to any of them. A rosewood chiffonier was next the object of his attentions. He tried a fresh experiment on this. Kneeling down, he pressed both hands underneath the chiffonier, and out darted a drawer that was perfectly invisible before—so invisible that in all probability neither the dealer who sold the chiffonier to Pétrus nor Pétrus himself suspected its existence. This secret draw contained some political letters, dated 1793 to 1798. Correspondence of those revolutionary times, however, seemed to have no attraction for the captain. He quickly replaced the papers, closed the drawer with his foot, and turned to the top part of the chiffonier. How could he open this? Even as the question flashed through his mind he involuntarily drew a bunch of keys from his pocket. He then instinctively tried key after key, until he found one which unlocked the door. There was only a little iron box inside, but it seemed to have the greatest interest for the captain. It was certainly a marvellous bit of workmanship of the time of Louis XIII., and this may have accounted for the close scrutiny he bestowed upon it. Merely as an amateur delighting in everything appertaining to art workmanship may it have been that he examined this iron box with more attention that he had hitherto shown. At any rate, the fact that this bijou of a box was inviolable, and that not one of his numerous keys could unlock it, did but increase his curiosity. It was, therefore, with a grunt of manifest dissatisfaction that he deposited the box in the chiffonier, and noiselessly reclosed the door upon hearing steps approaching the studio. The captain snatched the nearest volume from the bookshelf, sank into an arm-chair, and was in an instant as absorbed in reading as if he had pitched hap-hazard upon a favourite author of his. So deeply engrossed was he in the pages before him that he appeared not to hear the studio door open, and it was only when Pétrus rushed up to him and warmly shook him by both hands that he appeared able to break the literary spell that had so suddenly seized possession of him. Even then, however, the captain did not directly answer the warm-hearted greetings of his newly-found godson, but bluffly asked, "What time do you take breakfast?"

"At any hour you please," replied Pétrus; "I have a round of visits to make before breakfast, but you must make yourself quite at home. Every room in the house is open to you."

"Oh, this studio does very well for an old sea-dog like me," answered the captain. "Can I stop here?"

"By all means. Since it is by your generous gift that I am able to keep the pictures and things here, you have a perfect right to regard them to you heart's content."

"Very well, then, I'll make this my snuggery, save when you receive a visit from one of your pretty models or give a sitting to some fair lady. Shall that be the arrangement, my boy?"

"Certainly, captain. You'll not mind giving up the studio, then, on Sunday next? I shall on that day begin a portrait, for which I shall probably want about twenty sittings."

"A portrait of some great personage?"

"No; simply of a little girl—the youngest daughter of Marshal de Lamothe-Houdan."

"Ah!"

"The sister of the Princess Régina."

"I haven't the honour of knowing that illustrious lady."

"One day I hope to have the honour of presenting her to you, my dear captain. Now I must be off. The horse is at the door. And I am as anxious to pay my long-suffering creditors as they are to be paid. Au revoir!"

Captain Monte-Hauban remained seated till he was assured of his godson's departure. He then threw down the book in which he had feigned so great an interest, locked the door of the studio, and resumed his study of the chiffonier.

*   *   *   *   *   *

Sunday came, and it was a work of love with Pétrus to rearrange the ornaments of his studio and provide a profusion of those gems of nature—the choicest blooms of the garden—which were most likely to give pleasure to the Princess Régina, the queen of his heart and soul. Roses enframed the window, and filled the studio with their sweet perfumes, fuchsias drooped from beauteous Sèvres vases; graceful statuettes of nymphs and swains, gay in pink and blue, peeped out from masses of luxuriant ferns. The studio was, in fine transformed by the loving hands of Pétrus into as near a resemblance to the sweet floral boudoir of the Princess as was possible. As the hour for the arrival of Régina and Abeille drew near, Pétrus felt a sense of relief at the absence of the bluff, albeit generous captain, for he felt that his presence would have been a jarring element in what he hoped to look back upon as a day of perfect bliss. The longed-for hour at length arrived, and the heart of the artist gave a leap of delight as the Princess and her little fairy of a sister swept into the studio, with all the indefinable grace of good breeding, and there were exchanged those silent but precious greetings so dear to those in love. It was a true labour of joy with Pétrus to paint a living image of the bright, laughing features of Abeille, for was he not animated by the enchanting presence of Régina? Roseate were the hours, and they sped by all too quickly, leaving, however, a sweet fragrance that wrapped the painter's soul in bliss and made him but long the more for the ecstasy of the next sitting. The current of his life flowed on thus gladsomely for a week. One night, Pétrus returned home about eleven o'clock, and was somewhat surprised to find the captain was again absent. At an early hour the following morning his valet awoke him with the announcement that a veiled lady wished to see him without a moment's delay. Wondering who the lady could be,

Pétrus hurried down to meet his visitor, and found it was Régina, who was strangely agitated.

"Régina!" escaped his lips. "Can any misfortune have happened to you? Oh! I trust not, darling."

"A terrible misfortune, Pétrus!" answered the Princess, lifting her veil, and revealing a face which gave full expression to the anguish her mind was a prey to.

Chapter LXXXIII.—The Biter Bit.

THE cause of Régina's poignant grief was explained the same morning by Pétrus to Salvator, whose aid the painter sought as the one man who might best be able to relieve the distress that was consuming both the young lovers. Salvator (who had returned to Paris after a successful search for Rose-de-Noël, whom he had temporarily lodged in a convent with the consent of her lover) entered into his friend's trouble with wonted enthusiasm, and read with indignation the following letter, which had been addressed to Régina.

"To the Princesse Régina de Lamothe-Houdan.

"Madame,—

"It is with infinite distress I am constrained to inform you that I have gained possession of a batch of letters, the publicity of which would occasion you and your family deep mortification. To prove the vital importance of keeping this correspondence in utter secresy, I need only mention that the letters are those you have addressed to Monsieur Pétrus Herbel, whom you have informed, in passing, of the relation existing between your mother and Comte Rappt.

"This family secret shall be strictly kept by me, and the compromising letters shall be returned into your own hands upon your paying me the sum of five hundred thousand francs.

"The said letters shall be delivered up to you to-morrow, at midnight, at your garden gate, on your handing me the afore-mentioned sum.

"Wave a handkerchief from your bed-room window to-night, if you consent to this amicable arrangement; and believe me to be your devoted servant,   COMTE ERCOLANO——."

"Have you missed these letters, then?" asked Salvator of Pétrus, when he had finished reading this threatening epistle.

"That was *my* first idea on learning the terrible news from Regina,' responded Pétrus. "We both hastened to my studio. I flung open the chiffonier in which I kept the letters securely locked in an iron box. The box was gone! To our mutual horror, we both realised the fact that this was no vain threat. Some treacherous villain had evidently entered the studio in my absence and stolen the treasure. What can be done! Publicity of this family secret would be a deathblow to Régina's father. Yet it seems impossible to collect so enormous a sum as the wretch demands."

"Whom do you suspect?"

"A man who I have now every reason to believe has grossly deceived me—a man who palmed himself on me as my godfather, and who imposed upon me by a spontaneous gift of ten thousand francs to prevent his 'godson,' as he styled me, from putting up his pictures to auction!"

"Ah! I see. Ten thousand for *five hundred* thousand francs! A sprat to catch a whale! Never mind, Pétrus. I guess the hand which has duped you. Cheer up! Leave the thing to me and the money he wants shall be in the hands of the Princess, and the biter shall be bit."

* * * * * *

The handkerchief was duly waved that night from Régina's window; and at the appointed hour on the following night a white form stole to the garden gate of the Marshal de Lamothe-Houdan's mansion. Simultaneously, a tall muffled figure moved from the shadow of a tree outside the gate and thrust a letter inside the iron bars.

The lady in white snatched the letter with trembling fingers, and by the light of the moon satisfied herself that the missive was one of those she was to pay so dearly for. The Princess Régina (for she it was who was keeping this midnight tryst to shield the honour of her father) gave a bank-note in exchange for the precious document, which she hid in her bosom. One by one, each letter was thus restored to her by the stranger, who received the exact sum he had extorted. The Comte Ercolano pocketed the notes with evident satisfaction, and gave the Princess the following piece of counsel at parting. "And now, my dear Princess, take the advice of a veteran gallant. Love as much and as fervently as you please; but never love on paper again! Adieu!"

The last word had scarcely escaped his lips when he was felled to the ground by a heavy body which fell upon him like a thunderbolt from above.

Chapter LXXXIV.—The Human Aerolite.

COMTE ERCOLANO * * * was for an instant stunned by this sudden fall in the supreme moment of his triumph. He was as suddenly brought to his senses, however, first by a feeling of relief, as if the crushing weight which pressed him to the earth had been lifted from him, next by experiencing a violent wrench, as both his arms were bent behind his back by some irresistible power, and his hands pinioned so securely by an iron grasp that he was left completely helpless. The same occult power lifted him to his feet. Restored to the perpendicular, he strove to see who it was that had fallen upon him and felled him with such brutal force. In vain! The Mohican of Paris, who had been concealed in the tree overhead, from which he had quietly dropped on to the pretended Comte, had discreetly slipped behind his prisoner. One of his massive hands sufficed to grip, with a giant's strength, both hands of the Comte. The other stole round the Comte's waist, successively pulled a brace of pistols and a poniard from his belt, and flung them over the wall of the Marshal de Lamothe-Houdan's mansion. The hand next grasped the Comte's throat with a vigour which threatened to strangle him.

The pressure increased in intensity till the Comte thought his last hour had come, and he spasmodically tried to give utterance to a cry for mercy. Then, and not till then, his assailant spoke, slightly relaxing his hold, as he said, in the familiar voice of Jean Taureau,

"You cry for mercy, do you? Give me all the money you received from that lady, then!"

The Comte trembled as though his very life were demanded, but answered not a word. Was he strangled, or did he refuse? Jean Taureau repeated his demand, and emphasised it by a renewed pressure of the throat. The Comte, whose hands had been let free meantime, by a sudden effort endeavoured to seize his antagonist by the throat in his turn. Ere he could reach the collar of Jean's coat, however, the hand with muscles of steel again caught his fingers, this time nearly dislocated them by the invincible strength of its grasp, and let the nerveless hands fall limp by his side. Simultaneously he felt a firmer grip on his throat, and a thousand lights appeared to sparkle before his eyes, and his last breath seemed spent. With what he feared might be his very last atom of strength if he delayed a moment longer, the Comte quickly lifted his hand to his pocket, drew out nine of the ten packets of bank-notes, and dropped rather than flung them on the ground. Jean Taureau loosened his grasp, but did not quite let go the throat which he had held as in a vice. The Comte took in a deep breath, and as the pure air of the night entered his lungs a hope sprang up in his heart. On plunging his hand into his pocket for the notes, he had felt a knife at the bottom; and he confidently looked for an opportunity to open the blade, and by a quick stab to rid himself of his colossal adversary. Jean Taureau, maintaining his hold on the Comte's throat, stooped down and picked up the notes, but took the precaution to count the packets before pocketing them.

"Where's the tenth?" he sternly demanded, after satisfying himself he had but nine.

"Let me feel in my pocket; I may find it," gasped the Comte.

"That seems fair enough. Be quick about it, though!"

"Release me, then."

"Not till I have the last note."

"There it is, then!" exclaimed the Comte, flinging down the tenth packet, after he had managed to open his pocket-knife.

Jean Taureau, true to his word, let go the Comte directly he saw the last bundle of notes at his feet. The Comte's intention was to spring upon his formidable enemy the moment he bent down to pick up the notes, and to plunge the knife into him, and thereby have the chance of regaining the hush-money which he had been compelled to surrender. Suspecting some foul play, Jean Taureau was too wily to act upon the spur of the moment in this way, but kept one eye fixed upon the notes, the other upon the Comte, and thus caught sight in time of the flash of the blade in his hand. With lightning-like rapidity Jean shot forth his right arm, caught the wrist of the knife-hand in his iron grip, and pressed it so violently that the knife fell from the Comte's hand, and a cry of pain escaped his lips as he was once more smote to the earth.

Jean Taureau felled the Comte so deftly that there he lay close by the last packet of notes, which Jean was now enabled to pocket without danger, as he knelt with one knee on the recumbent figure. As a final, desperate effort, the Comte meanwhile stretched forth one hand to recover his knife. Perceiving this, Jean Taureau, as if resolved to have done with so treacherous an opponent once for all, clenched his fist, and dealt the Comte a blow on the head weighty enough to have felled an ox, accompanying the blow with the question, "Won't you remain quiet for a minute?"

The Comte was quiet and helpless enough now. He had been stunned, and he remained senseless for five minutes. Seeing that he would persist in giving no sign of life, and tired of such obstinacy, Jean Taureau politely saluted the log-like figure of the Comte, and took his departure with the satisfied air of one who had done his duty and a good night's work to boot.

CHAPTER LXXXV.—A CHASE FOR FIVE HUNDRED THOUSAND FRANCS.

EARLY the next morning, Salvator sought Jean Taureau at his lodging in the Rue de la Bourbe. Before arriving as high as the fourth floor, on which dwelt the colossal carpenter and the red-haired Fifine, Salvator could hear the old, familiar refrain. Mademoiselle Fifine was giving tongue to the most violent imprecations in her repertory, whilst Jean Taureau's oaths rang out above the shrill din of the woman's rancour. Salvator knocked loudly at the door. Fifine, her red hair hanging loose down her neck, her dress in deshabille, her face inflamed with passion, answered the knock.

"Quarrelling again!" exclaimed Salvator. "Do you *never* give Jean Taureau a peaceful moment?"

"'Tis his fault, Monsieur Salvator."

"She lies!" thundered out her infuriated mate, rushing towards her with fists clenched ready to strike her as heavily as he had struck the Comte Ercolano * * *.

"Come, come, Jean!" interrupted Salvator, to pacify the carpenter. "It is too early in the morning to strike a woman. It is too early to have the excuse that you are drunk."

Salvator at the same time stepped between the infuriated Jean and the now cowering woman.

"Ah! Monsieur Salvator," urged Jean Taureau, "if you only knew what an infamous creature she is, you wouldn't interfere to save her from my just vengeance, I know. Her proper place is the gaol or the scaffold. It is to spare her the ignominy of those punishments that I would exterminate her here."

"What has she done now?"

"She is faithless. She is shifty as the wind. She has made a new acquaintance in the neighbourhood, and there's no keeping her at home."

"But that's an old failing of hers."

"With this addition: she has robbed me."

"Of what?"

"Of all yesterday's money."

"Of your day's wages?"

"Yes, Monsieur; and my night's wages as well. She has stolen the five hundred thousand francs!"

"The five hundred thousand francs!" repeated Salvator, in a tone of amazement and anger, turning at the same moment to interrogate the woman he had interfered to protect from violence.

"Yes; she has the notes upon her now, the cursed jade. The cause of our quarrel was that I was about to snatch them from her when you arrived, Monsieur Salvator. But, see. The thief's run off with her booty, now!"

"Let's start after her, Jean. There's not a moment to lose."

The two men, without wasting another word, forthwith darted down stairs; Jean Taureau rushed up the street in the direction of the Esplanade de l'Observatoire, Salvator running at an equally rapid pace down the street. Salvator gained the bottom of the Rue de la Bourbe in a few seconds. A difficulty then arose. Which of the three thoroughfares before him should he take? He gazed down each street as far as the eye could reach. No Fifine was to be seen. He was looking round with a puzzled air, when a milkwoman at the corner of the Rue Saint-Jacques exclaimed,

"Monsieur Salvator!"

"Yes!" answered Salvator, impatiently, regarding the woman without recognising her.

"Ah! you don't remember me, Monsieur?"

"No."

"Not Maguelonne, of the Rue aux Fers? There's not much business in flowers just now, so I've turned milkwoman."

"Oh! I remember you well, now. But I haven't a moment to spare, Maguelonne. Have you seen a tall, red-haired woman pass this way?"

"Running like a mad woman? Yes."

"How long ago?"

"Only this instant."

"Which way did she go?"

"Down the Rue Saint-Jacques."

"Thank you!" cried Salvator, turning to hasten down the street in question.

"Monsieur Salvator! Monsieur Salvator!" called out Maguelonne.

"I haven't a moment to spare just now."

"Wait only half a moment, then. What do you want with the woman?"

"To speak to her."

"You'll not have far to go, then!"

"Where *has* she gone? Tell me quickly, if you know."

"She's gone where she goes every day. You'll find her there," replied the woman, pointing to a house in the Rue Saint-Jacques, bearing the numbers 297 and 299, and called the Petit-Bicêtre.

"Whom does she visit there?"

"An agent of the police. Jambassier, or Jubassier——"

"Gibassier!" exclaimed Salvator.

"That's the name!"

"*Ma foi!*" muttered Salvator. "I *am* in luck's way. I wanted that man's address, and Mademoiselle Fifine will have given it me. Ah! Monsieur Jackal, you were right when you said, '*Seek the woman.*' Thank you, Maguelonne. Is your mother doing well?"

"Oh, yes, thank *you*, Monsieur Salvator! She is very grateful to you for getting her into the hospital."

Whilst Salvator hurries in search of Jean Taureau's faithless paramour, we shall have time to tell in a few words how he succeeded in checkmating the Comte Ercolano * * *. The five hundred thousand francs which it was imperative the Princess Régina should have to pay the Comte for the return of her billets-doux were obtained by Salvator, under his rightful name of Conrad de Valgeneuse, from Monsieur Baratteau, whom he intimidated by a threat to reveal the villany by which he had prevented him from being the acknowledged heir of his father. This sum secured, and handed to Pétrus for Régina, Salvator next took steps to deprive the pretended Comte Ercolano of the fruits of his scheme, and engaged Jean Taureau to seek a hiding-place in the tree close by the gate which was the trysting-place of the Comte and Régina, and instructed him to fall (as he did, like a human aërolite) upon the Comte when he had delivered up the last letter.

The Petit-Bicêtre, which Salvator was not long in entering, was a lodging-house of the dingiest and squalidest type. There was a dirty court-yard. A staircase ran up to the left, and another to the right. Salvator ran nimbly up to the topmost floor on the left hand side of the building without discovering the woman he sought. On descending, he happened to glance out of the window on the fourth floor, and caught sight of the figure of Fifine near the window of the fifth floor on the opposite side. She was plainly waiting for admission to the chambers on the fifth floor, and Salvator thought he might catch her before she entered, if he made haste. He therefore flew down stairs, bounded across the court-yard, and ascended the right-hand staircase with such celerity that he was close behind Fifine before she was aware of his presence.

"Open the door, Giba," she was crying, vigorously knocking and kicking at the door. "It's me!"

But Gibassier was obdurate. He slept on, proof against the amorous calls to which he had previously responded with alacrity. He did not reach home till four o'clock in the morning; and he was not improbably dreaming over again the narrow escape he had, as Comte Ercolano, of being pummelled to death by his muscular assailant, besides being deprived of the spoil he had so fondly counted upon to end his last days in that luxurious ease which he had enjoyed so keenly as the nautical godfather of Pétrus Herbel. Mademoiselle Fifine was in the midst of her persistent appeals for admission when she felt a hand upon her shoulder. She started when she found herself face to face with Salvator. Guessing why he had followed her, she rushed to the window, and was about to throw it open to call for help.

"Keep quiet, woman," commanded Salvator. "If you make any disturbance, I'll have you arrested, and taken to prison in no time."

"Arrested! What for?"

"For robbery, first ——"

"I am an honest woman," she protested.

"An honest woman!" retorted Salvator, with contempt. "Why, not only have you stolen the five hundred thousand francs which are about you, and which belong to me, but——"

Salvator whispered the rest of the sentence in her ear.

Fifine grew deadly pale.

"'Twas not I who killed him," she answered, with 'bated breath. "It was Bébé la Rousse!"

"That is to say, you held the lamp whilst she beat the life out of him with a bar of iron. Therefore, you both had a hand in the murder. Now, will you call for help, or shall I?"

Trembling with fear and passion, Fifine drew from her pocket a handful of bank-notes, and sullenly gave them to Salvator.

"Good! They are all here," said Salvator. "And now go home and beg Jean's pardon, and remember that the first complaint of you I hear from him will ensure your being taken to prison, Joséphine Dumont."

The woman trembled afresh on hearing herself addressed by her real name, and tarried no longer on the scene of her mortification.

CHAPTER LXXXVI.—GIBASSIER'S COMMISSION.

HARDLY had Mdlle. Joséphine Dumont, or Mdlle. Fifine, disappeared, when the door of Gibassier's room was opened a little way, and the face of that worthy was projected to ascertain the cause of the altercation which had roused him from his slumbers. Gibassier no sooner caught sight of Salvator than he withdrew his face, and would have shut the door had not Salvator been too quick for him.

"I have the honour of addressing Monsieur Gibassier, haven't I?" said Salvator, stretching forward his hand to prevent the door from being shut.

"Yes, Monsieur," answered Gibassier, regarding his interlocutor with suspicion. "Whom have *I* the honour of speaking to?"

"My dress indicates what I am, doesn't it?"

"You are a Commissionaire, I see; but what's your name?"

"Salvator."

"The Commissionaire of the Rue aux Fers?" exclaimed Gibassier, recoiling in some alarm: "What do you want with me?"

"I want you to do me a service. I will pay you well for it," replied Salvator, entering the room and closing the door after him.

"What is the nature of the service?" demanded Gibassier, taking a seat and motioning to his visitor to do the same.

"It will be easy enough to perform. But first, tell me whether you can leave Paris for a week."

"Leave Paris? With all the pleasure in the world, Monsieur Salvator. My health is failing in Paris."

"Yes, it is clear enough you are not over well. There's a strained and bloodshot look about your eyes. The veins of your neck seem terribly swollen. You plainly want a change of air."

"Ah! that I do, my dear Monsieur. This very night I thought I was attacked by a fit of apoplexy."

"But you were bled in time, I hope," naïvely answered Salvator.

"Yes, copiously bled, Monsieur. But let me drop my egotism. What is the errand you want me to leave Paris on?"

"The errand will be simply to deliver a letter to a certain address in Heidelberg," replied Salvator.

"When must I start?"

"To-morrow morning."

"I'll be ready—that is, if the price suits me. It will be an expensive journey to and from Heidelberg, and I shall want a good sum for my time and trouble."

"Four thousand francs: will that satisfy you?" demanded Salvator, flourishing the notes before Gibassier, and filling his breast with pangs of regret and bitterness.

"Amply," was the reply Gibassier contented himself with, however, as he smothered his regret and endeavoured to look cheerfully on the promised four thousand francs as a sum to be by no means despised.

"Very well. Here, take the notes. The letter shall be delivered to you in good time."

Gibassier seized the notes with avidity, tested their genuineness, and, as Salvator was apparently about to take his departure, asked what time he would be expected to leave Paris in the morning.

"At daylight," answered Salvator; adding, as if the thought had only then occurred to him, "By-the-way, I may as well take your receipt for the four thousand francs."

"Certainly. It won't take me a minute to write it, Monsieur Salvator."

Gibassier, not noticing the smile of satisfaction playing round Salvator's lips, wrote out the receipt in his best style, and handed it to his new employer in perfect good faith.

One glance at the receipt was sufficient for Salvator's purpose.

"You consummate rascal!" he exclaimed. "What! has the cunning Gibassier being duped at last by an honest man? Is it possible that the skilful farceur, Captain Monte-Houban, the wily diplomatist, Comte Ercolano Threestars, has at length been outwitted by me?"

Gibassier bounded to his feet on finding himself thus unmasked, and would have snatched the receipt back. Salvator, however, was on the alert. Drawing a pistol from his pocket, he presented it at the head of the ex-convict, and exclaimed, in a commanding tone, "Sit down, my dear Comte Ercolano. Sit down, and listen to me a little while longer."

Gibassier appeared to recognise in Salvator the master-mind who had foiled him in his last swindling adventure. A man of ruse and low cunning rather than of courage, he deemed it prudent to submit at discretion, and therefore sank back into his chair and awaited what was to follow. Salvator sat down in the chair opposite him, and, still playing with the pistol, continued, "Now, let me come to the point with you, Monsieur Gibassier. Judge how much I know of you. You were tried for the murder of one Claude Vincent. You took part in that crime, but you escaped conviction, as 'it was not proven.' Your last imprisonment was for robbery. You escaped from your convict-prison. You came to Paris, and you were concerned in the abduction of a young school-girl from Versailles. Don't deny it. I am certain what I say is true. Then, after Heaven knows how many more base actions, you entered the house of Pétrus Herbel as his pretended godfather, stole from his chiffonier some love-letters, and extorted a large sum of hush-money from an innocent lady for their restoration. You see I have more than enough evidence against you to send you back to prison. Would you like to know the price of my silence?"

"Name it."

"I will. It is your help—I am in earnest now, mind—in an affair of life and death. What is the date fixed for Monsieur Sarranti's execution?"

"To-morrow afternoon, at four o'clock."

"It will be a race, indeed, against Death, then," muttered Salvator to himself.

"Do you know the honest Monsieur Gérard?" he added aloud.

"Yes—through seeing him with Monsieur Jackal."

"Has he ever asked you to visit him at his house in the suburbs?"

"Never."

"You have the opportunity of serving him out, then."

"How?"

"Easily enough. Monsieur Gérard is about to be nominated Mayor of Vanvres. He gives a dinner to his chief supporters this very evening. Now, Monsieur Gérard has been guilty of a murder, as you have. But there is this difference between you: you stood your trial and were acquitted; he has never been tried, but allows an innocent man to go to the scaffold without saying a word. Well, you can have no compunction in letting justice overtake such a base criminal?"

"Certainly not."

"Particularly when you can earn ten thousand francs in addition to the sum I have already given you?"

"*Sacrebleu!* Only tell me what I am to do, Monsieur Salvator, Shall you want a receipt this time?"

"Ah! I see you are yourself again, Gibassier. Well, what I want you to do is simply this: go to Vanvres this evening, call Monsieur Gérard away from his convives, and get him to return with you to Paris, there and then, on the plea that Monsieur Jackal has news of the greatest urgency for him. For the success of my project he must be kept out of his house for about two hours. May I count upon your help?"

"Rely upon my carrying out your wishes to the letter. At six I will be there, and Monsieur Gérard shall leave Vanvres with me."

Chapter LXXXVII.—Monsieur Gerard's Last Dinner.

THE summer air was so balmy that evening that M. Gérard entertained his friends at dinner in his garden. A well-spread table stood on the lawn, and round it were seated the host and his eleven guests. This select company comprised all the notabilities of Vanvres—retired bourgeois, who regarded M. Gérard as the pink of morality and respectability, and who would as soon have doubted the brilliancy of the sun as the virtue of their charitable host. Thus, as toothsome viands were washed down by choice wines, not the Mayor's chair, but a seat in the Legislative Chamber, or even in the House of Peers, was suggested from mouth to mouth as the fittest reward for M. Gérard's life of true philanthropy. The chorus of praise grew louder as the generous wines circulated; and the most loquacious of the party, a notary, at length gave voluble expression to the idea which had been echoed from lip to lip—their unanimous desire that their Mayor-elect should consent to be a candidate for the vacant seat in the Legislative Chamber. Mildly protesting he was unworthy of so great an honour, M. Gérard yielded to the voice of the charmer, and said he must of course obey the wishes of his neighbours. An hour swiftly sped by. Faces became flushed. Gesticulations were more animated. Tongues wagged merrily. The festivity was at its height, when a servant approached and whispered in his master's ear that a stranger wished to speak to him on business of the utmost importance.

"What name did he give?" demanded M. Gérard.

"No name, Monsieur."

"Tell him, then," said M. Gérard, majestically, "that to-day I am only at home to friends."

"Bravo! bravo! bravo!" cried the guests, looking admiringly at their host.

"How well he speaks," exclaimed the notary.

"How eloquent he will be when he is in the Legislative Chamber!" said the doctor.

"How dignified when he becomes a Minister!" chimed in a retired grocer.

The servant reappeared.

"Well, what is the answer?" demanded his master.

"He says he has come from Monsieur Jackal to inform you that the execution of Monsieur Sarranti takes place to-morrow."

M. Gérard turned livid. He rose abruptly, and with terror in his face, hastily quitted his seat, and ran to speak with his mysterious visitor. The guests waited in vain. M. Gérard did not return. Half an hour after his sudden departure, however, a dog bounded into the garden, and was closely followed by a young man, who bowed courteously to the company, and said,

"Gentlemen, I come to take Monsieur Gérard's place. He bids me say he is extremely vexed to have to leave you on important business which calls him to Paris. Let us enjoy ourselves, however, as well as we can in his absence. To your healths, Messieurs!"

At the new comer's bidding, all was presently gay again. The dog seemed alone uneasy. He ran from one side of the lawn to the other, whining dolefully. Circling round and round the table in ever-decreasing circles, the dog at last gave a deep growl, and rushed to a spot by his master's feet, and furiously pawed up the earth.

"Messieurs," said the new host at this juncture, "shall I tell you the cause of Monsieur Gérard's hasty departure?"

"By all means," answered the notary; "but do for goodness sake look after your dog. He seems a little mad."

"Mad!" came back the prompt reply. "Roland is sane as I am. See, he has by his sagacity discovered where Monsieur Gérard has hidden the remains of his murdered nephew!"

So saying, Salvator seized a spade close by, pushed the table on one side, and completed the work which Roland had begun. To the amazement and horror of M. Gérard's guests, he presently came to some human remains, which he gently lifted with the spade and placed by the side of their new grave. Resting at length from his labour, Salvator said, "Messieurs, you are all of you witnesses that I have found this skeleton of a child in Monsieur Gérard's garden?"

"All, all!" was the unanimous answer.

CHAPTER LXXXVIII.—GIBASSIER'S MANŒUVRE.

THE honest Monsieur Gérard had, meanwhile, fallen into the trap set by Salvator in the most natural manner in the world.

We saw him suddenly leave his guests at the height of their festivity. Let us follow him from that moment. The emotions aroused by the flattering compliments of his neighbours were quickly dispelled. It was with a sinking heart that he re-entered his mansion in search of Monsieur Jackal's messenger. In the hall he found a man in a long great coat, with his hat drawn over his eyes. The first anxious glance made it clear to M. Gérard who his unexpected visitor was.

"Ah! It is you, Gibassier!" he exclaimed.

"Yes, it's me in person, Monsieur Gérard," answered the escaped convict and police spy.

"And you came from?" asked M. Gérard, anxious to learn the gist of the news at once.

"From the master, of course," replied Gibassier.

"And Monsieur Jackal wishes to see me in relation to the execution of—of Monsieur Sarranti to-morrow?"

"Yes."

"Then let us start at once," said M. Gérard, snatching up his hat and leading the way to the carriage in which Gibassier had driven to Vanvres.

Chuckling inwardly, Gibassier bade his dupe enter first, gave whispered instructions to the driver, and was soon en route to Paris with M. Gérard.

"Why are you so disturbed by the message I've brought?" inquired Gibassier, after a long silence; adding, with well-feigned frankness, "If I were in your place, Monsieur, I should deem myself so deserving of my well-earned comfort that I wouldn't be called from a festive meeting of friends on any account."

"True! true! But you see riches bring responsibilities as well as pleasures; and an even mind bids me be always prepared for a reversal of fortune!"

"No doubt! no doubt! But what can *you* possibly fear?"

"Ah, my dear Monsieur Gibassier—— the unknown! None of us can guard against that."

"No; that is quite clear," said Gibassier, smiling to himself, and continuing the conversation with unabated zest.

The philanthropist of Vanvres could not account for his companion's discursive mood. It was in vain he strove to discover a reason for it.

"Here we are at the Barrière d'Enfer!" exclaimed the driver at length. "You wished to stop here, didn't you?"

"The Barrière d'Enfer!" cried M. Gérard. "I thought our destination was the Rue de Jérusalem!"

"Yours may be, but mine is not," coolly answered Gibassier.

"But did not Monsieur Jackal send for me?" demanded M. Gérard, white with anger.

"Not he. Not only does he not expect you, but I should think he would be very much surprised to see you."

"Then you have played me a trick in bringing me here. Why? What injury have I ever done you?"

"What injury! *Ma foi!* Have you not this very evening gathered round you a cluster of friends and acquaintances, and have you not omitted me from the list of invited to your garden fête? What! You ask to your electoral and gastronomic banquet a number of dull bourgeois neighbours, and leave your good friend Gibassier out in the cold! Is not that injury enough? *Ma foi!* As you deprived me of a good dinner, it is only quits that I have prevented you from finishing yours."

M. Gérard could only regard Gibassier with amazement as Salvator's emissary jumped out of the carriage, slammed the door in his face, and continued in the same tone of cool effrontery,

"I took the carriage at four o'clock precisely. I mention this fact so that the coachman may not overcharge you. Au revoir! my dear Monsieur Gérard."

"What! You leave me to pay for your miserable practical joke?" called back M. Gérard.

But Gibassier had disappeared.

"Drive back to Vanvres!" shouted out M. Gérard to the driver, enraged at being thus easily taken in.

During the return journey he was filled with a vague sense of impending danger. Was the ruse of which he had just been made a victim the first step of his Nemesis? What was the mysterious cause of his being drawn away from Vanvres? On the eve of M. Sarranti's execution for the crimes of which the honest M. Gérard was really guilty, so extraordinary an occurrence may well have called forth a feeling of grave uneasiness. To Vanvres M. Gérard accordingly hurried in the hope of discovering the clue to the mystery. A storm that had been brewing burst out. The thunder pealed, and the lightning flashed, adding to the indefinable sense of gloom which filled his breast and made him at once anxious and yet fearful as the jaded horses drew near Vanvres. Ten o'clock struck as M. Gérard re-entered his house, after paying the driver. The mansion seemed buried in a dark cloud, so black was the night. No light, no gay laughter, not the faintest sound of festivity greeted the host. A dead silence reigned supreme in the hall, throughout the house, everywhere that M. Gérard penetrated with fear and trembling. Plucking up courage, he lifted his voice and called his valet. No response!

"Ah! He is most likely feasting in the kitchen with the rest of the servants!" muttered M. Gérard to himself.

A flash of lightning more vivid than ever at that moment enabled him to see that the garden door was open. To the garden he seemed to be irresistibly drawn, shaken though his nerves were by the violent thunderclap. He lit a lamp, but the light was extinguished by a gust of wind before he had taken two steps on the lawn. Another lightning flash, however, served to reveal to him what had taken place in his absence. He was rooted to the earth for an instant by the sight of the pit which Salvator had dug. The next moment he threw himself on the ground, bent forward, and thrust his hands to the bottom of the pit, shivering as he did so.

"Lost! Lost!" was the exclamation that escaped his ashen lips as, his fruitless search at an end, he sprang to his feet, almost overpowered by the sickening dread that now filled his soul. "They have sought and discovered the skeleton in my absence. Lost! Lost! when I was so near being saved!"

"What shall I do?" ran his thoughts. "Fly the country? They would overtake me before I could leave France!"

What sounded like a yawn was the sole response. The yawn was followed by the appearance of a head from under the table, and M. Gérard recognised in him one of his late guests, who had dined not wisely but too well.

The toper had evidently been left to recover from the stupor of intoxication, and had only just awakened from a confused dream.

"Welcome back, my dear Monsieur Gérard," he hiccoughed. "Your deputy did very well, but, of course, he was not to be compared to the host himself."

"My deputy?" repeated M. Gérard, who suddenly resolved to glean as many particulars as he could from this rambling toper. "Well, and what did you think of him?"

"Oh! he was a good-looking young fellow enough; but his mode of entertaining was not the most cheerful in the world."

"Why?"

"Why! Well, his dog Brésil——"

"Brésil!" exclaimed M. Gérard, unable to govern the panic roused by the mention of the dog which had played so eventful a part in the darkest episode of his life. "Brésil! Brésil! Do you mean to tell me the dog's name was really Brésil?"

This disclosure was enough for M. Gérard. Justice was on his track at last, he felt convinced. He stayed only to help his besotted guest safely out of the house. The one remaining hope for him was the help of M. Jackal. He alone could procure him the necessary passport, and provide him with the requisite disguises to escape the fate that threatened him. M. Gérard tarried not an instant longer to search for any of his absent servants (whose apparent flight he did not stop to regret), but saddled the best horse in his stable with his own hands, and set off at a fleet gallop for the Paris Préfecture.

CHAPTER LXXXIX.—SALVATOR'S CHECK.

LEAVING the affrighted Gérard on the high road to Paris, let us follow our hero, who had borne off the ghastly piece of evidence in triumph from Vanvres. Salvator arrived at the Préfecture just as M. Gérard was setting out at full speed for the same destination. The Chief Commissioner received Salvator with the stereotyped smile of welcome, late as it was. The child's skeleton which Salvator had, with Brésil's aid, found in M. Gérard's garden, was inclosed in a bag, which our hero deposited in front of him, the dog being close by to guard the treasure.

"Glad to see you always, Monsieur Salvator; but I didn't know you had returned to Paris," said M. Jackal.

"Even the Paris police are not omniscient, then," answered Salvator. "I've been back some days now. What I have ventured to disturb you about at so late an hour is of the gravest importance. I have just come from a friend of yours at Vanvres, Monsieur Gérard——"

"Monsieur Gérard!" repeated M. Jackal, as if ignorant of the name, and re-echoing it wonderingly, as he sniffed a huge pinch of snuff. "Monsieur Gérard! You're mistaken, my dear sir, in saying he's a friend of mine. I don't know any Monsieur Gérard."

"But you must know him. A single sentence will enlighten you. Monsieur Gérard is the man who committed the crimes for which Monsieur Sarranti was sentenced to death."

"And think you I would make an acquaintance of an assassin? Impossible!"

"Monsieur Jackal, let us understand each other. You and I ought to know each other by this time. I am fully aware that you are trying your utmost to prevent what I am as earnestly endeavouring to accomplish. If you are a power, I am a power also. And it may be as well to let you know in good time that the man who raises a hand against me in the performance of what I deem a holy duty will not survive twenty-four hours ——"

"Monsieur, allow me also to say that I place duty before life; and that it is not by menacing me ——"

"Don't let us waste words, Monsieur Jackal. Tell me—the execution of Monsieur Sarranti is fixed for to-morrow, is it not?"

"Is it? I had forgotten it."

"You have but a short memory, then, for at five this very evening you bade the executioner be ready to-morrow for this very task."

"But why the deuce do you interest yourself so much in this Sarranti?"

"For two reasons. Firstly, he is innocent; secondly, his son is my best friend."

"Dominique Sarranti? Ah, yes! I remember he obtained from the King a reprieve of three months for his father, so that he might make a pilgrimage to Rome. Poor fellow! I'm afraid he has perished on the road."

"Then I am here to demand justice on his behalf, Monsieur Jackal. I have found the missing proof of Monsieur Gérard's guilt and Monsieur Sarranti's innocence."

"You have succeeded at last!"

"Yes, and in spite of you, Monsieur Jackal. I need not remind you of our vain search for the skeleton in the park at Viry. I need only inform you that I have recovered this lost link in the terrible tragedy. This night my good dog and I found this skeleton in Monsieur Gérard's garden at Vanvres."

Salvator thereupon showed M. Jackal the ghastly contents of his bag, and resumed, "And now, Monsieur Jackal, I swear before Heaven that if Monsieur Sarranti is executed to-morrow I will hold you responsible for his death. As for this convincing piece of evidence, I leave it, without fear, in your charge, for I have in my possession the procès-verbal, which is a sufficient check upon even so mighty a potentate as the Chief of the Secret Police of Paris. Monsieur Sarranti must be saved, and shall be saved, even if I have to beg for the intervention of the King himself."

Salvator then bowed stiffly to M. Jackal, and took his departure, leaving the Chief of the Police amazed and alarmed at the discovery and the menace. M. Jackal was soon put on his mettle. An angry light gleamed in his foxy eyes as he flew to the window, touched a secret spring, and set a dozen bells ringing.

"By this measure," he murmured, "I shall, at least, have time to consult with the Minister of Justice."

"Monsieur Gérard!" announced the usher, a moment later.

Honest Monsieur Gérard, livid and breathless, burst into M. Jackal's office, and, exhausted by his violent ride, fell back almost faintingly into the arm-chair proffered him.

"Good!" exclaimed the Chief of the Police, cool as the other was craven. Turning to the usher, he added, sharply, "You saw that young man leave a minute ago, with his dog?"

"Yes, Monsieur."

"They must both be arrested; but neither man nor dog must be harmed, on any account. Give the order at once. Quick! Go!"

"Depend on their both being arrested, Monsieur," answered the confidential usher, vanishing with the message as he spoke.

"I am lost ——," began M. Gérard, tremulously; but he was abruptly interrupted by the Chief of the Police.

"Look out of yon window," commanded M. Jackal.

M. Gérard meekly obeyed.

"What do you see going on in the courtyard?"

"A young man leaving the Préfecture."

"Well?"

"He is now assailed by four of your men."

"Well?"

"The young man fights bravely. He turns on them like a lion. He keeps them at bay."

"Look at him well, Monsieur Gérard, for that young man holds your life in his hands."

"A dog now flies to his assistance. *Mon Dieu! It's Brésil!*" exclaimed the trembling spectator, falling senseless on the floor before M. Jackal.

CHAPTER XC.—CHECK AND COUNTER-CHECK.

THE Chief Commissioner of the Paris Police took the place of the affrighted M. Gérard at the window, and noted with satisfaction that Salvator and the dog were at length overpowered by numbers and made prisoners by his agents.

"Good!" exclaimed M. Jackal, shutting the window and rousing M. Gérard from the dead faint into which he had been thrown on seeing Brésil. "And now for the business that brought you here at this late hour. Whatever induced you to leave your convives this evening?"

"Ah! Monsieur," stammered Gérard, in excuse, "it was the belief that I was summoned post-haste by you."

"A trick of the enemy! And to think you were gullible enough to leave your guests at table over the very spot in which you had buried the skeleton of your closet!"

"You know what happened, then? You know that on my return I found the remains had been removed? Would that you also knew their present resting-place!"

"See for yourself," answered M. Jackal, opening the bundle on his desk, and revealing the human remains which Salvator had deposited in his custody.

A terrible cry escaped the craven murderer on viewing once again this ghastly evidence of his guilt. He turned white, and would have fled had he not been held back by the politic advice of the astute Commissioner of Police.

"What folly are you about now?" exclaimed M. Jackal. "It would be impossible for you to take a dozen steps outside the Préfecture in your present agitated state without being arrested."

The trembling criminal sank back in his chair, and wistfully awaited the counsel that might be offered him.

"Just see now how utterly unreasonable your terror was a moment ago!" resumed M. Jackal. "The young man and dog I have just had arrested were the discoverers of your secret. It was he who left the skeleton in my charge, his aim being to open the prison door to Monsieur Sarranti, who is to be executed to-morrow for the crimes Brésil saw you commit. Now, say it is as much our interest to have Monsieur Sarranti guillotined as it is your interest to escape from France. If it is, there's no reason why I shouldn't hand you the passport you long for, is there?"

"A passport, my dear Monsieur Jackal! Give me a passport, and I can easily gain a seaport, and thence escape to England."

The Commissioner of Police touched his bell and an usher answered the ring.

"A passport!" M. Jackal laconically demanded.

"For abroad," M. Gérard timidly added.

"Yes, for abroad," repeated M. Jackal.

An icy silence ensued until the usher reappeared with the passport, which he handed to the Commissioner of Police, who placed it in the trembling hands of M. Gérard.

"It is not *visé!*" said the Mayor-elect of Vanvres.

"Nor does it need it, honest Monsieur Gérard. It is a special police pass; and, if you don't feel crushed by the honour of representing the police, you may make your mind easy while you have it in your possession."

"Thank you, thank you, my dear Monsieur Jackal," said M. Gérard, rising hurriedly, and not staying a moment after he had muttered, in a shaken voice, "Adieu!"

"The deuce attend you!" muttered M. Jackal after the retreating figure. "For if heaven does but concern itself with you, your race will soon be run, my fine fellow."

M. Jackal once again rang his bell.

"Is my carriage ready?" he demanded of the usher who answered the summons.

"It was ready ten minutes ago."

M. Jackal gave a glance at himself in the glass, was satisfied with the reflection, threw an overcoat over his shoulders, and lost not a minute in entering his carriage.

"To Monsieur the Minister of Justice!" he called to the driver, and then sank back in a cosy corner, with a smile of satisfaction at the easy way in which he had checked Salvator.

"But where is my memory?" he asked himself the next moment. "I forgot the King has a grand fête at St. Cloud to-night, and will have all his ministers around him."

"To St. Cloud!" was the new direction M. Jackal gave the coachman as he jerked his head out of the window.

The carriage flew through the Paris streets; and M. Jackal, who appeared to have as strong a hold over Somnus as he had over his agents, had fallen into a sound sleep before the Louvre was reached. A moment later he was awakened in the most abrupt and unexpected fashion. The carriage was stopped. Both doors were suddenly opened. A man leapt on each step and held a pistol levelled at M. Jackal's breast, whilst two others menaced the coachman. The four men were masked.

"Hallo! What's the matter?" exclaimed the astounded Chief of the Police.

"Another word—another gesture—and you're a dead man!" was the firm reply.

"What!" cried M. Jackal, disregarding the threat. "Is it possible that one can be stopped like this at midnight in the Champs Élysées? Where can the police be?"

"You ought to be able to answer that question yourself, Monsieur Jackal. But make your mind easy, we are not robbers."

"What are you, then?"

"We are enemies who hold your life in our hands. So, if you but attempt to give an alarm, I repeat you are a dead man."

"Do what you please with me, Messieurs," responded M. Jackal, making a virtue of necessity, and resigning himself to the inevitable.

The spokesman of this midnight band then blindfolded the Chief of the Police, whilst his companion still held his pistol pointed at M. Jackal's heart.

A bandage was then slipped round the eyes of the affrighted driver. One of the masked men took the reins from him, another jumped inside to keep M. Jackal company, and the two others sprang up behind the carriage.

"You know where to drive to!" said the carbonaro inside to the new driver.

The carriage was turned round, and, awakened by a smart cut of the whip, the horses darted of at a slashing gallop.

CHAPTER XCI.—M. JACKAL'S ADVENTURE.

THE masked driver who now held the reins in place of M. Jackal's coachman was certainly clever in his vocation, for in ten minutes he had made so many turns, and had succeeded so well in mystifying the Chief of the Police, that his mind was in a maze, and he had not the least idea as to which quarter of Paris they were in.

The carriage had, in point of fact, pursued a contrary route to that which M. Jackal had commenced. Dashing along the Quai de la Conférence, it had turned to the left, regained its starting place, and made the same circuit once more, after which it had crossed the bridge of Louis XV., M. Jackal's sharp ears then giving him the faint clue that they were crossing the river, but not enlightening him one jot further as to their whereabouts. Down the Quai d'Orsay rolled the carriage, and maintained its perplexing course through the Rue du Bac, the Rue de l'Université, and by a roundabout route to the Boulevard des Invalides. The first stoppage took place in the Rue de Vaugirard.

"Are we at our journey's end?" asked M. Jackal.

"No," was the laconic answer.

"You will allow me to refresh myself, then, with a pinch of snuff?" pleaded M. Jackal.

"Willingly, Monsieur," answered his companion; "but you will allow me in return to relieve you of the arms you carry in the right pocket of your overcoat—a brace of pistols and a dagger!"

"Monsieur," replied M. Jackal, not losing his sangfroid, "you could not have known the contents of my pocket better had you examined it before you spoke. Release my hand, and I'll surrender my arms without fuss!"

"Pardon me, but I would rather help myself," replied the masked stranger, at the same time taking possession of the pistols and dagger. "And now your hands are free, Monsieur Jackal, if you'll promise to remain quiet."

"Thank you for your courtesy, Monsieur——. I have not the honour of knowing your name; and rest assured that if I ever have the power to render you a similar service, I'll not forget your kindness of to-night."

"That occasion will never come," responded the unknown, in the same frigid tone which had characterised his previous terse remarks.

"The deuce it won't!" thought M. Jackal to himself. "Who can these mysterious enemies be? Only two men in France could have dealt me this blow—the Préfet of Paris and Salvator. The Préfet needs me too much at this moment to put me in durance. So I must be indebted to Salvator for this check. Ah! Gérard—honest Monsieur Gérard!—you shall pay dearly for this outrage! Yes; I see now. Salvator has kept true to his word. He must have warned his friends that if he did not appear at a certain time it would be because he was kept a prisoner. Ah! Mon Dieu! I remember his terrible words now, 'The man who raises a hand against me in the performance of what I deem a holy duty will not survive twenty-four hours!'"

This train of thought was interrupted by the fall of a heavy weight on the roof of the carriage with a shock which made M. Jackal tremble involuntarily. The speed of the carriage was not relaxed. On it sped, now rattling over the stones of a quiet street, and later rolling easily and almost noiselessly along the macadamised road. M. Jackal imagined they had by this time reached the suburbs, but was totally ignorant whether they were in the north or south, east or west, of Paris. As the carriage continued to bowl along smoothly, his curiosity increased, and he furtively raised his hand to lift the bandage from his eyes. The click of a trigger close to his right ear made him drop his hand more quickly than he had raised it, and led him to exclaim, in the most natural manner in the world,

"Air, Monsieur! Let me breathe the fresh air or I shall be stifled!"

"Certainly, Monsieur Jackal," replied his companion, letting the right hand window drop. "But pray, for your own sake, don't attempt to breathe through your eyes."

The Chief of the Police gave himself up once more to his secret thoughts.

"Unquestionably this forcible abduction comes from my not taking Salvator at his word," ran the reflections of M. Jackal, as he puzzled his brain with the riddle, how to get out of the trap into which he had fallen? An idea at length occurred to him. He brightened at the thought, and an exclamation of satisfaction escaped him.

"What is it?" demanded his stern custodian.

"I have just thought, Monsieur, that it cannot be your wish to do harm to an innocent party by making me enjoy this compulsory excursion. Just before my departure from the Préfecture it was my duty to cause a young man to be arrested for a short time as a mere matter of precaution. I intended to set him at liberty in a couple of hours—that is to say, on my return from St. Cloud. I was on the road to St. Cloud when you did me the honour to change my route. Will you permit me to return to the Préfecture to release the prisoner?"

"No!"

"Then, at least, allow me to write an order of release. My coachman can take it to the Préfecture, and Monsieur Salvator will be immediately set free."

M. Jackal had purposely kept the name of Salvator to the last. The hit told. His companion started on hearing Salvator's name, and abruptly sang out,

"Stop, coachman!"

"It will be the easiest thing in the world to write my message by moonlight if you will but unfasten this bandage," said M. Jackal, feeling somewhat reassured as the carriage came to a dead stop, and again lifting his hand to remove the handkerchief which blindfolded him.

The click of a trigger again made him pause.

"Stop till I'm ready for *you*," said his gaoler.

Closing the window, and drawing down the red silken curtains on both sides, the masked stranger then drew from beneath his cloak a dark lantern.

"Monsieur, you can now remove the bandage," he said.

M. Jackal was not long in obeying the order; but when the bandage was removed he was for a moment blind as Love or Fortune. He soon saw, however, that he was shut in a trap hermetically sealed. Loophole there was none. He had no option, therefore, but to produce his pocket-book forthwith and pencil on one page,

"Order to Monsieur Kanler, at the Salle Saint-Martin, to set Monsieur Salvator at liberty immediately.—JACKAL."

"Now," added the Chief of the Police, "if you will simply give this message to my coachman, he will deliver it without a moment's delay."

"We'll keep your coachman for some other service, Monsieur. For urgent duty such as this is, we have messengers of our own worth all the drivers in the world."

M. Jackal's custodian thereupon replaced his lantern in his belt, rebandaged his prisoner's eyes, drew up the blinds, opened a window to the right, and gave a call.

The acute Chief of the Police, his sense of hearing all the keener now he was blindfolded, instinctively knew that one of the men behind the carriage had answered the call, and had taken his message, though what orders he received with it he could not divine, as they were delivered in a foreign tongue, utterly unknown to him.

"All right!" shouted the mysterious stranger within the carriage, as his special messenger started off with the order for Salvator's release.

"The vehicle whirled along again with the speed of the wind, and the prisoner inside was presently startled by the noise of another heavy body falling on the roof of the carriage.

"The first sounded to me like a coil of rope," thought M. Jackal to himself. "This sounds like a ladder. What on earth do they mean?"

From the reverie into which he plunged in endeavouring to solve this weighty question he was roused by the stoppage of the carriage for a fourth time.

"Do we take some one up here?" he ventured to inquire.

"No; on the contrary, we drop some one."

M. Jackal was rather too soon in nerving himself to alight with coolness. It was his confidential coachman who was dismissed at this juncture after exchanging a word of farewell with his master. Utterly at the mercy of his unknown captors felt the Chief of the Police as the carriage dashed along with increased celerity, lightened as it now was. Not a word escaped him. He feared he might betray the sickening fear which was taking possession of his heart. Similarly silent was his masked companion until another half hour had glided by.

"We have arrived at last!" was the exclamation that made M. Jackal tremble, as the carriage was brought to a stop for the last time.

He heard the two burdens which had been dropped on the roof taken down. One was a coil of rope; the other, a ladder. The ladder was placed against the house opposite which the carriage was stationed, and it reached as high as the first floor. The carriage door was then opened, and M. Jackal alighted in obedience to the command of his fellow-traveller—the one who seemed to be the chief of the mysterious band. Led to the foot of the ladder, M. Jackal, still blindfolded, could not see that one of the band had already mounted, had cut through a pane of glass with a diamond, and had thus opened the window. The submissive Chief of the Police was alive enough, however, to the energetic order he now received: "There's a ladder before you; mount it!"

M. Jackal placed his foot readily on the first rung, and ascended as rapidly as he could with safety.

"If you utter a single cry you're a dead man!" his implacable companion reminded him in a whisper.

M. Jackal consoled himself with the muttered ejaculation "Thank Heaven! the dénoûment can't be far off!"

Arrived at the summit—he counted seventeen rungs in the ascent—M. Jackal was guided by the carbonaro who had preceded him to the room on the first floor. The ladder was then replaced on the roof of the carriage, which drove off, and left the Chief of the Police he knew not where.

"Here I am a prisoner," ran M. Jackal's reflections. "But where am I? Not in a cellar, because I had to ascend from the street."

"May I ask if we have at length arrived at our final destination?" he presently ventured to inquire.

"No. It will be three-quarters of an hour before we get *there*."

Laconic as ever, it will be seen, was the reply he had to rest satisfied with.

Another long interval of suspense, followed by a gleam of light, perceptible even through the bandage round M. Jackal's eyes. His guide then took his hand, and led him down a steep flight of stairs to a courtyard, at the end of which stood the circular wall of a well, surmounted with wooden uprights to hold the pulley from which a basket was pendant.

Arrived at the well, the guide bent over the low wall, and shouted down,

"Are you ready?"

"Yes," was the answer that welled up from what seemed the bowels of the earth.

M. Jackal then found himself in the grasp of a strong pair of hands, which quickly lifted him into the basket.

The hum of voices around him told him plainly that his guide had been joined by three or four comrades.

Grasping the rope to steady himself in the basket, M. Jackal was dizzy for a moment with the rapid descent. What reason they could have for thus making him pay a subterranean visit, just as if he were a miner, puzzled him somewhat till he remembered his previous underground adventure which resulted in his defeat of the Bonapartist plot.

"Ah! I see," he communed with himself, "they are conducting me by this roundabout route to keep me ignorant of the locality. I shall have to make another journey through the catacombs. Would it were voluntary, though, like the last!"

The moment the basket touched the bottom of the well, M. Jackal was promptly helped out.

The basket reascended and descended until the full number of carbonari had been deposited by the side of the wondering Chief of the Police.

A long and tedious march through the catacombs, the gloom of which was only relieved by the faint gleams of a lantern borne by the leader, brought the party with their prisoner to a low door.

The door was opened by the silent leader, and the lantern light revealed a flight of steps rising steeply in front of him.

One by one they mounted these steps; and, once at the summit M. Jackal felt insensibly relieved by a slight breeze, which told him he had again ascended to the surface of the earth.

What part of Paris he could be in he could not imagine. The soil was soft beneath his feet. Could he be in a wood? He was soon destined to see for himself.

"Your journey's finished at last!" said the voice which had grown so familiar to him.

"You may take off your bandage!"

M. Jackal took advantage of this permission, and tore off the handkerchief quick as thought. He could not repress an exclamation of astonishment at the spectacle which met his gaze. He *was* in the midst of a wood. He was the immediate centre, however, of a thick ring of men a hundred strong.

Not a single face did he know. The people and the place were alike a mystery to him. Our readers, however, will have recognised the gathering as a meeting of the carbonari, and the wood as the virgin forest of the Rue d'Enfer, whence Salvator and General Lebastard de Prémont started to rescue Mina and save Monsieur Sarranti.

"Brothers," said a man of commanding aspect who formed one of the living ring that encircled the terrified Chief of the Police, "you have before you one who awaits your judgment. In accordance with the wish of our brother Salvator, he has been arrested and brought hither."

"First let him write an order setting Salvator at liberty," replied another of the band.

"That I have already done, Messieurs," urged M. Jackal. "And I confess I sincerely regret I did not release Monsieur Salvator before my departure from the Préfecture."

"Your excuses are too late," was the stern response. "Your death has long been determined upon for a hundred other crimes against liberty, and our brother Salvator has alone saved you up to this moment. Prepare yourself now for execution. You have but a few minutes to live!"

* * * * * *

M. Jackal, blindfolded again, felt that life was surely ebbing from him half an hour later.

He was in the densest part of the wood.

Close at hand stood his brawny executioner, Jean Taureau, who smiled grimly as he grasped one end of a rope, which was slung round the stout branch of a tree, and the other end of which was tied round M. Jackal's neck.

Jean Taureau caught hold of the rope as high as he could reach, and prepared for the strong pull and long pull that was to launch M. Jackal into eternity.

"Stay, Jean!" shouted a voice at this juncture—a voice that sounded as sweetest music in the ears of the despairing Chief of the Police.

CHAPTER XCII.—SALVATOR'S PLOT.

THE word of command which saved M. Jackal from being strangled by the rope was the cause of as much pleasure to the executioner as to the trembling Chief of the Police himself. An exclamation of joyous surprise escaped the lips of Jean Taureau as he recognised the voice of Salvator. He loosened his grasp on the rope; and M. Jackal, feeling the loop encircling his throat slackened, hastily raised his hands and plucked the bandage from his eyes, to see the man whom he looked to for his deliverance, although he had deprived the Commissionaire of his liberty. Salvator stood before him, calm as ever. Near our hero was the messenger whom General Lebastard de Prémont had dispatched with M. Jackal's order for the release of Salvator.

"Ah! my dear Monsieur Salvator!" cried the Chief of the Police, transported with gratitude. "I owe you my life!"

"For the second time, if I remember rightly," was the stern answer, tinged with reproach.

"The second! No, the third!" protested M. Jackal. "Ah! put me to the proof, and see if I am ungrateful!"

"I will; and this very instant, too! With men of your nature, M. Jackal, one ought not to stay until the sentiments you express have time to freeze. So follow us!"

"With pleasure," answered M. Jackal, as Jean Taureau unwillingly unfastened the knot and freed his neck from its galling ligature. The Chief of the Police had to leap across the open grave which had been dug for him to follow in the track of Salvator; and he leapt over it with no little agility, the sooner to quit the company of the grim and lusty carpenter, who would have taken his life without the least compunction a few moments ago. They were not long in arriving in the midst of the band of carbonari, who remained still in consultation. The face of each member of this secret association was darkened by a frown. Clearly, the reappearance of the man they had sentenced to death was as unwelcome as it was unexpected. A dead silence greeted M. Jackal, whose heart again sank within him as the shadow of Jean Taureau, on whose arm was slung the fatal rope, fell upon him.

"Brothers!" exclaimed Salvator in the firm, mellow voice habitual with him. "I fully understand the cause of your great surprise. You are astonished to see Monsieur Jackal amongst you once more, when you thought he had gone to another place. Blame me for it, but hear my excuse first. Brothers, I simply acted on these grounds: With Monsieur Jackal dead, it would have been useless to hope for help from him; but with Monsieur Jackal living, he may be able to do us a great service, especially as he is most willing to perform any duty we may ask of him. Do I not speak the truth, Monsieur Jackal?"

"You may depend upon me, Monsieur Salvator. Still, I would beg of you not to demand from me a service utterly beyond my powers."

"Brothers, you hear him? Since he is the only man in Paris who can enlighten us as to the preparations for to-morrow, and since he is bound to tell us the truth on pain of death, let us take counsel from him."

There being no opposition to Salvator's appeal—only a rigid silence on the part of these Mohicans of Paris—our hero again questioned M. Jackal.

"Is the execution definitively fixed for to-morrow?"

"Yes; to-morrow afternoon, at four o'clock."

Salvator threw a searching glance round the circle till his eyes rested upon General Lebastard de Prémont, whom he next addressed.

"What arrangements have you made for to-morrow, brother?"

"I have engaged all the first floor windows on the Quai Pelletier, and all the windows looking on the Place de Grève. There are four hundred windows in all. With three men at each window we shall have a total of twelve hundred men thus advantageously placed. Then, I have ordered four hundred to be scattered along the Rue du Mouton, the Rue Jean-de-Léfine, and all the streets which lead to the Place of the Hôtel de Ville. Two hundred more will be echeloned from the gate of the Conciergerie to the Place de Grève, each man being armed with a poniard and two pistols."

"Peste! All this must have cost you a mint of money," broke in M. Jackal.

"You're mistaken. The windows cost us a mere trifle : a hundred and fifty thousand francs. Windows can be rented, but loyal hearts can never be bought."

"Proceed," interrupted Salvator.

"This is our project," continued the carbonaro. "The people will throng to the Place, and their numbers will be swelled by our men, who will on no pretext allow their ranks to be broken. The car, escorted by a picket of gendarmes, will leave the Conciergerie about half-past three, and will proceed to the Place de Grève by the Quai aux Fleurs. All will go well till they reach St. Michael's bridge. There one of my Indians will throw himself under the wheels of the car and will be crushed——"

"Ah!" broke in M. Jackal, who listened intently, and with the profoundest astonishment to these revelations. "Then I have the honour of being in the presence of General Lebastard de Prémont?"

"You have. Weren't you aware I was in Paris?"

"I was sure of it, General. But be good enough to continue. You were saying that one of your Indians would throw himself under the wheels of the car."

"At sight of which accident," continued the General, "the

people will raise shouts of fear and pity, the attention of the escort will be drawn exclusively to the poor Indian, and all our men gathered round will precipitate themselves upon the car and capsize it, at the same moment giving a preconcerted signal which will call all their comrades from the neighbouring streets and adjacent windows to the spot. In a minute a thousand men will be collected round the upset vehicle, the door of which will be burst open to liberate the prisoner, who will be borne off by a trusty band of ten men on horseback. I shall be one of the ten; and I'll answer for this: Sarranti shall be free; or, if he be retaken, it shall be over my corpse! That is my plan, Brother Salvator. Does it meet with your approval?"

"Monsieur Jackal alone," answered Salvator, "can tell us what chance your project has of success; and he will speak in all sincerity I believe I can guarantee."

"Mon Dieu!" replied the Chief of Police, regaining his sangfroid as danger seemed to recede from him, "I swear by all I hold most precious in the world—that is, my life—that if I knew any means by which Monsieur Sarranti could be set free I would reveal it directly. But, as fate would have it, unfortunately I myself took the precautions necessary to guard against an attempted rescue."

"We don't ask you to suggest a means of escape, my good man," said Salvator, impatiently, "we simply ask you whether the General's plan is likely to succeed."

"Precisely. That was what I was coming to. Well, to be brief, you can understand how anxious the Government is to execute Monsieur Sarranti by the anxiety *you* feel with regard to your project of rescue. The preparations I have made will, I am sorry to say, render that rescue abortive. I had learnt that General de Prémont had purchased arms for two thousand men. What did I naturally do? Why, I ordered six thousand to be armed, of course. Two thousand out of the six have been stationed since yesterday in the cellars of the Hôtel de Ville. Two thousand more have had Notre Dame for their barracks to-night. The remaining two thousand will march to the Place de Grève at three o'clock to-morrow afternoon. So that you can see that your eighteen hundred men will be surrounded by my six thousand. Your attempt was foreseen. Precautions have been taken. The rescue must, therefore, fail. I say it with sincere regret. From the bottom of my heart I beg you not to attempt it."

Salvator and the General exchanged a rapid glance, which was understood by all the brethren assembled.

"We thank you for your counsel, Monsieur Jackal," said Salvator. "We thank you in spite of the fact that you will be the cause of the failure. Forewarned, however, is forearmed. Let us now deliberate, brothers, upon the next scheme which occurs to any one of us."

No one answered. M. Jackal was again plunged into the depths of despair. The dark looks of the carbonari, the sombre figure of Jean Taureau, with the dread rope still round his arm, were anything but assuring to the Chief of the Police. Silence was at length broken by Salvator.

"I have a simple plan to suggest," he said.

"What is it?" broke in M. Jackal, seemingly more anxious now that any member of the carbonari to hear how Monsieur Sarranti might be saved.

"What was the object of my visit to you before my arrest, Monsieur Jackal?"

"You left with me what you said was a proof of the innocence of Monsieur Sarranti—the skeleton of a child found by you in the garden of M. Gérard at Vanvres."

"And why did I leave it with you?"

"To be shown to the Prosecutor-General."

"Have you done so?"

"I swear to you, Monsieur Salvator, that I was hastening to St. Cloud to speak to the Minister of Justice on the subject when I was arrested and brought here."

"Very well. You and I will make the journey together, then."

"As you please," said M. Jackal, in a tone of resignation not very encouraging to Salvator.

"You don't think the journey would be of much use?"

"I do not, Monsieur Salvator. You must see that if you can show the King and the Minister of Justice the most irrefutable proofs of Monsieur Sarranti's innocence there would still remain the fact that he had been sentenced to death on the verdict of a jury. To set aside that decision a new trial would be necessary. The trial might be delayed and prolonged as much as the Government pleases. Where would Monsieur Sarranti be meanwhile? He would be languishing in prison. Innocent, he would be deemed guilty till his innocence should be formally proved. Year after year might pass by. He would pine and probably die in prison. In face of these possibilities, I must confess I am not very hopeful of good resulting from your suggested visit to St. Cloud, Monsieur Salvator."

"Enough! You are right, Monsieur Jackal. Let that plan share the fate of General de Prémont's. Happily, I have yet another one that is the best of all, I believe."

The profound silence of the carbonari testified the interest felt by them in the third means of rescue to be unfolded to them.

"It is three months since this plan occurred to me," said Salvator. "It was during the trial even and before the conviction of Monsieur Sarranti. I had left the Palace of Justice one afternoon, and had descended to the river-side to take a boat for a row, when my attention was drawn to four or five openings in the river wall closed by iron gates. I examined these gates. My examination proved that nothing would be easier than to open them and so penetrate through the sewers underneath the Quai, and perhaps underneath the Conciergerie itself. The next morning I called upon a friend of mine at the Conciergerie (never mind what post he occupies, for the moment, Monsieur Jackal!), and I learnt casually from him that one of these subterranean passages did pass under the prison. The next thing to find was the particular sewer which led from the Seine to the Conciergerie. I made the attempt that very night. Three trusty brothers, well acquainted with the catacombs, joined me. It was a dark night. The first gate of the sewer I calculated would be *the* one was easily opened. But we had not made ten steps before further progress was stopped by another and stronger iron barrier. One of my men was fortunately armed with his tools. He soon forced a passage, and advanced along the gloomy sewer alone. We missed him for ten minutes. At the end of that time he came back, and fell at our feet, half asphyxiated. Leaving him, with his companions, at the mouth of the fetid tunnel to recover in the fresh air, I went up by myself about twenty paces, when I found still another iron gate barring our way. A second of my comrades was half suffocated before this third barrier was broken through. There was yet another iron gate a little higher up. This difficulty was surmounted in the same way, my third assistant being, however, nearly killed by the foul air. Our work had then to be interrupted till the following night. Meantime I carefully studied a map of the prison. We resumed our explorations armed with a chemical safeguard against the poisonous atmosphere of the sewer. With this we reached the third gate in safety. The tunnel then turned to the right. We overheard the tramp of soldiers overhead. I knew we were near the gaol. In another minute I had reached the angle directly underneath the cells of the prisoners condemned to death. Carefully closing each gate behind us, we retraced our steps to the Seine. Then began a herculean labour for my brave assistants. How hard it was you may imagine when I tell you that three men, relieving each other during the work, took sixty-seven nights to complete their task !"

A murmur of admiration rose from the lips of the carbonari, and of M. Jackal. Three men alone were mute : Jean Taureau and his two mates, Sac-à-Plâtre and Toussaint-Louverture. They sheepishly looked on the ground on hearing this involuntary tribute to their pluck and endurance.

"There stand the three performers of that terrible work !" added Salvator.

The three Mohicans of Paris appeared yet more confused as the eyes of the carbonari were fixed upon them with evident admiration.

"Whether we save Monsieur Sarranti or not, the fortunes of our three gallant brothers are made," said General de Prémont, stepping forward and shaking hands warmly with the bashful giants.

"Thanks to their heroic labour," resumed Salvator, "we penetrated to the very cell of cells. It was empty. It would remain so till Monsieur Sarranti should be put there a day or so before the date of his execution. That execution shall *never* take place, brothers. (Shouts of approval.) We have only to push up a stone in the floor of Monsieur Sarranti's cell, and he will be free. He will be able to descend to the sewer, at the mouth of which a boat will be ready for him, and he will soon be far away from the ken of the police. The moment has come to try this desperate plan. Will it do, think you, Monsieur Jackal? Speak quickly, for we must be prompt or it will be too late."

"The project is daring, Monsieur Salvator; but it is the only feasible one. May it prove successful!"

"Let us depart, then, brothers. Monsieur Jackal will be conducted to a place of safety, and every courtesy will be paid him. Now to the rescue of Monsieur Sarranti!"

Whilst two men seized M. Jackal by the arms and led him into the wood, Salvator, with General de Prémont, Jean Taureau, Toussaint Louverture, and Sac-à-Plâtre, disappeared in a contrary direction.

CHAPTER XCIII.—THE ATTEMPTED RESCUE.

WE need not follow Salvator and his companions through all the mazes of the catacombs. They left underground Paris by the Rue Saint-Jacques. Dawn was breaking as they gained the Quai de l'Horloge, and three of their number—the General, Sac-à-Plâtre, and Touissaint Louverture—stepped into Salvator's boat.

"Now," said Salvator in a low voice, which was yet so distinct that all could hear every word, "now, Jean Taureau, obey my last instructions implicitly. You will hasten up the sewer to the spot you know well enough."

"Yes, Monsieur Salvator."

"You will listen for a moment till you are sure all is quiet overhead. Then give a vigorous but sure and steady push with your shoulder, so as to gradually dislodge the flagstone in the centre of the cell without noise. I shall be close at hand, and will do the rest. En marche!"

Jean Taureau at once started off, and disappeared through the mouth of the sewer.

Salvator quickly followed in his footsteps. Ere he could reach Jean Taureau, however, the burly carpenter had, by a powerful muscular effort, raised the flagstone of M. Sarranti's cell.

"Ready?" was Salvator's laconic query.

"Yes."

"Push it aside, then!"

"It's done!" answered Jean Taureau, moving to give way to his master as a faint gleam of light shot through the aperture from above.

Salvator pushed his head and shoulders through the hole, and cast an anxious glance round the prisoner's cell. It was empty!

CHAPTER XCIV.—M. GERARD'S NEMESIS.

To understand the cause of M. Sarranti's unexpected absence from his cell at the very moment liberty was within his reach, the reader must follow "honest Monsieur Gérard" in his hurried flight to Vanvres. The ride from Paris seemed one long nightmare, albeit his horse went at a frantic gallop, spurred on by the maddened murderer. Home at last, M. Gérard flew upstairs to his bed-room, packed his travelling trunk with mad haste, locked it, and trembled as with fever when he stooped to lift the trunk on his back. He paused, and a terror-stricken look stole into his damp, pallid face. He heard what sounded like the rustling of a robe on the staircase. He looked towards the door, and beheld a white figure on the threshold.

"Who are you?" came faintly from his blue, dry lips.

"I," answered a grave voice.

The white figure drew nearer, and came within the circle of light cast by the candle.

"The monk!" exclaimed M. Gérard, as he recognised in the white, cadaverous features of the menacing figure before him the face of Dominique Sarranti.

"Yes; I have come to take the law into my own hands. I promised your confession should be kept secret while you *lived*. I will keep my word. Every means I could think of to save my father from expiating the crimes which *you* committed I have tried, even to humbling myself before the Pope. Your death alone will save my father——"

M. Gérard instinctively felt that a struggle for life or death was impending between him and the stern man confronting him.

"Let me pass!" he shouted, striving to grasp a pistol on the table near him.

The monk was too quick for him. Drawing a knife from his girdle, he plunged it into the murderer's heart. M. Gérard fell dead at his feet.

CHAPTER XCV.—BY ORDER OF THE KING.

SAVE a dense black cloud which obscured the moon, the blue vault of the heavens was clear, and the stars flashed like diamonds, when Dominique Sarranti, hiding the fatal knife within his robe, hurried from the corpse of M. Gérard to complete the task he had set his soul upon accomplishing. At St. Cloud—the palace the monk was bound for—King Charles X. was holding Council with his ministers. His Majesty—who wore the brilliant uniform of a General, glittering with orders—listened with an air of abstraction to the speeches. His looks were bent on the thick cloud which veiled the moon—presage to him of a stormy morrow, and a consequent postponement of the anticipated hunt in the forest of Compiègne. A sigh escaped him. The cloud seemed immovable as a rock. Would he be compelled to give up the chase? Even as the Royal sportsman asked himself this question, a breeze sprang up and swept the sombre mass away, and the moon shone forth in all its glory, and the King's eyes sparkled with delight. But his joy was only momentary. Whilst the heavens grew clearer, a cloud of earthly origin dashed the King's hopes again. The Préfet of Police was announced. Gloomier than his Majesty's brow a minute ago was the face of this high functionary. The Préfet bent his head with respectful reverence, and lost not a moment in addressing the King.

"Sire," he said, "I have the honour to solicit permission to take every measure necessary to preserve the peace of Paris to-morrow."

"The peace of Paris!" exclaimed his Majesty. "What can disturb that?"

"Sire," answered M. Delavau, one of the King's Ministers, "your Majesty is aware of the death of Manuel?"

"Yes," said the King, with some impatience. "A man of great merit, I understand; but as he was a Republican, his death should not trouble us beyond measure!"

"It is not in that sense, Sire, that the death of Manuel affects me. I fear the disturbances which will probably take place at his funeral. I fear a repetition of the riot that happened at the funeral of Monsieur de la Rochefoucauld-Liancourt. It is to nip this revolutionary feeling in the bud that I humbly beg of your Majesty to place Paris in a state of siege for a brief interval."

"Is the danger, then, so imminent?" demanded the King, with a troubled voice.

"It is, Sire," answered M. Delavau for the Préfet.

"Let us hold counsel together in earnest, then, Messieurs," said his Majesty, beckoning to his Ministers and the Préfet to follow him to the window.

"Now explain yourself more explicitly, Monsieur," said the King to the Préfet.

"Sire," was the answer, "it is not the funeral of Manuel alone on the morrow which alarms me. It is the fact that there will not only be one cause of disturbance, but also a second, and the more serious of the two."

"What do you allude to now?" asked Charles X., in surprise.

"To a Bonapartist movement, Sire!"

"Pure fancy! A bogey to frighten women and children! Bonapartism has lived its life. It died with Bonaparte. *Requiescat in pace!*"

"Allow me to undeceive your Majesty," replied the Préfet. "The Bonapartist party is far from being dead. It has great vitality. For the last month the Bonapartists have made quite a raid on all the gun-shops of Paris, and even on the manufactories of Saint-Etienne and Liège——"

"Can this be true?" uttered the King, in alarm.

"I will answer for its truth with my life, Sire. Not only are the Bonapartists ready, but they are on the eve of striking a blow. Tomorrow, Sire, will take place the execution of Monsieur Sarranti, and——"

"Sarranti!" interrupted his Majesty. "Why, I granted him a respite at the request of a monk."

"His son," resumed the Préfet. "He prayed for the respite so that he might have time to make a pilgrimage to Rome, thence to bring the proof of his father's innocence."

"Yes; I remember that was the case."

"The three months' respite expired to-day, Sire; and, in accordance with the orders I have received, the execution is fixed for to-morrow."

"Still, the monk seemed positively certain of his father's innocence," mused Charles X.

"May be, Sire; but he has not proved it. He has not even returned to Paris yet."

"And to-morrow will be the last day of grace accorded to the condemned man."

"Yes, Sire. To save Monsieur Sarranti, however, one of the Emperor's most devoted followers, the man who failed in the conspiracy to bring the King of Rome to Paris, has expended over a million during the past week."

"Do you believe a man who was really a thief and an assassin would inspire such devotion?" questioned the King.

"Sire, he has been condemned."

"Well, well! What force has General Lebastard de Prémont at his disposal for to-morrow?"

"A strong one, Sire."

"Then oppose him with a force of double the strength—nay, three times, four times as strong."

"Those measures I have already taken, Sire."

"Then what have you to fear?" said the King, with some impatience, as he again looked up at the clear blue and starry vault of the heavens, which gave promise of a fine morrow.

"The coincidence of Monsieur Manuel's funeral and Monsieur Sarranti's execution, Sire: the union of the Jacobins and the Bonapartists. That our enemies are determined will be clear to your Majesty when I add that one of the most clever and devoted agents of your Majesty has been boldly carried off by them."

"Whom do you allude to?"

"Monsieur Jackal, Sire."

"What!" exclaimed the King with a start. "Can they have had such audacity? When did this happen?"

"About three hours ago, Sire. He was seized near the Louvre, whilst en route to confer with me and the Minister of Justice at St. Cloud. Will your Majesty now prevent any further outrages by the prompt and effectual remedy I suggest? Will your Majesty declare Paris in a state of siege?"

The King remained silent. The Ministers—faithful apes that they were—imitated their master's silence. The King did not answer immediately, for two reasons—first, the measure appeared too grave to be adopted with haste; secondly, it would be impossible for him to enjoy a day's hunting in the Forest of Compiègne on the morrow were he to place Paris in a state of siege.

"Well, Messieurs," said the King, after debating with himself for some moments, "what think your Excellencies of the proposition of Monsieur le Préfet?"

To the great astonishment of his Majesty, they unanimously pronounced in favour of the state of siege. The King shook his head, however, feeling instinctively that the step would be unwise. As if struck by a happy solution of the difficulty, he brightened up the next moment as he said, "If I were to pardon Monsieur Sarranti, not only should I diminish the chances of an émeute, but probably gain some friends by the act."

"Sire," said M. de Peyronnet, "Sterne had good reason for saying that there was not a grain of hate in the soul of a Bourbon."

"*Who* said that?" demanded Charles X., visibly flattered at the compliment.

"An English author, Sire."

"Living?"

"No, Sire; he died sixty years ago."

"That author knew us well, Monsieur de Peyronnet; and I only regret I had not the pleasure of knowing him. But that is beside the question. This Sarranti affair seems to me so obscure that I repeat I think it would be advisable to pardon the condemned man."

This merciful view was overruled, however, by the Minister of Justice, whose opinion was shared by the other Ministers.

"Let it be as you decide, then," cried the King at length, with a sigh.

"Then your Majesty will permit me to declare Paris in a state of siege?" said the Préfet with an air of relief.

"Alas! I suppose you must, as you are all unanimously against me on the subject, though I must repeat I think the measure far too rigorous for the occasion."

A deep sigh came from the King, and seemed to say, "There goes a good day's hunting."

Even as he was regarding the sky with a look of keen regret, however, an usher entered the room, and addressed the King.

"Sire," he said, "a monk asks permission to see your Majesty."

"Did he give you his name?"

"The Abbé Dominique, Sire."

"It is he!" murmured the King, adding aloud, "Conduct him to my private room!"

"Messieurs," resumed the King, turning to the Ministers, "I have to request you will await my return here. This newcomer may alter the face of things altogether."

The King found Dominique already in his private room. The monk stood straight and motionless, pale and rigid as a marble statue.

"You have returned at last, then!" exclaimed Charles X., in a tone of pity, for the deadly pallor of the phantom-like figure touched him deeply. "But you seem very ill!"

"The journey was a long and painful one, Sire. I fell ill in the defiles of Mont Cenis. In traversing the Marennes I was seized with fever, which detained me a month in the bed of a country inn. To make up for lost time I walked the last fifty leagues in forty days, and I only reached Paris two hours ago!"

"Why, why did you not ride some part of the way?"

"Sire, I made a vow to walk to Rome and back on foot."

"Brave man! What was the object, and the result, of your mission to Rome?"

"My mission was to appeal to the Pope to remove the seal of silence which prevented me from revealing the secret of a confession. I failed."

"And you bring back no proof of your father's innocence after all," sighed the King.

"On the contrary, I possess an irrefutable proof, Sire."

"Produce it."

"It is here," answered the monk, drawing from his bosom a folded paper.

"But you dare not reveal the secrets of the confessional, you say."

"Pardon me, Sire. I have the right to speak freely now. This confession was signed by a man who is now dead. Some time ago I was called suddenly to Vanvres to receive the dying confession of a Monsieur Gérard. I went. Directly I heard his name I recoiled with horror. It was Gérard Tardieu, the man who had accused my father of robbery and murder. Despite my protests, he would persist in confessing to me the secret of his life. He told me how, step by step, he was led into crime by a cold-blooded schemer who passed as his wife. Tempted by her, he murdered his little nephew, leaving the woman to make away with the little girl. But a faithful dog rescued his young mistress. The girl was saved—she still lives—but the dog strangled her would-be murderess!"

"The proof, the proof of all this villany!" interrupted the King. "Give me the proof, and justice shall be at once done to your long-suffering father!"

"This *is* the proof," answered Dominique Sarranti, bending low, and handing to his Majesty the paper, indorsed with these words:—

"This is my Confession before God and man, to be made public, if necessary, after my death.   GERARD TARDIEU."

"And how long have you had this terrible document?" inquired the King.

"Since the assassin gave it me, in the belief that he was dying, Sire."

"And having it in your possession, you kept it secret, even when your father was condemned to death!"

"Sire, you will see yourself that this confession could only be published after his death. He died but three-quarters of an hour ago. He was assassinated."

"Assassinated!" exclaimed the King, with horror. "By whom?"

The monk sank upon his knees, and drew forth the knife still red with the life-blood of Gérard Tardieu.

"I was the assassin!" answered the monk below his breath, trembling with emotion. "It was the only means of saving my father. I stabbed him to the heart. The scaffold is ready, Sire; let me mount it instead of my father!"

There ensued a moment of suspense. Charles X. broke the silence in a voice soft as a forgiving judge's.

"Rise, Monsieur," he said. "Your crime is, undoubtedly, a fearful one. But your heroic devotion to your father excuses you. Let the law judge you. I cannot blame you, Monsieur."

"But my father. Every moment in prison must be an age to him now!"

The King touched a bell. To the servant who answered the summons he said, "Tell Monsieur le Préfet and Monsieur the Keeper of the Seals that I wish to see them at once."

Charles X. then raised the exhausted monk from his recumbent position, and bade him rest in the arm-chair. The Minister of Justice and the Préfet now made their appearance.

"Messieurs," said the King, "there need be no state of siege. Monsieur Sarranti must be set free. He is innocent. His innocence has been conclusively proved to me by his devoted son here. Monsieur le Préfet will have the goodness to lose not another moment in conducting the Abbé Sarranti to the Conciergerie, and in liberating Monsieur Sarranti."

"Sire! Sire!" cried the monk, holding out his hands in token of his heartfelt gratitude.

"You have a week to recover from the fatigue of your pilgrimage," replied the King. "At the end of that time the law will claim you as a prisoner."

The face of Charles X. then brightened like that of a joyous schoolboy. Summoning his Master of the Hounds as the Préfet and Dominique Sarranti hastened from his presence, the King gleefully exclaimed,

"The hunt is to come off to-morrow, after all. Mind horses and hounds are ready early!"

It was thus by order of King Charles X. that Monsieur Sarranti was liberated from prison some hours before Salvator's desperate attempt to rescue him.

Chapter XCVI.—Salvator at Home.

SOME days after the release of M. Sarranti—days ominous for King Charles X., for Paris had been disturbed by an émeute, fomented by the police, threatening prelude to the Revolution of 1830!—Salvator was enjoying what was to him a rare treat : lunch in his modest home, with Fragola. Roland shared their light meal, which had been spread by the dainty hands of Fragola over the whitest of tablecloths. It was a charming dejeûner. Love's glamour brightened the feast. The peaceful calm was unspeakably refreshing to Salvator after the adventures humanity had led him into ; and the glowing eyes of Fragola, and her flushing cheeks and animation, sufficiently proved that the tête-à-tête was the acme of happiness to her fond heart. The idyllic lunch was interrupted by a ring at the bell.

Roland (as was his wont with strangers) did not give utterance to an angry growl. He simply pricked up his ears, and leisurely walked towards the door. Sensitively modest as she was, Fragola nevertheless fled to her room at the ring, and left Salvator to receive his visitors. They proved to be General de Prémont and M. Sarranti. They had come to bid Salvator farewell. Their host received them with characteristic warmth and cordiality, and there was a secret smile in his frank face as he heartily shook hands with the General.

"The time has come, alas! when we have to bid our best friend good-bye," sighed General Lebastard de Prémont.

"We have yet time for a friendly chat together, I hope, for I have something particularly interesting to say to you, General," answered Salvator.

"I don't know what you can say to interest me, my friend, now that my dear comrade here is free, except it be that you see the means of placing Napoleon II. on the throne of his father."

"There should be a subject which would concern you more deeply than that even."

"It certainly does not occur to my mind. I have no relations to trouble me or to trouble. I *had* a daughter—poor darling !—but she is long since dead."

"What if she lives?"

"Lives ! Lives ! Oh, speak out, my friend, I beseech you !"

"Pray relieve the suspense of my poor friend," added M. Sarranti.

"Let me ask you a few questions first, General?"

"Quick, then."

"Were you ever at Rouen?"

"Yes," answered the General, his heart giving a great leap, and tears springing into his eyes.

"How long ago?"

"In 1812—fifteen years ago."

"You arrived there in a post-chaise?"

"Yes."

"You tarried but a short time at Rouen, and then sped to the village of La Bouille?"

"I did. Can it be that you know——"

"I know all the circumstances, I am happy to say, General. Your daughter lives. The Mina you helped me to rescue from the Park of Viry was your Mina. The kiss you gave her in remembrance of your lost darling was a father's kiss. The lover into whose arms you delivered her was the noble student who had maintained her from childhood to womanhood, who had kept her pure in wicked Paris, and who even now awaits your consent ere he weds the idol of is heart."

"Mina ! Mina ! My darling still lives, then ! Thank God !" cried the General, burying his agitated face in his hands to hide the tears of joy which streamed from his eyes. A hand which had saved the General from death in the heat of battle clasped his hand with true-hearted sympathy ; and M. Sarranti shared the General's joy as a brother would have done.

"And where is my little daughter?" asked General de Prémont, calming himself.

"In Holland."

"Then I must start for Holland at once. Will you accompany me, Monsieur Salvator?"

"I would with all my heart, were not Paris in so disturbed a state."

"Au revoir, then, my dear friend, for I cannot bring myself to say adieu now. Stay ! There is one person I *must* see before leaving Paris !"

"Whom?"

"The villain who would have ruined my Mina!"

"But Monsieur de Valgeneuse is, unfortunately, absent from Paris at this moment!"

"Then I'll await his return!"

"That would probably retard your journey to Holland sadly, my dear General. Monsieur Lorédan de Valgeneuse is in pursuit of a new flame. He would make a conquest of fair Madame de Marande, and has taken flight to Picardie to pay court to his new idol. Leave your revenge till you return to Paris, General. He will be here then, there is little doubt."

"You are always right, my dear Salvator. I'll follow your advice. Au revoir! au revoir!"

* * * *

An hour later a post-chaise left Paris by the Saint-Denis Barrier, where Salvator waved his hand in farewell to the General and M. Sarranti, and watched the carriage until it disappeared in the distance. There flashed past the post-chaise shortly afterwards a carriage speeding to Paris as rapidly as the General was flying from the city. The occupant of the carriage was Madame de Marande, in whose wake rode a cavalier whom a father's vengeance would have laid low had but General de Prémont recognised in the breathless rider Lorédan de Valgeneuse.

CHAPTER XCVII.—THE ROUE'S END.

WE must be indiscreet enough to penetrate the seductive sanctum of Madame de Marande on the night of her return to Paris to see the web Fate was fabricating for that moth of folly and fashion, Lorédan de Valgeneuse. A vision of beauty seemed Lydia de Marande in her soft, white loveliness. A dim light—which seemed to blush at its own daring—glowed from a crimson-globed lamp, sending amorous shafts of light through the silken curtains which parted to reveal the perfect form of this alluring Queen of Night. What was she musing on, as, with eyes half-closed, she dreamily reclined in undulating beauty? On the void in her life? On the continual round of pleasure which gave her scarce time for reflection? On the singular union which had brought the penniless orphan the wealthiest husband in Paris? On the love that was involuntarily taking the place of mere dutiful regard and affection for her middle-aged husband, whose never-changing courtesy and fond adoration shone forth in such bright colours when contrasted with the empty compliments and attentions lavished upon her by more than one idler of Parisian society? Who can tell? A faint noise, no louder than the rustle of a curtain, roused Madame de Marande from her reverie. The next moment the door opened, and Monsieur de Marande appeared. His face wore an unwonted look of care as he entered. The look was displaced by a smile as his young wife uttered a warmer greeting than his heart had been touched with for some time, Moving the silken curtains aside, Monsieur de Marande lifted his wife's soft hand to his lips, and imprinted upon the white taper fingers a tremulous kiss, which sent a strange thrill through the heart of Lydia.

"Since your visit to Picardie, dear," he said in a tone of unusual gentleness, "I have given much thought to our mutual relations. The honour the King has done me in choosing me one of his Ministers after the elections has not driven from my mind the vow I made to beg your forgiveness, dearest, for any seeming neglect I may have been guilty of in devoting myself too exclusively to worldly affairs, and not taking that care which I ought to have taken of my wife——"

"Oh, I assure you, I have never, never been so selfish as to think I could monopolise your attention. You have ever been too good——"

"No. On the contrary, my neglect has brought upon you attentions which must be insufferable from——"

"Monsieur Lorédan de Valgeneuse?"

"Yes. But you shall be no longer open to the insult of his attentions. I am your husband, Lydia. Let us be more to each other than we have been. If you could but love me a little——"

"I do! I love you with all my heart and soul. Do I not owe everything to you! Ah! fresh as yesterday comes back the time when, blighted by the cruel flight of my first love, I accepted your generous offer, and, a girl of seventeen, became the wife of the richest banker in Paris. Duty has now developed into love. Thank you, thank you for breaking the ice. We'll let warm love take the place of coldness now."

Husband and wife were locked in their first really loving embrace.

"Now I feel I can tell you a secret which I have long kept from you, Lydia," said M. de Marande a moment later. "The first love, who so basely forsook you because your father had lost your dowry in an unlucky speculation, was shot dead by me in a duel. I have a deadly aim, Lydia; and if this De Valgeneuse ever persecutes you with his attentions again, he shall share the fate of De Bedmar."

The rustling noise which had before disturbed Lydia again attracted her notice. It was accompanied by the sound of footsteps in her boudoir. M. de Marande dropped his wife's hand and bounded into the boudoir. Voices in hot dispute reached the ears of the anxious wife. She listened, and could distinguish the thin voice of De Valgeneuse mingling with the deep tones of M. de Marande.

* * * * *

Pale and restless from a sleepless night, the young wife rose the next morning. She gazed before her as if in a stupor. Her vision seemed to pierce the tapestry. The dream-picture that met her rapt gaze was a glimpse of the Bois de Boulogne, with two men facing each other—one calm and nobly erect, the other nervously impatient as he turned to his second, as if awaiting a deadly signal.

CHAPTER XCVIII.—THE DUEL.

THE dream-picture of Lydia de Marande was realised that morning in the Bois de Boulogne. Monsieur de Marande naturally regarded the intrusion of Lorédan into the boudoir of Madame de Marande as an insult to his wife, demanded satisfaction for the outrage to his honour, and fixed the morrow for a hostile meeting. The persistent but unencouraged lover of Lydia de Marande had penetrated to the boudoir through the treachery of Nathalie, the lady's maid, a creature of his sister's; and, not wanting in courage and daring, he looked upon the duel as a most satisfactory issue from the embarrassment his escapade had led him into, especially as he prided himself on being a good shot. The first to arrive at the Bois de Boulogne was Salvator, or Conrad de Valgeneuse, as we ought henceforth to call him. His cousin's last shameless adventure had reached his ears, and he was present at the rendezvous to receive what might prove to be the dying wishes of Lorédan, or to act as surgeon in case of need. There was an anxious wait for some minutes. The next to appear were M. de Marande and his seconds, General Pajol and Comte Herbel. Calm and placid, as if he were simply keeping a business engagement, looked the new Minister of the King as he opened a packet of leters which his servant handed him, and read them phlegmatically through one by one, destroying those that were of no importance, and scribbling memoranda for his secretary's information on the missives he handed back to his man. Regarding his watch, M. de Marande said, "Ten minutes to spare. If our opponents should not arrive till nine I shall have time to sign a few orders the King wishes to be executed. Meantime, Generals, will you do me the favour to measure the ground and charge the pistols? Then I can take up my position and not keep them waiting a second."

The two generals had given valiant proofs of their bravery on many a battle-field, and Salvator was the incarnation of courage. Both the seconds and the unseen observer, however, were alike astounde by the heroic sangfroid of M. de Marande. Punctually at nine o'clock the party was completed. Lorédan de Valgeneuse, nonchalant as ever, was accompanied by Camille de Rozan and another friend. A courier rode up at the same moment, and handed to M. de Marande the looked-for orders, which the banker signed, unmoved by the arrival of his adversary.

"We are sorry if we have kept you waiting," said the creole to General Herbel.

"Not a moment!" was the terse reply. "We were rather early!"

"Then we will make up for lost time," added the other second of Lorédan de Valgeneuse.

The latter caught sight of his cousin Conrad at this juncture, and a shiver ran through him involuntarily as this figure of ill-omen met his gaze.

"Messieurs," exclaimed Lorédan, impatiently turning to his seconds, "I don't know whether it is to insult us they have brought this Commissionaire here as a looker-on."

"I am here in the interests of humanity, Monsieur," answered Salvator coldly. "I am here as surgeon."

Lorédan de Valgeneuse shrugged his shoulders with a gesture that was meant to intimate that *he* had no fear of the result of the duel.

M. de Marande, still busy with his papers, was writing away, yet imperturbably. There was no idle assumption of indifference on the part of the Minister of State. The maintenance of this unalterable sangfroid appeared to have its effect before many moments on the young duellist, his nervousness being plainly discernible beneath his mask of indifference.

"Monsieur," General Herbel ventured at length to say to the busy banker, "have the goodness to make ready!"

"I am quite ready," was the quiet rejoinder of M. de Marande, who still wrote on serenely.

"You misunderstand me," replied the General. "I would have you rest a moment before the signal is given. Pray, don't throw a chance away."

"Bah!" was the stolid answer. "I *must* finish signing these papers. The King waits for no one, you know. Make your mind easy about me, General. Something tells me I shall kill De Valgeneuse. So, charge the pistols and measure the forty paces."

The arms loaded and the distance settled, it was agreed that General Pajol should give the signal by smiting his hands thrice, the principals to advance fifteen paces at the third clap, or to fire from where they stood, whichever course either might prefer.

"Very well, Messieurs," said Lorédan de Valgeneuse, "I am quite ready."

General Herbel handed M. de Marande his pistol, which he simply placed under his arm whilst he signed the last two papers, saying at the same time, "Monsieur Lorédan can take his fifteen paces and fire as soon as he likes."

"He is a dead man," muttered General Pajol.

Not a muscle of the banker's face moved as he rose to his full height, and placed himself in position as he gave a final glance at the orders before handing them to his courier. General Pajol gave the signal to march and fire, but M. de Marande continued to regard the papers in his hand, although he withdrew his pistol from underneath his arm.

"Enough of this comedy!" exclaimed Lorédan de Valgeneuse, fairly irritated by his opponent's composure. "I shall fire! Let him die like a dog if he wishes!"

Grinding his teeth, the young man took the fifteen paces and fired at M. de Marande. The ball missed. The banker then raised his pistol and fired. Monsieur Lorédan de Valgeneuse reeled and fell, face downwards, to the earth.

"So I have not wasted much of the morning, after all," said M. de Marande. "The earth is well rid of a villain, and the King's business has not suffered delay!"

Salvator sprang to the side of the wounded man, whose face was livid, and whose last hour was evidently near. His cousin tore open his shirt, and found he was wounded in the breast.

"Is the wound fatal?" tremulously asked his pallid second, M. de Rozan.

"Yes," answered Salvator.

"Is there no hope of his surviving?" asked the stricken creole.

"None whatever."

Salvator rose, and hastened to Generals Herbel and Pajol, to whom he communicated the same tidings.

"Can you do nothing for him?" asked M. de Marande, guessing the purport of the message.

"Absolutely nothing! He has only ten minutes to live!"

"Then, may heaven have mercy on his soul!" murmured M. de Marande.

CHAPTER XCIX.—FATHER AND DAUGHTER.

LET us now take flight to Amsterdam, the Venice of the North, so picturesque in its varied colouring and labyrinth of canals, so fantastic in its quaint Dutch architecture. Tranquilly flows the river of life in Amsterdam. Placidly beats the pulse of this peaceful city—a city to live and love in. He who said, "See Naples and die," would have said of Amsterdam, "See Amsterdam and live!"

Such, at least, was the opinion of two young people not unknown to the reader—Justin and Mina, who dwelt in Amsterdam, as lovingly as two doves in their nest. Madame Van Sylper was their one friend. Mistress of the chief boarding-school for young ladies in Amsterdam, Madame Van Sylper willingly accepted Mina as a boarder and Justin as French master. A golden dream was it for the loving couple till a certain morning, fraught with a new joy for Mina, brought a moment of painful suspense to the heart of Justin. Justin trembled with a vague fear when word was brought him one Sunday that two gentlemen from Paris wished to speak with him. He found them waiting for him in Madame Van Sylper's dining-room. Almost before he had entered the room one of the strangers had risen and warmly grasped him by both hands, whilst the other bowed with marked respect.

"Don't you remember me?" said the stranger, who still held his hands firmly grasped.

"No, Monsieur."

"Yet you have seen me before, and on an occasion memorable enough for you, inasmuch as your fiancée was then released from captivity and restored to your arms, Monsieur Justin."

"I remember now," answered Justin, his eyes brightening with gratitude. "It was you who helped me and my good friend Salvator to save Mina from the Park of Viry. You are General Lebastard de Prémont."

"I am," said the General, with renewed heartiness. "And you, Justin, shall be my dear——"

General de Prémont was about there and then to acknowledge the faithful, loving guardian of his daughter as his son, but he abruptly paused as the word was on the tip of his tongue.

"My dear friend," resumed the General, "did Salvator ever speak to you of Mina's father? Did he ever tell you her father was still living?"

"He did give me that hope. Can it be that you know him General?"

"Yes," murmured the General. "But what could you think of a father who deserted his little girl?"

"I thought he must have been very unfortunate, General."

"And you never blamed him?"

"Never," answered Justin, glancing curiously from the General to his friend, for something seemed to tell him that one of these men was Mina's father.

"The father of Mina has returned," continued General de Prémont, "and one day he will, doubtless, ask you to restore his daughter to him. Tell me, will Mina be worthy of whomsoever her father might choose for her husband?"

"She is as good as she is lovely," stammered Justin, touched to the heart by this last question, for it seemed to him impossible that he should be ever deemed worthy the choice of Mina's father.

"Oh, let me see her, my own dear little Mina!" exclaimed the General, no longer able to restrain the overpowering feelings of a father.

"My dear Justin—my son [what joy shot through Justin's heart at this fond word!]—bring her to me, only break the news gently; for, remember, she is but a young girl. My darling!"

Justin flew to obey the General's order. He speedily returned with Mina, whom he thus introduced, "Let me present you to two friends of mine, dear!"

Mina graciously saluted the two visitors. The General pressed his hand to his heart to still its violent beating, and two tears ran down his cheeks as the ravishing beauty of his daughter dawned upon him.

"Prepare to receive the most gladsome news in all the world, Mina, from these gentlemen," whispered Justin.

"They bring news of my father!" cried the young girl, her bright eyes flashing with joyous expectation. "Oh, Monsieur, tell me, do you know my father?"

Each word sounded like a bitter reproach to the General; but his heart was too full for speech. Mina looked from one to the other with an air of perplexity.

"Answer me, I beg of you," appealed Mina. "Does my father live? Does he care for me? Does he—love me?"

"He does live; he is here; he loves you with all a father's love, Mina, darling!" cried General de Prémont, holding out both arms to receive his daughter's embrace.

"Father!"

Mina sprang forward, and was folded in the arms of her soldier father, who, mastered by his emotion, sank back into his chair, whilst his daughter knelt at his side and devoured with loving eyes the bronzed and battle-worn face of her father. Justin softly opened the door, and, motioning to M. Sarranti to follow him, retired, and left the General and Mina to enjoy alone their first sweet interview.

Chapter C.—Camille and Suzanne.

Lorédan de Valgeneuse, whom we left mortally wounded in the Bois de Boulogne, breathed his last in the arms of his seconds a few minutes after the departure of Monsieur de Marande and the two Generals. The following letter informed General de Prémont of the roués tragic end :—

"My dear General,—In order that nothing may interrupt the supreme happiness you must feel at the restoration of Mina to your arms, I hasten to tell you that Lorédan de Valgeneuse, your daughter's abductor, has been killed in a duel by Monsieur de Marande.

"Allow me to express my satisfaction that it will no longer be necessary for you to expose your valuable life to obtain the punishment of that worthless member of society.

"My kindest regards to the two lovers.

"Your sincere friend,
"Conrad de Valgeneuse."

Even this trifler with life—even Lorédan de Valgeneuse—however, had two friends who mourned his sudden death. In face of his still form—in face of the white, rigid features from which the familiar mocking smile had fled—Camille de Rozan, shallow-natured though he was, felt, equally with his fellow-second, a pang of self-reproach at the hand he had had in the fatal duel. Fear of the law—stern enough against duellists at that period—at length roused the two seconds to action. It would be necessary to convey the dead body back to Paris without its being detected. The corpse was therefore lifted into the carriage which had brought De Valgeneuse and his friends to the Bois de Boulogne full of confidence as to the issue of the duel; and the driver and footman were intrusted with the delicate duty of driving their charge safely through the Barrier de l'Etoile, whilst Camille de Rozan and his companion walked back to the city. The two young men parted at the Barrier de l'Etoile. Camille, having sent a message to his wife by his friend, slowly directed his steps to the Rue du Bac, for he had before him the painful task of announcing the sad tidings of her brother's death to Suzanne de Valgeneuse. It was half-past ten when he gained the fine mansion of the Valgeneuses. The house bore its usual aspect. In the courtyard Nathalie was laughing at the jokes of the groom. The current of life flowed easily as ever, in spite of the cloud which would presently darken it. Camille demanded whether he could speak with Mademoiselle Suzanne.

"Mistress is not up yet," answered Nathalie, with a sly look.

"Do you wish to see her on business of importance?"

"Of the greatest importance and urgency."

"In that case, Monsieur, I suppose I must awaken Mademoiselle."

"Do so at once. I will wait in the drawing-room."

Suzanne De Valgeneuse was roused from a sweet dream by Nathalie.

"Camille! Dear Camille!" murmured the dark beauty, but half-awakened.

"Monsieur Camille is here," answered Nathalie, gently shaking her mistress. "He is waiting for you in the drawing-room, Mademoiselle."

"Is he?" exclaimed Suzanne de Valgeneuse, springing up in her bed. "Show him into my boudoir, then. Stay!"

Mademoiselle de Valgeneuse thereupon seized a hand-mirror from her toilet-table, gave a coquettish glance in the glass, and inquired with a self-satisfied, languishing air, "How do I look this morning, Nathalie?"

"Beautiful as ever."

"Now be frank, and don't flatter, Nathalie. Am I not a little weary-looking?"

"A little pale, Mademoiselle, that is all; and are not the lilies pale, and does anybody ever think of reproaching them with their pallor?"

"Very well," sighed the mistress, with a sigh of pleasure, "as you declare I am not absolutely ugly this morning, conduct Monsieur de Rozan to my boudoir, and say I will be with him in a minute."

Suzanne cast another coquettish glance in the mirror as she tied her hair in a careless knot. Crowned thus with a richly-luxuriant natural coronet, and dressed in a gracefully-flowing morning robe of cashmere, she was, a moment or so later, fully armed for conquest, and swept with a well-assured air from her room to meet Camille de Rozan.

"Camille!" she exclaimed, in a soft tone of delight; as she entered the boudoir, to be received in the arms of the creole.

"Suzanne," replied the young man, with unwonted gravity, after the first salute, "I have sad, very sad news for you."

"Your wife knows ——"

"No, no, no!"

"You no longer love me, then?"

"Suzanne, can you doubt my love? Alas! it is Lorédan ——"

"My brother! O, Camille! relieve me of my suspense. Lorédan was to have fought a duel this morning, I know. Did it take place?"

"Yes."

"Well?"

"Lorédan was ——"

"Wounded?" cried the stricken sister.

Camille de Rozan could not answer the appeal of anguish.

"Killed?" gasped the young girl.

"Alas! Your poor brother is no more!" replied the creole, with a voice full of pity.

"Lorédan! My poor Lorédan!" was the heart-stricken cry that escaped the lips of Suzanne de Valgeneuse, as she sank for sympathy on the breast of Camille, and wept passionately.

Camille allowed the passion of grief to exhaust itself ere he attempted to console the girl whom he illicitly loved. The storm of sorrow melting by-and-by into sobs, he led her to the sofa, and sat beside the sorrow-laden Suzanne with his arms still around her agitated form.

"So I am left all alone," said Suzanne at length, in a weak, broken voice; "without relatives, without friends."

"You forget you still have me by your side, Suzanne," whispered Camille de Rozan.

"True; I have *one* friend, but one; and he loves me, at least he says so."

"Let me prove it, Suzanne! Show me how I can prove my love, dear Suzanne, and no sacrifice will be too great for me!"

"*No* sacrifice?"

"None, I swear to you, Suzanne!"

"I will try you. Listen! My brother being dead, I have nobody, nothing to bind me to Paris. I am free. If you really love me let us fly together. Choose between *her* and me! But, oh, Camille, weigh well your words before you answer, for your answer may be life or death for me!"

The faint heart of the creole sank at the suddenness of this passionate proposal. For a moment an absent face seemed mirrored before him. Then his fickle nature yielded to the temptation of the moment, and he summed up his faithless answer in a kiss.

"Ah, it is me you have chosen," continued Suzanne de Valgeneuse in the same tone of nervous excitement. "Then let us quit Paris tonight, Camille. Let us fly to Havre, to Marseilles, Bordeaux, or Brest, whichever port we can leave soonest for America, our future paradise."

"But have you any idea of the fortune that would be necessary for all this! The bulk of my fortune came to me with my wife, and ——"

"We will let her enjoy every sou of it. Realise mine, Camille. We shall have at least two million francs. With that sum, surely the future should not alarm us."

"Are you quite certain you have two millions, Suzanne?"

A shiver passed through the young girl's frame, and left her pale and cold as marble.

"Ah! you, too, have heard of him!" she exclaimed, casting a searching look at the creole. "Is it possible this rumour of the discovered will is true? If so, I shall be ruined, and my dream of happiness with you, Camille, will be at an end."

"Is there another heir, then?" asked the creole.

"There is. Alas! my poor brother was about to realise all our fortune. We should have been safe, Camille, if this cruel duel had not taken place."

"What is the name of this heir?"

"Conrad de Valgeneuse is the name we know him by. He is more publicly known, I believe, as Salvator."

"Salvator, the mysterious commissionaire! Suzanne, I fear our flight would be hopeless indeed."

CHAPTER CI.—A JUDAS KISS.

A MEETING of a very different nature took place on the evening of the same day between Camille and Madame de Rozan. A glowing brunette from Cuba, a beauty who idolised her husband, Madame de

Rozan had at first entered into the fashionable dissipations of Paris with great ardour. She loved the empty gaiety of Parisian society as fondly as she loved the sparkling gaiety—the surface polish—of Camille de Rozan. She loved him, and implicitly believed he returned her passion till his frequent absence aroused her jealousy and led to her setting a watch upon him. It was almost a fatal blow to her when she discovered more than one proof of his faithlessness. Desperate was the resolve of the jealous wife, and easy enough to divine by any one who could have beheld her for a moment that evening seated in an easy-chair in her bed-room. The shaded lamp on the little table near her gleamed on a pale, determined woman, and on an open pistol-case. She carefully loaded and capped the brace of bijou pistols, replaced them in the case, and as minutely examined the point of a miniature poniard. Her work accomplished, Madame de Rozan leant back and fell into a reverie; and her pallor became more intense, her brows more contracted, and a cold, deadly look of hate flashed from her eyes. She was presently interrupted by the sound of a well-known step on the stairs.

"'Tis Camille!" she exclaimed.

And, with the rapidity of thought, she closed the pistol-case, and hid it with the poniard in the drawer of the table, which she locked, and then slipped the key into her pocket. Madame de Rozan rose as her husband entered.

"What! still up, mignon?" cried Camille, lightly.

"Yes," answered Madame de Rozan in an icy tone.

"Foolish one! Do think of your health for my sake!" said Camille, as he imprinted a kiss on her dry lips. The Judas kiss sent an icy tremor through her, and she involuntarily shrank from her faithless husband.

"What is it, love? Are you ill?" demanded Camille, with a well-feigned air of anxiety.

"I am not ill in the sense that you mean," she responded.

"Then why this sternness?"

"Camille, have you not noticed a great change in me during the last few weeks?"

"You have grown a little pale, love; but you look all the lovelier for that."

"Camille," answered the poor wife, melting into tears, "you will kill me with this mockery, with this deception. Why, oh why do you leave me so?"

"What! still suspicious of your loving Camille?" laughed the creole.

This stung Madame de Rozan to the quick. She possessed a proof of his infidelity, and she resolved to show him she was fully aware of his faithlessness and falsehood. "Will you swear you do not love Suzanne de Valgeneuse?" she demanded.

"Of course I will, love. I swear it!"

"Then you lie, Camille! You are a hypocrite, a perjurer, and a traitor!"

Camille sarted back and looked amazed, as he was thus unmasked by his wife.

"Enough of this falsehood!" continued Madame de Rozan. "It is useless to attempt to deceive me. I have kept a watch upon you for several days past. I know that night after night you have been a constant visitor of Suzanne de Valgeneuse."

"Don't let us have a scene," replied Camille, with a sneer. "I tell you I swear there's nothing whatever between me and Mademoiselle de Valgeneuse. I swear there is not, and that ought to convince you."

"Then what is the meaning of this note?" asked the outraged wife, suddenly handing him a letter, the sight of which astounded him.

The billet-doux ran as follows:—

"Camille, my dearest Camille!—Why art thou not near me, when I think only of thee, dream only of thee, love but thee?"

"Oh, this espionage is unbearable!" exclaimed the creole, petulantly, tearing the note angrily into bits. "So, not content to dog my footsteps, you even break open my desk and examine my papers!"

"And have I not a right to do so?" answered Madame de Rozan, furiously. "Am I not your wife? Ah, you are grievously mistaken if you think I am a woman to be deceived with impunity!"

Emphasising her words with the intensest passion, her eyes burning with indignation, the agitated wife would have admirably served as a model for Medea.

Recoiling before her, the creole had recourse to a fresh falsehood.

"Listen to me a moment," he pleaded. "What if Suzanne de Valgeneuse is over head and ears in love with me? Can I help it? Can I prevent a woman from falling in love with me if she will? Be reasonable, love, and you will see I am not to blame after all."

"But do you not return her love?" persisted Madame de Rozan.

"No. I may regard her with the affection of a brother because she is the sister of my dearest friend, poor Lorédan de Valgeneuse!"

"Would that I could believe you, Camille!" sighed the wife. "But I must have proof positive of your love for me before I can trust you again."

"What proof?"

"Let us leave Paris together."

"Why on earth should we leave Paris?"

"To remove a great temptation from Mademoiselle de Valgeneuse!"

"Very well, let us go by all means."

"We will start to-morrow, then."

"To-morrow!" exclaimed Camille, taken aback. "Impossible! so soon as that! We have a hundred things to purchase, visits to pay, and friends to take leave of."

"I have already left our cards, Camille. We have everything necessary for our voyage. Let us depart to-morrow, and all shall be forgiven!"

"I repeat, it will be impossible to leave Paris at so short a notice."

"How long will your engagements detain you, then? Two, three days?"

"A week at least."

"A week be it then. But I warn you, Camille, that if you play me false it will not only be a death-blow to me, but to you and to *her* also!"

The wife uttered these last words of menace in a tone of stern determination, the deadly meaning of which was clear enough when she instinctively threw a glance at the drawer in which she had hidden the poniard and pistols.

Chapter CII.—A Wife's Vengeance.

THE day after Camille's stormy interview with his young wife there came a temptation the fickle creole was powerless to resist. It came in the shape of the following brief note from Suzanne de Valgeneuse :—

"Dearest Camille,—Salvator has proved our benefactor. My cousin has given me a fortune of a million francs. Be ready this afternoon. Let us start for Havre at three o'clock.   "SUZANNE DE V."

"I will be ready," was the reply Camille de Rozan returned. The messenger gone, he tore up the fateful missive, threw the pieces into the grate, and left the house to complete his preparations for flight.

With the suspicion born of her husband's faithlessness, Dolorès de Rozan stole into the drawing-room a minute later, and felt her worst fears realised as she recognised the hated handwriting of Suzanne de Valgeneuse on the bits of paper that littered the fireplace. The fire had not even scorched the cream-white paper, but each word seemed to burn itself into the wife's soul. To gather up the shreds of the love-letter was the work of a moment. In the privacy of her bedroom, Dolorès was not long in piecing the note together, and in discovering how near her husband's treachery was to its culmination. The tears started to her eyes and welled over as her heart sank hopelessly within her, and life seemed a blank and death a welcome relief from her misery. Then passion and vengeance gradually took possession of her, and steeled her for the deadly task she had set herself when she had uttered last night's terrible menace in Camille's hearing.

"I will follow them," she cried, in an icy tone that told only too plainly that love had utterly left her bosom. She rang, and the bell was promptly answered.

"Madame's not ill, I hope," exclaimed the girl, alarmed at the snowy pallor of her mistress.

"No, Marie. I am—quite well. I rang for you to learn a few things about Normandy. You were born there, were you not?"

"Yes, Madame, at Rouen."

"Is that far from Paris?"

"About thirty leagues."

"And Havre?"

"Nearly the same distance, I believe."

"Thank you, Marie. Now make haste and dress, and get a cab, for I want you to go out shopping with me this morning."

"What can be the secret of this woman's fascinating power over Camille?" asked Dolorès to herself, as, the maid gone, she caught sight of the reflection of her own beautiful face in the mirror. "By what subtle means can this Suzanne de Valgeneuse have made Camille love her so devotedly and so speedily? What is her spell? She is not so young, she cannot boast of beauty. Still, I have proof positive, alas! that she has completely captivated him. How can I foil her? Further appeal to him will be fruitless. He would swear fidelity to me one moment, to her the next. Traitor! Yes, I will follow him and his paramour. Be calm, my heart, and nerve me for this supreme trial!"

"The carriage is waiting, Madame!"

The girl's announcement was welcome to Madame de Rozan. It suggested immediate action, best of solaces for grief. A few seconds, and Dolorès and her confidential maid were being driven down the boulevards to the Palais Royal. There the first purchases were made. To a carriage-maker's in the Rue de la Pépinière she next sped to buy a travelling-chariot.

"I want one light and very strong, Monsieur," she said.

"For a long journey, Madame?"

"No; about thirty leagues."

"Madame wishes to arrive quickly at her destination, perhaps?" further inquired the maker.

"As quickly as I possibly can."

"Then here's the very carriage for Madame—light and strong at the same time. It will *fly* along the road."

"That will suit me. Now, Monsieur," continued Madame de Rozan, handing him her purse, "do me the favour to engage the best driver and horses you can find in Paris, and send the carriage all ready for the journey to my address this afternoon. I think you will find enough to repay you in this purse."

"Your wishes shall be attended to by myself personally," answered the coachmaker, his eyes twinkling as he helped himself to three notes of a thousand francs each. "But at what hour would you like the carriage to be at your door?"

Madame de Rozan reflected for a moment. The departure of Suzanne with her husband, she remembered, had been fixed for three o'clock. Dolorès therefore deemed it advisable that she should not start in pursuit till an hour or half an hour later.

"Half-past three," she said, finally, as she gave her card to the coachmaker, and received back her purse, lightened of the three notes.

"At half-past three exactly it shall be there," answered the man, rubbing his hands and bowing obsequiously as Madame de Rozan drove off.

She found Camille awaiting déjeûner when she returned.

"Been out shopping, Mignon?" asked her husband, gaily kissing her cold lips with well-assumed affection.

"Yes."

"For our journey?"

"Yes," repeated Madame de Rozan, accompanying her reply with a significant look, the meaning of which the shallow Camille thought he divined.

Déjeûner over—it was then about half-past two—Camille de Rozan rose, giving the excuse that he was off for a ride in the Bois de Boulogne.

"Shall you return to dinner?" asked Madame de Rozan coldly.

"Why, no. We have lunched so late, Dolorès. Let us sup together instead, darling. Adieu, till to-night," added the creole, saluting his wife with more than wonted warmth, and then, hastening from her presence abruptly, as if fearing a longer stay by the side of his young wife might make him break his promise to Suzanne de Valgeneuse.

"With a lie on his lips he has left me," murmured the determined wife as she regained her room, and with an unfaltering hand lifted from the case the deadly weapons she had set aside as a last resource.

Time flew swiftly, but none too quickly for Dolorès, who was soon equipped for the journey she was nervously anxious to begin. Welcome to her ears, then, was the noise of approaching wheels and the clatter made by the sudden stoppage of the expected carriage at her door. Followed closely by Marie, Madame de Rozan lost not an instant in springing into the chariot, which forthwith dashed off and bowled along the streets of Paris for the high road to Havre. Absorbed in gloomy thoughts of vengeance, Madame de Rozan had no eyes for the villages they flashed through, nor the wintry landscape, nor the darkening heavens. They travelled at so furious a pace that at six o'clock they came in sight of the fugitives, and late at night they arrived at Havre almost at the same time as Camille and Suzanne de Valgencuse. Learning from her husband's postillion that he had put up at the Royal Hotel on the quay, to the Royal Hotel Madame de Rozan hied. Ten minutes later she was installed in a room in the hotel. It was No. 10. The chambermaid was busily tidying the room when Madame de Rozan interrupted her with a sudden question.

"Will you do me a service for five hundred francs?"

"Five hundred francs!" stammered the chambermaid, staggered by the mention of so large a sum: a whole year's earnings to her. "What do you want me to do for so much money?"

"Nothing very dreadful. First, tell me the number of the room occupied by the two travellers—a gentleman with a lady—who arrived here by post-chaise ten minutes ago."

"Certainly, Madame. Number 23—at the end of the corridor."

"Is there a room empty next to theirs?"

"Yes, Madame."

"Let me have that room, and these twenty-five louis shall be yours. My maid can have this room."

"Oh, certainly, Madame," replied the girl, with alacrity, seizing the candlestick and curtseying low as she pocketed the gold.

"Will Madame make the change at once?"

Madame de Rozan followed the active chambermaid along the dark and silent corridor, and trembled as she entered No. 22, for she overheard voices which stabbed her to the heart. When the girl had taken her departure Dolorès flew to a door communicating with the adjoining room, and which, though closed, was so thin that she could without difficulty hear the conversation going on between her husband and his paramour. The wife's hatred of Suzanne de Valgeneuse grew stronger as she listened.

"You are incorrigible, I fear, Camille," was the first sentence Madame de Rozan caught. "You have wrecked one poor woman's life and been the cause of her lover's death, I know ; and now you have deceived your wife. How can I be sure you will not play me false as well?"

"Because you are not my wife. But let me never hear you allude to Carmélite or Colomban again."

"Then promise me not to mention your wife's name again. Why, nothing but Dolorès—Dolorès has been ringing in my ears since we left Paris."

"Pardieu ! What more natural than to think of a blooming young wife, fresh and lovely, whom one is leaving after only a year of married life ?"

"It is surely not in good taste, however natural it may be, to sing the praises of your wife even before the woman who has left everything for you, and whom you professed to love. But, perhaps, you no longer love me?"

"No longer love you !" exclaimed Camille, amorously, accompanying the exclamation with a shower of kisses that made his wife involuntarily draw her poniard from its sheath and with one violent blow break down the frail door that separated her from the lovers.

White as ghosts, Camille and Suzanne looked thunderstruck by the sudden appearance of Madame de Rozan, the image of vengeance, with her bloodless face cold as marble, her bosom heaving with scorn and indignation, and her hand firmly grasping the hilt of the poniard.

"Camille," cried Dolorès, with a voice cold and implacable as fate. "You have shamefully and treacherously deceived me. You cannot now have the audacity to say you have not proved false to your marriage vow. You have deserted me for this creature, and she shall be your punishment. Your life with her will be a slow and painful death, for my image shall haunt you even as the ghost of Colomban haunts you now. Keep your paramour, Camille, and may the phantom of the wife you have killed haunt you to your dying day !"

And Dolorès stabbed herself to the heart as the last words escaped her lips, and fell a corpse at their feet.

"Dolorès ! Dolorès !" exclaimed the creole, kneeling down beside her and raising her lifeless form in his arms, the little heart that he had filled with compunction as he remembered the thousand loving caresses his dead wife had bestowed upon him in the early days of their union. "Dolorès ! Dolorès ! Live, live my wife, to see my repentance !"

But not a breath came from the ashen lips; they had closed like the petals of a flower that has lived its day.

Chapter CIII.—A Villain Unmasked.

WHILST this tragic event was being enacted at Havre a scene of deep interest was taking place in Paris in the palace of Marshal de Lamothe-Houdan. Fate was about to dissipate at last the clouds which had so long obscured the future of Régina and Pétrus. The Marshal's wife was on her death-bed, and could no longer keep from her husband the secret that had embittered her life: the fact that she had, when first married, been tempted to lend a favourable ear to the flattering attentions of Comte Rappt during the Marshal's absence. Though the Princess Rina, inexperienced as she was in the world's ways, shrank instinctively from the precipice, to the brink of which she strayed, and endeavoured to make amends for a brief period of folly by a lifetime of faithful love and affection for her husband, yet there remained the sting of remembrance, and the proofs of her momentary fickleness in the letters full of passionate avowals of love from the Comte. And when, by the Marshal's desire, Comte Rappt was affianced to Régina as a most desirable match, woman's weakness, and the desire to appear blameless in her husband's eyes, kept the wife silent till the approach of death was hailed by her with thankfulness, in that it gave her the longed-for opportunity of relieving her heart from the weight which had shortened her days, and of freeing her daughter from the engagement which she still believed to be in existence between Régina and the man who would have betrayed her.

The sands of the Princess Rina's life had run low indeed when she began this tardy confession. She had little breath left to tell Marshal de Lamothe-Houdan the story of his friend's intended treachery; and that little failed her when the dread moment came for her to mention her own culpability in listening, even in the ignorance of girlhood, to the slightest breath of dishonour. She could only point to her desk and utter the one word, "Letters!"

The Princess then passed into the Silent Land; and the bereaved husband, dismissing all thought of the dishonour his wife's intended avowal might have portended, gave himself up to the overwhelming grief occasioned by the loss of his life's partner, the one joy of many a lonely bivouac, the mother of his darlings. His daughter's tears soon mingled with his at the bedside of the Princess. On their sacred privacy the Abbé Coletti would have trespassed. He was stopped on the threshold, however, by the stricken Marshal, who forbade him to intrude his unwelcome presence into the silent chamber of death. The claim of one at least of the living upon him, however, was suddenly brought home to the Marshal by the appearance of Comte Rappt, whom he hastened to meet ere he could enter the room.

"Villain!" hissed the aged Marshal in the Comte's ear. "At last I know you. I know not the full extent of my wrong, but my poor wife told me, with her last breath, enough to prove that the man I looked upon as my trusted friend was no better than a serpent. Leave my house now. One of my true friends will wait upon you to arrange a meeting for the morning after to-morrow."

Crestfallen and overwhelmed by the suddenness of this revelation, Comte Rappt descended to the drawing-room, where he tarried for a while in the hope that Régina would presently rejoin him. Nor was he disappointed. He had quite regained his composure when the Princess Régina stole into the room, having nerved herself to demand from the Comte any letters he might possess of her mother's. Restraining her sobs she pleaded earnestly for their restoration to one who wished her mother's fair fame to remain unsullied in the world's eyes. The Comte saw his opportunity. He promised compliance with her request on one condition—that she procured for him an interview with Pétrus in her garden on the following evening. Régina consented. She had no fear for her lover's safety, and wrote without hesitation the letter which the Comte counted upon to deliver his rival into his hands.

CHAPTER CIV.—THE COMTE'S TRAP.

THE Comte did not close his eyes that night. The remorseless man, hopelessly deprived of Régina's hand, had resolved to compass the death of his favoured rival before his duel with Marshal de Lamothe-Houdan; and this deadly theme was the burden of his thoughts till morning. He rang for his valet at seven, and bade him summon Bordier—one of the most unscrupulous tools of Comte Rappt. Whilst Bordier was being sought the Comte carefully examined a brace of pistols which he took from a secret drawer in his cabinet. He loaded them, and replaced them with a sinister smile. Three light knocks at the door then smote his ears. "Come in," he said.

Bordier accordingly bowed himself in.

"You have learnt the news of last night, I suppose?" demanded the Comte.

"I have heard, to my great regret, of the death of the wife of Marshal de Lamothe-Houdan, Monsieur le Comte."

"You have! Apropos, then, I may tell you I have a hostile engagement for to-morrow. Don't start like that, Bordier! You ought to know by this time that I am very well able to defend my life. But it is not of the duel, Bordier, I would speak to you. I want your assistance in another matter."

"You have only to name it, Monsieur le Ministre. My life is yours."

"I know it, my faithful Bordier; and in token of my gratitude here is your nomination to the vacant Préfetship."

"Oh! how can I ever repay you for your bounty, Monsieur le Comte?" exclaimed the delighted Bordier.

"Let me tell you. You know Monsieur Pétrus Herbel?"

"Yes, Monsieur."

"I need a trusty friend to place a letter into his hands, and I count upon you doing it for me; Bordier. Have you a couple of men upon whom you can rely?"

"As upon myself, Monsieur."

"Very well. You will instruct one of them to take up his station on the Boulevard des Invalides, and not to budge therefrom till he sees Nanon, the nurse, leave Marshal de Lamothe-Houdan's mansion. He will then follow her at a distance. If she goes in the direction of Rue Notre-Dame-des-Champs, in which Monsieur Herbel lives, he will walk up to her and say, 'Hand me that letter, or I arrest you.' Nanon is devóted to the Princess; but, being an old woman, it is only natural that her devotion will give way to her timidity and weakness."

"Your wishes shall be carried out to the letter, Monsieur."

"Good! Your second man will take up his station in the Rue Plumet, opposite the door of the Marshal's mansion, and will follow and accost Nanon precisely in the same manner and with the same words, if she should leave by that street."

"And when shall I put them on duty?"

"This instant."

"Rely upon me, Monsieur," answered Bordier, again bowing low and moving towards the door.

"One moment, Bordier!" cried the Comte. "You forget the principal thing." Then, handing to Bordier the letter for Pétrus, written by the Princess Régina, he added, "You will yourself give this to Monsieur Herbel's servant, and tell him to let his master have it as soon as possible."

Bordier quickly departed, and lost no time in stationing his men at the appointed places. Whilst the Comte's envoy wended his way to the residence of Régina's lover, a Government messenger of the humblest kind—the postman—handed to Nanon a letter which was destined to frustrate Comte Rappt. It was simply a billet-doux from Pétrus, announcing, in lover-like language, that he would for three whole days be kept from seeing the idol of his heart, being called to the bedside of his uncle, who was stricken with gout. Far from plunging Régina into the depths of gloom and sadness, the missive lifted a heavy load from the heart of the Princess. She had awakened with the direst presentiments; for in her dreams she had beheld her lover prone on the snow, a corpse, and had recognised in the phantom murderer, Comte Rappt. The dream-clouds of night were swept away by the sweet missive of morning. Love's instinct told her that chance had saved Pétrus from some impending act of treachery. To make assurance doubly sure, however, Régina flew to her writing-desk, and hurriedly penned the following note to her lover:—

"MY WELL-BELOVED PETRUS,—Your letter came this morning like a ray of silver light in darkest night. My poor mother died yesterday evening. The reassurance of your constant love has been sweetest balm to my heart. Sorrow does but bind us more closely. Let us, however, resign ourselves to absence from one another for three days, since Fate will have it so; and be sure of the true love of
"REGINA."

The letter sealed, the Princess instructed Nanon to take it to Pétrus.

"Rue Notre-Dame-des-Champs?" asked the faithful nurse.

"No, Nanon. Rue de Varennes, at Comte Herbel's, this time."

The moment the front door closed behind Nanon, the spy stationed by Bordier in the Rue Plumet caught sight of her, and prepared to dog her footsteps. The route taken by the nurse puzzled him, however. Joining his comrade on the Boulevard des Invalides, he said, "The old woman has not gone in the direction of Rue Notre-Dame-des-Champs, after all."

"She fears she may be followed, perhaps; and is going by a roundabout way, possibly. Let us start in pursuit!"

Nanon was followed at a short distance by the two spies. They saw the nurse enter the courtyard of Comte Herbel's mansion; and, after a short wait, they had the satisfaction of seeing her retrace her steps to the Rue Plumet. Their first journey was, therefore, in vain; and they, accordingly, again took up their stations to be on the alert for Nanon's re-appearance. Bordier himself handed Régina's letter to the servant of Pétrus. He ran against a commissionaire as he was leaving, and bestowed no gentle epithet upon M. Herbel's new visitor. The commissionaire, on his part, cast a piercing glance at the man who had roughly hustled against him, and murmured to himself as he mounted the stairs, "Bordier! What the deuce does that rascal want here? No good, I'll be bound."

The commissionaire was Conrad de Valgeneuse, who had once more found it necessary to don his disguise as Salvator.

"Monsieur Pétrus is not in," said the valet, as Salvator was about to enter his friend's studio.

"I know it. You will see by this note that he has commissioned me to see his letters during his absence. First, tell me what business brought the man who has just left here."

"He brought this letter for master, Monsieur."

"Then I must find out what villainy is at the bottom of it," thought Salvator to himself.

CHAPTER CV.—CAUGHT IN HIS OWN TRAP.

SALVATOR, authorised to open and answer the letters of Pétrus Herbel during the painter's enforced absence, hesitated not a moment to break the seals of the gossiping notes from his friends Ludovic and Jean Robert. Sacred to him, however, for a moment was the billet-doux of the Princess Régina. "The contents of *this* letter," Salvator thought to himself, "are plainly for his heart of hearts alone."

"The man who was leaving as I was coming in brought this note, you said, didn't you?" asked Salvator of the valet.

"Yes, Monsieur—the man in a cloak."

"But how came Bordier—the tool of Comte Rappt—to be chosen as the Princess's messenger?" communed Salvator with himself. "Instinct told me his presence was of ill omen directly I saw him. A serpent lurks among the roses of love, I fear. So I must even venture to read this love-missive to guard my friend against any danger which may threaten him."

Salvator scanned the note in which the Princess begged Pétrus to grant Comte Rappt an interview in her garden that evening. It was clear to him that the hand which wrote the note trembled greatly. One who loved deeply himself, Salvator gathered from the absence of terms of endearment usual in billets-doux that Régina must have written it under pressure. Reading between the lines he came to the conclusion that the letter had in all probability been inspired by Comte Rappt to serve some secret purpose. What that object might be Salvator resolved to discover by attending the trysting-place himself in place of his friend, whom he inly believed to be threatened by some indefinable peril.

The night came—a wintry night, with sky steel-blue, snow on the ground, and every tree of frosted silver. The appointed hour found Salvator at the gate of Marshal de Lamothe-Houdan's garden, impatient to ascertain the dénoûment of the strange rendezvous which he was now certain was intended as a death-trap for Pétrus. Forewarned, he was forearmed for the meeting. Fragola was the means of putting him on his guard. The young girl no sooner heard from Salvator of the strange messenger who had delivered Régina's letter than she hastened to the Princess to learn whether the missive had been sent in good faith.

"I was forced to write it," was Régina's reply. "Beg of Pétrus not to come now, for I fear for his safety."

Thus it was that Salvator, learning that some unknown danger threatened his friend, concluded the visit would not be without peril to him, and so came provided with a loaded pistol. How should he enter the garden? The question was soon answered for him. He saw that the small gate was open. By accident or design? Whichever it might be, he resolved to use the greatest caution. Noiselessly stepping in by the little iron gate, he threw a searching glance around, and, perceiving no one, ventured a few paces up the snow-clad pathway. The white form of a woman met his gaze when he had advanced a few steps farther. The figure was half concealed in a grove to the left. Salvator recognised in this mute lady—white as the mantle of snow that covered lawn and tree alike—the Princess Régina. Walking towards her, but cautiously looking all the while to the right, Mohican of Paris that he was, Salvator suddenly discerned the face of a man projecting from the trunk of a chestnut-tree.

"That's my enemy," thought Salvator to himself, at the same moment drawing his pistol from beneath his cloak.

It was the enemy of Pétrus Herbel. It was Comte Rappt who thus treacherously awaited his rival in ambush, a pistol in each hand. He had kept his appointment early, and observed with surprise that Régina was already in the garden.

"Régina!" had the Count exclaimed in his astonishment.

"Yes," answered the Princess coldly. "Did you not promise that I should assist at your interview?"

"But consider how icily cold the night is," urged the Comte. "Let me beg of you to retire for the sake of your health. I have only a few words to say to the young man."

"No, I have made up my mind to stay, Comte. All day I have been troubled with some vague presentiments, and I must satisfy myself that they have no foundation."

"Presentiments! Presentiments of a severe cold, very probably; but nothing more, surely! If you have determined to stay out the interview, pray seek the shelter of yonder grove, and draw your mantle closely around you, for we may have to wait some time for the appearance of your laggard lover."

Comte Rappt pointed to the bushes to the left as he closed this appeal. Thither the Princess hied without suspicion; whilst the Comte, unable to repress a sinister smile, took up his station behind the chestnut-tree. It was not until the Princess Régina saw Salvator approaching her, and at the same moment observed the look of deadly hate on the face of Comte Rappt, that she divined the Comte's murderous object. *She was to be the bait,* her woman's instinct told her. Not without an effort on her part, however, should Salvator fall into the trap set for Pétrus, determined Régina. She flew from the grove to warn him. A pistol-shot rang through the air that very instant. A cry of anguish escaped from the Princess, and she fell fainting on the snow-white ground. The shot struck Salvator full in the breast, but rebounded therefrom with a metallic sound. It had hit the Commissionaire's badge.

"I have to thank my stars I chose my humble vocation," thought Salvator, raising his pistol till it covered the Comte's breast.

Firing in his turn, Salvator anticipated the Comte's second shot, and had the satisfaction to see his adversary fall to the earth. Régina next demanded Salvator's attention.

"Princess! Princess!" he cried, kneeling and gently raising her unconscious form. "Princess, awake!"

The white lips of Régina moved not. Snow was softly pressed upon her brow. Its revivifying effect was soon evident. A sigh escaped her. Her eyes opened. Finding her voice, she asked of Salvator, as a puzzled look stole into her face,

"That shot! Were you not wounded, then?"

"Not in the least. I was saved by this metal badge. My dastardly assailant has fallen, however, Princess."

"You have killed the Comte!" exclaimed Régina, now fully restored to consciousness.

"Possibly. If you will allow me to leave you for a moment I will ascertain for certain."

Salvator was soon by the Comte's side. He lay prone on his back, his cruel visage livid, a crimson patch on the snow near him. A warm hand stole down his left breast. Not a throb! He was shot through the heart.

"He is dead, Princess," was the message Salvator brought back to Régina.

The tidings came as a painful shock to Régina, albeit the man now cold in death was he who had wrecked the life of her mother and would have rendered her existence as miserable. There was dead silence for a moment. It was interrupted by the stern voice of Marshal de Lamothe-Houdan, who stood beside them, and demanded, "What is the meaning of these shots I heard a minute ago? Who is this stranger, Régina?"

"Father!" cried the Princess in alarm.

"If Monsieur le Marshal will allow me, I will endeavour to give an explanation," said Salvator, bowing deferentially.

"Speak, Monsieur, although it was not to you I addressed myself, and although it appears to me passing strange to find you here alone with my daughter."

"Rest assured, father, that this gentleman is the soul of honour," broke in Régina.

"Explain, explain, then, Monsieur," said the Marshal with impatience. "But first who are you?"

"Conrad de Valgeneuse."

"What! As a Commissionaire?"

"I will explain this inconsistency another time, Monsieur le Marshal. For the present, let me refer you to the Princess Régina, who has known me for a long time."

"Father, Monsieur Conrad de Valgeneuse is the most loyal and sincere friend I have next to you," pleaded Régina.

"I may now venture to account for my presence here to-night," resumed Salvator. "One of my best friends was invited to meet Comte Rappt here at ten o'clock. He could not come. I took his place. But something told me it was a trap for my friend, and I came armed."

"Through whom did Comte Rappt dare to send this invitation?" demanded the Marshal indignantly.

"Through me, father. The Comte forced or persuaded me to write the letter in a moment of weakness after mother's death."

"What was his object?"

"That I was in entire ignorance of until to-night. I know now only too well. His object was to assassinate him."

"Whom?"

"Monsieur Pétrus Herbel," answered Régina, timidly looking up in her father's face as she mentioned the name of her lover.

"So I came," continued Salvator, "in place of my friend, fearing some treachery. Scarcely had I entered the garden when a pistol-shot hit me here, but fortunately this piece of metal saved my life. My assailant was about to fire a second shot from behind yon chestnut tree when I fired in my turn, and shot him dead."

"The Comte?" exclaimed the Marshal, in a tone of agitation.

"Yes."

"Dead!" cried the Marshal. "Dead! Killed by the and of another! Dead, when I had looked forward to revenging myself upon the traitor with my own hand! Where is he?"

"Father! Father!" pleaded the Princess, anxious to save the Marshal the pain of seeing the Comte again. "Come indoors with me, let me beg of you!"

"Where is he?" demanded the Marshal angrily. "I must see the villain who stole from me the heart of my wife, who——"

"Father! Father!" cried Régina, piteously, vainly endeavouring to lead the aged Marshal to the palace.

"I am not your father! He——"

"Oh, my poor mother! At least cast no slur on her fair name!" exclaimed Régina, roused in her turn at the aspersion thrown by her father in his passion upon the character of his wife. "Did she not show you those letters?"

"No. Do they explain the matter fully, Régina? Speak, child! It is life or death to me."

"Read them, father. Read them, and never doubt my mother again!" sobbed Régina."

The reaction from despair to hope unnerved the Marshal. Clinging to the Princess, he suffered himself to be led by her, murmuring, "Forgive me, darling! I knew not what I said. Passion and revenge overcame me. Let the villain lie there, Régina, whilst I read his letters. Let me at once satisfy myself that you are right, and I am wrong, Régina!"

"Monsieur de Valgeneuse," added the Marshal to Salvator, who had drawn on one side at the first intimation of the terrible dialogue between father and daughter, "pardon my rudeness. I would have sent a traitor to judgment myself, but you have anticipated me, and——"

The voice of the Marshal grew faint. He staggered, and would have fallen had not Salvator hastened to aid Régina in leading the stricken Marshal to the palace. He was gently led into his study. Sinking feebly into an arm-chair, he whispered for writing materials to be brought to him. A bright smile of infinite sweetness flickered in his pallid face as he looked up at Régina.

"You love Monsieur Herbel, my darling, don't you?" he asked,

"I do, father," was Régina's low reply.

"Receive my blessing, then. May you both be happy!"

Turning to Salvator, the Marshal with difficulty murmured, "You are a worthy son of a worthy father. You are a noble friend, for you have risked your life to save his life. The friend whom I trusted——"

A rush of blood to his face betokened the emotion which any reference to Comte Rappt called up within him.

"Quick! The paper!" he gasped out.

Salvator wheeled the writing-desk in front of the Marshal, who wrote with feverish haste the following declaration:—

"Let no one be accused of the murder of Comte Rappt. It was I who killed him, this evening, in my garden, in punishment for an outrage he had done me.

"MARSHAL DE LAMOTHE-HOUDAN."

CHAPTER CVI.—BICETRE.

MARSHAL DE LAMOTHE-HOUDAN had hardly signed the declaration whereby he voluntarily made himself responsible for the death of Comte Rappt than he sank back into the arms of Salvator. The waves of emotion that had swept through his soul brought on the fatal attack of apoplexy which ended his noble life. Whilst the stricken Princess, weeping at his feet, was thus deprived of father and mother, both within twenty-four hours, the King lost one of his most trusted Ministers by the death of the Marshal. The change of Ministry that ensued was marked by a reversal of the police policy of the Government. M. Jackal was retained as chief, but was warned to rid himself of all questionable subordinates. Gibassier was one of the first victims of this new order of things. Summoned before the Chief of the Police, the escaped convict and quondam detective was thus addressed by his late employer, "I deeply regret, Gibassier, I assure you, to have to put you under restraint for some time. The heat of Paris has, I fear, turned your brain. When you stopped the mailpost, by which an Englishman and his wife were travelling, between Nemours and Château-Landon, you forgot that you might have embroiled the Courts of France and England. In short, you have interpreted too literally the liberty I granted you."

"But, Monsieur Jackal," pleaded Gibassier, "I had no idea of ill-treating the islanders when I stopped the mail post."

"I see you have the courage of your opinion, as usual, Gibassier. That's just what I like in you. Unfortunately, however, frankness and wisdom don't go hand in hand, as a rule. This outrage on an Englishman cannot be overlooked. A little change of air will do you good, Gibassier."

"Rochefort, Brest, or Toulon?" asked Gibassier, in a subdued tone.

"Which you please, Gibassier."

"For how long?"

"As long as you please. You have only to conduct yourself well; and I appreciate your services too highly to suffer you to remain away from me long."

"Very well," sighed Gibassier. "Since I must perforce leave town, I will choose Toulon. Am I to go by way of Bicêtre?"

"Naturally. That is a matter of routine. Colombier," added M. Jackal, taking a huge pinch of snuff, and then introducing Gibassier to his servant with a wave of the hand. "Colombier, I recommend Monsieur Gibassier to your special attention and care. You see, Gibassier, I am doing everything for your comfort."

"I really cannot find words to thank you sufficiently," replied Gibassier, with a grimace, as he bowed himself out of M. Jackal's presence.

The Chief of the Police regarded him with a melancholy air as he departed, murmuring to himself, "There goes my right hand."

The ancient Castle of Bicêtre, situated near the village of Gentilly, about a league to the south of Paris, offers to the tourist one of the most sombre spectacles that can be imagined. Viewed from a distance, the black and frowning walls have something fantastic and even terrible in their suggestiveness; and at night particularly it would not be surprising if there should rise up phantoms of all the victims and criminals incarcerated within the dungeons of Bicêtre since the time of King St. Louis. The gloomy castle, indeed, resembled those old German châteaux, said to be haunted by ghouls and sorcerers when wrapped in the veil of night. It was in the courtyard of Bicêtre that took place the ceremony of shackling in iron fetters the prisoners condemned, like Gibassier, to Rochefort or Toulon for their sins. Gibassier was not the only Mohican of Paris, loaded with chains and fetters worthy of Tubal Cain or Vulcan himself. There were a few other tools of M. Jackal, who, having served their turn, had now received their reward in a hard term of imprisonment. Brin-d'Acier and Longue-Avoine, Papillon and Carmagnole, were Gibassier's companions in misery. The one noble figure among these criminals was the Abbé Dominique. Murmuring to himself a prayerful appeal for mercy towards his unfortunate brethren, Dominique Sarranti, still wearing his garb of a monk, walked up to the chief gaoler.

"Why, Monsieur," he demanded, "do I not wear chains as these miserable men do, when I am equally guilty with them?"

"Monsieur l'Abbé," answered the gaoler, "I have acted in accordance with my orders."

"Were you directed, then, to leave me unfettered?"

"Yes, Monsieur l'Abbé."

"By whom?"

"By the Préfet of Police."

At this moment a carriage entered the court-yard. The gentleman who descended from it hastened straight to Dominique Sarranti, to whom he said, handing him a roll of parchment at the same time, "Monsieur, from this moment you are free. His Majesty has entrusted me with your pardon."

"An unconditional pardon?" asked Dominique, tears of gratitude springing to his eyes.

"Entirely unconditional. The King has ordered me, moreover, to carry out whatever instructions it may please you to give me."

The Abbé Dominique turned aside to hide the emotion he felt. What should be his future path? The moment had arrived to determine, thanks to the King's magnanimity. He recalled to mind the grand mission of charity accomplished during the reign of Louis XIII. by a monk like himself, Saint Vincent de Paul, who was appointed Almoner-General of the Convict Prisons.

"I will be his disciple," he thought, the Divine light of humanity shining from his eyes. "I will fill their sin-stained souls with hope. Monsieur," he added aloud in a firm voice; "since his Majesty has given me the opportunity, I should like to be Almoner of his Prisons."

"The King anticipated your decision," was the answer. "And here is your nomination to that holy office. You can commence your duties from this moment, Monsieur l'Abbé."

Dominique Sarranti had gained his heart's desire. And there was need for his ministration at once, for the convicts on the eve of departure were chanting an ominous refrain that might have passed for the "Marseillaise" of crime. All the tenderer to human frailty, may be, from his own terrible experience, the Abbé began his merciful functions with a trembling voice; and the pity and sympathy of his address as his eloquent tones reached the ears of the prisoners about to depart may have sunk deeply into the hearts of not a few. Seated in groups on the straw that littered the bottom of the long prison-cart, the fettered convicts left Bicêtre for Toulon or Rochefort with a new look in their stern faces—a look of quiet seriousness awakened by the farewell words of true humanity spoken by Dominique Sarranti.

CHAPTER CVII.—ROSE-DE-NOEL'S FORTUNE.

LA BROCANTE, the fortune-teller, who had adopted Rose-de-Noël, and brought her up in misery, suffered no slight heart-wrench when the time came for her to part with the sweet maiden. It was Salvator who informed her of the necessity of sending Rose-de-Noël to a boarding-school to fit her to become the wife of Ludovic.

"She belongs, body and soul," urged Salvator, "to the man who saved her life and won her love. It is, therefore, indispensable to prepare her by education for the world she will have to move in as my friend's wife. So you must permit me to take charge of Rose-de-Noël."

"Never!" replied La Brocante, resolutely.

"I tell you it is absolutely necessary that she leaves at once," said Salvator, firmly.

"But you would never conduct her to a boarding-school, Monsieur Salvator! Wasn't little Mina carried off from a boarding-school?"

"Yes. But it will be impossible to carry Rose-de-Noël off from the one I have in view. Come, come; you ought to be proud of her being educated, if you really love her. I promise you shall see her whenever you please. Will that satisfy you?"

"Thank you, thank you! Monsieur Salvator," cried la Brocante. Then, rising and going to the door of the inner room, she called,

"Rose! Rosette! Rose, dear!"

Rose promptly appeared. She was no longer a pale lily of a girl. She had budded into the ideal of all that is most graceful; and as her figure had developed into the perfection of undulating beauty, her face had acquired a new loveliness, for the beautifying touch of love had made her eyes glow with new life. A rosy blush flew to her cheeks directly she recognised Salvator. Was he not the friend of Ludovic? There entered, unobserved, at this moment four ladies. They indicated their presence by a sign to Salvator, who bowed, and at once introduced them to La Brocante.

"Madame," he said, drawing forward the Princess Régina, "will undertake to teach Rose-de-Noël drawing. Madame Carmelite, here, will be her music-mistress; and Madame de Marande will instruct her in the mysteries of housekeeping. As for this lady," added Salvator, lovingly regarding Fragola, "she will teach you——"

"How to make a loving and happy home," broke in Régina. "Will you not come with us, Rose?"

"With pleasure," answered Rose-de-Noël.

A shiver ran through the old fortune-teller at this answer, and she would have fallen to the floor had not Salvator supported her.

"Brocante," said he, "Courage! Heaven has sent these four ladies to save Rose-de-Noël from—— well, you know Paris, and you can well imagine from what she will be rescued."

La Brocante could only bow her head in agreement, and suffer Rose-de-Noël to be reinstated into her rightful place in society. Left a fortune of two million francs by M. Gérard, in spite of himself, Rose-de-Noël had, besides these riches, the sincere love of the man who had wooed and won her in her poverty. His loving care as much as his medicines, doubtless, cured her of the malady from which she had so long suffered; which proves that Molière is still the most illustrious of doctors, since it was he who created the "Love Doctor."

CHAPTER CVIII.—THE LAST ACT.

WE meet our heroes and heroines for the last time at the Théâtre Italien towards the close of the year 1830. The occasion was the début in Paris of a cantatrice who for two seasons past had gained celebrity in Italy—la Signora Carmélite.

"All Paris" assembled at the theatre to do honour to the débutante, who had chosen the rôle of Desdemona in the opera of "Othello." Not only the undoubted talent of the renowned artiste, but also her fair repute and the charity of her private life, made the Parisian public generally most anxious to give her a warm and enthusiastic greeting, whilst the few friends acquainted with Carmélite's private history had a yet deeper reason to prompt a hearty reception of the prima donna.

Jean Robert and Pétrus had contributed greatly to the marked popularity of Carmélite; the former had sung her praises in impassioned odes, the latter had awakened fresh interest in her by his lifelike portrait of the débutante. Judge whether she merited all this sympathy. Music, it will be remembered, became Carmélite's one solace when the desertion of Camille de Rozan and the death of her true lover made life a burden to her. The seclusion of a convent was recommended to her by the Princess Régina. Our old friend Müller, however, delighted with the talent his pupil showed as a singer, accompanied Carmélite to Italy. Arrived at Milan, he led her to the great Opera House La Scala.

"That shall be your convent," he said; then, pointing to Rossini, present in a private box, Müller added, "And that your god."

Carmélite made her début at La Scala a fortnight later as Arsace in "Semiramide," and Rossini welcomed her as the prima-primadonna of Italy. Three months after, she played "La Donna del Lago" at Venice, and the young Venetian nobles gave her a serenade by moonlight, the brilliancy of which the gondoliers long treasured in their memories. During the two years she remained in the land of melody, Carmélite marched from triumph to triumph, gained the rank of *Diva* and the warmest admiration of Rossini and Bellini; and Russia tempted her with the offer of a most lucrative engagement, whilst an Italian Marquis, German Barons, Polish Princes, and a host of Comtes threw themselves at her feet, and declared their love for her. But Carmélite was true to her one dead love. Paris still held her heart and soul, and to Paris she was irresistibly drawn when there remained no laurel wreath for her to win in Italy. Never was the Théâtre Italien more brilliant. The house was one blaze of beauty and diamonds on the night of Carmélite's first appearance. The Court was present. The Ambassadors occupied the balcony boxes; the ladies of the ministers, the boxes facing the stage.

The fifth box from the stage to the left was an object of particular attraction. Its occupants were Pétrus Herbel and the Princess Régina (married a twelvemonth since) and little Abeille, all three pictures of happiness. Directly opposite there was an equally gladsome couple in Ludovic and Rose de Nöel, who had not come dowerless to her loving husband, the fortune of M. Gérard having made her a millionaire. Another box to the right was also the centre of much attraction. It contained a lady of dazzling beauty, attired in a dress of snow-white gauze, resplendent with pearls and diamonds —Rosenha Engel, the danseuse, who had won the heart of the young Napoleon at Vienna. Next her sat a gentleman in whom, wearing as he did an evening suit, it would have been difficult to recognise the turbaned figure, with a robe of white cashmere smothered in gold and pearls and emeralds, first introduced to the reader at the Theatre Imperial of Vienna. General Lebastard de Prémont was not the only companion of Rosenha Engel that night, Monsieur Sarranti sharing the box with them. Justin and Mina, now one another's for life, were in the box beneath with M. Müller, nervous enough at his pupil's début, confident as Justin and Mina were of Carmélite's triumph. Salvator and Fragola, in the adjoining loge, were not less sanguine of their friend's success, which was the subject of their animated conversation with Jean Robert, now at the height of his popularity as a dramatic author. Monsieur and Madame de Marande, without whom the fashionable circle would scarcely have been complete, were also notable among this brilliant audience; whilst in the centre of the orchestra—lonely as a pariah—Monsieur Jackal was seated, philosophically refreshing himself with huge pinches of snuff pending the first strains of the overture.

Giving a last glance at the principal personages in this drama of Paris as the first heart-moving notes of "Othello" swept like waves of harmony through the theatre, one's eyes could not fail to dwell for a moment upon *the* hero of our romance : Salvator, now in the full enjoyment of his title and wealth, sharing both with the sweet partner of his life, Fragola, the fairest and most loving of wives, and yet by his presence there that night still keeping true to the Divine instinct of human sympathy and fraternal help constantly displayed by him throughout the multitudinous adventures of "The Mohicans of Paris."

With warm friends such as these to encourage her, the success of Carmélite's début would have been assured even if her Desdemona had not been one of the most fascinating and touching impersonations ever seen on the operatic stage. The applause was enthusiastic. Her triumph transcended the fondest hopes of her admirers. Bravos more hearty could never have greeted even a Pasta, Catalani, Malibran, Grisi, or Pauline Viardot. The grand scena in the third act was thrice redemanded, for the voice of Carmélite reached the very souls of her spell-bound listeners, and each sweet tremulous note seemed to tremble on their heart-strings, and tears started unbidden to bright eyes. Public ecstacy found vent in a perfect shower of bouquets and laurel wreaths at the end of the opera, and in repeated calls for the sweet singer who had enchanted the audience. Her victory was exceptional ; and was not her life? Having reached the uttermost depths of anguish in her youth, Carmélite insensibly threw a great earnestness into the ideal representations which formed her one relief from an ever-present sorrow. She lost herself in her part, and carried her audience away by her thrilling and impressive performances. And popular recognition of her talents did not end with floral tributes.

Carmélite found a throng of admirers awaiting her as she was taking her departure from the theatre. To press the hand of the gifted artiste, even to touch her dress or gaze upon her features, was deemed a crowning honour. A grateful smile had she for Salvator and Fragola, Justin and Mina, and the venerable Monsieur Müller, who had guided her to this crowning triumph. Stepping eagerly towards M. Müller, and affectionately grasping his hand, she modestly asked, "Are you satisfied with me, Master!"

"You sing as Heaven prompts you, my dear, and, as Weber wrote, to perfection," answered M. Müller, gallantly saluting his favourite pupil, whom all Paris had pronounced the most successful of prima donnas.

* * * * * *

It only remains to add a few lines as to the fate of "The Mohicans of Paris" who have figured in this story. In a theatre as gloomy as the one we have just left was brilliant, the St. Vincent de Paul of the nineteenth century, the Abbé Dominique Sarranti, could have shown you the withered figure of a man ending a worthless life in the prison of Rochefort. This was Camille de Rozan, whose elopement with Suzanne de Valgeneuse had resulted not only in the death of his wife, but in his murder of his paramour, for which crime he was condemned to penal servitude for life. Gibassier, who daily performed his allotted task without a murmur in the same prison, was wont to declare Camille de Rozan to be a hundred years older than himself, so much had the heartless creole roué aged. Jean Taureau, definitely renouncing Mademoiselle Fifine and all her works, retired to a little cottage out of Paris, the fruits of his herculean labours and latter-day thrift. As for his evil genius, she received a fatal blow during a carnival-quarrel, and expired in a Paris hospital unregretted, unmourned. Fafiou, whom Jean Taureau so long regarded as a rival, married the pretty columbine of the Boulevard booth, and became famous as Colbrun, one of the most popular comedians in Paris. Toussaint Louverture, the dusky Mohican of Paris, who was Jean Taureau's right hand in the brawl with which the romance opened, rose to be a foreman in some large gasworks. Sac-à-Plâtre was promoted to the rank of master-mason, and was one of the most active builders of the barrack-like buildings adorning the environs of Paris. Croc-en-Jambes, the ragpicker, struck up a lucrative partnership with La Gibellotte, the firm undertaking to exploit all the cats of the twelve quarters of Paris. Finally, Brésil-Roland, not the least interesting personage in this history, it is to be hoped, spent the rest of his days as luxuriously as his faithful services entitled him to in the home of Salvator or Rose-de-Noël, who vied with each other in duly honouring so noble and devoted a friend.

THE END.

Made in the USA
Middletown, DE
26 January 2025

70249627R00163